praise for
the Bystander
an Amy Prowers book

Saudi Arabia is a mystery to most of us, a mystery not much revealed in the hyperbolic treatment it gets from our media. Ms. Burlake knows it well—the good, the bad, the not so pretty. She weaves a complex fantasy, rooted in reality ranging from skyscrapered and freewayed Riyadh to the wilds of the Empty Quarter. With sensitivity to the moral uprightness of the Saudi desert people worthy of Wilfred Thesiger, she warms to the rivalries in an over large royal family hoarding vast oil wealth and how they play out in the transition from an aged first generation to ambitious and ruthless young princes. Saudi faith and its use of Islam become a central plot device as she moves us through one royal couple's pursuit of the big prize. Western diplomats and archeologists find themselves used as pawns in the more devious, savvy, morally tainted ploys of an ambitious prince and his wife. We are drawn into a story of intrigue and violence but leave with a richer sense of how Saudi society works.

—Charles Brayshaw
Senior Foreign Service Officer

After reading The Bystander, *the pacing and the way Katherine Burlake eases in history and culture makes me eager to read her next book.*

—Mary Ellen Gilroy
Senior Foreign Service Officer

the
Bystander

an Amy Prowers book

Katherine Burlake

Edited by: Barb Wilson, EditPartner.com
Book Consultant: Judith Briles, The Book Shepherd
Cover and interior design: Rebecca Finkel, F + P Graphic Design
eBook conversion: Rebecca Finkel, F + P Graphic Design

ISBN hardcover: 978-0-9989734-0-1
ISBN softcover: 978-0-9989734-3-2
ISBN eBook: 978-0-9989734-1-8
ISBN audio: 978-0-9989734-2-5

Library of Congress Control Number: 2017908805
Fiction | Political Thriller | Middle East

First Edition
Printed in the USA

Glossary

Abaya Is a loose over-garment, a cloak or robe like dress worn by some women in the Muslim world, the Arabian Peninsula and North Africa. Covers the whole body except head, feet, and hands. Can be worn with the niqab, a veil covering the face except for the eyes. Rational comes from a Qur'ran verse saying believing women cover themselves with a loose garment and no harm will come to you.

Call to Prayer Muslims are called to prayer five times a day. Once at dawn, once at midday, once about the middle of the afternoon, once just after sunset, and once at night about two hours after sunset.

Caravanserai Large guest houses used for rest, safety, and exchange of cultures along the Silk Road countries from Turkey to China.

Crown Prince First in line for the throne.

Deputy Crown Prince Second in line for the throne.

Djinns Is a type of spirit in Islam, like an angel. Some Muslims believe they can take the form of an animal or human. Also called jinn.

Empty Quarter The al Rub' al Khali means quarter of emptiness and is named for the vast sand desert across Saudi Arabia, Oman, Yemen, and the United Arab Emirates (UAE). It is the largest continuous body of sand in the world.

Gutras Is a headdress worn in countries on the Arabian Peninsula.

House of Saud Is the ruling royal family of Saudi Arabia comprising thousands of member, all descendants of Mohammad bin Saud, founder of the first Saudi state. Today the descendants of Ibn Saud, the modern founder of Saudi Arabia, rule the country lead by the King.

Jeddah Is the second largest city in Saudi with a population of about 4 million people, an important commercial hub, and the gateway to Mecca, Islam's holiest city and Medina the second holiest place in Islam.

King of Saudi Arabia Is the most important member of the Royal family and Custodian of the two Holy Mosques in Mecca and Medina.

Mecca Is the holiest city in Islam and the birthplace of the Prophet Mohammad as well as the religion. Only Muslims are allowed in the city and millions come annually for the Hajj pilgrimage

Medina Second holist city in Islam and burial place of Prophet Mohammed.

Nejd Plateau Is a rocky plateau in central Saudi Arabia, bound in the south by the Rub 'al Khali and the east by the capital of Saudi, Riyadh.

Riyadh Is the capital of Saudi Arabia with more than six million people of the thirty-two million living in the kingdom. It is located on the edge of the Najd Plateau in the center of the Arabian Peninsula.

Shamal A wind blowing from the northwest over the Persian Gulf, including Saudi Arabia that is strong during the day and decreases at night.

Thobe Traditional white dress, a robe, worn by men on the Arabian Peninsula.

Wahhabis Wahhabism has been Saudi Arabia's main faith for over two hundred years. It is a form of Islam that interprets, literally, the Qur'an. Strick Wahhabis believe those who practice other forms of Islam are heathens.

Preface

In Saudi Arabia, life revolves around the desert and Islam. Riyadh, a city of over five million, exists on air conditioning. The outside heat is dry, but over a hundred degrees. In all Islamic countries, the call to prayer is five times a day, yet commercial activity continues however, in Saudi Arabia, businesses close until prayer is over. The economy functions in the 21st century where one can buy anything, from popcorn to a Mercedes. Women wearing black abayas, aren't allowed to drive, and men are required to dress in a white robe and checkered head-dress. The people are quiet, refined, honest, and hospitable. Enjoy the ride, and be glad you're not on a camel crossing the kingdom.

Prologue

The Bystander is one who watches in silence.

From the beach of the Royal Doha Hotel in Qatar, Amy Prowers looked over the blue water of the Persian Gulf. The view was a contrast to the wrangling of oil executives and Middle East princes at the North Arabian Oil Conference in the hotel.

"*So this is the Middle East,*" she thought, wishing she had skipped the conference and gone to Saudi Arabia. Her friend, Princess Hassa, had asked her to excavate the ancient city of Ubar, though she hadn't a clue why Hassa, an archeologist, needed her help.

In the distance, alone on the water, was the triangular sail of a wooden *dhow*. The boat slowly tacked back and forth. She put up her hand to feel the direction of the wind, looking back at hotel, then at the *dhow* which was heading toward the dock in front of the hotel.

Someone was shouting in Arabic and then in English. Turning around, she saw a hotel security guard running toward her waving a phone. He gestured to a walkway around the hotel. Instinctively, Amy ran toward it, with the guard behind her.

"The boat house, the boat house," he screamed, "is the safe house!" And he continued to shout into his phone in both English and Arabic.

Overcome by curiosity, she turned and took a last look as the *dhow* approached the dock. The guard grabbed her arm, pulling her into the small building he called a boat house.

The sound of the explosion seemed to last an eternity and then the rumble of debris hit the roof.

"We're safe, we're safe," repeated the guard.

Amy felt anything but safe. "Alive," she said, "we're alive."

• • •

In his Riyadh palace, Prince Rashid took the phone call from his security service. The Royal Doha Hotel had been bombed. Details on who and how many were killed were still unknown.

Looking at the sun setting over the wadi, he heard the lyrical call to prayer from nine mosques echo over the desert in a symphony of sound.

He felt no regret or guilt for those who died at the hotel. The dead were not a threat to him. Eliminating many of his cousins and half-brothers from the pool of potential successors to the aging King improved his odds of succession. He reminded himself nothing was guaranteed until the vote. Even then, nothing was certain.

If he learned anything from his father, who was the Crown Prince, control was everything. *I never wanted to rule*, he thought, *but if not me, who else?*

• • •

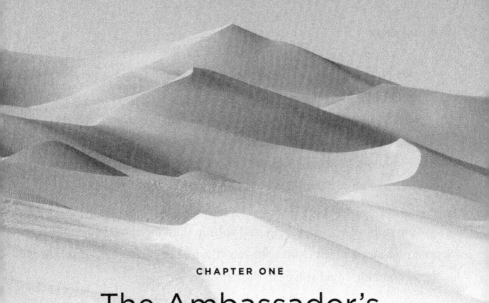

CHAPTER ONE

The Ambassador's Residence

*She wasn't happy about being asked
to spy on her Saudi friends.*

The sky above Riyadh, Saudi Arabia's capital city, was beginning to turn blue. Amy looked out the window at the beige-on-beige desert landscape. *What have I gotten myself into,* she thought. *Why did I come? Am I bored or just curious? No, I promised Princess Hassa I would come and help her excavate Ubar. That's why I'm here. Or is it something more? Am I trying to come to closure on Vince's life?*

Following the smell of coffee, she headed downstairs.

"Coffee, American brewed, but from Kenya," beamed Sonny, the Philippine butler. "Ambassador says you like coffee."

"I'm a coffee-holic." She sipped it. "This is exquisite, even for a coffee-holic."

Looking around at the cathedral ceiling, marble floors, antique furniture and paintings, the ambassador's residence reminded her of a hotel rather than a home.

He finished laying out the food on a buffet table as Amy helped herself to eggs and toast.

As Sonny poured another cup of coffee, Sam Preisell, the US ambassador, swept into the room. Tall, and wearing his trademark cowboy boots, he scooped up the mug of coffee Sonny had waiting for him and gulped it down.

"Caffeine is what we need in the morning. Glad to see you up early. We are really old ranchers at heart. I've been thinking about your cousin and wish Ace had left Doha with you. The bad guys responsible for the hotel bombing could still be in the city."

Amy knew he was right.

"I wanted him to leave. If he and Olen hadn't been at the camel races, they easily could have been killed or injured. But my cousin has always been addicted to danger, Sam. What worries me is that Olen is with him. I need our partner alive to manage the leases and the rest of our company business."

Sam laughed and sipped more coffee. "Our company business, ha. All those tankers. I made a mistake when I didn't buy into your transportation corporation."

"You're still as rich as Croesus, Sam."

"How true. I may be richer than that ancient Turkish king."

He was looking out the glass patio doors, and she could see he was worried. Maybe she should have skipped Saudi Arabia and gone to Dubai, which was safe.

"Princess Hassa called yesterday and wants to meet at the Riyadh Antiquities and National Museum. My go-to guy, Ali Giovanni, will be your driver."

"Great, Sam. I hope to find out why she asked me to help on the excavation of Ubar. I'm no archeologist, but she's been a friend for years and never asked a thing, until now."

Amy thought a shadow crossed his normally smiling face.

"I wanted you to come to Saudi, but my spies are telling me it can get hot, and I don't mean the weather. The Empty Quarter is the largest sand desert in the world. The sand swallows people and caravans."

He chugged another cup of black coffee.

"For centuries, the Rub' al Khali has hidden its secrets under sand dunes a thousand feet high. So, the legend goes that under the sand lies the city of Ubar, famous for frankincense which in ancient days was more valuable than gold. Amy, today frankincense is still harvested in Oman. Gotta tell you, the first time I saw the trees they looked like east Texas scrub brush. But that little brush brought Alexander the Great and Roman emperors to this peninsula. What Hassa expects to find is anyone's guess. For sure it isn't frankincense."

Amy knew Sam was right. "Somewhere I read that frankincense was burned for its scent and for medicinal powers. But, like you, I am sure that's not why Hassa asked me."

Sam agreed.

"The Ubar excavation is Hassa's and Rashid's show. I don't pay much attention to these things, but the Doha bombing, especially with Saudi royals killed, including Rashid's cousins and half-brothers, has the kingdom on edge. My embassy staff is, well, let's just say nervous. You need to know that Rashid has a security alert on his movements."

Sonny poured Sam another cup of coffee. With his coffee injection, Sam continued.

"The security advisories from my protective detail, the spooks, and military advisors could make me paranoid. On paper, they all work for me, but the truth is, they run their own shows. The CIA director for the kingdom, Bob Morris, is a good friend. I trust him and take his warnings seriously."

Amy could tell from his expression he had more to say.

"A wind comes out of the northwest and blows across the sand. The Bedouins call it the shamal. On it rides the future of the kingdom. Maybe today or next month, but soon, the King will be dead. Bob believes Prince Rashid is the leader of a group, small but powerful, called the Black Princes."

"What do they want?" asked Amy. The Rashid she knew was a Muslim, but not a radical.

"The problem is the line of succession. The King of Saudi Arabia—who is also the Custodian of the Two Holy Mosques in Mecca and Medina—has the responsibility for all Muslims. Today that's more than a billion people.

"Can you imagine, Amy, a billion? Two million of them make the pilgrimage to Mecca and Medina every year. Those pilgrims don't care about the Saudi succession. In fact, many of them think the Turks should be controlling the Two Holy Mosques, as they did for centuries."

He went over to a table loaded with books. "You've been friends with the Prince and his wife for years."

"Decades, Sam," said Amy, remembering how Rashid and Vince were buddies at the university.

"After Vince was killed, and even during my other two marriages, I've met them in London every year for dinner and drinks. They are a great couple who believe Allah has a plan for their lives. What it is, I have no idea."

Sam smiled. "While you're in Saudi, maybe you'll find out. Your success in business is obvious, but out here, Amy, you're a bystander. I'd like you to read the CIA Red Book on the succession which will give you some background on the royals. Frankly, it's hard to keep the Arabic names straight, but you'll get an idea of what's going on. Traditionally, the selection process is tightly held in the royal family. The sons of the kingdom's founder, Abdul Aziz, are dead or dying.

Who will be king is anyone's guess. Until they complete the selection process, the interests of our country are at risk."

He picked out a spiral notebook with a red cover. She noticed it was labeled unclassified, but was it? Sam had a reputation for ignoring security procedures. He often boasted about it. More likely his staff just labeled the book unclassified.

"The Red Books are summaries, a thumbnail sketch of where Prince Rashid fits into the succession. Remember, your friend may appear to be a laid-back Prince, but the word is, he will let nothing get in the way of his ambition to be king. He's the undisputed leader of the Black Princes. Their name was taken from the eighteenth century when Mohammed bin Saud, the first ruler of the House of Saud, named his loyal soldiers the Black Princes. Today we need to know more about that group. Whatever you learn, the spooks would like to know."

He paused and then said emphatically, "I know he's your friend, but times change. People change. And my God, I keep thinking you should be with your aunt in Berlin, instead of here. Something strange is going on in the Empty Quarter. So far even the spooks can't figure it out."

"Sam, I needed to make the trip. And don't forget my stepdaughter is going to join us. Audrey is a real archeologist, and well-qualified in ancient excavations."

He sipped more coffee and smiled. "After Vince died I couldn't keep your husbands and stepchildren straight. If you say she's good, then I'm a believer. We'll take care of her whenever she arrives from Turkey."

Sonny motioned to him from the door. "Secure phone, sir."

"Speaking of spooks, that likely is one of my staff giving me an update. Every time there's a bang, even if it's a car backfiring, I hear about it."

He headed for the door and stopped. "If you talk to Ace, tell him to get out of Doha."

Amy settled into a leather chair, sipped coffee, and thought how little influence she had over her cousin. She wasn't happy about being asked to spy on her Saudi friends. But then regardless of what she heard, she didn't have to report to Sam or the spooks. That made her feel better.

Turning to the title page, she saw the book wasn't put together by one of Sam's staff, but by a Washington-based institute specializing in the Persian Gulf and energy policies. No wonder it wasn't classified. But then, she often thought the fetish with classified information got in the way of real business.

She skipped to the chapter on the Saudi royal succession. It occurred to her that one day, Rashid might be the King of Saudi Arabia. Vince always said he could be king, but she never quite believed him. Her dead husband was the reason she was here. Questions still surrounded his death in Northern Pakistan. Over the years she'd resigned herself to not knowing how or why. In some way, she saw her visit to Saudi as a way of doing something he would have wanted her to do.

The first page was uninspiring.

The King and Crown Prince are in poor health and both nearly ninety. No royal has been appointed deputy premier, the third in line for succession.

Amy wondered how much of this she could skim. As she looked out the window at the sculptured grounds of the residence, Sonny brought her a pot of coffee. She took a sip hoping it would help her concentrate on the dry material in the Red Book.

She made a decision and slapped the notebook shut. The succession could wait. She was looking forward to seeing Hassa and hearing her opinion on the royal rulers of Saudi Arabia. They'd have a lot of time to talk about succession on their way to Ubar. Sam said she was a bystander; somehow, she didn't feel like one.

• • •

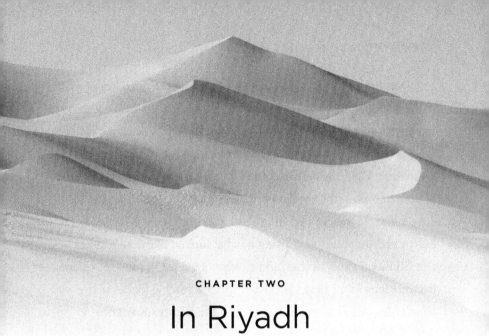

CHAPTER TWO

In Riyadh

At the Museum of Archaeology and Ethnography—
the King is very ill and could die at any moment.

Ali Giovanni, known as Ali G, waved at the Saudi National Guards to open the gate of the Diplomatic Quarter. From the back seat of the armored car, Amy looked back across a desert wadi to distant mountains.

"Ali G, are those the mountains where Riyadh gets its water?" she asked.

"Yes, Miss Amy. Here in central Arabia, the Nejd region and the mountains of the Tuwaiq Escarpment go from Riyadh five hundred miles south to the Empty Quarter, the world's largest sand desert."

She recalled from stories Rashid and Hassa had told her that centuries ago, forests and mountains covered today's desert. And in those mountains, the local tribes believed Adam and Eve had lived. No real proof existed as to where the first couple lived, but she knew at least a dozen locations claimed their residency.

"It is a rugged landscape, Ali G." To her, the blue sky behind the rocks looked like eternity.

They turned on to a six-lane highway that reminded her of roads in the US. Looking back to the west, Amy could see the road cut through the limestone rocks like a knife.

Looking east toward the city of Riyadh, Amy wasn't sure what was more impressive, the herd of camels grazing in the desert or a backdrop of domed tops of the royal palaces.

"What are the camels eating?" All she could see was dirt and gravel, but something must be growing in what looked like desert to her.

"They eat small bushes, and clumps of grass if it rains. No plants live very long in the heat. Camels are smart at finding food, and live wild all over the desert, even in the sands of the Empty Quarter."

"You're not a Saudi, are you?" she asked.

He laughed. "No, I am Sudanese. My mother was Italian so I took her name. I am called Ali G for Giovanni. There aren't many Italians in Saudi, but the Sudan is like Saudi, a lot of desert."

Her cousin Ace had a Sudanese girlfriend, a polite term for the owner of a bar, in Dubai. From the girlfriend's visits in Mexico, and discussing the Sudan, Amy learned a lot about the upper Nile River, which flowed through Sudan.

"The Blue and White Nile flow into the Sudan and join just south of Khartoum. Is water more prevalent than here in Saudi Arabia?" Amy asked.

"Maybe. The Nile is huge, but in Riyadh the springs of the Wadi Hanifah are underground. You can't see the water, but it is like the gold you might find at Ubar."

Amy wasn't so sure. "My guess, Ali G, is that the gold is long gone from Ubar. But I could be wrong."

As they exited the highway, Amy looked across gated white stucco housing compounds stretching across the desert city. The palaces were for the royals, but according to Ali G, nationalities from other countries, known as third country nationals and essential to the economy of the country, lived in these stucco compounds. Before she knew it, they'd arrived at the Riyadh Museum of Archaeology and Ethnography.

Princess Hassa greeted Amy dressed in the traditional abaya. Amy would never have recognized the woman she'd met in London so many times over the years. In western clothes, Hassa looked like a model. Today a black gown covered her entire body, and a black scarf concealed her hair.

Her face wasn't covered, though Amy had noticed many other women covered their faces. Apparently, face covering was optional.

"Today is women's day at the museum. If we wait a few minutes, we can avoid the crowds. We have until prayer time at noon, when the museum closes. The dates are in season and the coffee is hot," said Hassa, pointing to small tables in front of a food bar.

Amy tried to remember what she knew about the gahwa, the traditional Arabic coffee. One didn't just pour a cup and drink it. There was something about the server holding the coffee pot, the dallah, with the left hand and offering the cup with his right. True to Arabic tradition, Hassa poured with her left hand.

Amy slowly sipped her coffee. "What's in this coffee?" she asked.

"They strain the grounds, reheat them, and add the spice cardamom. I can tell you like it."

"Hassa, you know I drink coffee all the time. This is different than Western coffee, but I love it. Dates have always been a favorite fruit of mine. They are chilled, my favorite way to eat them."

"Saudi is full of date groves. The trees live forty or fifty years, but the best dates are from Iraq. The wars hurt production, but the Iraqis still export some. Did you know dates once were more important to the Iraqi's economy than exporting oil?"

As they sipped coffee, Amy asked, "You don't cover your face, but some women do. Any reason for the difference?"

"Covering your face is optional. If I was going to the mosque, I would cover it. Sharia law can be ambiguous, but still is enforced by the matawi—that's the name of our religious police. Their official title is the Committee for the Promotion of Virtue and Prevention of Vice. Fortunately, their power was clipped and they aren't in the Empty Quarter."

"They go around all day monitoring dress?" Amy asked.

Hassa laughed. "They have a bunch of responsibilities, like seeing businesses are closed during prayer call. But if you're in a store or restaurant, you can be served, you just can't leave until prayer call ends. They banned Barbie dolls and are against black magic, which has come from African Muslims. What we call fate, or say is written, the Africans call magic."

"How do I recognize them?"

Hassa poured more coffee. "Look at their beards. They are long and unkempt. But don't worry; you're dressed fine and their power is cut."

Amy knew she was dressed conservatively.

"The ambassador's residence has abayas for visitors, but I wanted to wear this skirt and jacket because the fabric protects my skin from the sun. Years ago, visiting Vince and my father at excavations in Iran and Pakistan, I dressed like this. Sun is bad for you."

She sipped her coffee. "I love this Saudi coffee, so light, but a lot of caffeine. So how did their power get cut?"

Hassa laughed. "The matawi messed with the wrong people. Two princesses, cousins of Rashid, are active in charities. They're nice, responsible women. For a reason no one knows, the matawi called them whores. Their brother, a powerful prince, demanded an apology and got it. Today, a government bureau monitors matawi activities. More coffee?"

Amy nodded yes, after all, the cups were small, but she was wondering what was it that determined a prince from a powerful prince. She was ready to go to the Empty Quarter and the ruins at Ubar, but knew Saudis never rushed. Hassa seemed to read her mind.

"It may seem odd to you to visit this museum. I wanted you to learn the customs of the Bedouin people and the history of life in the Empty Quarter. The museum is a series of scenes showing how the Bedouins live, and a short film. Riyadh has many souks and museums you can visit when we return, unless you want to go today."

Amy was listening to her and starting to feel jet-lagged. "I have a long evening tonight, so back to the ambassador's residence is best. Sam wants me to attend a reception at the French ambassador's residence. I never take a nap, but I am jet-lagged and will need to rest for the event."

Hassa's face lit up. "That's great. Rashid and I are going, too. He wanted to say hello before we left for the desert. He's been so busy with the business of succession. You know the King is dying, and for the first time, a grandson of Ibn Saud will be selected to be the deputy crown prince since all the sons are dead."

In spite of herself, Amy found herself asking the question that seemed to be on Sam's mind. "Hassa, could that be Rashid?"

The princess laughed. "Oh, my friend, more is required than just being a royal grandson. The selected prince must be the most upright among princes. What that means, who knows."

She looked away for a moment and changed the subject. "The good news is we leave for the Empty Quarter tomorrow."

"I'm ready, Hassa."

A thin man dressed in a white thobe, the robe, and ghutrah, the traditional Saudi red-checked headdress, was standing next to the door near their table. To Amy, his head gear reminded her of a table cloth at a pizza parlor.

Walking past the man into the museum, the two women assumed he was a security guard. They also assumed he didn't understand English and hadn't been listening to their conversation.

The museum guards were watching the man. He hadn't bought a ticket to enter the museum, and seemed to be waiting for someone.

Before they could ask, he walked slowly out the entrance to a waiting car.

"We know their schedule," the man said to his driver. Taking a cell phone out of his thobe, he called a mining camp in the Empty Quarter. His brother, a smuggler, was very interested in knowing when the royal party would arrive in the Empty Quarter.

• • •

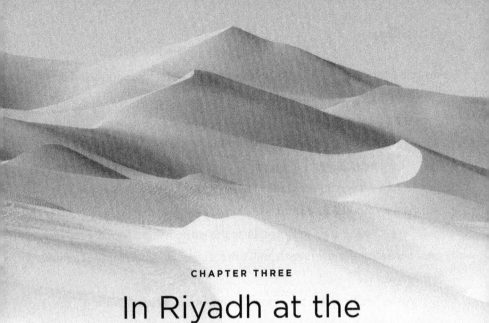

CHAPTER THREE

In Riyadh at the French Embassy

She didn't want to be pumped for information used in cables to Washington.

On the patio of the French Ambassador's residence, the evening temperature was still above one hundred. Nevertheless, it was pleasant, thanks to plastic tubing woven around the patio lights and plants. The tubing spraying water into the air helped lower the temperature and made the evening temperature comfortable. It was November, late fall in Riyadh, but the temperatures were still around a hundred degrees. Without humidity, the natives thought it was cool.

Amy turned from the misting tubes, to the bartender pouring a glass of champagne. The blue and white-striped label made the bottle look like it came from a French one-euro store. *At least it's bubbly*, she thought, and took a sip. The taste was exquisite, dry and light, fitting for the weather.

She glanced around the room. Sam's security detail was at the far end of the patio, chatting with two men whom she suspected from their haircuts were embassy staff. Then Sam was at her side introducing her to Bob Morris, the head of bilateral programs. His title sounded like some spook operation and she remembered he was the embassy's top spy, the one Sam trusted.

"I saw you looking at the label on the bottle," said Morris.

Amy laughed, and then remarked, "The label looked like a cheap bottle. Obviously, you can't judge French champagne by its label, because this is the smoothest champagne I have ever had."

"Wait," said Sam, "until you taste the white wines. They are famous and bottled under the French ambassador's private label from his family vineyards."

An aid interrupted. Sam looked calm, but Amy saw his jaw tighten. He motioned for the two men at the edge of the patio with his security detail to join them.

"Amy, Bob and I have to leave for a couple of minutes, some problem in the city. Skip Watson, my political officer, and Bangstorm Brewer, Bob's deputy, will keep you company."

Amy wanted to protest she didn't need an escort, but knew objecting was pointless. She looked at her escorts. Watson and Brewer were an odd couple of embassy employees.

Watson fit the profile of a political officer. Tall, impeccably dressed, he looked ready to pose for a photograph, a wine glass in his hand. Brewer was the opposite and reminded her of Ace. No matter what he wore, her cousin always looked rumpled. Ace and Brewer were both overweight, only the spook was short. Brewer was someone no one would notice. Then she looked at his face. Above his beard, his dark eyes saw everything.

Amy was curious what problem pulled the ambassador away, but the two men seemed unconcerned about their boss's abrupt departure. Each took another glass of champagne from the waiter.

"The ambassador told us you were in Doha when the Royal Doha Hotel blew up," said Skip. "Your cousin, and the German guy with him, who has a Mexican passport, are working with some of our staff on what happened in Doha."

Amy knew that sounded like her cousin.

"I left Doha within hours after the hotel blew up. Ace and Olen, our partner in Mexican oil leases, were at the camel races or they would have been in the hotel when the bomb hit. If I know my cousin, by now he knows the terrorist's profile. He would have learned everything about the attack from the oil conference attendees and could brief your contacts."

Amy sounded calm, but felt shaken when she remembered it. When she saw the *dhow* approach the hotel dock, she didn't think anything would happened to her. Ace once told her everyone in dangerous places think nothing will happen to them. She knew he was right. On some level, you had to think the other guy will get killed, not you.

She didn't want to be pumped for information that would go back to political appointees at the State Department in Washington and for Brewer, back to the CIA. It wasn't that she didn't want to help, she just didn't think she had any information that was news to them.

"I am not sure what to say. Though I was at the hotel, I was, as Sam would say, just a bystander. Do you have an update on the dead?"

Skip was able to rattle off the grisly statistics. She expected nothing less from him.

"So far, the total is over one hundred seventy dead and some two hundred injured, including the oil conference attendees and staff working at the hotel."

Amy asked, "Can you trace the *dhow*?"

"Tracing," said Skip, "is impossible because local fishing boats aren't regulated. *Dhows* travel in and out of all the Persian Gulf ports as they please, unregulated."

The two men ordered more drinks while Amy sipped her champagne and thought about why her cousin stayed in Doha.

Ace had to be dragged to the conference, protesting how much he hated the Middle East. To her, that was rather hypocritical. He lived like a king off the family income from oil leases, and for years hadn't worked in the family business. Aunt Sonora believed the time had come for him to step up to some role. Coming to the conference showed he was the face of the Prowers family, even though Amy was the brains. So, Ace came with her to Doha.

Now Amy wondered if he would ever leave Arabia. A born danger junkie, she had gotten out of Doha on one of the first planes; but Ace stayed, looked at the bodies, saw how the investigation was going, and was using all his old contacts for information. He was genetically programmed to follow danger.

Bangstorm—who said everyone called him by his last name, Brewer—interrupted.

"Let's call Doha what it is, a mess. The bombing is the work of one of al-Qaeda's children. They're cropping up all over now that bin Laden is dead. Our business here is the future of the kingdom, and who will rule it. We argue about it all the time. How stable is the royal family? No one knows."

"Forget Doha," said Skip. "Amy, you're going to the Empty Quarter and we'd love to tag along on Hassa's excavation. To some, the desert is a big empty space, but the border with Yemen is a mess. The guards are paid to look the other way as the smugglers cross, and there aren't enough of them to police the border as it is. It may sound crazy, but as embassy officials, we still need Saudi government permission to freely travel to the Empty Quarter. We could go, but we'd be followed by Saudi intelligence officials and see nothing. With all this security, we wonder what the Saudis are doing in the 'Sand', as the Bedouin call the Empty Quarter."

Brewer continued for him. "The Bedouin are insular and don't trust outsiders. As part of Hassa's party, we are able to look around and not raise any red flags."

"Let me bore you with a quote," said Skip, "from one of the first explorers in the Empty Quarter, a Brit of course, Wilfred Thesiger. I will paraphrase."

He looked around to be sure Brewer and Amy were attentive.

"I'll also make it generic so no sexual discrimination. Old Wilfred, who knew this country like a Bedouin, said if you live here you'll be changed. The desert casts a spell and you will want to return."

While Skip performed, which is what Amy thought he was doing, she found it odd that the Rub' al Khali, the Empty Quarter, was off-limits to diplomats. Why not ask Rashid if these two embassy staff could come with the group to the ruins at Ubar?

"Either of you know any geology or archeology?"

Skip and Brewer said yes. Amy wasn't surprised. The ambassador must have briefed them. If they went to the Empty Quarter with her, she'd be curious what they actually knew. She doubted their knowledge of archeology was greater than hers. Why were the two men so eager to go? What was going on in the world's largest sand desert? In time, she'd find out.

"Let me ask Rashid."

"He's out by the swimming pool." Skip paused. "We were standing right beside him yesterday at the Clock Tower Souk, which you probably don't know, is the main square in Riyadh. There is a mosque, a museum, and many upscale shops."

Amy looked confused. "So it's a souk, a shopping area?"

"Yes, it's a prominent public square surrounded by a mosque and a museum, where the executions take place," said Brewer.

"We were at the square to witness and report on the executions to Washington. It's one of our duties, and not one we enjoy. Why Prince Rashid was there, well—we have no idea. It's unusual for a royal to attend an execution, especially one for espionage. Executions for espionage aren't that common."

"Doesn't sound like fun," said Amy, as she opened the patio glass doors heading to the giant swimming pool.

Standing beside the pool, Rashid, elegantly dressed in a white thobe and the ghutrah, the traditional red and white headdress, was chatting with several Saudis and an older man. All the men were obviously deferring to the very tall prince, who Amy wasn't sure she'd recognize Rashid on the street. The headdress changed a man's entire facial structure.

The older man, as Rashid introduced her, was the French ambassador. Of medium height, he was very thin.

Why are the French never fat? Before Amy could speak, Hassa was at her side.

"Amy, you'll be delighted. The papers are in order for your stepdaughter to join us at Ubar. Rashid called our embassy in Istanbul and got her a visa. We leave tomorrow, and she will join us at the ruins. The embassy staff said Audrey is fluent in Arabic and learning Turkish. I am thrilled she is coming with us."

Amy smiled. "She loves languages and tries to learn all of them."

Audrey coming to Saudi was good news. Someone with technical knowledge would be useful. According to Hassa, nothing had been found at the site, but the locals were clearing out the debris in the cavern for the arrival of the royal party from Riyadh. Amy waited for an opportunity to ask if the American embassy staff could tag along. She didn't have to wait long.

Rashid wouldn't be going with them. "I have too much work with meetings on the royal succession. The Majlis Al Shur, Amy, is the Consultative Council which meets with the princes to select the third in line, the deputy crown prince. Very soon one of us, the grandsons of our founder, Abdul Aziz Ibn Saud, will be selected. A meeting could be called at three in the morning and if I'm in the Empty Quarter I'd miss it. The King is very ill, could die at any moment, and the Crown

Prince is in a coma in Spain, so the selection by the Council is expected soon."

Amy saw her opening, and asked if the two American embassy staff could go with Hassa's party to the Empty Quarter. Despite her misgivings, she found herself saying they were archeologists.

"Great," said Rashid, and didn't question their credentials. "If Hassa and her team find ancient artifacts, from the days of the caravanserais, like old Qur'ans, or any of the rumored gold of Ubar, having American embassy staff as witnesses will be helpful in verifying the origin of what might be found."

Amy motioned to Skip and Brewer to join them. She wanted to say they'd seen each other at the execution, but that was hardly cocktail party talk. After introductions, Rashid asked where the ambassador was. Both men were honest, but vague. And their non-comments made Amy wonder again why Sam and Bob Morris left so abruptly.

• • •

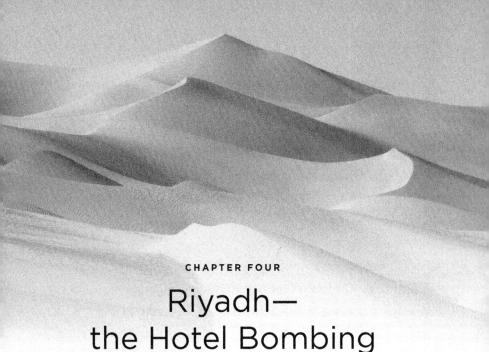

CHAPTER FOUR

Riyadh—
the Hotel Bombing

The royals are all over this hotel.

Smoke was everywhere and darkness obscured any view of the road or the hotel. The never-ending screech of emergency sirens was in the air.

Asif parked on the side of the road, careful to stay out of the steep ditch. Walking to the Raj Hotel, he felt the buzz in his jacket pocket. The text message was from Bob Morris. Did the CIA chief already know about the bombing? The text said yes. *How Morris did it,* wondered Asif as he texted back that he was at the scene and would be in touch with more information.

The two men worked together for more than fifteen years, starting when Morris was a young agent in Lahore, Pakistan. The assignment in those days wasn't a plum for an ambitious young operative, but with Asif's sources, Morris made a name for himself. He never forgot his source and had Asif assigned to Saudi Arabia as a translator. The thin, nondescript Pakistani with the perfect Arabic accent was presumed by everyone to be a Saudi. His salary and bonus paid for his four brothers and three sisters to go to the university in Karachi.

Asif showed his embassy identification to the hotel security guard standing on the highway and walked toward the bomb scene.

I arrived in time, he thought, watching two military trucks with Saudi National Guards pulling up on the roadway. He knew their job was to guard the perimeter from onlookers like himself. Since he was within the perimeter, they'd initially think he was an official. He had a little time before Saudi guards started checking IDs and forced him to leave.

He walked past an ambulance parked beside the hotel and a row of burnt cars. The front of the hotel was surprisingly untouched. Broken glass was all he saw. The head doorman, Mohammed, another Pakistani, motioned him over.

"Asif, I know you want information. Most of the dead are Saudis. I think there are two or three Americans, more Europeans. The worst news or best news, I guess for some, is many of the dead Saudis are royal princes. Many more people were injured. I don't know the count."

"Terrorism?" asked Asif.

The doorman shook his head no. "Some might say yes to discredit certain groups, but the hotel's coffee shop is a meeting place for the smugglers."

"Liquor, drugs?" asked Asif.

Mohammed spoke quickly without emotion.

"Yes and more. I hear only bits of conversations, which are in English, the language they all speak. Weapons, my friend, are the real prize."

Asif knew his older Pakistani friend didn't approve of smuggling. The old man had worked at the hotel for thirty years and was a devoted Muslim. "That's something neither of us wants to know. I'll be careful with the information."

Then he asked, "Yemeni?"

"Yes, you know all the borders are open. I hear them talk about their trips in the desert to Dubai, to Muscat, and to the Empty Quarter.

Everyone thinks Yemeni, since so many live here in Riyadh. They are poor and here for the work, like us. I am not certain other nationalities aren't involved."

Neither of the men liked the Yemeni. To them, they were untrustworthy, and had flooded into the kingdom for work over the years. Asif then asked the important question and one that could put them both in a Saudi jail.

"Are Saudis involved?"

Mohammed looked around, watching the Saudi National Guard beginning to cordon off the hotel. They obviously thought Asif was one of the hotel staff, even though he didn't have a uniform like the doorman. He moved closer and switched from English to their native Urdu. He was a tall man and bent over so only Asif could hear.

"The royals are all over this hotel. They claim the coffee is the best with beans flown in from Guinea and Kenya. They brew it like western coffee. It's good, but the coffee isn't why they're here. Asif, I believe the Raj Hotel is a central Riyadh meeting place to exchange products. Some rent suites in the hotel and drink a lot of liquor. Housekeeping staff won't talk. They're afraid and—I am sure—paid for silence. A Pakistani leaving the kingdom to go home to Lahore told me when they cleaned those rooms, the closets are locked with padlocks and bars. Asif, the man was scared. Still he told me many weapons are hidden in this hotel."

Asif looked around. So far, the Saudi guards continued to ignore them. But soon he would be questioned and perhaps detained, even with his US embassy identification.

"*Shokran*, my friend, I need to get out of here. Call me on my cell phone if something else comes up."

Mohammed said yes, then added. "One more thing. Saudi royals are into smuggling, but something else is going on."

"You don't know what?" asked Asif.

"No, but something is going to happen, I swear."

Then, Asif slipped into the hotel and walked to the kitchen. A back door opened onto an alleyway, and he walked slowly down the road until he was sure the Saudi National Guards couldn't see him. He climbed up the bank to the main road near his car. He needed to get out of here and call Bob Morris.

• • •

At the palaces of the royals, Prince Rashid watched the smoke spiral in the black sky. Here and there he could see sparks of a flame around the Raj Hotel. Another successful operation completed.

• • •

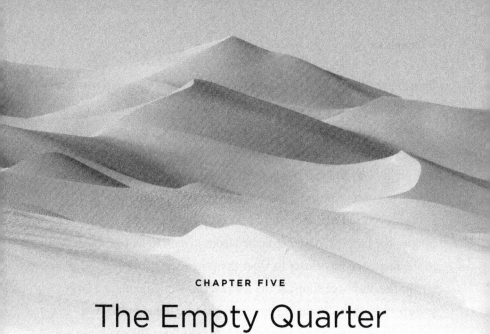

CHAPTER FIVE

The Empty Quarter

Sea of sand, as the Rub' al Khali
was called, certainly fit.

The SUV was vibrating from the force of the wind as Princess Hassa's expedition headed to the Empty Quarter. Amy was wide awake, looking for sand dunes. From her reading, she knew the wind was called the shamal and blew from the eastern Turkish mountains across Syria, Jordan and the Arabian Peninsula, creating sand dunes over eight hundred feet, the highest in the world.

Somewhere ahead were the sands of the Rub' al Khali, the world's largest sand desert. Hassa had fallen asleep before they left Riyadh. Amy wondered how she could miss this desert.

The blacktop road ahead shimmered like a snake in the sun. Looking back, the line of SUVs behind them also were shimmering in the sun. *No camels, just SUVs. We are a modern caravanserai*, thought Amy. That was what Sam had called them as he said good-bye.

Today Riyadh, with its modern buildings, was behind her. All she saw out the windows were flat gravel plains. Where were the sand dunes? She picked up her phone, though she'd been told the Empty Quarter didn't have reliable phone reception. So why texting worked made no sense to her. A communications tower had to exist somewhere, because she was looking at a text message from Ace.

He and Olen were flying to Dubai and Aunt Sonora told him she was on her way to Ubar. He ended the text saying she was nuts. How typical of Ace to think she shouldn't have come to Saudi.

Amy opened her phone and pulled up the map of Arabia on her phone. The Empty Quarter stretched from Riyadh to Dubai. According to the map, Ace was closer to Ubar than she was in Riyadh.

In the duty-free shops at the Doha airport, she'd bought a large picture map of the Arabian Peninsula, because it had both paved and dirt roads, and the oases. She folded it to see where the road was from Riyadh to the village of Shisur where the party was staying. Ubar wasn't on the map, but the highways—heading south to Oman and Yemen, and east to Dubai in the United Arab Emirates—were. Since the days of the caravanserai, over two thousand years ago, Bedouin tribes lived along the routes.

Looking out at the beige landscape passing by at sixty kilometers an hour, she thought the desert also hadn't changed since 1000 BC. In those days, gold and frankincense were brought by caravans, from Egypt in the west and from China in the east, to this southern Arabian Desert. Ubar's secrets, the city's life, went back to those days. She wasn't an archeologist, but was excited to be a part of Hassa's expedition to find lost treasure.

The blacktop road crested a ridge, and Amy finally saw the sea of sand, the Rub' al Khali. The name fit. The road was two lanes, but along both sides large piles of sand, perfectly sculptured by the wind, slowly edged across the road like snowdrifts. The SUV slowed, shuddering in the wind, as the driver moved to the center of the road to stop sliding in the sand.

The driver pointed ahead into the distance. "We will stop for a break at this last village before we get to Shisur."

Amy was ready for a stretch and to use the rest room. The so-called village was one compound with several homes behind a stone wall. In front of the compound, what looked to her like a truck stop, were eight gas pumps and a small store.

Hassa woke up as the Rover slowed. "We need this stop. Without it, our vehicles would have to carry gas to reach Shisur. Gas smells, is dangerous, and we couldn't carry our other luggage. Rashid's family has known the Awads, who own and operate the stop, for centuries."

Spoken like a princess was Amy's thought.

"*Salam Alaikum.*" Hassa entered the store speaking to the young man operating the cash register. They exchanged words and Amy picked up from their voices that something wasn't quite right. The man seemed sad. Hassa confirmed her feeling.

"Amy, this man is a cousin of the Awad brothers. All the Bedouins are cousins. He says one of the Awad brothers is being buried today in Shisur, so the owner of the store isn't here."

Hassa looked surprised. "I had no idea one of the family had died and the young man says his cousin was executed in Riyadh. Keeping up with such news is impossible."

As she left to use the toilet, Skip and Brewer came out from behind one of the many counters. The store was a combination of a grocery store and a department store.

"Her conversation with the clerk had more to it than she told you. The execution Brewer and I attended was for an Awad. Rashid was there with several royal princes standing not twenty feet from us. Royal princes rarely attend executions."

Brewer added, "Something is going on with the Awads. Our agency regularly follows the family because their village is the gateway to the Empty Quarter. The family has other business besides this rest stop. We think smuggling, but no evidence yet. It's no surprise that the prince didn't tell his wife. The executions in Riyadh's infamous chop-chop square are brutal."

Amy couldn't imagine seeing someone killed in such a way. She knew blood wouldn't bother her, but the death would. Without thinking, she asked, "Did you watch the actual execution?"

Skip was honest. "No," he said. "We wore our sunglasses and baseball caps. No one could tell if our eyes were closed."

Amy changed the subject. "I need to pick up a few things and the store seems to have everything."

She walked up and down the aisles finding tissues, always needed, when Hassa returned and ordered coffee for everyone. The young man seemed to have anticipated their arrival, likely one of the drivers had texted him, and he had several fresh pots brewing.

Amy sipped her coffee looking out at the dusty, empty road that lay ahead. Then they were off.

Another hour went by as Hassa slept, and Amy found herself again watching the beige-brown sand go by. At one point, she was surprised to see a convoy of SUVs heading north. The driver said they were the Awads returning to their compound from Shisur.

Amy wasn't so sure. With all the talk of smugglers and executions, anyone could be in the convoy.

Then through the haze, in what should have been a blue sky, she saw what looked like a rocky ridge. Slowly the Land Rover began to climb. Almost on cue, Hassa woke up.

As they reached the top of the ridge, the two women looked out the windows toward the oasis surrounded by rocky cliffs. Amy could see date palms and white stucco homes silhouetted against the brown stone cliffs. To her, this was how a village at an oasis should look.

The driver pointed to his GPS, and said, "Shisur oasis, our destination, ahead."

Hassa pointed east to the base of the sand dunes. "Ubar is that way, Amy. I've been told when we see the ruins of the city, we'll realize why no one found it. Without the sinkhole, it would still be lost today. The entrance was buried in sand; but once we are inside, you'll see for yourself what we will discover."

Who, thought Amy, *could have told Hassa this?* Hassa was hiding something about this excavation. Her friend seemed so sure they would discover something. Whatever was found, she knew she was here to be a witness.

• • •

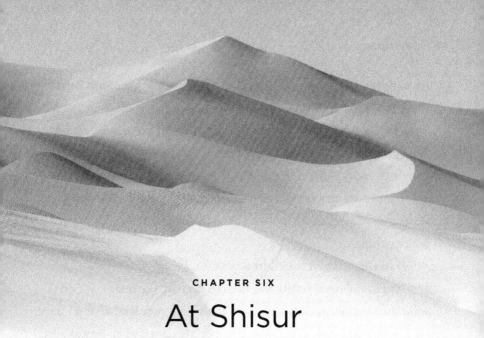

CHAPTER SIX

At Shisur

She asked herself what was so important
about an ancient city on the camel trails to Asia
at a time when Christianity exploded into the world.

By the time the modern caravanserai of SUVs reached Shisur, the sun
was setting and dinner was ready to be served. Tired from the drive, Amy
was glad Hassa's driver alerted the village to their arrival. Underneath
the date palms behind the housing compound, Mohammed Ishaq, the
village leader of his tribe, had laid out a feast of lamb, vegetables, rice,
dates, figs, and baklava.

She looked up at the sun setting into the sand, and wished she
could have a beer with the lamb and rice. Alcohol was likely available
somewhere on the oasis, but for her to ask would be an insult to Bedouin
hospitality.

As if reading her mind, Ali G came out of what appeared to be a
small tent carrying a case of beer, followed by a tribesman with two
more cases.

Hassa declined and Amy regrettably followed her lead. She knew
the princess liked to drink, but the custom of her Muslim country was
no drinking. Skip and Brewer had no inhibitions and eagerly said yes.

Ali G opened their beers, as M. Ishaq poured apple juice with Perrier water for Hassa and Amy. This mixture was called Saudi champagne. Though she didn't know the tribal leader, Amy instinctively liked him. Something about him said he was trustworthy, a word that fit so few people today.

The two women toasted glasses of Saudi champagne. "To our good times in London," said Amy, who liked the drink, but could have used the real thing.

Hassa sighed as if the effort was acute.

"I'm in the royal family and need to keep up the image. We don't want the religious zealots—the Wahhabis—after us. Rashid and I must set an example when we're in our country. My father, when he was alive, did the same. In London, we live as you do."

Hassa hadn't mentioned her father for some time, but Amy knew how much she missed him. Hassa's father and three brothers had died in a freak accident in the south of Saudi Arabia near the Yemen border. Out hunting, their SUV rolled down a sand cliff. They were killed about the same time as Amy's own father, Benton Prowers, died in a plane crash.

After her father died, Amy dedicated her life to his last request, following his clues to find the Shroud of Turin. She found it, and knew her father was proud of her. What would he think of her going to Ubar? Again, she asked herself what was so important about an ancient city on the camel trails to Asia at the time Christianity exploded into the world. No one had given her an answer.

While the men drank beer, including most of the Bedouin tribesmen, the two women switched to mint tea. It was light and refreshing in the desert.

M. Ishaq's daughters, who managed what seemed to Amy was a Bedouin bed and breakfast for their father, assured them the tea was good for sleeping. Ali G brought the two women a plate with more lamb, which they refused.

"Your accommodations are okay?"

They both replied yes. "It's time to say good night," said Hassa. Amy took her clue and the two headed for their separate rooms. Hassa was staying in a private wing of the house. Amy suspected it was fit for a princess. Her own room was bare bones without a phone or TV, but clean and neat. It was all she needed. The room had a private bathroom which made it a little less like camping out.

She stopped for a moment to say good night to Skip and Brewer, who were still drinking beer and absorbed in conversation with one of the Bedouin tribesmen. What information could they gleam from the tribesmen? Fortunately, Skip was fluent in Arabic because she doubted the tribesmen spoke English.

During the night, Amy woke up and went to the windows, taking a moment to orientate herself to where she was. The full moon reflected off the red sand.

What existed at this oasis or at Ubar, so many years, centuries ago, she wondered. *And little seems to have changed.*

The hour was late, but she sent a text message to her stepdaughter Audrey to see if she had arrived in Riyadh. Audrey answered immediately, saying she was still in Istanbul. The plane had a mechanical problem. Amy knew whenever Audrey arrived in Riyadh, Sam would take her to the Empty Quarter.

Amy wanted to send a text telling her to stay in Istanbul, but didn't. Hassa would think it odd—or worse, an insult—that Audrey wasn't coming to excavate Ubar. She wished she'd never mentioned the excavation to her stepdaughter or Hassa. Something wasn't quite right, and she couldn't put her finger on it.

Next, she had a text from Ace. He and Olen had arrived in Dubai. For a moment, she wished she was in Dubai. She had no facts, just an uneasy feeling about this entire expedition.

• • •

A fading white moon was sinking in the early morning sky as Amy headed outside for a walk. The sand was cold in the desert in the winter until the sun was up.

Ali G was on his prayer rug. Beside him, praying, was Hassa's protective detail. Rashid had sent another SUV with four men to guard his wife. Hassa told her they were following their convoy to Ubar and were supposed to act like they were invisible, whatever that meant. And, Hassa laughed.

Amy didn't pray. The silence of the desert created a feeling of solitude. The only way she could describe it was like eternity.

Gazing up at the cliffs, she recalled the Mayan ruins she had explored with Vince and her father when finding relics of the ancient civilizations—dead people is how she thought of them—they hoped to understand the culture. Today, both her first husband and father were dead. She hoped it wasn't an omen, but then she never put much stock in superstitions. The rest of her family did. How she acquired such a rational view, she didn't know.

Prayers were over, and Ali G brought her a cup filled with strong coffee, an espresso. It was just what she needed.

"Today, Miss Amy, a good day to go into the ruins."

"Yes," said Amy, wondering what, if anything, they'd find in the ruins.

"It will be light soon, and we go. Security people said Hassa will come early. I'll get the SUV ready."

As he left, Skip and Brewer emerged from the house. "Good night's sleep?" asked Amy.

Both men rolled their eyes and headed for the pot of coffee on the grill over an open fire.

"Thank God," said Brewer as as he sipped coffee. "American."

"So, you bonded with the Bedouin," said Amy. Ali G snickered.

Skip managed a smile now that he had a cup of coffee. "They're the descendants of the original Arabian tribes."

Amy laughed, thinking he was sarcastic, and told him the tribesmen must provide good information for his cables to Washington.

"That too," replied Skip. "After Ubar, they're going to take us to another older cave in the cliffs, the tomb of Hud."

There was a loud bang from the front of the house, almost an explosion.

"What was that?" asked Amy trying to sound calm.

"Not a bomb." Brewer's voice was calm and he sounded like an expert.

Skip was already heading around the house.

Brewer looked at the table of doughnuts. "I'm going to have another, maybe two."

Amy was surprised at his lack of reaction to the bang, but asked, "Who was Hud?" So many gods, tribes and ancient cities were out in this so-named empty desert. She'd never heard of any of them.

Brewer took a bite out of a chocolate doughnut. "Hud was a direct descendant of Noah, and a prophet in ancient Arabia of a great tribe called Ad who lived in a city called Iram. They were rich, forgot Allah, and didn't listen to Hud who was telling them how Allah wanted them to live."

"So, what's in Hud tomb, or at Ubar?"

"No one is sure, maybe nothing. You almost get to Hud tomb on the same road to Ubar, only his tomb is further east."

Listening to him, it occurred to Amy that Brewer and Skip didn't care about Ubar or even this Hud guy's tomb. They came to the desert for something else.

Skip returned from investigating the bang, shaking his head.

"Bad news. One of Hassa's SUVs, a Land Rover, has sand in the engine. It's busted. Mohammed Ishaq is looking for another SUV."

"The embassy's SUVs are okay?" asked Brewer.

"Yep."

"So we can go to Hud tomb today instead of Ubar."

"Works for me."

"Want to come?" asked Brewer looking at Amy.

Her instinct was to skip the trip unless Hassa went. She wasn't glued to Hassa's side, but felt a commitment to stick with the princess. Hassa was her friend while Skip and Brewer were embassy staff. If Sonora and Ace were here, they'd tell her to ditch the diplomats. Stay with the royals.

Skip poured another cup of coffee. Ali G returned. He seemed on edge, not his usual relaxed self.

"Anything wrong?" she asked, thinking he was concerned because Hassa hadn't appeared.

"Miss Amy, please don't go traveling with the tribesmen. I know the Americans are from the embassy, but the ambassador trusted you to me."

Amy smiled. "Don't worry, Ali G. I'll go only if Hassa does."

Ali G relaxed and said, as if there was no doubt, "Hassa won't go."

They drank more coffee and chatted with Mohammed Ishaq. Who else would know more about this region than the tribal leader of Shisur?

"Mohammed Ishaq," asked Amy, "what should we know about Ubar for tomorrow's trip."

"It's all about geology, Miss Amy. The city was built over springs that were once part of an inland sea. Ubar was a great city on the caravanserai, and the springs were the source of fresh water."

He smiled. "The desert always gets you. The city was surrounded by a fortress built on a limestone cliff. Over centuries, the water receded due to overuse. One day, no one was sure when, about three hundred to five hundred years after Christ, an earthquake sank the city. Straight down it went. Bedouin legend says if the city is found, it should be intact, layer and layer on top of itself. Like a pancake."

While he talked, Amy saw Ali G motioning to her from the date palm trees. When her host needed to attend to the food, she headed his way. Two of Hassa's protective detail were standing under the date palms smoking.

Ali G started discussing how important dates were for the desert. They were food, firewood, and fiber for thatching roofs. To discuss dates wasn't why he dragged her away, but he obviously didn't want anyone to overhear their conversation. Finally, Hassa's men moved back to the table with the food.

"Amy, you must not go off into the desert with the Bedouin to Hud's tomb. The desert isn't safe, even with tribesmen as an escort."

Amy wondered if he didn't mean, *don't trust the Bedouin.* Amy reassured him the drive on the blacktop road across the Empty Quarter was enough for Hassa. She couldn't see her friend tramping across the desert to any other tombs.

As they walked back to the house, Amy heard a roar of motor gears. Looking back at the road, she was surprised to see a huge semi-truck pulling a double trailer heading east on the blacktop road, not north to Riyadh. The grinding of gears told her whatever was under the canvas on the trailer was heavy.

"Where did that truck come from and where is it going?" asked Amy.

Ali G shrugged, noncommittal.

Brewer heard her question. "We monitor truck traffic on this high-way, and I gotta say it's continuous. Our route from Riyadh came down the north-south route, but other highways run west to Yemen; and the Red Sea, and east to the United Arab Emirates border, and to Dubai. Out here in the sand, the borders are fluid. No one really knows where the border is."

Amy had more questions. The size of the truck made no sense. She was missing something.

"What are they hauling?" She wasn't going to let him slide out of this one.

Brewer seemed to wince, perhaps wishing he'd kept silent.

"There are mines here in the Empty Quarter, though their location is not known by many. Under the sand lies every mineral in the world, including uranium. These huge trucks are likely hauling mining equipment. We think they get the equipment from the Port of Aden. In Yemen, no one watches the port. Security is less than in Saudi Arabia."

Then he quickly changed the subject to how the Arabian Peninsula was formed, first being covered with water.

"The reason everyone gets sick in the kingdom is because the blowing dust we breathe is really particles of seashells thousands of years old."

Amy was tired of hearing about the geological formations and wondered why he switched subjects.

"Brewer, forget about the ocean covering the peninsula. Oceans once covered all the land masses, even North America. This area we are in right now is where King Solomon's mines were and his gold, or so legend has it."

Brewer was cryptic. "That's what the royals would have you believe. Trust me, Amy, the real treasure today is the minerals the sand covers. The most necessary and needed mineral is uranium."

Amy thought she knew about commodities. "I never thought of uranium as a commodity everyone wanted. Isn't there a limit to its use, and after the mess in Japan at Fukushima Daiichi, no one wants nuclear power plants?"

Amy's perspective on the use of nuclear power was shared by many people, but she listened to his explanation to try and understand the importance of uranium.

"The deactivation of nuclear weapons by America and Russia is finished. For a time, uranium from those weapons flooded the market and made the mineral cheap. Those days are gone and today uranium is scarce and will soon be impossible to obtain. That's why it's important, Amy.

Now she asked the key question.

"What are they doing with it? Are they shipping it out of the country like their oil and gas?"

Brewer should have known Amy would ask the tough question. He looked around. No one was listening to them, but he still lowered his voice.

"That's what Skip and I'd like to find out. We need to know exactly what is going on in this mining camp on the road to Dubai."

"What about drones?" she asked.

"Right, only their imaging doesn't work in the desert if the site is disguised to look like the desert. It's impossible to see from a satellite because the site doesn't have any distinguishing features. The desert is hot; but if they use a camouflage cover, the core buildings can't be distinguished from the desert."

Now Amy understood why the two men had wanted to tag along to Ubar, and why they were traipsing off across the desert with the Bedouins. They were looking for the mining camp. Going to Hud's tomb was a ruse. Hud was a mythical figure. If he did exist, it was a thousand years ago. Who cared today? Obviously, the two embassy men had another agenda, the mining camp. Everyone had an agenda. She wondered, did the agendas intersect?

Brewer was watching her closely, and she hoped he trusted her.

"When we go off with the Bedouins, just tell Hassa and Mohammed Ishaq we're looking for Hud's grave, and we may actually get there. Saudi intelligence has spies everywhere, and Skip and I assume someone in this village works for them. Looking for Hud's tomb is a reasonable side trip while we're here at the Shisur oasis."

"No problem," she said.

Her own role in the expedition was still a question. Why was she here? If Hassa was searching for Solomon's gold, or gold that had been at Ubar when the city sunk, qualified archeologists could help excavate. Something was missing. She hoped Hassa would tell her soon. Sitting at Shisur for a day was boring.

Maybe I should go to Hud's tomb.

• • •

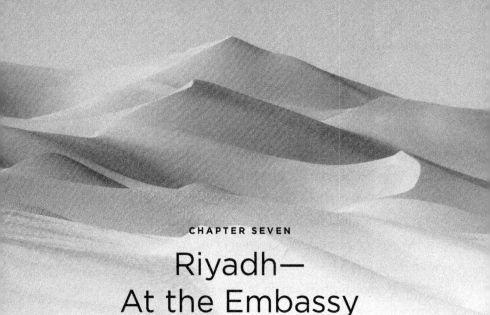

CHAPTER SEVEN

Riyadh—
At the Embassy

If the Black Princes are involved,
they're making a fortune.

In the morning, the classified reports stared back at the ambassador and the embassy chief of the CIA stationed in Riyadh, Bob Morris. Neither man was pleased.

"Crazy sons of bitches," said the ambassador.

"That's polite," replied Morris, watching the computer screen in front of them continuing to spit out information on the hotel bombing in the center of Riyadh which killed three Americans and at least four Brits.

"I'll contact the duty officer and the consular officer. Americans were killed. Families must be notified and arrangements made to take the bodies to the states."

Sam looked at Morris. "I hope they cremate the bodies. So much easier to transport ashes than a body."

"No way," said Morris, "it's haram in Islam, forbidden." Looking at his phone, he saw he had a text message from Asif. "Sam, this gets interesting. My source at the hotel says the bombing wasn't a turf war over booze and drugs. It was over arms."

"Weapons!" exclaimed Sam.

"Yep, my source says booze and drugs are the cover. Explains where they got the material to make the bomb. No surprise—the source thinks it came over the border from Yemen. The tribes in the southwest part of the kingdom are thieves. If they were Islamic fundamentalists, we might be able to tap the source of funding. But they're simply criminals."

"They are more Yemeni than Saudi, unfortunately."

Morris was pleased his education of the ambassador was not wasted.

"Right, not much we can do, but rely on the Saudi military, who are as pissed as we are about the illegal border crossings."

"Bob, my best friend's daughter is in the Empty Quarter with Prince Rashid's wife. Is it safe?"

"The Black Princes, led by Prince Rashid, are moving arms in and out of the Empty Quarter for more than a year. The good news is the Prince would never put his wife in danger. Amy will be as safe in the Empty Quarter as she can be in one of the most remote places in the world. Skip and Brewer are with her."

Morris wasn't really sure how safe Amy was even with the embassy staff. This was Arabia, and the big desert was full of bandits and Bedouins who lived off the land.

The ambassador had doubts, too.

"God, Morris, I worried the day our satellite maps went online that every goon in Arabia would figure out how to navigate across what was once an impenetrable desert."

Bob agreed.

"At the French Embassy's reception, Prince Rashid gave his permission for Brewer and Skip to join the trip to Ubar. No one in the diplomatic community was allowed into the Empty Quarter in several years. This was almost a coup, and Amy was responsible for making it happen."

The downside for Morris was Skip was also invited. He thought Skip, the ambassador's senior political advisor, was useless, except for his fluency in Arabic. His accent was called high Arabic. His own organization had many Arabic speakers but not with that accent.

He groaned thinking about it. The accent they learned at language school mirrored that of the instructor, usually from Morocco, which the Gulf countries considered a gutter version of Arabic. But Skip, the son of an oil executive, lived in Jordan as a child and sounded like a native.

Too bad, thought Morris, *he had so little common sense.*

"Bob, Skip and Brewer are additional protection for Amy. I sound prejudiced, but I trust my own staff more than the royals."

Sam opened a drawer from what looked like a desk and pulled out a bottle of scotch and two glasses.

Bob looked up from his phone to see a bottle of high-end single malt scotch from the Island of Islay. Sam had liquor contacts for sure. Maybe he should get Sam's contacts to look at the routes his agency had for the smugglers. But he couldn't. They were classified, and Sam had no reason to know that level of detail. Why did classification always get in the way of sound intelligence?

"Bob, this is my last bottle, and I saved it for a special occasion. Did I tell you the French Ambassador told me French archeologists have found bones and heads of spears and drawings on the walls of caves showing gazelle and antelope in the Empty Quarter dating back to 1000 BC?

"In ancient times, the Arabian Peninsula was attached to Africa. Under all this sand, ancient sites, villages, and burial grounds exist. One of the French archeologists at the French Embassy reception said they found the tooth of a hippo buried in what once was a swamp. Apparently, teeth don't disintegrate."

Morris knew the French findings were interesting, but he needed Sam to focus on today.

"Sam, what I can't figure out is why Ubar is important to Rashid and Hassa. I don't see the purpose. The site is south of the oasis at Shisur and the ruins were built centuries ago around an ancient well producing water. The Ubar well was the last stop for the caravans before crossing the desert. It was a short cut across the Arabian Peninsula, to Jeddah and the north, skipping Yemen."

He went up to the oversized map of the Arabian Peninsula on the wall and pointed to the Yemen-Oman border.

"On the other side of the Empty Quarter are the Dhofar Mountains that border the Indian Ocean. The beaches are wide, sandy, and easy for landing craft. Neither the government of Oman nor Yemen patrol the beaches. They choose to ignore them. Today, weapons are being dumped on those beaches and transported across the desert. The bandits must have a way station where they store weapons and ammunition until they move them across the desert. At least that's one of our scenarios. If the Black Princes are involved, and we think they must be, they're making a fortune. Liquor alone would make smuggling valuable. Estimates of the resale value of booze in the kingdom is five hundred million dollars. What the weapons are worth is anyone's guess."

Bob finished his scotch and Sam poured him another.

"To bring contraband across the Empty Quarter from Oman or Yemen, they need a place to get gas and water. Shisur is perfect."

Sam asked why they didn't use the oceans to move the weapons.

Bob laughed. "Every navy in the world has a ship in the Arabian Sea. They come out into the Persian Gulf, look around, and go back. This includes our navy, the Iranians, the British, the French, and whatever ships the small Gulf States can float. And unlike the beaches, the ports are closely guarded."

Bob pointed to a road coming into the Empty Quarter from the west. "The only other way to bring contraband into Saudi is through North Yemen. That part of the world is controlled by the Shia Houthis. They began as a preaching group, and now with Iranian support, are a political and military power in North Yemen. The Saudis are fighting them, with few positive results. If smugglers come north on that road, they have a clear shot to Riyadh from Najran, the Saudi border village, or they can go further north to Jordan."

The ambassador looked worried.

"Makes me more nervous letting Amy go down there. She still doesn't really know why Rashid and Hassa asked her for help. It's very unusual."

He thought a moment. "With all the money the princes have, you'd think they wouldn't need to smuggle."

"Right," said Morris, "but liquor sales are all off the books, let alone what they might be getting from the sale of weapons. None of the other royals see that money. With it, the Black Princes are able to finance whatever they need, perhaps their own army. The rest of the two thousand or more princes, who control the wealth and are in the line of succession, are none the wiser. Our problem now is we don't have even a guess as to how many royals belong to the Black Princes. Worse, I suspect the women—the princesses—are also involved in some way."

The ambassador concurred with Morris. He was surprised to learn Saudi laws allowed women to inherit and control their own money, if their father decreed so. They couldn't drive a car and always were covered in a black abaya, but they were rich in their own right. His concern, like Morris's, was if the kingdom was overtaken by the Black Princes, American interests would be in trouble.

"Should we share our concerns with the governor of Riyadh?" asked Sam.

Morris suggested instead they give the information to a trusted general in the Saudi military.

The choice was marginal, but they agreed it was less likely the military was involved in smuggling than the royals. Sam said he'd have the embassy defense attaché contact General Ibrahim, deputy commander of the Saudi National Guard.

"One last question, Bob. Have your contacts turned up anything on the whereabouts of our favorite al Aziz grandson, the one who is also a bin Laden, Abdul bin Mischel?"

"Not yet, we think he might be in Africa. It's the perfect place to hide. He'd have an entire continent."

The ambassador smiled. "Or he could have been in Doha at the hotel bombing."

Bob nodded yes. "He's dangerous and not being able to locate him is a problem."

Morris felt the vibration from his cell phone and opened up another text message from Asif. It was short and not what the ambassador or Morris wanted to hear. Americans and British nationals weren't the only ones killed in the Riyadh hotel. Members of the royal family were also dead.

Sam was still talking.

"Bob, liquor and drugs are fine, but weapons are trouble for us and the Saudis. The trafficking of persons, especially the women from the subcontinent, India and Asia, makes me sick. How do we stop that commercial activity?"

"The women come willingly, Sam, believing they will have a better life. We can't stop them from coming. If we could do anything, believe me, we would."

Sam wasn't so sure and said so. "What about the women standing in the immigration lines at Riyadh International Airport? My staff and I are whisked through by expeditors, while the women wait hours for their sponsors to pick them up. We do little to change the practice. Wealthy Saudis need houses cleaned, children tended, and often an extra woman will accommodate the head of the household."

Bob knew Sam was right and was upset. To the ambassador, these women weren't servants so much as they were slaves. Yet no one ever talked about the trafficking of people for sex. That was against the Qur'an, as was drinking and drugs. The Saudi society made women expendable, but weapons were not. The kingdom had plenty of all four: liquor, drugs, weapons, and illegal women.

Both men knew smuggling weapons into the country, even a few at a time, could create havoc but not overthrow the kingdom Abdul Aziz ibn Saud built. Bob took every opportunity to lecture Sam, since this was how the ambassador liked to get information. Sometimes Bob wished he could write a memo, but Sam never read papers.

"The Saudi border guards are part of the scam and bought off. It's always about following the money. The problem for us is the relief organizations who launder the money. The offshoots go in every direction. They use hawalas and no one can track them all. Some think the hawala money transfer system is unique to the Middle East and the Asian subcontinent. Did you know hawalas are in the US, often in grocery stores near where the immigrants live?

"To them, the hawala system is an open-ended invitation to launder money. Centuries ago, when the process was invented in South Asia, it made sense. Today, it also makes sense for illegal activity. Keeping the exchange of money out of the banking system, allows money laundering using the hawala system."

"Amazing, Bob," said Sam shaking his head. "A man could set off a bomb killing dozens of innocent people, but would never cheat in the hawala system. They give money to a third party and then someone overseas picks it up?"

"We don't see the fraud," said Bob. "The irony is how the process works as well as it does."

The phone rang from the Marine guard post informing them the embassy consular officers were at the hotel working with the Saudi authorities to identify the Americans and contact their families. Sam and Bob paused a moment, both thinking about the families of the dead Americans. The door opened and the on-duty communications specialist, one of Bob's staff, handed him a stack of cables.

"Some of these cables from Washington are important."

To Bob, that was code to at least look at them. Quickly he scanned the cables which said the same thing as his text from Asif.

"Our embassy in London says the deaths of the Americans and Brits in the Riyadh hotel bombing has everyone's attention. So much for interest in weapons smuggling."

• • •

While Bob read the cables, Sam thought about London. The city was a center for European-Middle East operations. The leaders of many terrorist groups preferred a base in the English suburbs. With their families and children in school, they lived comfortably and yet were close to the action. The time zone was almost the same in London as the Middle East, only two hours earlier.

Sam reached out to turn off his computer when he saw a new email had arrived. He never ignored emails from Ace. With Amy in the kingdom, he wasn't surprised her cousin was keeping tabs on her. Sam hoped Ace wasn't spying for his Aunt Sonora's Committee. He expected Ace would be requesting a visa for Saudi soon.

Opening Ace's email, he read Ace's new information. Abdul bin Mischel bin Laden had been seen on the Arabian Peninsula in the mountains near the Yemen-Saudi border.

He closed the email. Now was the time to check on how reliable Bob's bilateral mission intelligence information was. He would see how long before they told him about Rashid's half-brother. All of them were supposed to be on the same team, but sometimes he wondered.

• • •

Bob was relieved that Sam returned to his residence for a few hours' sleep. He took another pill; not sure what it was, but it kept him awake. Washington would expect an assessment of the hotel bombing. His analysts would write a report for his signature. He could edit his staff's work, but usually didn't. They were competent. His job was to lead, and as the leader, he had something more important to set in motion. His office was monitoring the smugglers traveling through the Empty Quarter, but the plan needed to be improved. Obviously, using drones was not working. He needed a person on the ground.

Asif was his ace in the hole. He could travel across the desert and though not a Bedouin, fit in as a fellow traveler. He spoke Arabic and looked like a Saudi.

What cover would work? It wasn't like there were a lot of occupations or reasons to be in the desert.

He walked out into the hallway of the windowless office. His staff was busy in their cubicles. One of them was a photographer and his black and white photos lined the hallway. Most of the photos were of mosques and animals, since taking photos of people, especially women, was not allowed.

His answer to an occupation for Asif was framed on the wall. Asif would be training hawks. How simple. Only Asif would need equipment, traps and what else? Oh yes, he'd need a falcon.

Back at his desk, Bob buzzed one of his analysts. "Can you find a list of what a guy who tends hawks needs, besides his truck? All I ever see is the man with the protective piece on his arm where the hawk sits. Something more must be required."

He shut the intercom off. Finding the right vehicle was important. With it, Asif could camp in the desert and avoid staying in Bedouin villages. The less contact he had, the better.

Unfortunately, all his trucks have diplomatic license plates. One person could help him, Jan Forester, the embassy general service officer, and supervisor of the motor pool. She had to have a truck or two, legally licensed in Saudi Arabia without diplomatic plates.

As a young girl, Jan had grown up in the Middle East, moving around as her father was a petroleum engineer. Speaking fluid Arabic, and with dark hair and eyes, thanks to her Italian mother, she looked like a local, and was always able to find out what was happening. Bob's staff called her the souk gossip, but her instincts and information were always right on.

She was in her office and immediately answered the phone, which was connected to Bob's private number.

"Bob, I have two Toyota pickups, legal in Saudi with Riyadh plates."

"Thanks, Jan, I only need one. And I'll come over and pick it up myself within the hour."

"Great."

What he liked about Jan was she'd wonder why he needed the truck, but would never ask, and better yet, wouldn't discuss issuing him the truck with anyone.

• • •

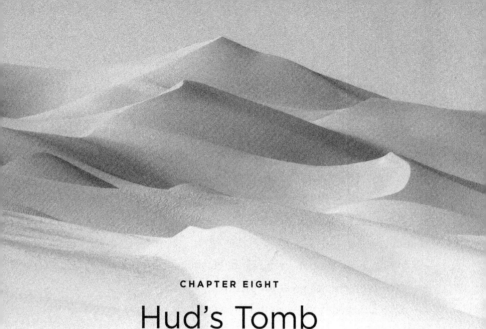

CHAPTER EIGHT

Hud's Tomb

Had a drone spotted them
taking pictures of the mining camp?

"I know the way." Hassan, M. Ishaq's brother, was pleased to be driving the Americans. It showed his brother trusted him.

Skip and Brewer looked at each other, knowing they had to divert him. But how? They were driving across a ridge on the east side of the Shisur.

"Hassan, we have this map," said Skip, as Brewer opened a large topographical map. "Pull over, and let's take a look."

"Okay." Hassan sounded very upbeat. He just wanted to please the Yanks.

Brewer's finger followed the blue line as they showed him the map. "We know this road goes south to Hud's tomb."

"Over here, this dashed line is a dirt track heading a bit north, then looping around back to the tomb. That's the road we want to take."

"I know the road," said Hassan. "It's the long way."

"Yes," said Skip and pulled out a camera. "We will have a better view of the desert on the track. Our pictures will be unique."

Hassan looked doubtful. "The track takes us near the mines. It's not so pretty."

Skip didn't miss a beat. "It's the angle looking back at the ridge where the tomb is. The light is better for photos."

"Okay." Hassan smiled. "It's good we have an SUV."

They headed off shortly reaching the point where they left the road to take the track across the sand. Hassan slowed for the deep soft sand that covered the road.

As the SUV slipped in the sand, Hassan apologized for slowing.

"No problem, it's great for pictures."

Skip adjusted his lens, as did Brewer. Their cameras were high-tech digital with long distance lens almost a foot long. Each had a special filter to take out the haze and glare of the sun on the sand. No store sold them; only the military used them.

As the SUV climbed up the road toward the ridge, Hassan's attention was focused on keeping out of the drifts of sand. Skip and Brewer were focused on the view of the compound that housed the mines north of the ridge. The track looped around and took them directly above the town.

"These pictures are good," said Skip. "We can get them developed and analyzed back in Riyadh."

Brewer was about to speak when the SUV came to a halt. The gears ground as Hassan switched back and forth from neutral to four-wheel drive. Nothing happened. They were stuck in a huge drift of sand. The three men got out and Hassan opened the back door to get to the emergency kit and shovels.

After an hour of shoveling, the wheels were still stuck. They had decreased the air pressure in the wheels and tried to jack them up. They put aluminum sand ladders underneath, but the jacks kept sinking in the sand. They were deeper now than when they started.

At this rate, the SUV would sink by midnight. Brewer didn't see a way out without help. Another vehicle was needed to pull them out of the sand.

"At least we have water," he said, as the sun beat down on them.

"I bet our phones work," said Skip. "We are close to the mines."

"Yes." Hassan, as if it just occurred to him, pulled out a phone. "I'll call my brother."

Skip and Brewer just looked at each other, thinking they should have thought of that.

When Hassan finished the phone call, they took pieces of canvas, designed for a tent, and tied them to the SUV to provide shade. Hassan had a thermos of iced tea, which helped their morale.

Brewer lit a cigar and pointed to the sky. "What the hell is that?"

Hassan laughed. "It's a drone. The mine uses them for security."

"Wonderful," said Skip. He looked at Brewer. They were thinking the same thing. Had a drone spotted them taking pictures?

"Nothing we can do now," said Brewer, "except hope Mohammed Ishaq arrives soon."

Hassan looked up at the sky. The sun was disappearing as the wind swept the sand into the sky.

"I hope my brother hurries."

• • •

Asif was looking for a place to camp. He would sleep in the back of the truck, but needed to build a fire and heat up the leg of lamb he'd brought from Riyadh. But before he could eat, he needed to bed down the falcon.

When Bob Morris described his cover, it sounded easy enough.

"Asif," he'd said, "falcon training is the perfect cover in the desert. Falcons are part of the Bedouin life. They are used to hunt rabbits and desert quail."

What I didn't know, he thought, *was how much work the Saker falcon would require.*

The bird was beautiful. Asif knew it could fly at speeds up to a hundred kilometers an hour. A trained falcon was worth thousands of dollars. He'd almost asked Bob if the bird had a name, then realized he wasn't going to bond with it. The falcon was his cover.

He put on the gauntlet and looked at the falcon in his mew, the cage. The bird was striking with its hood and seemed calm. On the side of the cage was a block. He tethered the falcon to it using leather straps designed to restrain the bird, but not injure it, and took off the hood.

Starting a fire using a small gas stove, he could feel the eyes of the falcon watching him. Throwing the lamb on the grill, he turned and opened up a cooler filled with dead quail. Unbelievably, he'd carried more food for the falcon than for himself.

He was glad he had the heavy gauntlet on his hand and forearm. The falcon eagerly gulped down the two quail. At this rate, he was going to need more food to keep his cover alive.

The imam at the mining camp should be able to help. That was Bob's last advice. If you need anything, he said, ask the imam.

The lamb was almost done when he heard the sound of a SUV grinding on a low gear without its lights on. Too late he realized his fire could be seen for miles. He just didn't think there was anyone around for miles.

The night was clear and he saw the silhouette of an SUV almost upon him. Asif was sure they were smugglers until he heard their voices. They were speaking Farsi.

Iranians? No, they had to be north Yemeni, the Houthis. They were the Shia minority and had been fighting the Saudis since about 2004. Now he wondered if they were Iranian, or Yemeni.

He stood up and greeted them in Arabic. "*Salam Alaikum.*"

They responded in Arabic, not realizing he had heard them speaking Farsi.

After the usual pleasantries, they asked him for water or an engine coolant needed to keep their SUV from overheating. Asif had extra gallons. According to the two men, both of whom carried a pistol and two knives on their belts, with a rifle slung over their shoulders, a mining camp was just up the road. At the camp, they had friends who could repair the SUV or get another vehicle.

"We are going to Dubai."

Asif nodded yes, while thinking they weren't going to Dubai.

"Have a piece of lamb. I have more than enough, and it won't keep out here."

"Shokran." They each ate a piece, then hurriedly drove off to the east.

As he watched them go, Asif reminded himself he wasn't in the city. He needed to think like a nomad. He had to laugh. The desert wasn't as empty as city dwellers thought.

For now, he needed to focus on a camping site near the mining camp and off the main road. Bob had suggested the ridge behind both the camp and near the tomb of an ancient legend named Hud. He gave the falcon another chilled quail and turned the gas stove off. Tomorrow he'd find the camp site Bob suggested.

• • •

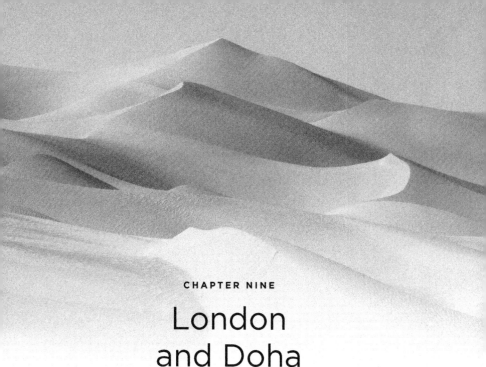

CHAPTER NINE

London and Doha

Political control and who ran the Saudi oil fields was the prize.

Clouds and puffs of fog obscured the full moon in the London sky. Shishi shops on Edgeware Road north of the Marble Arch were busy serving coffee while the patrons smoked pipes or cigarettes. No one would remember the man of medium height with a cap obscuring his face and hair.

Taking a drag on an unfiltered cigarette, Guy logged onto his computer to open his emails. He had more than seventy, and quickly scrolled through the list until he found the one he wanted. The contacts weren't supposed to email him unless something significant happened. Their idea of significant and his were two different things. They sent him everything, afraid some tidbit was the real story, and they missed it. Later, he would go through and answer each one. Selling information was his job.

When he opened his email, he saw his old friend, Ace, was in the Middle East. He was surprised, because he never thought Ace would travel outside Europe or the USA. He bet Ace's Aunt Sonora dragged him into her Committee, and had him traveling the world. Sonora was too old to travel and enjoyed her life in Berlin. Maybe life had gotten too dull. A hotel bombing was more exciting than running the Prowers's family ranching and oil interests.

He looked back at the computer screen. Thanks to his contacts, he had the information Ace needed and began typing.

• • •

In Doha

Ace hadn't left the Doha International Airport. He was still meeting with oil executives. The corporation had leases to sign requiring both his signature and Olen's. Since the bombing at the hotel, the airport was the most secure place. *Of all things,* he thought, *camel races had saved them from the hotel bombing.* His computer dinged, and he checked his email.

In London, his friend had information that a turf war over control of weapons smuggling was going on in Saudi. He read the email again and deleted the part that said Abdul bin Mischel bin Laden, the top suspect in planning the attack on the oil conference and the hotel in Riyadh, was back on the Arabian Peninsula. Not everyone needed that information, at least in his judgement.

He was ready to forward the email to Sam and Amy with a note saying he was on his way to Dubai and would be at the corporate condo. He knew Amy might have left for the ruins at Ubar. To him, she should've stayed in Riyadh, but he knew she'd go with Hassa. He sighed. He could hope. She was a Prowers and like him, she couldn't stay out of the action. He understood his own addiction to danger, but Amy was still in denial.

Abdul was the question. One of the Doha airport officials whom he'd bonded with told him Abdul left for South Africa on a flight scheduled about an hour after the hotel was bombed. He remembered, when he was still active in the military, how he met Abdul.

His Army special operations unit was in Khartoum, when Abdul's Uncle Osama was still alive and living there. Ace always thought the meeting was too convenient, even though his unit had a mission in the Sudan. What struck Ace, even then, as he got to know Abdul, who was proud of his grandfather Mohammed bin Laden and the empire he had built, was that he could be his Uncle Osama's likely heir.

The real irony, and on this Ace knew his Aunt Sonora would agree, was that Abdul was a Saudi royal, a grandson of Ibn Saud, the founder of modern Saudi Arabia. Rashid and Abdul were half-brothers. Abdul was not in the line of succession, because his mother was from Yemen, but stranger things had happened.

For now, he saw no reason to concern either the ambassador or Amy about Abdul. It might be nothing. Sam was a political novice, and Amy need to concentrate on Ubar and why Hassa wanted her for the dig. If Sam saw a threat, he would stop Amy from going with Hassa, which would be a red flag to everyone that something was wrong. The hotel bombing in Riyadh put the diplomatic community on edge.

He read the email attachment provided by Guy Melville, his London friend. More was at stake than liquor and drugs. Political control and who ran the Saudi oil fields was the prize.

Olen von Hagen, whose family partnered with the Prowers on Mexican and North African oil leases, and was his traveling companion to the Doha conference, interrupted his thinking. Often reserved and controlled, Olen could hardly contain himself.

"Another bombing has occurred, this time in Riyadh. It's all over CNN and Al-Jazeera where Arabic talk shows are discussing every aspect."

Ace grimaced, though he was glad the international Arabic station broadcast in English as well as Arabic. He didn't have the inconvenience of hiring a translator. Both men paused, thinking about how fast the international news had the story.

"Olen, this is the land of bad neighborhoods. Something is always blown up or someone executed. I know Mexico is a battleground right now over the drug traffic, but in the Middle East it's in their genes. They don't even need an excuse to fight."

Looking at Olen, he said, "It is written. That's something from out of T.E. Lawrence's book. What it means is nothing matters, because whatever happens was already written, predestined."

Ace knew Olen was beginning to understand the Middle East. People were crazy over here. What would Olen's adopted father, an old German general, think about oil deals in the Persian Gulf, when there was so much oil in the Gulf of Mexico? No one could ask him, since the old man was dead.

"Ace, I'm skeptical and to me nothing is written. We have to convince Amy to leave. It's nuts that she's running around this country for archeology. Didn't she get enough of that when she was looking for the Shroud of Turin for her father, or when Vince was killed in Pakistan?"

They both knew how difficult it was to persuade Amy to do something she didn't want to. But Olen was right.

"I haven't been pushy enough, Olen. What's that old expression on things that can never be? My Uncle Benton use to say it all the time, like getting water from the moon. I figured it was impossible to get her to leave, but it's time I did something. When we get to Dubai, I'll try to get her on the phone."

Dubai was looking good to both of them, like a port in the storm, or a sandstorm, since they were in the desert. Their flight was called and Olen closed his computer. Ace took a minute to send one quick email to Sam. The news about the Riyadh bombing changed his mind. He added what he had cut out—that Abdul was rumored to be on the Arabian Peninsula.

Something was going on and he suspected it was being orchestrated by the royals in Riyadh. One royal he was sure was involved was Amy's dead husband Vince's old pal, Prince Rashid. He didn't have any proof, only the feeling in his gut.

With that, he picked up his carry-on bag, and, with Olen, headed for the boarding gate at the Doha airport.

• • •

.

CHAPTER TEN

To Ubar

After fighting against the wind,
the cliffs above Ubar emerged.

In the morning, the only trace of the sandstorm was a light haze on the desert. Everyone was focused on getting to Ubar. Amy would like to have kidded the embassy guys about getting stuck in the sand, but getting back to Shisur was not easy. By the time M. Ishaq arrived, they were almost out of water.

Today the caravan included four SUVs, one for Hassa and Amy, one for the embassy guys, and two for Hassa's protective detail, certainly enough manpower to pull an SUV out of the sand. Each vehicle carried extra water and tents in case they had to spend the night in the desert. M. Ishaq was taking no chances.

After two hours of fighting against the wind, the cliffs above Ubar emerged in the hazy horizon. Looking at the desert and cliffs, Amy thought no one had been here for a hundred years, except for the two pickups sitting at the base of the cliff.

Thanks to M. Ishaq, Bedouins from his village arrived early to set up ropes in preparation for the descent. Skip, surprisingly, was an experienced caver. He explained to Amy and Brewer that ropes were set from rods in the ground tied to boulders. If the fragile limestone cliffs caved in, the ropes would be the caver's escape route.

Amy looked up at the dirt trail ending in what looked like a cave in the opening of the cliffs. She hoped they didn't have to rely on the ropes. To her, they looked like an unreliable security net. She had more confidence in Allah protecting them than in the ropes. For the moment, she was glad Audrey wasn't here. Maybe by the time she arrived, they'd have more knowledge of the fragility of the limestone ruin.

She put on her hat, as the sun was almost overhead, and followed Hassa up the trail to the entry of the cave. The princess, like Amy, wore a safari shirt and long skirt with boots. Hassa's face was uncovered. To Amy, her friend could appear at home in Italy or Spain.

As they slowly climbed in the heat, the Bedouin tribesmen pointed out drawings on the stone sides of the cliffs.

"Very old."

Amy knew they were probably right, but didn't care about drawings. Inside, what looked like a cave in the cliffs was the entrance to Ubar. The ruins of the ancient city were all that mattered.

Finally, they reached the opening surrounded by rocks. Thanks to two spotlights provided by M. Ishaq's men, they could see a path winding down inside the cavern. The path stopped at a stone door a few yards from the opening of the cave.

"We need to open that door," said Hassa.

Amy thought the rock door looked modern, almost new. She didn't think even the dry desert could preserve it for centuries in that condition. Two Bedouin took metal bars and pushed it open. As they did, the rock door swung open and dropped. For a moment silence was all they heard, and then a dull boom, like a shudder.

Amy stepped up to the opening next to Skip and Brewer. The three of them looked down into a seemingly endless abyss. She thought she was seeing the bottom of the world.

"What are we looking at?" asked Amy, as lights illuminated the shadow of ruins, though the bottom was still in darkness.

Hassa acted as their guide, pointing below to a limestone ledge and rock wall made by man.

"On that rock ledge, so the story goes, was the fortress of Ubar, until it slid down the mountain in an earthquake. Somehow the fortress stayed intact, but it crushed the homes of the town below, which fell to the bottom of the abyss. Finding the fortress intact is good news," said Hassa, "because the room with the safe is in the fortress. The cavers have to get to the ledge and find it."

Amy wanted to ask Hassa how she knew what safe and what room, but said nothing. The so-called excavation was getting weirder by the minute. Did Hassa already know what she was going to find? She seemed to.

Skip and Brewer pulled out cameras to take pictures of the interior. One of the Bedouin brought another spotlight and now they could almost see a faint shadow at the bottom of the pit. Amy guessed the plan was to go down on ropes to the room with the safe, wherever that was. How they could go down in the dim light, she didn't know. This dig was more like caving than an archeology excavation above ground. Caving was something she'd never wanted to do. She had no desire to go down into the hole.

Then Hassa, who she knew used to go caving in France, made a decision that surprised them all.

"We don't have enough rope or gear to excavate. Rashid will have to send more equipment and experts at caving."

She looked discouraged. "I've done caving, but this is way above my level."

Amy refrained from saying "good decision." Common sense prevailed, that was enough. She took a last look into the hole and followed Hassa to the opening in the cliff. As they came out of the darkness into the sunlight of the desert floor, Amy blinked. The sun seemed too bright, but she could see a goat roasting. She looked at her watch. It was nearly noon. The walk up the path to the stone door and opening it had taken longer than she thought.

"I need to call Rashid, but all of you go ahead and eat." Hassa headed for the SUV and the powerful satellite phone would work in the Empty Quarter, thanks to the communication satellites that circled the globe.

Amy poured a cup of coffee. Skip and Brewer returned and were watching the goat turn on the skewer and plotting. Though it wasn't the hot season, the sun at midday was warm.

"Rashid won't be able to get the climbing gear down here for a couple of days, even if he uses a helicopter. He needs to find rock climbers who know what they're doing to get down to that fortress," said Brewer.

"Riyadh has a climbing club with many rock climbers, but the question is, does he want them on this dig? Does he have any choice? No one else is going to climb down this unstable mess."

Listening to him, Amy asked, "Does anyone know or can tell how stable that fortress is?"

Skip and Brewer both shrugged.

"I use to cave," said Skip, "but nothing this dangerous. The key is to find out if the rocks that sank so many years ago are stable. I doubt even experts can tell. I've been on a dozen caving trips, and never seen anything like this. Hassa is right, we need expert cavers."

"She's calling Rashid on the satellite phone, which is a secure line. She could have texted him on her cell phone," said Brewer. "What is the reason for all the secrecy?"

No one answered, because no one knew.

Ali G handed them bottles of chilled water, then headed over to the tribesmen. Drinking water was a requirement for everyone in the desert.

Skip sipped water as they continued to watch the goat roasting. Looking around, he saw that the three of them were alone.

"Amy, you should know why Brewer and I came with you. We needed more information on the mines, even if all we did was talk to the desert tribesmen. Mining equipment is being hauled in, and we doubt it's to mine gold. I know all the stories about Solomon's mine, but that was two thousand years ago. Now that we're here, it appears as if something is going on besides mining. We just don't know what. Maybe the tribesmen will tell us. Going to Hud's tomb was an excuse to get close to the camp."

Amy sipped coffee and was silent. This trip suddenly seemed like a dead end. First Hassa, who seemed to know exactly where to go in the ruins, now Skip and Brewer with their own agenda.

Ali G returned from where the SUVs were parked. "Hassa's on the phone to Rashid, but from what I heard, he wants us to wait here another day. Hassa is ready to return to Riyadh. She's right. Getting down this abyss won't be easy."

To Amy, returning to Riyadh would be better than sitting around the oasis. She brought a couple of books in case she had down time, but maybe she should see something else in the desert. She doubted she ever be in the Empty Quarter again.

Skip and Brewer were talking to one of the Bedouin they met the night before. They walked over to her and Brewer repeated what he had said earlier about Hud's tomb. This time everyone at the roasting pit heard about Hud.

"The Bedouin are willing to take us to Hud's tomb. Amy, you're welcome to come along. We'll be back later tonight unless we get stuck in the sand again."

He and Skip both laughed, but Amy didn't. The two had gotten stuck once and could again. Besides, they really wanted more pictures of the mining camp. Maybe they hadn't spent as much time as she had in the deserts in the US. Amy didn't hesitate to say no. She'd stay with Hassa now that she knew looking for Hud's tomb was more or less a ruse to see the mining camp. She caught Ali G's look of approval when she said no.

With Ali G, Amy watched Skip and Brewer drive off in the embassy SUV. Hassan, M. Ishaq's brother, was again driving.

"How did they know they'd be going?" she asked. Ali G shrugged, but didn't seem surprised.

To Amy, taking off at a moment's notice with desert tribesmen they had just met seemed odd. She pulled out her phone and sent a text to Audrey to stay in Riyadh. Her stepdaughter had no business coming to Shisur until the excavation had a plan. Next, she sent a text to the ambassador telling him his staff had driven off into the sunset.

As she and Ali G walked back to the SUV, she heard her phone. Pulling it out, she read the text from the ambassador. "Tell Skip and Brewer not to leave Shisur." She texted back that it was too late, they'd left. Why the ambassador wanted them to stay, she didn't know. But she knew it would have been the right decision.

• • •

"Skip and Brewer are heading again to Hud's tomb. Am I supposed to know who Hud is? I had never heard of him until I came to the desert," said Amy, filling her plate with goat meat and bread. She wondered over the centuries how many graves were in this desert, and how many ruins were still to be found.

Hassa had just arrived at the roasting pit and laughed at her friend.

"You're not alone, my dear. Today hardly anyone knows about Hud. Back in BC times, when the water finally receded from the peninsula, the people of Ad were living here. Hud was their leader and Ubar was their center. Legend tells us the people were of low morals or no morals and worshiped more than one god. When Hud died, their empire ended."

Amy bit into another piece of flat bread as Hassa continued.

"When Ubar fell, the people scattered and Hud was forgotten. Over the centuries, whenever there was a crime in this part of the world, Bedouins would threaten to take the accused to Hud's tomb. The threat often brought an immediate confession because his tomb is believed to be haunted and the source of evil djinns. Hud's tomb also has more than one location. I wonder to which location the Bedouin are taking Skip and Brewer."

"I have no idea," said Amy. "I wish I'd asked more questions—stupid me. I texted the ambassador that they were going and he answered saying they should stay here. His text came after they'd left. I texted them, but they haven't responded."

"The ambassador is right," said Hassa. "They have their own agenda. Don't you agree?"

"They jumped at the chance to come to the Empty Quarter with your expedition. Now they are interested in everything but your excavation," said Amy, wanting to ask Hassa her agenda. But she held back. Knowing Saudis, she'd find out soon enough.

Hassa said nothing. They finished eating and Amy was thinking about what book to read when her friend surprised her with a new outing.

"There is a local market down the road toward the Dhofar Mountains. My security detail tells me the road circles back to Shisur. The market could be interesting. The native women make handmade trinkets to sell to the smugglers."

Amy agreed immediately. Any excuse to be out in the desert was better than sitting at Shisur. Hassa's protective detail in another SUV followed them down the road. Looking out at the never-ending dunes reminded Amy of how the Arabian Peninsula was formed.

"Hassa, Ali G and I were talking about the history of the peninsula, how the sea once covered all of this."

"Amy, no one knows why, but coral fossils and fish scales have been found in the sand. Over three hundred million years ago, in the Jurassic era, this desert was a sea. Once rivers ran through the peninsula and formed the many wadis. Near Jizan, south of Jeddah on the Red Sea, French archeologists found bones of a moeritherium."

"I'm not up on bones. What's that?" asked Amy.

"I know. I just learned the name, too. It is a hippo-like animal that is now extinct. At one time, the Arabian Peninsula was connected to Africa, but we are talking millions of years ago. All this odd stuff makes me wonder what we might find at Ubar. It's historically important as a stop on the caravanserai, and it hasn't been mauled by man."

Hassa paused as if she was thinking, then continued. "We also believe we might find important Islamic artifacts. In a way, Ubar is our heritage."

This was the first time Hassa had mentioned what sounded to Amy like the real reason Ubar was important. What Rashid and Hassa wanted in the ruins of the ancient city must have something to do with religion. Amy's intuition told her whatever they found was why they'd asked her to be on the excavation.

To her, that meant one thing. The royals needed her political connections to verify the finding to establish the provenance. She would verify the source, where they had found the artifacts.

• • •

CHAPTER ELEVEN

To Sanaa— the Yemen Connection

Abdul's obsession fit Rashid's ambition
to be selected as deputy premier.

Holding automatic weapons, security guards were posted every twenty feet at Sana'a International Airport, or as it was known in the Arab world, El Rahaba. Like many third-world countries, the guards looked at the passengers, but paid little attention to detail. What got their attention was the beep at the electrical gate, which told them someone was carrying a weapon.

The plane from Johannesburg, South Africa, arrived every day at seven in the morning. At that early hour, the Yemeni guards weren't quite awake. Most suffered from the effect of smoking qat, a mild narcotic plant, the night before.

Abdul bin Mischel, a tall, thin man dressed in a beige safari suit, walked past the guards with ease. Through his sunglasses, he noted the security guards barely looked at his heavy leather bags. According to his passport, he was Syed Rahman, born in Johannesburg. As a South African businessman from Durban, he was prepared to recite a long litany on the merits of chemical waste disposal. Today the Arabian Peninsula simply buried waste. However, the truth was Abdul—or Syed—wasn't going to make a living from waste disposal.

His business, chemical waste disposal, was a free pass to bring chemicals into the Gulf countries where they weren't available. The complex mix of chemicals required to dispose of waste required a degree in chemistry, something few, if any, Yemeni had. Civil or electrical engineers wouldn't be knowledgeable enough to question what chemicals a freighter was unloading at the Port of Aden, or the destination of the chemicals.

As planned, Abdul's cousin was waiting for him. They drove to one of the nondescript housing compounds near the airport. Abdul pulled out a packet of documents.

"Muktar, you'll need these papers to get the chemicals through customs, though I doubt the Aden officials will pay much attention. Be sure you have an SUV, or a pickup. Do you need any money?"

"No, you sent more than I needed through the hawalas, and I bought this pickup."

Abdul smiled. "We have more to do. I sent you extra funds as a backup when I left Durban. You did well with the purchase of the pickup. It looks very used."

They both laughed.

"I bought it in Saudi," said Muktar. "It is good to have you back, my cousin."

"I'll be at the oasis of Shisur by nightfall," said Abdul.

"*Ma'assalama.* See you outside Najran on the road to Riyadh."

• • •

The phone call
Rashid's satellite phone was beeping. Quickly, he unlocked the desk drawer where he secured it, and he punched the button on the phone to take the call.

It was Muktar in Aden. "Your Highness, our friend has arrived from South Africa and is on his way to Riyadh. The supplies came in this morning."

"Any trouble with customs?" asked Rashid.

"No."

"You know where to go?" Rashid's question was carefully phrased without details. The satellite phone was secure, but the kingdom had many hackers. The best security was to avoid discussing where and when on any electronic device.

"I do," replied Muktar.

Rashid wanted to send his security men to escort the SUV with the chemicals, but knew that would be a flashing light to security, customs, smugglers and thieves that the cargo had value.

"My cousin, you know the road and where to meet our friend?" Rashid called Muktar cousin, though he was Abdul's cousin, not his.

"Yes."

"*Assalam Alaikum.*"

"*Walaikum Assalam.*"

Rashid turned the phone off, locking it back in his desk. Who would ever have imagined how complicated the relationship would become with his half-brother Abdul and the family of Mohammed bin Laden.

Interesting, thought Rashid, *how everyone loses track of the girls. When I rule, their talents will be used. Abdul and I have the same grandfather, ibn Saud, the founder of modern Saudi Arabia, and the same father. Such irony in families. We are half-brothers, but he's not a royal prince. His mother was the daughter of a Yemeni commoner and billionaire Mohammed bin Laden, and the sister of the man made famous by the Americans, the dead terrorist, Osama bin Laden. So his half-brother, while royal, was not in the Saudi line of succession. He was the heir to one of the largest fortunes in the world, the bin Laden's.*

Today, their father was dead, and Abdul was one of the few people Rashid trusted. Though not a member of the Black Princes, his half-brother's obsession was to see the kingdom ruled by Rashid. Then and only then, according to Abdul, the Saudi King would stop being a pawn of the super powers. He believed, as did his Uncle Osama, they would drive the infidels from the Middle East.

The first step was for Rashid to be named as deputy premier, second in the line of succession to be king of Saudi Arabia. Many royal grandsons were competing for that title, and the royals would make a decision soon, as to who would be appointed deputy premier. With both the King and Crown Prince ill, the deputy premier, once appointed, would rule.

"I see my path, Allah be praised."

As he said it, realized he was parroting the mantra of his countrymen, what so many of them said on any occasion. Only in his heart, he wasn't sure Allah had anything to do with it.

Abdul had worked with Osama for years, and his uncle successfully radicalized his nephew's political and religious beliefs. Abdul, in many ways, converted Rashid to terrorism as a pathway to power.

Now, Rashid knew, was the time to tap into what his half-brother had learned about using violence to rule. The two hotel bombings were the first successes. The next one would be the real test. For a moment, he was sad. Abdul's destiny was to give his life.

• • •

Abdul drove slowly through the Dhofar Mountains. Occasionally, a speeding pickup truck passed him. He could afford to hire a plane to Najran, but driving was autonomous. No one knew he was going to the oasis except Muktar and Rashid.

Muktar would take the road to Najran, which looked like he was going to Dubai. Outside the town the road split, and that was where they'd meet. From there, he alone would take the explosives into Riyadh to wherever Rashid had selected.

The blacktop road ran north through a wadi, where once rivers flowed. Ahead, he could see the top spire of a mosque. It was eleven in the morning, and he could use a coffee.

Entering the village, he saw SUVs and instantly slowed. They were clean with no dents, obviously belonging to officials. With the wind and sand, driving was often a challenge. Usually desert vehicles were rolled a couple of times. These SUVs looked as if they'd just come from the factory.

Turning around to leave would be conspicuous, and if he did, where would he go? His pickup was old and if he went off-road, he'd never get over the dunes. Other cars were parked along the road looking like a desert traffic jam. Then he saw why. A market was set up beside the mosque.

Bedouin women were sitting behind wooden crates with umbrellas shielding them from the sun. Getting out, Abdul was glad he changed into the traditional clothes; the long white thobe and ghutrah, the Saudi red plaid headdress. No one paid any attention to him.

Locals were sitting at small wire tables drinking coffee. He saw two women next to a table of men, most likely their husbands. Whatever the relationship, they must be the occupants of the SUVs.

He walked over to one of the tables selling water and took a closer look at the group. He didn't see any weapons on the men. Women, with their heads covered, all looked the same. He took another look, and realized one of women was Hassa, his half-brother's wife. What could Hassa be doing here in the desert? He couldn't hide. She'd seen him.

She acted as if he was expected. "Abdul, how nice to see you."

Her friend Amy was introduced and Hassa ordered Abdul a coffee. He told them he had come from Yemen and was going through Shisur and Layla on the way to Riyadh.

"You're less than an hour to the guest house at Shisur. You must come and stay with us, Abdul, it's dangerous to be driving these roads alone. We're ready to leave unless Amy wants more coffee."

Amy shook her head no. Hassa briefed her protective detail, who didn't look pleased, but said nothing. They climbed into the vehicles and Abdul followed.

"So, Hassa, who is Abdul?" asked Amy, as they climbed into the Rover.

"He's Rashid's half-brother who lives in South Africa. I have no idea what he is doing in the Empty Quarter. Maybe tonight we will find out. Rashid may know. I'll text him right now."

Amy thought about the map of the Empty Quarter she had in her head. There wasn't much to remember. At Shisur, the road split. One branch went north to Riyadh and the other headed east to Dubai. There must be an easier way to get to Riyadh, like flying. She found it curious that no one questioned why Abdul was driving. No one, except tourists, usually Anglos, drove through the Empty Quarter for the view.

• • •

Waiting at Shisur

That evening, in front of the guest house, a goat was turning on the spit. Amy liked the meat, but found a steady diet tiring. Goat was a staple in the Middle East, and obviously contributed to a long life, since so many of the desert people lived to an old age. Today, the meat tasted great.

Almost on cue, Skip and Brewer appeared.

"We never got to Hud's tomb," said Skip. "We took the wrong turn, and spent the day digging the SUV out of the sand again."

"Tomorrow morning we're leaving early to try again."

"Would you like to come this time?" Brewer asked, adding they intended to only go to the tomb.

"Yes, unless Hassa goes back to Riyadh."

Walking up to join the group, Hassa said, "Rashid vetoed a return to Riyadh. He wants us to wait here. He's sending equipment and a couple of rock climbers. They're Norwegian diplomats. He says they know what they're doing."

Skip asked Hassa if she wanted to visit Hud's tomb.

"Why not."

"We leave at sunrise."

Hassa shook her head no. "I don't do early, so count me out."

Hassa saw Abdul and waved at him to join them. He waved back, then opened the hood of the pickup.

"I'll take him some apple juice. He ought to eat unless he is living on dates and water. It isn't Ramadan, so he isn't fasting."

To Amy, water and dates sounded like a healthy diet. She watched Hassa and Abdul. Driving across the desert in a beat-up pickup still struck her as odd.

Abdul closed the hood, drank some apple juice, and got in the pickup. Hassa pointed to the tent covering the gas pumps from the sun and walked back to the barbeque pit.

"He's going to drive to Riyadh, but he has a problem with the engine in his truck. He thinks it's been fixed, but is checking again."

Hassa went on to explain to Amy how driving across the desert at night was something those who lived in the desert enjoyed.

"The sky at night is spectacular. You feel as if you can touch the stars. As long as he stays on the blacktop road, he'll get to Riyadh before morning prayer. If his old pickup breaks down, someone will come along and help him, even if it's smugglers."

Silently, Amy questioned why he would drive on alone. To her, the pickup belonged in a junk yard. Whatever, now it was time to head to M. Ishaq's guest house. Sunrise would come early.

• • •

CHAPTER TWELVE

At Hud's Tomb

Local Bedouins think Hud's tomb is here.

"Assalam Alaikum," Hassan greeted Amy as she climbed into the jeep to join Skip and Brewer. It was predawn, and they drove in silence.

Amy looked up at the darkened sky. By this time of the morning, the desert sky was always clear.

Funny, she thought, *how often the windstorms came early in the evening, but by early morning the desert was usually as clear as cleaned glass.*

Looking east, she could see the horizon turning to a red glow. She watched Hassan shift gears and head down a dry lake bed.

Slowly the sun climbed high in the sky and she looked at her watch. They'd left Shisur at predawn, and now just an hour later, the sun was beating down on them. It was hot, but no one turned on air conditioning. This was the desert: you lived with the heat.

According to their driver, Hassan, who was M. Ishaq's brother, and Brewer's handheld GPS, the tomb was only a few kilometers away. She hoped Ali G wasn't upset she'd left. The last thing he said to her was "please don't go".

To pass the time, she read the book Hassa had given her to learn about the prophet Hud.

Hassan interrupted her reading. "The road follows the sand shoals to the base of a flat flint ridge."

"And," said Skip, "in the ancient scriptures, flint was the key to finding Ubar. Here we are on our way to Hud's tomb, and we have a flint ridge. Don't believe we saw flint going to Ubar. And that's why many mistake this tomb for Ubar."

They got out of the pickup and climbed up about forty feet to what looked like the entrance to a cave. Hassan flashed a light inside to clear the area of any bats that might have taken refuge for the night. They wouldn't need the lights once the sun was up.

Amy looked inside the opening at the rocky ledge that headed downward into the earth.

"What is it we're looking for?"

Brewer seemed to know. "The pieces of pottery are good, but we need something called cuneiform, writing on stone. That would be the crucial evidence it is Hud's tomb." He sighed, disappointed. "This place looks like it's been picked over."

The sun crept up higher into the sky. Amy and Brewer looked at each other, thinking the trip had been wasted.

Then the two heard a shout from Skip. He had walked across to a ridge that looked like it led to another opening in the cliffs.

Years of corrosion had made the limestone shelves fragile. The weight of the flint rock could cause a sinkhole. The rocks would crash into the earth and the cave would be closed forever.

Carefully, they climbed down to join Skip. There was a slab that looked more like a door covering an entrance. Skip put the light on it and Amy carefully rubbed the slab. She could see marks on it, and thought it might be writing.

They looked again to their left wondering if the flint ridge was going to collapse. As they watched, the rock and sand collapsed around them. Somehow the ledge they were on held.

Slowly, they edged around the slab door to an opening in the ridge wall. Carefully Amy, Brewer, Skip, and Hassan stepped on the broken shards, pieces of pottery, and entered a room carved out in the limestone.

"How simple," said Amy, looking up at the ridge. "We could have looked all over, but this is the opening."

The stones in the center were blackened. Obviously, this had been a fireplace or site for rituals. Against the wall was a stack of flat stones, which she recognized at once.

"Cuneiform tablet writing," said Amy. She wondered why the stones were stacked so conveniently, almost as if waiting to be found.

"Praise be to Allah and Mohammed, his prophet," replied Hassan.

Amy was thinking they couldn't possibly transport all the stones back to Riyadh. They needed a helicopter. The question was, which stones were important?

They noticed three were scattered in front of the others. She carefully picked them up and wrapped them in gunnysacks.

Will we ever be back, she thought. *Who knows?*

So far, they were lucky, and the rock ledge they were on was solid. But with earthquakes, they weren't sure the ridge wouldn't collapse at any moment.

Her foot had hit something in the sand. She moved the sand around what appeared to be more stone slabs with writing on them.

Amy brushed the dust and sand away. "It has the same writing as the door."

She pulled out a digital camera. "We also have to take detailed pictures of the door. We may be able to identify the language. What if this is Ubar and not the other ruin?"

They were all silent, thinking if this is Ubar, where was the gold?

• • •

They left the tomb believed to be Hud's, and Hassan said, "I apologize, but I know where another tomb is on the way back to Shisur. Some think its Hud's tomb."

Without hesitation, they all wanted to check it out.

"In the Middle East," said Skip, "every place in history has another story."

Amy added, "It's because so many thousands of years have passed. Who knows what really was going on?"

"No one," chimed in Brewer.

Hassan turned east, away from the road to Shisur. The road began to descend and Hassan slowed. The road was blacktop, but full of pot holes. To their right was a rocky ridge peaking up above the sand dunes. Hassan said there was a cave on the side of the sand ridge and where some Bedouin believed was the real tomb of Hud.

"Many local Bedouins think Hud's tomb is here, and the cave we were in was where the locals lived."

"How far?" asked Amy.

"Just up the next ridge. If it's opened," said Hassan, "we might walk in, but many of these tombs have been sealed shut. The Bedouins seal them to keep the evil spirits, the djinns, inside."

Skip was squinting up the ridge as if he could already see the tomb.

"The Bedouins who live here believe the spirits are just as old as the Nabataeans who lived in the first century BC. Their dead are buried at Madain Saleh near the Jordanian border."

"Interesting," said Amy. "I may never see those ruins, but I'm finding all these buried ridges in the desert fascinating. No tourists are here, for sure."

Looking up at the barren ridge peeking out of the sand, she was glad the drive had only taken an hour. They'd be back at Shisur by late morning. She could see the tomb opening above them on the ridge. The road ended, and they parked on flat gravel.

"This is the perfect place for tour buses," joked Brewer.

Getting out of the SUV, Amy felt the silence of the desert. The wind was blowing, but nothing was moving. Brewer was taking pictures. She could see an entry, like a cave opening. Skip had taken a flashlight from the pickup, and was heading up the ridge.

Amy watched him, not sure why she was hesitating, when a dusty white pickup swirled from behind a sand dune with two men standing in the back. It took a moment for her to realize they had automatic weapons pointed at them.

Hassan started to speak and a shot rang out from inside the pickup. For a moment, Amy froze. Then she realized this was real and watched his body slowly float to the ground. He was face down, not moving. The sand around him was turning wet with what she knew was blood.

A tall thin man, his face and head covered with a black hood, got out of the pickup. Holding a semi-automatic rifle in his hands, he walked over and kicked Hassan.

"Those who work with infidels will die."

He looked up at the three Americans, turned Hassan over and shot him again, this time through the head. One of the men chased after Skip, who had ducked into the opening of the cave to try and hide. Within minutes, he was dragged down the trail to the vehicles.

"We go. You," he pointed a handgun at Brewer, "driver's seat SUV. Others get in back. Try to leave, I shoot him."

He walked back to the dirty white pickup, keeping his gun on Brewer. Switching to Arabic, he spoke to the driver and the two men who had been in the back of the pickup.

Skip, who spoke Arabic, understood what he said. He turned to Amy. "They're taking us to some house. Sorry we got you into this. Now whose wife do you want to be?"

Amy thought the straight-laced political officer was quite relaxed, considering Hassan was dead, and they were being held at gunpoint. She grimaced, acutely conscious of Hassan's bleeding body lying on the gravel, yet knew there was nothing any of them could do. She still felt cold, even in the heat but needed to focus on how to get out of this mess.

She'd been kidnapped years ago in Mexico. Somehow this incident seemed different. Probably because Hassan had been killed.

"I'm going to tell them the truth. They're in control and we have to go along until we see a chance to escape," she said.

"No, you're not. Forget the truth." Skip was adamant. "If they ask, you're my wife, which may save you from being sold as a slave. That's what happens to captured women. They may sell off married women, too; but if you pretend to be married, you have a better chance of staying with us than if you're single. Right now, they want something from us, or they would have killed us with Hassan."

Amy realized she had no options. Survival was her goal.

"I've been married three times, why not a fourth. We are going to get out of this, right?"

Neither Skip nor Brewer answered. Amy realized they didn't know any more than she did.

The leader opened the door. His face was covered, but his eyes glared at Amy and Skip. "Everyone, hand me your cell phones, now."

They fumbled to find their phones, then he took the butt end of his weapon and smashed each one. He tossed the phones to his men who put them under the tires of the pickup to run over them.

Pointing the gun at Brewer, he said, "drive, follow the pickup," and pointed down the blacktop road as he climbed into the front seat. The pickup ahead of them drove over the phones, crushing them.

Amy knew it didn't matter if the phones were destroyed, everyone at Shisur knew they'd gone to Hud's tomb. She was sure when they looked for them, they would follow the road to the other tomb and find Hassan's body and the phones.

Where they were being taken was what was important. The djinns had done their work. The tomb was an evil place.

Under her sleeve of her safari jacket, Amy felt her plastic watch. The watch looked cheap, something no one would be interested in taking off her, like a Rolex. Nevertheless, she kept it covered and felt for the tiny button on the side. The leader was watching the road and Brewer, not looking in the back seat at her or Skip. She pushed the button, hoping it activated the GPS.

Once M. Ishaq realized they were missed, a search would begin. Hassa, the embassy, Sam, everyone would be looking for them. If the watch worked, the signal would identify where they were. She took a deep breath, realizing the problem. Ace was the only one who knew she had the watch. He'd given it to her, and one to Olen, saying they had to protect themselves if they got lost in the Middle East.

Would Ace get the signal in Dubai? Amy didn't know, nor did she have any idea what Ace would do. She hoped he would call Sam in Riyadh. But with her cousin, there was no telling if he'd take finding her into his own hands.

The watch was a long shot. The real question was how long it would take Hassa, Ali G, and M. Ishaq to find Hassan's body and realize they had been kidnapped.

· · ·

CHAPTER THIRTEEN

Shisur Again

Not every Bedouin was pleased to have
a nuclear power plant in their desert,
let alone what it really was, a weapons factory.

Abdul woke up and looked at his watch. It was nearly noon. He should have left at dawn. The flight and the drive across the desert had tired him more than he realized. And then he'd been delayed by repairs to the pickup. He headed out of the house to his pickup.

"Coffee, Abdul?" Hassa was sitting on the front patio with M. Ishaq. A large pot of coffee was sitting on a burner between them. Without hesitation, M. Ishaq poured him a cup and explained that the Americans had left for Hud's tomb. Abdul sat down and enjoyed the coffee. What good would it do to protest?

"I know you need to go. I hope the repairs hold," said Hassa. Her voice was smooth and calm. If she knew why Abdul was in the Empty Quarter, she didn't show it. Her demeanor was the same as when he met her in the village market.

How much Hassa knew about Rashid's plans, Abdul could only guess. His half-brother often said his wife shared everything, which was the reason he only had one wife. The more wives, the more trouble, a philosophy Abdul understood. He had no wife. His life's mission was his life.

For now, he had to be careful, because of M. Ishaq. The tribal leader was believed loyal to Rashid. With his village on the main smuggler's route to the port of al Mukalla in Yemen, he had to be connected to them, if not one of the leaders. He thanked Allah that Muktar had taken the road to Najran to the west.

He decided not to trust M. Ishaq's loyalty and would create an illusion.

"I'm thinking about heading east to Dubai."

Hassa interrupted. "But Rashid is expecting you."

"I have cousins in Dubai, and can fly to Riyadh."

Hassa smiled. "Of course, that is the best way to go."

She listened while he and M. Ishaq discussed the drive. It would be about seven hours, and all Abdul had to do was stay heading east on the blacktop road. Her intuition told her in some way Abdul was involved with her husband's plans for succession. Whatever it was, soon everyone would know.

"When I call Rashid, I'll tell him your plans have changed," she said.

Abdul smiled and thanked M. Ishaq for his hospitality.

"*Allah Ma'ak*, God go with you."

Hassa replied, "*Ila al liqa'a*, see you later." To herself, she thought, *I'll never see him again.*

Abdul nodded yes, and quickly got into the truck.

• • •

Turning east to Dubai, he calculated the mining camp would be an hour away. Once at the camp, he could circle back to the Najran road because the area was flat and graveled, not the sandy dunes. The pickup should be able to manage the hard gravel, *Inshallah*.

At the intersection where the road to the east went to Dubai and north to Riyadh was a wooden sign board. There really was no need for the sign. Still, the sign made him smile: New York, 5400 kilometers; Moscow 4200 kilometers; Sidney 7200 kilometers. He turned east to the mining camp.

• • •

Brewer saw the main road at the same time as the leader. Bluntly, he was told to turn east, the opposite direction from Shisur. In the rearview mirror, he could see Amy and Skip sleeping, or at least pretending to be. Now was as good a time as any to engage the leader. Who was this guy speaking almost perfect English with an American accent?

"Someone is ahead of me up the road."

The leader took a pair of binoculars out of a small briefcase at his feet, and peered ahead.

"Slow down. Don't get any closer. We don't have far to go."

Brewer hoped Amy and Skip heard what was said. Not that they could do anything. Knowing what was going on was the only way they were going to get out of this mess.

• • •

M. Ishaq knew something was wrong. It was nearly two p.m. His brother should have returned by noon. He walked over to Hassa's guest house. Forcing himself to sound unconcerned, he said. "They probably have broken down, or are stuck in the sand. I'm sending another vehicle out to find them. Only one road goes to Hud's tomb, so they'll be easy to find."

"M. Ishaq, take part of my protective detail."

He thanked her. "I want to carry weapons."

"No problem," said Hassa. "My protective detail wanted to bring weapons when we left Riyadh. You have weapons here?"

"Yes, we hide them in a cache under the date palms."

"My detail will be pleased."

Two hours later, no one was pleased, as Hassa's protective detail and M. Ishaq, with the villagers, returned with Hassan's body.

Hassa couldn't contain herself, even with a dead body in the pickup.

"How could an SUV disappear with Amy, Skip and Brewer? Who would be so stupid to take them?"

Nothing anyone could say would stop her from ranting. And none of them had an answer. She was adamant.

"I'll get the royal family and the Americans to search. We will find them."

• • •

M. Ishaq knew the Americans would never give up. As for the royals, he couldn't read Rashid's mind, but his wife obviously thought he'd use Saudi National Guard to find them. His own motive in the search would be different.

Regardless of what happened to the Americans, he knew he'd kill whoever took his brother's life. The kidnapping was a blot on his reputation, but nothing was more important than vindicating his brother's death. Someone would pay.

As the tribal leader, he had relationships with everyone, the Saudi government, and the Yemeni smugglers out of al Mukalla, the port on the Yemen side of the Empty Quarter. Every group needed something from him, and he was in the position to provide whatever support they needed.

For the past thirty years, I've fed Saudi intelligence information on smuggling operations including Saudi government officials and royals. My cut has been good, and I have used it to help my tribe. No one who lived in Shisur would tell any tales.

Now he wasn't so sure. The execution of the Awad brother made him nervous. Someone had to have a side deal. Otherwise, no one, certainly not the Black Princes, would have executed him.

He looked out the window at the sandy sky. Who would be stupid enough to commit this kidnapping? Why take three Americans? The only ones who didn't care about power struggles in the Saudi government.

Or someone had screwed up. Could it be Prince Rashid had lost control?

• • •

Rashid received Hassa's text, which was more secure than the phone. He had never trusted the Yemeni and now he knew why. They were idiots. Their greed and stupidity had betrayed him and the Black Princes.

All they had to do was leave Hassan and Amy tied up and take the two embassy men. Adrenaline had taken over, and they acted as common criminals, which is what they were at heart.

To Rashid, the embassy staff got what they deserved. Why did the Americans want to go to the Empty Quarter? Was it the mining camp? How would they know? The camouflage was perfect. Still, no other reason made sense.

He never understood diplomats, not just the Americans, but any of the international diplomats in Saudi. They didn't care about smuggling. Weapons or booze illegally brought in didn't matter. Smuggling, to them, was the Saudi National Guard's problem. Smugglers didn't touch diplomats.

How wrong all of them were. Embassy officials should be concerned with smuggling because it was destabilizing the kingdom. Where would they get their oil?

He set up the Black Princes to use smugglers to move weapons around the kingdom. And if they made some money off the smuggled weapons or booze, who was to care? Saudi government officials were always ready for a handout. Some got greedy, like the Awad brother. Such was the cost of doing business.

Amy, the wife of an old friend and in many ways, his friend, was different. Finding her was his responsibility since he'd hired the Yemeni who kidnapped her. If the succession meeting in Riyadh wasn't due, he'd go to the Empty Quarter and track down and kill these criminals himself. But he couldn't take the chance.

The royal family would meet any day to settle the succession. They might not want to meet, but it was a must. A deputy crown prince, third in line, would be selected. Whoever was picked would likely be the next king. He couldn't afford to miss any meeting.

Rashid hit the intercom to get Salah, his administrative assistant, and explain to him what was needed to start the search. There would be endless coordination with the embassy, and he wanted his own people out in the desert ahead of them.

Now he had to phone the ambassador. As a personal friend of the Prowers family and the supervisor of the two missing embassy staff, Sam would be pissed off and want action now.

Salah poured coffee while Rashid thought about the madhouse the search would become once the Yanks were involved. There would be briefings, more briefings, and endless coordination of task forces. What poor timing, with Abdul arriving with the chemicals.

The phone rang, Salah answered. It was the American ambassador.

After the usual "oh my God," Rashid told the ambassador all the resources of the palace would be used in the search. Salah would handle the details.

"Anything you need, Mr. Ambassador, tell me. Amy is our family friend, and I owe her dead husband."

He put the phone down and looked out the window. The kidnappers had to be part of Awad's gang. The execution had cut off his head, but the gang had grown a new one. Later he would take care of them, but now he had to find the Americans.

The Empty Quarter had few roads. Hassa's security detail saw no signs of a track across the desert from Hud's tomb. That meant whoever took them came back to the main road, which went to either Riyadh or Dubai. On the road to Dubai was the mining camp. The imam at the camp would know.

Rashid took a long breath. His grandfather, Abdul al Aziz, had not conquered all the Bedouin tribes in the Empty Quarter because of dumb luck. The imam at the mining camp was loyal to his family and had been a friend of his father's. Most important, the imam knew the Bedouin who lived at the camp year-round.

The Bedouin thought they owned the desert. The mine infringed on their authority. Not every Bedouin was pleased to have a nuclear power plant in their desert, let alone what it really was, a weapons factory. One tribal leader had sworn the so-called mine would never be operational.

Along with the Bedouin dissidents, his worry was that the Americans had the ability to cover the area with satellite coverage or drones. They'd be all over the mining area. So far, the camouflage had worked, but under extensive scrutiny, maybe not.

Could my plans to rule depend on camouflage? Rashid hoped not. As a royal prince, his ambition was to rule, not like many royals who believed their role was to consume. His father was at the top of the succession pyramid, but as his son, he had to prove himself. And he had.

Educated in America as an electrical engineer, he returned home and developed cheap electricity for the Saudi people. Then he sold what was left at a profit to the other Gulf States, donating the money to charity.

Providing cheap electricity helped. *I am on track to be selected the deputy premier and ahead of my half-brothers and cousins who are still alive.*

To be considered for deputy premier, two heartbeats from being king, he had to be seen by the Saudi people, by the religious zealots, the wahhabis, and those who worked in the Saudi government as a person of substance—sympathetic to commoners.

Only his Black Princes, one whom was the deputy chief of the National Guard, knew building a power plant and mining in the Empty Quarter was a cover-up. The real work being done was happening in the weapons factory at the camp.

The final step to show his worth as a leader would be when Hassa completed the dig at Ubar. The Qur'an she'd find would knock out the rest of his competition. The kidnappings could cause the next phase of his plan to collapse.

I can't allow that to happen. Where was Abdul?

According to Hassa's text, his half-brother was supposed to be at the mining camp or near it, supposedly going to Dubai. The camp had a cell tower though service was intermittent because of the wind and the blowing sand.

Where the chemicals were, he didn't know. But he was confident Abdul would know how to conceal the chemicals from aerial surveillance. To date, everyone, except the Bedouin and smugglers, had been kept out of the Empty Quarter. The kidnappers had put the desert on the Americans' radar. The sooner the three were found and returned safely, the better. His hope was that the Yemini criminals would realize the Yanks were worth more alive than dead.

Calling Abdul was worth a try. Surprisingly, he got through to Abdul's phone on the first ring, then the line went dead. Because it rang, that meant his half-brother was at the camp. If the phone worked, the camp, which had communication towers, was near. Then his phone rang.

"*Salam Alaikum*, my brother, I was almost to the camp when the phone rang."

"*Salam Alaikum.* A sandstorm cloud has appeared on the horizon," said Rashid.

He knew Abdul understood the codes. They never used the word *sandstorm* unless they had a problem. Something had happened and sandstorm stood for hostages.

"A treasure has disappeared, and if not returned, will bring the sand down on us. You know what that means."

He knew Abdul would work out that hostages were taken and someone was searching for them. The search could accidently uncover the real purpose of the mining camp.

Rashid was explicit. "Help them out of the storm. Do whatever it takes. It is up to you, my brother. Contact the imam. *Mas as salaam.*"

Though supposedly a non-smoker, Rashid picked up a pack of cigarettes he kept in his desk and lit one. He praised Allah for the insight to make the plant appear to be a mining camp. Aerial photos should reveal little; or so he hoped.

He still had to worry. The Americans would cover the Empty Quarter from the ground and the air looking for Amy and the two men. *I am an idiot,* he thought. If they knew what went on at the mining camp, they'd bomb it for sure.

• • •

After taking Prince Rashid's call, no one watching the American ambassador or Bob Morris, his top spook, would think they had a problem. But to say the two men were pissed off didn't come close to their anger or determination. They immediately called a meeting with the US military detailed to the embassy, to be sure everyone was on the same page.

Bob Morris summarized the situation.

"No publicity. Prince Rashid will use the Saudi National Guard who know the Bedouin, but we will rely on our own satellite photography.

The planes on the aircraft carriers in the Persian Gulf can take reconnaissance photos. We have satellites and drones. We'll find them."

There was no disagreement.

After the meeting, Bob called Asif on his satellite phone to tell him about the kidnapping.

"I don't want you involved looking for them. Stay neutral, but if you hear or see anything, let me know. You're right in the middle of where it all happened."

Asif's reply told Bob once again his contact—his friend—was in the right place.

"I saw them, Mr. Bob. They didn't go to Hud's tomb, but to another tomb; one where the rumor, even in Riyadh, is the smugglers store their liquor and weapons on the way from the Yemeni coast to Riyadh. I haven't seen them since."

Bob knew that tomb and Asif was right. One of the drones had picked it up and the traffic in and out of it. Where would they hold hostages? Kidnapping was an income-producing business in the desert. The tomb was too remote and Anglos would look out of place. Holding them at the mining camp made more sense, as they would blend in if seen.

What Skip and Brewer were doing out there at the tomb with Amy? He credited Brewer with more common sense.

"Asif, stay low and keep me informed. Thanks again for you input. Oh, and how is the falcon? I hope it's still alive."

"He is alive and well. But Mr. Bob, he eats so much."

Bob laughed. "See our contact in the camp. You'll keep him alive."

• • •

CHAPTER FOURTEEN

Kidnapped

*What she knew was that she was pissed off
and wasn't ready to die.*

Amy pretended to wake up, but she hadn't slept a wink. On the
horizon ahead of the SUV, she saw what looked like communication
towers. The mining camp must be near since they were driving east.

By now she was sure M. Ishaq, Ali G and Hassa had sent a search
party to find them, realizing they were in trouble. She had no idea if
Ace had received the signal from her watch.

She thought about how everyone had to die sometime. Rationally,
her mind told her this shouldn't be happening. But the vision of Hassan's
body lying in the sand forced her to confront reality. Her options were few.

Is this kidnapping my end? She never thought death would come in
the desert. Feeling this way wasn't negative, but realistic. The sun seemed
darker, but she realized it was the reality of facing death. Was she going
to be killed? Women were expendable in the desert and in Saudi Arabia.
Did being an American save her or curse her? She didn't know.

What she knew was that she was pissed off and wasn't ready to die.
Her reality was she would do whatever it took to escape and live. And

for that, she had to be alert and thinking. One opportunity might be all she and the guys got.

The SUV drove slowly through the camp, which seemed to go on forever. There were tents, groups of stucco prefabricated housing, and bulldozers. Whatever was going on here wasn't immediately apparent. Mining, Amy suspected, was a cover for some other purpose of the camp.

• • •

Amy looked around the room at the blank cement walls of the prefabricated house, thankful at least the three of them weren't tied up. That was the good news, but they were still locked up. The high windows kept them from seeing out and anyone passing by from seeing in.

Why she wasn't separated from the men must be because she told her captors she was Skip's wife. Thankfully, she always wore her mother's wedding ring, which her father had given her on her eighteenth birthday. She'd worn it through three marriages and now the fourth.

Coming into the camp off the main road to Dubai, Amy knew they were still on the edge of what appeared to be a large mining camp. The main problem was that the leader hadn't given them any idea of their fate. Death or ransom was the obvious choice.

"My guess," said Brewer, "is the leader isn't in charge. He's the action man for whomever is calling the shots."

Neither Amy nor Skip spoke. Amy was watching Skip pace around the two small rooms. Nothing was in the room but a couch, two chairs, and a refrigerator. The bathroom was in a small room, and Middle Eastern, with a hole in the floor and a jug of water beside it. Fortunately, they all had taken jackets with them to the tomb. The desert was cold at night, and night was upon them.

Amy took off her watch and looked at the dial. The arrow indicated the GPS was on. She explained to Skip and Brewer how Ace had given her this watch for just such a situation.

"It's working. Question is whether or not Ace is receiving the signal."

Brewer said if the watch worked, Ace had gotten the signal when they entered the camp.

"The Empty Quarter has no phone service, other than satellite phones, just text. But when we came into the camp, I saw a couple of communication towers. If we had our phones, I bet they'd work."

They stopped talking as a key turned in the front door lock. Two women followed a man, all three with their faces covered, into the room carrying lamb kabobs, rice, humus, and bread. The man carried six large water bottles.

"You eat and drink."

Skip turned toward him as if to ask a question, and the man backhanded him. Skip fell to the floor in a heap.

"No questions," said the man as he left.

Skip started to get up. "I'm okay. Let's see what the food is like for us captives."

The three ate all of the food on the platters, including the bread, in silence. Amy knew they were trying to anticipate what was going to happen next. Maybe they'd find out why they had been kidnapped. Hassa and the group at Shisur were their best hope for rescue. By now, surely someone was looking for them. Amy had to believe that was happening; otherwise, there was no hope. Their situation still seemed like a dream to her.

"This isn't a dream, but a bad nightmare, or the evil djinns caught up with us," she said.

"Yep," replied Brewer, "but djinns or no djinns, we have to be ready for any chance to escape."

"It's ironic," said Skip. "We wanted to see this mining camp. Never thought it would be so up close and personal."

• • •

Abdul had to think about what to do next. He was focused on meeting Muktar, picking up the chemicals, and heading to Riyadh. Now he had to figure out where the three Americans might be.

This is what happens, he thought, *when the Saudis allowed smugglers to operate even in the remote desert.* Many of the royals were corrupt and used the profits from liquor sales to fund their extravagant lifestyles. When Rashid was king, that would come to an end. What he had seen of the Saudi royal family made him proud to be a bin Laden.

The problem was, the smugglers melted into the Bedouin tribes in the Empty Quarter from where they had originated. He couldn't crack those tribes.

One thing was in his favor, the imam at the mining camp was a friend of his father's and close to Rashid. If something was amiss— smuggling weapons, liquor, trafficking in kidnapped Americans—he would know.

Finding the imam was no problem. Everyone knew his compound. Abdul thought explaining would be difficult, but it was easy. The religious leader knew why he had come. Better yet, he knew where the captives were being held.

The imam stroked his beard and poured tea for the two of them.

"They aren't guarded except when the Bedouin bring them food. The kidnappers are in and out of the camp. If you try to help them escape, you better have a plan, because this group of thugs will come after you. They own the house and no one is sure why."

"What do they want?" asked Abdul.

"Who knows? They're a rogue group of bandits who smuggle guns, drugs, and women from the coast. Some of them live in the desert and others live in the camp. No one knows for sure who they are or who may be a new recruit. I don't like it, but I have to put up with them."

Abdul didn't buy that explanation and said so. The imam threw up his hands.

"It's true. This group has taken many hostages and they simply disappear. Those of us who work at the camp believe they sell the hostages in Dubai."

He paused. "They sell men as well as women. You'll need outside help as anyone in camp could be one of their spies, on their payroll."

The imam's explanation made a case for why the three were taken, although Abdul thought it was much too easy. He was a natural skeptic and had to orchestrate their escape and soon. Any day the royals could be meeting on the succession plan and he had to get the chemicals to Riyadh before the meeting. Rashid said there was a delay in the meeting, as the King had another fainting spell. This delay was fortunate. Allah be praised. The imam had a plan.

"More tea? My men will show you when it's safe to rescue them. You could wait until tomorrow, but I have no way of knowing these thugs' timetable. The house where they are kept is often used for transients. It's the easy part, as the lock on the door is weak. Where you go from there is up to you. Allah be with you."

Abdul continued to sip his tea and listen to the imam discuss the Islamic school at the mining camp. But his mind was also going over his options for capturing the Americans. He couldn't confront the smugglers. For all he knew there might be more. What was his best option?

• • •

Sam Preisell, the US ambassador, and Bob Morris were in the embassy control room working with the military who handled most of the drones. Morris's CIA drones were committed to Yemen, and it was frustrating to think he couldn't use them when his employee was in trouble.

Sam felt the vibration of his phone. It was from Ace.

"Ambassador, the watch I gave Amy works. She triggered it, but the signal required a communications tower, so I never got it. Now she is near a tower, and I have her coordinates. But tell me how long has she been..." he paused, almost stuck on the word, "...lost."

"Amy was taken in late morning, along with Skip and Brewer. What are the coordinates?"

As Ace read them, Morris tracked them on a map. He handed the map to Sam with a note that said "mining camp."

With no thought to security, the ambassador said to Ace, "mining camp." After all, any number of mining camps were scattered throughout the Empty Quarter. Then with more confidence than he felt, said, "We'll go in after them. You stay put. We'll keep you informed."

Ace thanked him and hung up.

"Do you think he'll follow those instructions?" asked Morris.

"No, but what can he do?"

In Dubai, Ace was already plotting how to get to the Empty Quarter.

• • •

CHAPTER FIFTEEN

Dubai

They couldn't just sit in Dubai watching the sun rise
and set over the high-rise condos.

Ace looked out over an array of luxury hotel towers to the blue water
of the Persian Gulf. First, the Royal Doha Hotel was bombed, next the
hotel bombing in Riyadh, and now Amy and two embassy employees
had been kidnapped. Riyadh and Doha, he understood. The Saudi
royals were meeting at both places. But Amy? Taking her and the two
embassy staff didn't make sense.

Where was this so-called mining camp? He needed a map of the
desert, and the concierge of the condo-hotel should be able to find him
one. There couldn't be that many routes in and out of the Empty Quarter.
The concierge also ought to be able to put together a couple of SUVs
and a driver who knew the Empty Quarter. The more he thought about
it, his local driver, one he'd used for years, might be able to make the trip.

The part Ace dreaded most was calling Aunt Sonora. He looked at
his watch. Berlin was an hour earlier, though the time was irrelevant.
Sonora rarely slept, and then only in the late morning—the dull part
of the day, as she called it.

When he spoke to his aunt, she was remarkably calm. "You and Sam are on it. I'll see if the Committee has any contacts in the local area who can help. Stay in touch by your phone."

Ace explained the limited reception in the desert. Contact was only possible when there was a communications tower.

"Do your best and don't get kidnapped, too."

Sonora still didn't sound upset, but Ace knew better. She was worried. And he couldn't risk asking about local contacts. "The phone might be monitored. I'll text you soon with updates."

That was his aunt telling him she knew someone, likely part of her Committee, who had contacts in the desert or at least with the Bedouin. He sat back and waited for her text.

• • •

Ace was right. Her text confirmed the Committee members included a shipping magnate who owned ships that docked in Oman, and Yemen at Aden, as well as a port Ace didn't know, Al Mukalla.

Sonora's text said she called the Committee member who was looking into the issue. She emphasized to him that time wasn't on their side. Kidnappers were unpredictable and could kill the three any time. Very little was known about the tribes in that area, so nothing could be assumed about what the kidnappers wanted.

He looked out over the high-rise mania that had become Dubai and thought about all the years his uncle, Benton Prowers, and Amy's first husband spent excavating remote sites around the world.

The world was dangerous then. True, Amy already had been kidnapped once trying to track down the Shroud of Turin, her father's last request. Never did either of the kidnappings seem to be for money, and she had plenty of it. *Rather,* he thought, *this one was like the first one, for a political reason.*

He didn't understand why now, and why in this desert. His Uncle Benton once mentioned there were many secrets hidden in the sands of such an expansive desert that had never, in modern times, been explored. The Saudi royal family saw to that.

Benton also was fond of quoting Wilfred Thesiger, an early British explorer. Ace thought a moment, trying to recall the words. The quote went something like: no man can live in the desert and remain unchanged. The imprint of the desert and the desire to be a nomad will follow him casting a spell.

His phone buzzed. It was Sonora. It must be important for her to make a call.

"I know an archeologist in Paris, an Iranian, who excavated in Oman and Yemen. He might know what is so important for Rashid and Hassa to ask for Amy's help excavating the ruins at Ubar. The prince's request for Amy's visit was odd. We never checked out why the excavation was so important. The Ubar excavation could be tied to the kidnapping."

"You're right," said Ace. "I hope more information answers that question."

As he hung up, he knew what he had to do. Where was Olen? They couldn't just sit in Dubai watching the sun rise and set over the high-rise condos on the Persian Gulf. The Empty Quarter was their next destination.

He called the concierge. Three visas to Saudi, including one for their driver, should be easy to get for a price. He doubted they would be needed in the desert, but having them was better than an encounter with the Saudi or United Arab Emirates border guards.

• • •

The mining camp
Bob Morris's five SUVs carrying two junior CIA agents and ten military personnel from the embassy arrived at the mining camp at dawn.

"We're too late," said Morris to his team. The imam stood next to him. His men, watching the road through the camp, had alerted him when the obviously official SUVs arrived.

"How did they get out of here? By helicopter? SUV? And where did they go?" asked Morris.

The imam shrugged. "There were no helicopters last night, so they had to have left by SUV. You see," he sounded apologetic, "the camp is small and quiet. We hear everything."

Morris pulled out a map of the Arabian Peninsula. He looked at the roads in the Empty Quarter.

"One road goes east-west and one north-south. They had to go south to avoid running into us. Ubar and Shisur are both south, and the Yemen border, undefined for miles in this desert, is southwest."

Morris took out his phone and called Prince Rashid. It seemed unusual that the man in charge of CIA operations for the peninsula would have the phone number of a royal prince. The imam noticed, but said nothing.

Rashid insisted he be kept informed and had given Morris his private number. The prince was worried about Hassa, who refused to leave Shisur until Amy was found. He told Morris that he was sending a helicopter to bring her back to Riyadh.

Now Bob was sure something else was driving the royals. Why would Hassa want to stay? He also knew Rashid had asked two Norwegian rock climbers to excavate Ubar. But the prince had said the Norwegians were still in Riyadh, supposedly on their embassy's business. Whoever took the three, he believed, were renegade members of a desert tribe.

The worrisome part to Bob was such a group would know the desert and likely travel off the main road. The prince had the answer. Bob didn't realize he knew the border area so well. Rashid pointed out to keep from sinking in the soft sand that shifts with the wind, they would have to follow one of the rock ridges that outline the valleys, the wadis.

Then Rashid described what Morris knew had to be the route. The mountains on the rugged Yemen-Saudi Arabia border, at the town of Najran, had one narrow pass guarded by the Saudi border patrol. To get to Yemen, the hijackers with the hostages must cross the desert and pick up the road beyond the pass where the guards were posted. The prince called it a tricky drive on a treacherous trail. Then, he gave Morris approval to use drones in the area, knowing it was an issue of protocol. The Americans operated drones all over his country illegally.

"We'll find them," Morris told the prince before hanging up. Then he was on the phone again to Sam. The call was short.

"My agency has two drones at a Saudi base near the Saudi-Yemen border. The Saudis don't like it, but allow it. Prince Rashid gave me permission to use the drones to search the desert."

Then Sam spun a new wrinkle.

"Bob, I know no one remembers the past. But while I was talking to him, I thought about Rashid's name. The prince's name is the tribe that fought the House of Saud for control of Arabia at the turn of the century. Am I crazy?"

"No, his father, Mischel, married one of the Rashid daughters and they gave their one son his mother's name. His father had numerous wives and children, but among the royal princes, Rashid is the only prince and grandson from a tribe that fought the House of Saud."

Bob knew Rashid's linage wasn't important right now, but made a mental note to check it out.

"What we need to do is find Amy, Skip, and Brewer."

Sam reminded Morris that Amy had activated her watch.

"I remember, and the drones should pick up her signal. At least I hope they can. Nothing more I can do here, so I'll be back in Riyadh by morning."

"Thank God you've got staff to drive you," said Sam. "See you tomorrow."

• • •

Amy slowly woke up and tried to remember what had happened. Above her the desert sky was filled with bright stars. She knew she was in the back of a pickup, but couldn't move. It took a moment for her to realize her hands and feet were tied with some type of cloth. Twisting on her side, she could see Skip lying beside her, not moving. Brewer was pulling himself up the side of the truck.

"Are you still groggy?" he asked.

Amy groaned. "Yes." There was still no movement from Skip. "Is he okay?"

"Not sure. These guys are likely amateurs with drugs, and when they shot us up may have overdosed him. Probably was a tranquilizer cocktail of some type. Since he is still knocked out, he may be allergic to the drugs."

Amy rolled over to Skip and twisted to put her ear on his chest. "He seems to be breathing."

"Great," Brewer sounded relieved. "Do you remember what happened?"

Amy didn't. "It's a blur."

She paused as the pickup seemed to hang on its side and then straighten back out. Looking up, she saw a huge sand drift that resembled a wave in the ocean.

"We're traveling across the desert, avoiding roads in a pickup that isn't as steady as our four-wheel drive SUVs."

Having lived on a ranch, Amy knew what a pickup could do. She pulled herself up on her hands and knees, and slowly moved over next to Brewer. They said nothing and looked at the sky. Knowing the stars, they seemed to be going southeast. What, she wondered, would they do when daylight arrived?

"You don't seem to be bothered by any of this," said Brewer.

Amy drew a deep breath. She didn't feel like explaining, but maybe it would help their situation if Brewer knew she wasn't going to fall apart.

"Years ago I was in southeast Asia during the Vietnam war, working with private development organizations. One thing I learned was that I can cope in a crisis. You have to stay alert, appear to go along with them, but look for a way out."

She paused a moment before telling him that she'd been kidnapped once before trying to find the Shroud of Turin.

Brewer thought a moment after listening to her.

"Your ability to cope can't be bought with money or taught. You're born with it."

"I learned about myself and not really good stuff. Give me a gun and I can kill a bad guy, never feeling guilty about it."

"Thanks for that," said Brewer. "I wouldn't have expected a rich girl like yourself to, well, understand."

"Remember, I was raised on a ranch."

Amy felt confident that he knew he could trust her to take part in any escape. "Let's figure out how to get out of here. I don't think they want my money, but who knows what it might buy."

• • •

Abdul had lost control a couple of times, but managed to keep his pickup upright. The desert night was lit up with a full moon. Its light allowed him to carefully watch and avoid spots with soft sand. He needed to text Rashid, but couldn't do that and maintain pace with the kidnappers. He looked at the dial on his dashboard and followed the needle.

When he located the house where the imam said the three Americans were being held, he saw their pickup. No one was around. Carefully, he circled the house to come up beside the pickup without being seen. Who would be watching, he didn't know, but he was careful. The tracking device he put underneath the kidnappers' pickup would allow him to track them.

Allah be praised, he thought, *for the foresight of having the monitoring device.* He couldn't stop the heavily armed men he'd seen in the camp, but he could track them and wait for his moment.

• • •

The pickup began to slow and Amy leaned over the side. "There's a road that looks traveled, not a camel trail."

Brewer took a look. "In these mountains are many remote villages. What might be a road can become a trail. You're right, this is a dirt road."

Whatever the track was called, it was not smooth and they bounced back and forth in the back of the truck, which seemed out of control. Then there was a bump and in slow motion the pickup flipped on its side sliding down the soft brown rocky ridge until the sand stopped it.

Amy and Brewer rolled over the side of the truck into the sand. Skip was not as fortunate. Still unconscious, unable to protect himself, he was thrown out on the sand and smashed his head on a large rock. Both his head and the rock were covered with blood.

Amy and Brewer were about six feet away.

"His neck is broken." Brewer spoke slowly. "We have to get out of here."

How Brewer knew Skip was dead, Amy didn't know. Her medical knowledge was limited, but Skip's body didn't move. Brewer was right. Now was the time to escape.

The ties on their hands were made of soft rotten cloth. Anything sharp would cut their bindings. There was no sound from the cab of the pickup.

They both crawled to the cab of the truck, as their feet were tied. Using his tied hands, Brewer opened the door. The two Bedouin were either dead or unconscious. The leader was nowhere to be seen.

"Who are these guys?" asked Amy.

"Don't know. What I need is a knife."

Brewer searched the glove compartment, under the front seats, and then their bodies.

Amy looked at the shattered glass windshield and said, "What about a piece of glass? Or would we just slash our wrists?"

Brewer was already rubbing the rotting cloth on a piece of glass. In a moment, he was free and used a small piece of glass to cut Amy's bindings. She closed her eyes, thanking whatever the gods might be for freedom.

Almost in unison they asked each other where the leader was. Getting out of the truck, and looking over the sand, they saw him crawling toward a dune. He'd been thrown out of the truck, but was still alive.

Brewer went back into the truck. "They have to have weapons, and the leader must have one."

Searching the driver, Brewer found a cell phone. "The only way to see if it works is to try, but first we need their weapons."

The sound of gears grinding caused Amy to look up the sand ridge. A vehicle was coming over the ridge the same way they'd come. The pickup came into view, moving slowly in the soft sand on the road. Whoever was driving it knew what their driver didn't; that one had to be careful in the soft sand.

For a moment they both froze, unsure who it was. The pickup stopped, and a tall thin man got out. He was dressed in a Bedouin robe, but his English had a British accent.

"Amy, may I be of help? I am Abdul, Rashid's cousin, and I met you with Hassa. Rashid asked me to get you out of the camp, only the kidnappers moved you. So I have been following the truck."

Suddenly, Abdul pulled out a gun. Two shots rang out. The leader who was trying to get up the sand dune had stopped. He was dead.

The three walked over to him. None of them had ever seen him before. Amy paused a moment longer. Had she seen him at the museum? No, she couldn't be sure. With the ghutrahs, they all looked the same, but still she wondered.

"Abdul, thank you." She sensed that Brewer was suspicious.

"Where is the next village?" he asked Abdul.

Apparently, it was just around the next ridge and almost on the Yemen border. Amy knew if they ended up in Yemen, their rescue might be more complicated, although she doubted Sam would let a vague border in the desert stop a rescue mission. She watched as Abdul and Brewer went over to Skip's body, confirming Skip was dead.

"To leave him may not seem right, but I think we should get to the village where Rashid has contacts. Out here, none of us is safe. The border guards work for the royal family and can come back for the bodies and the pickup. The trail is in bad condition, so I doubt there will be any traffic on it. The soft sand on the dirt track is why the pickup flipped."

What Abdul said made sense to Amy and Brewer. The two men lifted Skip's body into the back of Abdul's truck. Amy took Skip's hat and placed it over his face.

Brewer was searching the pockets of the leader for identification. He found nothing. The three kidnappers were put in the back of the pickup next to Skip.

"We'll leave the pickup with the bodies here. The villagers will come for the bodies, and will bury them."

Then Brewer, who was still searching the pickup finally found a cell phone, two rifles, and three handguns wedged behind the seat.

"We're taking the weapons. Nothing can be done here."

They got into Abdul's pickup and headed for the village on the Yemen border. Amy took one long look back at the crumbling sand dunes and the truck. The kidnapping was over. What lay ahead?

• • •

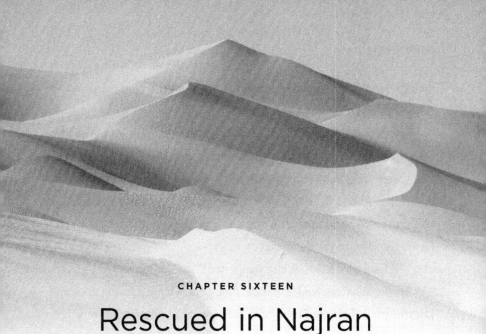

CHAPTER SIXTEEN

Rescued in Najran

Maybe we stumbled into something
at the grave that wasn't Hud's tomb.

Brewer turned on the phone he and Amy had taken from the dead
driver. Time to call Bob Morris. The dial tone worked and he waited
for what seemed an eternity for Bob to answer. He knew Bob didn't
recognize the number. Finally, he picked up.

"My God, Brewer, where are you? We've been all over the desert
looking for you."

"We're safe, Bob. Well, Amy and I are. I don't know how to say this,
but Skip is dead. We're in a village outside of Najran, close to the Yemen
border. Our pickup rolled in the sand. Skip was killed and so were our
kidnappers. Locals are bringing in Skip's body."

There was a pause as Bob digested the information and finally
asked the obvious question. "Thank God you and Amy are okay, but
what happened?"

"The kidnappers were taking us who knows where, when we
had an accident. The road was nothing but a sand trail. Even an SUV
would have had trouble staying upright. No way could the light Toyota

pickup handle the sand. The wheels got caught in a sand ridge. We rolled down a rock ridge and flipped.

"We were tied up in the back and thrown out. Skip hit his head on a rock. The driver and one of the kidnappers were also killed. Amy and I were lucky, we escaped with only bruises. We'd still be out in the desert, but Abdul, Rashid's half-brother, was on the trail and helped us. He's our Good Samaritan. Amy met him with Hassa at a village market. He ought to be in the database."

"I'll take a look. What else happened?" asked Bob.

"Abdul killed the leader of the kidnappers, who was trying to escape. I'm using a cell phone I took off a kidnapper. I'd ditch it, but our tech guys might be able to get some intel off of it. I need to stop using it, as it might be tracked. Bob, this place is brutal and unsophisticated. Getting a signal was difficult because of the mountains. I figured a drone went over and we pinged off it to get this call through."

Brewer wasn't finished.

"Abdul talked the border guards into collecting pickup and the bodies. They sure wouldn't do it for me. He told them he was related to Prince Rashid and that motivated them. The guards told us we weren't in Yemen, but on the Saudi side of the border, thank God."

Brewer's commentary on what happened sounded crazy to Bob, but Brewer had been held captive for two days. His thinking could be a little screwy.

"I'll let the ambassador know what's happened. We'll get a plane or helicopter to pick you up as soon as possible. I've got the coordinates of the village off your phone."

Brewer added, "There's a runway right next to the village. It's blacktop, so likely built by smugglers."

"Okay. Now tell me about this Good Samaritan, this Abdul. Where did he go?"

"He drove off heading north in a white Toyota pickup."

"I'll call you back when we know what time the aircraft will arrive. If the phone doesn't work, it won't matter. I have your GPS coordinates. Our staff will have aerial photos of the village within the hour. It would be helpful if you and Amy can draw us a sketch of what Abdul looks like."

"No problem, he looked just like Prince Rashid. Both Amy and I thought at first it was the prince."

• • •

Bob thought Brewer's story strange. No way had a Good Samaritan happened by. Coincidences didn't happen in the desert. The description of the truck was useless. White Toyota pickups were driven by nearly everyone who lived in the desert. Only the infidels drove silver, black, and grey vehicles. He picked up the secure phone—not to request the plane, he could take care of that in a minute, but to call his agency's unit operating the drones based on the Yemen border. His message was short.

"Keep the drone flying and look at the pictures of the road out of Najran in the last hour. We are looking for a white Toyota pickup heading north. I know it's the truck of choice of all locals, but find all of them and track them."

He looked at the clock on his desk. Amy and Brewer should be back in Riyadh by nightfall. Now to call the ambassador. The defense attaché worked for Sam and using the plane wouldn't be a problem. He'd use his agency's plane, but didn't want to compromise its value as a covert asset. And Sam, would have to call Prince Rashid.

• • •

"Shokran." Amy thanked their host for the tea and water. She drank the hot tea but skipped the water, not knowing if it was safe.

"Bob's going to tell Sam?" asked Amy. Brewer nodded yes.

"What else did Bob say?" She listened to Brewer rehash the conversation as she sipped tea.

"Amy, we have to figure out why they took us. We have to focus on today, and what's going on in the Empty Quarter. Maybe we stumbled into something at the grave that wasn't Hud's tomb."

To Amy, Brewer's words were positive, but he didn't sound enthusiastic. This kidnapping was stressful and had taken a toll. They were both exhausted.

"How can we know?" she replied. "The group that took us is still out there."

Amy was thinking about Skip. One minute he'd been their cocky leader, and then he was gone. She knew Brewer was right. She had to focus on today.

Clean clothes would feel good. Then she realized after being kidnapped, clothes were unimportant. If a plane didn't pick them up today, she'd look for something to wear at the local market.

"If Bob calls back, ask him if Hassa is still at the site. If she is, why can't the plane that picks us up take us to Shisur?"

The Hassa she knew wouldn't let a kidnapping keep her from going back to Ubar.

"It can't land there because Shisur doesn't have a runway. The feat of landing in the sand or on the bouncing paved road is fiction. You want to go back? Haven't you seen enough of the desert?"

"I came to Saudi for a reason, Brewer."

Amy was thinking about the reason why Hassa asked her to come to the kingdom.

"I can't focus on who kidnapped us, because I still don't understand the reason to excavate the ruins at Ubar. I'm now more determined to complete the excavation than I was previously. Maybe this was a distraction to keep us from Ubar."

She stopped. Her reaction sounded cold even abnormal. "I know I don't seem to be as upset as I should be, but like I told you, I was kidnapped once before in Mexico. I was held a little more than a day. It was stressful because others were killed."

Brewer almost smiled. "You're tougher than you look."

"I am when I'm pissed off. Now we have a dead American and who's going to explain why he's dead?"

"Amy, Bob will never give up until he finds out who was responsible for the kidnapping and Skip's death.

Amy closed her eyes and tried to rest. Sam certainly couldn't call her a bystander any more. Then, as if a bolt hit her, she remembered her stepdaughter. Audrey Melville was arriving in Riyadh the next day.

"Brewer, my stepdaughter is on her way to Riyadh. With all of this going on, I think she should stay in Turkey."

Even as she said it, Amy knew once Audrey said she'd come, nothing would deter her. But it was worth a try. The two women weren't related by blood, but might as well have been. They were so much alike.

"When we get back to the embassy, I'll get a call through," said Brewer. "What's her role in the expedition? I forget."

He stopped a moment. "I guess it just occurred to me you've had more than one husband."

"Yes." Patiently Amy told him Audrey was her second husband's child by his first wife, who died in childbirth.

She added, "I also had a third husband no one ever mentions. He also died. Keeping my spouse alive wasn't something I was good at."

"When Hassa asked me to come and excavate, I called Audrey. She's an up-and-coming archeologist, at the beginning of her career. She jumped at the chance to get into Saudi Arabia. I know she is looking for an unusual archeology angle so she can publish. I'm not an archeologist."

"I'm lost. So why did Hassa ask you to come?"

"She and Rashid knew my first husband, Vince. Hassa has some notion that since I traveled around the world with him, I know archeology. Maybe I know more than I think I do. But it's not enough. So I am still waiting to see what Hassa really wants. It is just a feeling, Brewer. I don't have any facts."

Amy looked at him. "I've learned a lot out here. Facts are used to support positions to prove a point whether it's right or wrong. Often a feeling, an instinct, is all you have."

"Yes, and the plane needs to arrive soon. My bet is this village isn't even on the map of the Saudi and Yemeni border. Nothing feels safe about this place."

Amy agreed. She started going over in her mind what had happened from the time she arrived at the embassy to when they were kidnapped. She hurried over what had happened at the museum to the cocktail party at the French Embassy. Someone could have heard the royals' conversation about the trip to Ubar. Who was around them? She remembered the waiter hovering near with a tray of cheeses and olives so Hassa and Rashid didn't have to wait to snack. Was he up to something else?

I'm frustrated, she thought, trying to remember who was at the party. The memory was gone. She made a mental note to be more observant. Ace and Sonora would approve of that decision.

· · ·

CHAPTER SEVENTEEN

Ace and Olen

Ace never doubted he was going into the desert.
It was a long shot to think he could find Amy
and her kidnappers.

As the sun rose on the Rub' al Khali, the dark road was a contrast
to the beige dunes that rose and fell in no particular manner. Every
time the car crested a hill, Ace could see what looked like an ocean
of pointed and sculptured sand dunes in rows across the horizon. He
looked at Olen, quietly snoring, and wondered how he could sleep
through a sunrise on the world's largest sand desert.

He owed Olen, who'd gotten them seats on the local UAE airline
out of Doha to Dubai. Ace could only guess at how he had done it. The
flight attendants told him the flight was the last one out of Doha. The
city was closed until the government decided who to blame for blowing
up the hotel and its guests.

Oil executives had more pull than anyone thought, at least that was
Ace's impression. He was sure the attendees at the conference had long
left Doha in their private jets.

He'd tried to get visas into Saudi Arabia, but in the end, it was his
aunt's connections who made arrangements for both he and Olen to

travel across the Empty Quarter to Shisur. She, or one of her Committee members, knew some sheik in Dubai who got the visas.

Ace never had a doubt he was going into the desert. It was a long shot to think he could find Amy and her kidnappers, but he also knew he had skills, training, and could get lucky. He was mildly surprised that Olen insisted on going with him.

At first, he thought Olen was making the trip to see what the desert was like. But looking at him sleep, that couldn't be the reason. Olen knew Prince Rashid requested Amy come to Saudi Arabia. Their Mexican partner was curious as to what the Royal House of Saudi wanted with Amy. Olen knew Amy's expertise was oil and gas leases. He'd want a piece of those Saudi leases, if indeed that was what she was up to.

Ace knew his cousin. She wasn't here for oil and gas. His best guess was it was for something more symbolic, obviously to be found at Ubar. What the site meant for Prince Rashid, he didn't know. For Hassa to ask Amy to come and help excavate Ubar, his cousin must have some role to play.

Could that be why she was kidnapped? He shook his head. His text from Bob Morris saying they were found was a relief, but he wasn't pleased.

Looking at his phone, he saw Amy's text asking where he was. The date was before the kidnapping. He texted her back, asking her where she was. If she had her phone and a signal, he'd get an answer. Then there was her watch. Of course, she'd have to be near a communications tower for it to work, and out here, the desert seemed to be empty. He thought it was well named.

Ace looked at the blacktop road going up and down the dunes and then at the sky looking for drones. The CIA, the military, and the Saudis all must have drones. Using them in the desert made common sense. He didn't think the desert was made for man or beast, yet both lived out here.

The text from Bob Morris on Amy's rescue said some passerby, who was Rashid's half-brother, rescued Amy and Brewer. The drones were still out trying to track where he was.

Ace grimaced. The story was too much of a coincidence. He didn't buy it, but was in no position to question who had helped his cousin. More likely, it was the two embassy employees the kidnappers wanted, and Amy and Hassan just happened to be in the wrong place. Or maybe they were taken by smugglers, or desert bandits grabbing Anglos for ransom. Who knew the truth? He looked at his watch, and their Dubai driver, Shafi, saw him.

"We will be in Shisur soon, Mr. Ace."

He looked at the horizon with the sun beating down on the sand. Ahead, he could see what looked like towers that drilled for oil or water.

"Is that Shisur up ahead?"

Shafi, who drove for Ace over the years in Dubai, replied. "Mining, sir, some type of mining. Not oil and not gas. Shisur is the next village."

Ace thought for a moment. "Do they mine gold?"

"Not sure, sir, they keep it very quiet."

"So Shafi, you have made this trip before?"

"Yes," said the driver. "I work for a driving service in Dubai and go all over the UAE, Oman, and Saudi."

"Ever see anything like this?" Ace was asking as they began driving through the so-called mining area. He counted at least twelve drilling rigs and though he didn't see all of them, counted at least twenty large construction trucks.

For a moment, Shafi was silent. Then he shook his head no. "Nothing like what is here. Usually mines have an open pit, but here they are using those rigs."

Ace didn't see many people in the camp. Then he heard the call to prayer, saw the small mosque, and assumed that's where everyone was.

Beyond the mosque were buildings he knew were not part of a mining operation. Rolling warehouses were lined up to the tops of the dunes and beyond. Warehouses were usually associated with manufacturing, not a mine.

The car zipped by, and then they were on top of the long rows of tents which were part of the housing area. As they passed by, three men came out. They were Asian. Ace used to be able to place every Asian in his or her country of origin by looking at their faces, but it had been years since he was in southeast Asia. If he had to guess—and it was a guess—they were Chinese.

Just as quickly they were out of the mining and housing area. He was again looking at the dunes. What were Chinese doing out in this part of the world in the largest sand desert? What was going on in those low buildings? He told himself to ignore it, but couldn't. His instincts told him it was funny business.

Even though they were on the equator, the sun had almost set. According to Shafi, they'd be in Shisur in about forty minutes.

The sky darkened and the stars came out. To Ace, the night was the most interesting time in the desert. Looking out the window, he felt as if he could see into the universe. Could the universe see him? Who could say?

• • •

CHAPTER EIGHTEEN

The Good Samaritan—Abdul

He didn't know the royals in the House of Saud well enough to figure out who had killed his father.

Abdul had camped overnight in the desert. He used a camouflage canvas cover to hide the pickup. Now it was wet with dew, but he had no time to wait for the sun to burn off the moisture. He threw it in the back of the truck.

Aerial surveillance would be in place the closer he got to Riyadh, and the truck would be picked up immediately. *Maybe,* he thought, *there was a use for the cover.* He picked up the canvas and tied it to the back window. The truck was partially covered, which was better than nothing.

Today, he knew his best course of action was to avoid roads, even dirt trails, and rely on his GPS, global positioning satellite. GPS was invaluable, but it didn't tell you if there was soft sand, hard dirt, or desert gravel ahead. There was no way to be sure where the soft sand dunes were or how high they were. He trusted in Allah that the pickup would make the trip.

Aeolus, he recalled, was the name of the Greek god for wind, and the wind was tricky, the way the dunes were formed. The windward side faced the wind that on the Arabian Peninsula came out of the northwest. The leeward side was the reverse, out of the wind. And most important, the side to watch was the slip face, on the leeward side, where the sand ran down. On that side, the road would be unstable.

Driving would be like sailing a ship; keep to the leeward side, the south side, and avoid the soft sand. Several times he had heard singing, supposedly caused by sand falling slowly down the dune. Once when he heard the sound, he thought it was a real desert djinn.

Years ago, in the desert with his stepfather, they came to a ridge over a thousand feet high. No SUV could get down the soft sand so they went around the ridge, always looking for hard desert gravel. GPS showed the ridge, but not the soft sand. Today he knew his GPS would be picked up by a plane or a drone immediately.

Who would think telecommunications were important in the world's largest sand desert? The Americans, the Saudis, the Iranians, and every oil company drilling in the sand had some type of communications system.

The mine was a good example. Rashid had upgraded phone lines using some type of radar in Riyadh. The Saudi National Guard were very happy with the upgrade, because they wanted to monitor the Yemen border. Realistically, that was a joke. There was no threat from Yemen itself. The government was in chaos for decades. But the border was as porous as the sand that formed the border. Everything smuggled into Saudi Arabia crossed those sands.

I learned that, he thought, *from my Uncle Osama. And from these sands came my inheritance from my grandfather, who made a fortune in Saudi and then in all the Gulf countries.*

In today's desert, I have to dodge the drones. The GPS will work because the mines are not far away. Still, the drones will pick it up. If I'm careful and keep the conversations short, I can use the phone.

He knew he was being unrealistic, and shut the GPS off, taking the battery out. Pulling out a map of the desert, he looked up at the sky. Centuries before satellites and global positioning, his people had navigated by the stars. He remembered how the Bedouin traveled across the desert. Without a map or compass, they crossed the vast desert and repetitive terrain with seemingly no problem.

In the sandy horizon, the shifting sand dunes made judging distance difficult, if not impossible, and visibility could be nonexistent. At night, Polaris, the North Star, was used. The Bedouin were familiar with the patterns of the wind, and used dune shape and rock erosion to plan a route. They also used detouring, a technique the Arabs had used for centuries.

The way it worked, Abdul thought, was so simple. His stepfather had shown him when they camped years ago in this desert.

Detouring followed the Arab proverb that three sides are the quickest way across a square. Take a ninety-degree departure to the right from the original route, then two more ninety-degree turns to the left, and you are back on the original route and around the obstacle.

Abdul remembered stories about Lawrence of Arabia, who used a compass. The Bedouin used stars to traverse the desert.

In his pack he had a compass, the old-fashioned type, connected to nothing electronic. With it and the stars, he knew he was going north. Using detouring, he plotted a course across the desert to the Jeddah road coming into Riyadh from the west. The route was almost a thousand kilometers, but doable.

He had water and gas. Taking out a chilled bottle of apple juice, he thought again about the journey, and then looked at the map.

To the north was a town called Najran. And the road continued north heading into Riyadh.

In Najran, he'd meet Muktar and take the pickup truck with the chemicals that his cousin had driven up the coast, and on to Abha on a winding mountain road.

Muktar was a Yemeni and the border guards—who were unsophisticated to say the least—believed him when he said his truck contained a new type of feed for goats. Amazingly, the more outrageous the statement, the more the guards were likely to believe it.

His responsibility was to get the pickup to Riyadh. If he didn't, he couldn't help Rashid. From Najran, the road to Riyadh would have traffic. In the pickup, he'd be just another traveler, concealed in the traffic. It might work. Tomorrow he'd risk a call to Muktar, to be sure he'd made it to Najran.

Abdul got out of the truck, and knelt in the sand. It was graveled, a hardpan. Confident, he drove off across the desert in a northwest direction.

The hardpan held up for an hour until he came over a ridge and found himself in a village with five tents, and a few palm trees. Obviously, there was enough vegetation to live.

"Assalam Alaikum."

A Bedouin man, obviously the village elder, greeted him. Abdul looked around and saw among the trees a dented pickup truck and a small trailer.

He thought for a moment. Cash was something he had a lot of—euros, dollars, riyals, even gold coins. These people traded everything all the time.

In a few minutes, he had negotiated for a trailer and two goats using the euros he brought in on his flight from South Africa. Fortunately, the pickup had a trailer hitch. Pulling the trailer would slow him down, but now he had a real cover.

"Shokran." He was on his way. Then the old man stepped in front of the SUV to stop him.

"You go to Najran?" he asked. Abdul nodded. "I know best road for you to take."

He took the map Abdul had on the front seat and sketched the route to Najran with his finger.

"There are some mountains, you be careful. Take you about three hours. Not far."

Abdul pulled out another bundle, this time of Saudi riyals, and thanked the old man. The route the man showed him was direct, and had a hard gravel trail, making it easy for a pickup pulling a small trailer with goats.

From Najran, he knew it was another ten hours or about a thousand kilometers before he got to Riyadh. Anyone coming in from the southwest would be suspected as a smuggler. His cargo of goats and industrial chemicals, as the labels said, would let him breeze through the check points on the highways into Riyadh.

He headed off, though at a slower pace with his load. *Praise Allah,* he thought, *his mission was going to be a success.* He would take these goats all the way to Riyadh, and then sacrifice them in the name of the prophet.

• • •

Abdul drove into the night. It was cool and the stars were streetlights on the sands. He arrived in Najran in the early morning hours, just as the market was opening. The mosque was calling the faithful to prayer, but he needed water and fresh fruit. He praised Allah and saw a gas station open.

As he loaded up with supplies, he looked around. No one was paying him any attention.

"You have water for the goats?" he asked. The attendant quickly brought out a pail and filled it from a pump. The goats eagerly drank it. Abdul congratulated himself. The goats were going to be his salvation. What a perfect cover. Rashid would be pleased.

"Coffee?" asked the attendant, and Abdul nodded.

Further up the road, he planned to take a nap. The highway was modern with pull-offs for trucks along the road that headed to Riyadh. He knew because his grandfather built the Saudi roads. For a few kilometers, the mountains in this region were covered in pine trees, making it harder for the drones to search. But the drones shouldn't be flying because the Americans had been found.

He pulled out his phone to call Muktar and was pleased to get him on the first try.

"I'm almost to the highway. I'll be in the pull-off. Look for a pickup pulling goats."

As he parked in the pull-off, Abdul leaned back in the seat, trying to nap. For a moment, he thought about the dead American and the dead kidnappers on the windswept trail to Yemen, not with any feeling of sorrow, but more curiosity. A freak accident, but the American shouldn't have been in his country and the kidnappers deserved their fate. The man was an infidel. The fate of the other two who lived was not his responsibility.

Still, he would ask Rashid why it was so important to help them. His half-brother must have some reason to risk their mission to aid the Americans.

He looked at the sky, remembering. Often Rashid joined them on desert treks. Their father was too busy, but never objected, because he wanted his sons to understand and be comfortable living in the desert.

In Syria, his stepfather traded spices. Traveling from Yemen to Oman and then Dubai and Doha, he learned the desert roads of the ancient travelers. In the Arabian Peninsula, they traded frankincense and myrrh to the oil men in ports on the Arabian Sea. His favorite route was the old Incense Road that flourished in the third century BC to the second century AD.

In those days, the route was important because the empires of old Egypt, Rome, and Babylon wanted the scents. The Arabs sold frankincense as an incense and perfume, and myrrh as an antiseptic to embalm.

To trade for spices, his stepfather swapped flour and salt. The route traded Indian, Arabian, African, and East Asian goods.

Often his stepfather's truck grumbled up the sandy ruts, and it was a relief to find blacktop again. Sometimes they stopped to look at old ruins.

Every water well in every oasis, seemed to have a set of ruins beside it. Often foreign groups of archeologists were at the ruins in the blazing sun, digging in the dirt.

"Looking for King Solomon's gold is fool's gold," said his stepfather, who believed other treasures were more important.

From a senior imam in Damascus, he learned that replicas of the Qur'an, written in later years, when the route was not as important, were left at stops along the way of the caravanserai.

"Keep a lookout, you never know what the Bedouin want to sell. Buy a Qur'an if you can."

Over the years, as they trekked along the ancient spice trail, he watched the ruins disappear in sinkholes covered by windswept sands. When Rashid told him Hassa was excavating the ruins at Ubar, he understood. He knew Ubar was a sinkhole.

Rashid had been with them on a trek across the desert when his stepfather told the story about Ubar, and that an ancient Qur'an might have been in the ruins when the city collapsed in the earthquake.

Did he know Rashid would become obsessed with finding the prophet's book, the Qur'an, the Damascus manuscript believed lost for centuries? If it was found, Rashid would be first of all the royal princes to find such a treasure. Finding the Qur'an, along with what Rashid had done to produce cheap electricity in the kingdom, would put him on the top of the list to be selected as deputy premier.

I loved those days, he thought, remembering the sand trails and the markets in villages. He never had such memories of his father, the Crown Prince, who died in a car accident when he and Rashid were in their twenties. To Abdul and Rashid, it was no accident.

The police report did not make sense. The car supposedly ran off the road on the west side of Riyadh and dropped a thousand feet into the Wadi. The imams said it was God's will.

One day, when Abdul went to the site of the crash, he saw an old man tending his camels. The man told him he was sitting on the side of the road the day of the crash and saw the accident but said nothing because he believed djinns caused the crash.

"Why were you silent?" he asked.

"I saw the djinns. They dug holes and left with many black bags. A few hours later, I heard the pop, an explosion. I think the black bags held explosives."

Abdul, a chemical engineer and a graduate of the American University in Beirut, knew if the explosion was small, little trace would be found.

"I saw the truck." The herdsman's voice was firm and confident. "It came down the track that goes up the ridge."

"Djinns don't live in trucks," he said. The herdsman insisted it was the djinns in the truck.

Believing in djinns was not part of Abdul's world but he knew they must exist. His father, Prince Mischel, believed in djinns. Forget the djinns, likely it was a Saudi dissident who set the charges and killed his father.

When he died, his father was the Crown Prince, first in line to be the King. His sons would be in the best position one day to be considered to be King. Raised in Syria, he didn't know royals in the House of Saud well enough to figure out who killed his father, but his half-brother, His Royal Highness Prince Rashid did. And Rashid wanted the Saudi throne.

Together they vowed to avenge their father. The two believed that the death was no accident. Someone in that group of descendants of the House of Saud killed their father. Their revenge was to kill the royals, as many princes as possible.

Abdul looked up at the sound of a truck. Muktar had arrived with the pickup loaded with the chemicals. They attached the trailer with the goats.

"We meet again in Yemen when you're done in Saudi, cousin," said Muktar.

"*Inshallah*," Abdul replied.

• • •

Rashid looked at his watch. Abdul should be in Najran by now. The road to Riyadh would be filled with cars and trucks. His half-brother, with his beat-up truck, would look like a local as cover. If it was anyone but his half-brother, he'd be worried.

Abdul assured him it was secured. Rashid had less confidence in Muktar. He was a Yemeni. Otherwise, Muktar would never get the truck across the Yemeni border into Saudi.

One of the family desert cats, now living in a palace, walked across his lap and flopped on the couch. The cats were their children. Somewhere in the palace were three others, probably sleeping with Hassa. His wife, back from Shisur said nothing could keep her from returning to complete the excavation at Ubar. That was the Hassa he knew and loved.

He told his wife the kidnappers were desert bandits, and Abdul rescued Amy and Brewer. Rarely did he keep something from her, but it was important that she looked surprised and worried. To Hassa and the Americans at the embassy, the kidnapping must look like another terrorist attack.

He poured more tea and, out of a bottle he kept locked in his desk, added brandy, and lit a cigarette. Never again would he trust the Yemeni.

All they had to do was leave Hassan and Amy tied up at the tomb. But no, they killed Hassan, M. Ishaq's brother, and kidnapped Amy. He was glad they were dead because if they weren't, he'd have them killed.

Bob Morris and the ambassador would focus endlessly on Skip's death; of that he was sure. Nobody cared about the dead kidnappers. M. Ishaq was his man. He'd take care of him and avenge the death of his brother.

The cigarette tasted good and he took another drag. The foul-up hadn't changed anything. Nothing had happened to change the plans of the Black Princes. *Inshallah*.

He knew Amy would go back to Ubar with Hassa. Like his wife, when she set her mind on doing something, it was impossible to stop her. His secure phone rang. It was Abdul, "I'm on the road to Riyadh. Muktar's heading back to Yemen. The product is secure."

All good news to Rashid. He asked for details on how Brewer and Amy had been found.

"Hassa is sure to ask me. Her father and brothers were killed in an SUV rollover in the Empty Quarter. She will be quite upset to hear Amy had the same type of accident."

They both knew Hassa needed to believe she had all the details of the kidnapping.

"The imam helped me locate them, but they left during the night. I put a locator device on the truck the night before, so I was able to follow them as they headed to the Yemeni border. There was an accident. Three kidnappers were killed, and one of the Americans from the embassy, a guy named Skip."

"What about Amy?" asked Rashid.

"She and the other American are okay and in a small village near the border with Yemen. I left them there. They're going to get a plane from Riyadh to fly them out. Now, my brother, tell me about the road to Riyadh. I don't know the capital very well. Checkpoints are everywhere, right? Our product is in the back of the pickup and for some cover, I am pulling a horse trailer, with two goats."

Rashid thought rapidly. "You're right about the checkpoints."

Then it came to him; the golf course, Dirab, owned by Khalid bin Rashid, a multi-millionaire and almost as rich as the royal family. He conveniently happened to be Rashid's mother's older brother.

"Do you know the Tuwaiq escarpment?"

"The what?" Abdul spent most of his time in Lebanon and Africa. His father might be a royal prince of the House of Saud, and be fluent in Arabic, French, Swahili, and English, but he knew little about the country.

"Stop the truck and get off the road. Pretend your tire is low."

Rashid was not conscious, he had been holding his breath. He waited for Abdul to tell him he was off the road.

"Okay, I am off the main four-lane road headed east and west, and I am parked between the gas station with a little store and a mosque."

"Great. I keep forgetting how little time you have spent in this country. You're nearly to the Jeddah highway. It's four lanes, and you can't miss it. The checkpoint is just above the escarpment as you come into Riyadh. You can turn off the highway onto a side road and come into Riyadh through the wadi the royals use to raise goats and grow vegetables. No guards are on the road, but we have a caretaker who operates the gate. I will see that he lets you through."

"What is the route again? I want to be sure." Abdul didn't sound surprised at Rashid's plan. His half-brother's trademark was he always had an answer.

"Get back on the Jeddah Road. It will take you to Riyadh. After you cross the flat desert and start to climb the ridge, that's the escarpment, you'll see a sign to a village called Dirab.

"Exit. Don't miss it. You'll find yourself at the guard station on the Riyadh-Jeddah highway. This side road will take you past the Dirab Golf

Course and then it will split. Turn north, to your left, and you will begin to wind into a wadi. About a mile down the road is a barrier like you see at railroad crossings.

"Drive through the wadi slowly, so as not to attract attention. Ignore the side roads and continue north. There is a village right on the edge of the escarpment. Only a few houses and compounds exist. Turn into the second compound."

"Got it. Can the compound board the two goats?"

"Yes, you will see that when you get there. It's really a small farm, though we keep some horses there. I may not get to the compound right away to see you. Hassa is insisting on returning to Shisur and I am sending extra security. Keep your phone charged. The staff is just one family. They work for me and are loyal. They worked for our father, too. I will see you before we finalize the proposal. *Ma a as-salaam*, good-bye."

"*Assalam Alaikum*. Peace be with you," said Abdul.

• • •

CHAPTER NINETEEN

Waiting in Najran

*Nothing was moving in the village,
not even the hot desert air.*

Amy and Brewer sat on a shaded patio and looked at the dirt road
that ran through the town.

"If we look long enough, do you think someone will come down
the road?" asked Brewer.

Amy realized he was being funny, except it was true. Nothing was
moving in the village, not even the hot desert air.

"It's hard to believe we were kidnapped in the Empty Quarter,"
said Amy.

Brewer agreed. "I wish this sheik had a phone that worked."

The sheik told them the border police had called the US embassy
in Riyadh to check on when the plane was coming. When, the border
police said, was anyone's guess.

Amy held up a dirty knapsack that the border police found under
the seat in the wrecked pickup truck. In it was the bound paper on the

expansion of Arabia under Islam. Or as Morris said when he gave it to her in Riyadh, how Islam won the Bedouin hearts and minds.

"This is a perfect time to read about Islam," said Amy.

"Read it and weep," said Brewer as she took the binder out of her bag.

"When you're finished, we can discuss it if you like. Sam and everyone in the agency have read it. The paper is one of Morris's pet projects. He uses it to train staff who are new to Saudi. When they arrive in this country, their knowledge of the area, to put it mildly, is zip."

"Don't they get training in the United States?" Amy didn't think the CIA would send newbies overseas.

"Yes and no. It isn't the real thing and that's why we send staff overseas to live outside America twenty-four hours a day. Most have at least two different country postings."

"Where was your second posting?"

"I've done two tours in both Vienna and Moscow, and one in Helsinki. But most of my time in Moscow, I spent traveling to the Stans."

Amy's expression said she had no idea what Stans meant.

"They're the former provinces of the old USSR: Kazakhstan, Kirgizstan, Turkmenistan, and Tajikistan. We just refer to them as the Stans. They are a long way from Moscow, and I spent a lot of time on Aeroflot. No frequent flier miles on that airline."

"I always thought you were a Middle East expert," said Amy.

"Russia and the Middle East are my two areas of expertise, but for the past year, I've been in Saudi or traveling to one of the Gulf countries."

Now Amy knew why Brewer's Arabic wasn't as good as Skip's.

"Do you still study Russian?"

"Yep, because I likely will be back there. Never know how long I will stay in Riyadh. Ever visited Russia?"

"Just Moscow, and when St. Petersburg was called Leningrad. It was a long time ago. My first husband was on the trail of some ancient treasures."

Brewer was intrigued. "What treasures?"

"Helen of Troy's necklace."

"Did he find it?"

"We weren't sure, and then he died. I will tell you the story of the search when we have a bottle of vodka to drink."

"It's a deal if the vodka's Russian. Now I will sit here, drink coffee, and meditate on how long it will take the plane to get here. It won't be a jet, but some prop-job."

He pulled out of his knapsack a small book, holding it up for Amy to see. It was a Russian language book. "I practice the verbs."

Amy laughed. "I'll read Morris's paper." For a moment, thinking about Russia, she'd forgotten where she was.

Amy didn't care where Sam and Bob got the plane. She wouldn't feel safe until she was out of this village and learned who had kidnapped them, and why? There were no answers yet. She looked at the bound papers Morris gave his staff.

That Morris would have his staff read history didn't surprise Amy. He wanted them to understand Saudi history, and to her, that spoke volumes about the kind of manager he was. The spooks were never high on her list, even though her father had been a covert operator in World War II and was proud of it. She enjoyed John le Carré's books, because he wrote about Europe after World War II. In spite of herself, she liked Bob, Brewer, and Skip.

Enough of the past. Now she could say she knew a real live chief of station for the CIA. Sonora's Committee would like that. The more she thought about telling them, the more she worried they'd try to recruit Bob. She'd have to ask Brewer how close Bob was to retiring.

Her relationship with the Committee was tenuous. She was sure they thought of her as Sonora's puppet. Maybe she was, but both she and her aunt knew at some point Amy would contribute. After all, she was a Prowers, as Sonora always said.

Amy put the notebook down and poured more tea. The sun had crept over the horizon and the day was beginning to warm up. Brewer was not optimistic on how long it would take to get a plane to the village. At least they were free. She might be free, but didn't feel safe. Looking around, any bandit could roll into this village and kidnap them again. That made her worry.

While they were being held, she was always sure they'd be released. Skip's death was an accident which could have happened anywhere. The pickup rolled over and he was unlucky his head hit a rock. She didn't feel like she really knew him, so there wasn't a real sense of loss. Yet death was permanent, and she should feel something more.

Looking down the road to the edge of the village, all she could see was a sea of sand. Maybe being surrounded by nothing made death seem like nothing.

She took a sip of tea which had a smooth aroma and flavor. Skip's death was depressing, but it couldn't be changed. You could never go back. She'd learned that with the deaths of three husbands. She opened the book again.

The next section was titled *The Umayad and 'Abassid period*.

What is this crap, she wanted to say to no one in particular. These names were only known to scholars and theologians. Yet in this part of the world, it was their history. There was some quote about history she always heard from her father and Sonora. It was on how studying the past helped you understand the future. The past was important. It never leaves you. Somehow, one day it must.

No way would the kidnapping keep her from helping Hassa, who she knew would go back to Ubar. She began to read, hoping to learn something that would help her understand whatever her role was to be at the excavation of Ubar.

"Enlightened yet?" ask Brewer, coming back into the room. The patio had warmed up and with it, the wind. He was hoping the dusty air and wind wouldn't delay the plane.

"I am on the last section and at least I recognize one of the names, the Ottomans. *The Mameluke-Ottoman-Modern Times* is the title."

Brewer laughed. "Now you're getting to the rise of the House of Saud and the wahhabis. It began in twelve hundred fifty-eight AD when Baghdad fell to the Mongols. Then the leadership of the Muslim world was taken over by the Turks. It gets more interesting as we get closer to today."

"Okay, I'm listening," said Amy.

"In the eighteenth century, everything changed. A reformer, Muhammed Abd al-Wahhab, came to power. His preaching was radical and modeled on Islam in the early years. He tossed out Shi'ism and Sufism as heresy because they believed in saints and holy places. But his biggest conquest was the conversion of Muhammed ibn-Saud in 1745. He spread wahhabism by force across most of Arabia."

"Politics and religion make the world go around," said Amy.

"Right," said Brewer. "And then ibn-Saud, know as Abdu al-'Aziz with the wahhabi backing, united all the Bedouin tribes in the Peninsula in 1930, creating the state of Saudi Arabia and making Riyadh the capital."

"Yes, I learned that at the museum in Riyadh. How oil had changed the country and impacted the Bedouin culture. As I understand, Brewer, the Bedouin are worried about their survival as a culture in the Middle East. What have I learned? Abdu al-'Aziz and the wahhabis joined forces to unite Saudi Arabia."

"That's about it," he said.

Politics and religion makes for power. What else is new, she thought. The British had used their position as a colonial power to try and control the Middle East. Maybe if they had added religion, they'd still be in charge.

"And," said Brewer, "Abdul al-'Aziz wanted to meet Roosevelt and have the Americans develop his country. We leave even when we should stay."

"What I don't get," said Amy, "is how it's okay to bomb an airport, but the good Muslim can't cheat or overcharge interest? They kill innocent bystanders in the name of Allah, which is fine with their religion. I guess that makes us all bystanders."

Their conversation stopped as, out of a silent desert, they heard a plane's engines. Looking up, Amy saw a two-engine prop plane circling in the sky.

"Where is the runway?" Amy questioned.

"It can land on a dirt track anywhere the track is flat. Over there, behind the houses, it looks like it is flat.

They headed toward the direction of the sound of the engines. The dust made it difficult to see, as the wind blew dirt in their faces. Then they saw the runway. Behind the low-slung stucco houses was a flat dirt strip.

The plane circled again. "The pilots are likely checking the wind," said Brewer.

As they waited, peering at the runway, a back door to what looked like a warehouse opening. Out came two men carrying a stretcher. The body was covered with a blanket. They both knew it was Skip.

"Don't they cremate bodies? Ashes are easy to carry."

"Would be easier," said Brewer, "only its haram, forbidden in Islam."

The plane pulled to a stop a few yards away, churning more dust and dirt. The door opened, and Bob Morris stepped out climbed down the wobbly stairs.

Walking over to Amy and Brewer, he gave them both a big hug. "Glad to see you two. The ambassador won't relax until you're back in Riyadh. Hassa is back, but the drivers heard her say she is ready to return to Ubar."

They were interrupted by the sheik and several village elders joining them on the dusty runway. Behind them, the stretcher brought Skip's body wrapped in a blanket.

The cargo door opened and two airmen came out, each with a rope around a goat. Then Skip's remains were stored in the hull of the plane. Everyone stood a moment in silence, as Bob handed the goats to the village elders. Goats were worth more than money as a thank-you.

"Let's go," said Bob, heading back up the steps. "There is nothing here for us."

Amy and Brewer thanked the Sheik and the elders for taking care of them. Within minutes they were seated, and the plane was racing back down the runway, never having shut off its engines. By the time they were airborne, Bob had poured three glasses of scotch.

They were silent, savoring the taste.

"Any luck finding Abdul, the guy who helped us out, the Good Samaritan, as Amy and I called him?" asked Brewer.

Morris shook his head no. "He seems to have disappeared."

Brewer didn't like that answer. "He wouldn't stay in this area, but he was heading somewhere."

Bob understood Brewer's frustration. "It's impossible for the drones to follow each movement of every banged-up Toyota pickup across the desert. We have a team reviewing drone film. They think he was going to Riyadh. We are looking at the vehicles coming into the checkpoint on the southeast side of Riyadh. Frankly, I am not sure they'll find anything."

"Aren't there checkpoints?" asked Amy.

"Yes, all around the city on every road into the city," said Brewer. "Nothing enters or leaves without being checked. They're looking for weapons, and sometimes checkpoints find handheld rockets. No one is allowed a weapon in the kingdom, and it's enforced."

Amy wondered about that statement. When weapons were illegal, to her that meant everyone must have one.

Bob poured more scotch. "When they find contraband, it reinforces the need for more security."

"I don't get it," said Brewer. "Our Samaritan was driving the classic Bedouin car, a somewhat beaten-up white pickup. I know there are a lot of them, but give me a break, they ought to be able to find him."

"Agreed," said Bob. "But tell me this, did he really look like Prince Rashid?"

"Yeah, he did," said Brewer.

Amy tried to explain. "The men all look the same with their head-dresses, but Abdul looks like Rashid. He has the same height, same eyes, same beard, and Rashid's face. The eyes were the main thing. I usually see Rashid in western clothes, but the resemblance was still there."

"Good news," said Bob, "is that if we find him from the drone tapes, we know what he looks like."

Amy sipped her scotch and looked out the window. The plane was only about ten thousand feet up and she could see the desert landscape in detail. A book on Saudi Arabia was stuck in the back of the seat. She pulled it out. It couldn't be any drier reading than the notebook on the expansion of Islam. Opening it, she began to read.

Seen from the air, the Arabian Desert looks as one would expect— sandy terrain with an occasional indistinct line of escarpments or moun-tain ranges.

Amy looked back out the window. Somewhere, among the ridges, was the ancient city of Ubar. Wanting to laugh, she realized she hadn't seen any of these desert animals listed in the book. The next chapter was "Geological Features."

The Tuwaiq escarpment is a region of eight hundred km (five hundred mi) arc of limestone cliffs, plateau, and canyons.

Amy remembered the Tuwaiq escarpment was outside Riyadh and so were the desert camps of the royals. In the camps, falcon hunting, a Saudi Royal obsession, took place. She turned the page to the chapter on Ecology and Natural Resources. This looked like something that was her family business. She read one sentence that said it all.

Natural resources in the Arabian Desert include: oil, natural gas, phosphates, sulfur, gold, zinc, and copper.

She thought for a moment and looked back at the page. That was it—one sentence on natural resources?

"Bob, who produced this book? The name is in Arabic."

"Saudi Today. Usually they have their name blazed across every book. Some Saudi scholar must have written this one. You can keep it. They publish a magazine every quarter circulated to thousands."

"You're going to read it all?" asked Brewer.

Amy laughed, "I'll let you know when I finish it."

The table of contents listed one chapter entitled "The History of the House of Saud." She recalled what Vince had said about history. He was talking about the Russians, but the point applied to all nations. Those who ignore it were destined to repeat the mistakes. Now that she was a part of Sonora's Committee, Saudi history might mean something. Just what, she didn't know.

• • •

CHAPTER TWENTY

Back in Riyadh

Thinking about the kidnapping
made Amy tired.

For a moment, looking around her room at the ambassador's residence, Amy felt like the kidnapping never happened. But it was real, and she was going back to the Empty Quarter with Hassa, determined to complete the excavation, even if no one knew why they'd been kidnapped.

To her, it was odd that Sam, Prince Rashid, and Bob Morris couldn't find who snatched them at the tomb next to Hud's. Skip was killed. They should be scouring the desert to find out who did it.

Right now, she needed another phone, and Ali G said he'd get her a cell in the electronics souk. She picked up the residence house phone to call Ace. The call went to voicemail, so she dialed Sonora in Berlin. As the ambassador, Sam had phone service to the world via satellite.

Her aunt was sympathetic, not what Amy expected, but then Sonora always surprised her. She didn't mention she'd been against Amy's trip to Saudi Arabia from the beginning.

"I'm pissed, Sonora. Brewer and I were kidnapped for God knows what, and they killed Hassan and Skip. I'll be here until the kidnappers are caught."

Amy expected Sonora's next words. She knew her aunt wasn't going to let kidnappers take her only niece without paying a price, preferably with their lives. They both knew someone, some organization, was behind the three dead Yemeni who took them.

"I started a search the day Ace called and said you were taken. Now I'll double my efforts to find out who took you. Ace and Olen are on their way to the Empty Quarter and may be in Shisur by now."

Sonora began to reconstruct what had happened. Listening to her, Amy felt tired just thinking about the kidnapping.

"Who knew you'd be at Hud's tomb? Someone in the village of Shisur is an informant, or someone employed by Rashid, Hassa, or the ambassador? Think about it, Amy. There's an informant."

Amy didn't have to think, she knew Sonora was right and said so.

"Technically, Sonora, we were at another tomb just down the road from Hud's. Being there may have caused a problem for someone, especially if smugglers were involved."

She thought a moment.

"A number of people could be informants. At the French ambassador's reception, Hassa, Rashid and I discussed our trip to Ubar. Everyone stands right next to each other and everyone understands English. Anyone could have heard us; other guests, and staff. The reception included the managers of international companies in Riyadh, local business men, and diplomats."

"You might be right," said Sonora.

"Just remember, diplomats can be spies. In fact, they usually are. Don't overlook the local Bedouin at Shisur. My bet is someone at the village is involved, and knows the group who took you. It's not like the Empty Quarter has a freeway going through it. SUVs need gas and water.

"The real question is why. Was it for a ransom, or were they going to execute you in a public square, not to put too fine a point on it all."

Amy knew she had to tell her aunt sometime.

"We're going back to finish the excavation."

Sonora paused for what seemed like forever.

"I figured as much. Neither you nor Hassa ever give up."

Now Sonora became the concerned aunt.

"Amy, these tribes in the kingdom live by the Bedouin code. It's me against my brother, and me against my cousins, then me and my cousins against strangers. That saying describes the hierarchy of loyalties, from the nuclear family to the tribe. Disputes are settled, interests are pursued, and justice and order are maintained according to an ethic of self-help and collective responsibility."

Listening to her aunt, Amy wondered if Prince Rashid and Princess Hassa were urban Arabs? They were cultured, hospitable, but she always felt at heart they were tough and could endure.

"You, Ace, and Olen are outsiders. You must be very careful, my dear. It's a hostile place for outsiders," said Sonora.

Her aunt made a legitimate point, yet all Amy had seen was their hospitality. It was built into their culture. In the desert, strangers were welcomed. They served Arabic coffee, a thin smooth drink that she loved.

True, women were second-class citizens, but that was her view. To Saudi women, the focus was on the home and their needs were provided as part of the culture.

"Good-bye, Sonora. I'll call you from the Empty Quarter if the phones work."

As she hung up, Sonny appeared with a tray of iced tea and cold beer. She skipped the beer and poured the tea thinking about what Sonora had said.

So Ace had left Dubai. Since he ate, slept, and drank with his cell phone, not answering meant he likely was in a dead zone in the Empty Quarter. She was glad Olen was with him.

She knew her oil partner well enough to know he wouldn't miss what was going on in the desert. He was a loyal friend, and smart.

After the bombing in Doha, he'd stick tight to Ace. No way would he let her cousin go traipsing off to the Empty Quarter alone. As a friend, she knew he'd be worried about her, though there was more to it. Business was business.

Olen had read the Committee report of the two Belgian geologists who worked for the Saudis. The Empty Quarter was loaded with mineral resources. Neither she nor Ace had the nerve to ask Sonora how she got it. They were both sure she had someone steal it for her.

"Another note, Miss Amy."

She looked up as Sonny brought her a note from Hassa, telling her the head of Prince Rashid's security detail was on his way to talk to her and Brewer.

As she read it, the head butler came in and announced M. bin Malik had talked to Brewer and was on his way to the ambassador's residence.

"He is the royals' security chief. Right?"

"Yes, Miss Amy. I will tell you when he arrives."

Amy was not getting a good feeling about the security chief. She looked around the room. It was the residence library. There were black and white photos, old ones in brass frames mixed with the books. She walked around the room to get a closer look. One was a massive photo almost four feet across. She bent over to read the inscription at the base and realized she had seen it before in one of Bob's books.

The Tuwaiq Escarpment, South of Riyadh, a prominent escarpment on the edge of the Rub' al khali.

The photo was of a crumbling rock ridge that descended into the desert floor. Sam had not picked out these books and photos of the Arabian Peninsula, of that she was sure.

The books must be part of the residence library and was here for years. One book title intrigued her: *Social Customs: Since the Time of Lawrence of Arabia.*

The cover was tight. She was sure it had never been opened, reinforcing her opinion that probably no one had read any of the books. *Well,* she thought, *finally someone is going to read one. And if I don't like it, there are plenty of other books here.*

She opened to the introduction and skimmed down the page. One of the powerful tribes was the Rashid family she knew was the tribe of Prince Rashid's mother.

For what seemed like the hundredth time, she though how odd that he suddenly needed to have her in the kingdom to help Hassa on the excavation. She was an outsider and had no allegiance and no knowledge of any other royals. Maybe that was why they'd asked her to come. Whatever they found at Ubar could belong to the Rashid tribe, not the House of Saud.

Sonny interrupted her to announce the security chief had pulled up to the residence gate.

Waiting for Rashid's security chief, she wondered what news he could have on Abdul or the goons that kidnapped her. She didn't have a great deal of optimism. It was a big desert.

• • •

CHAPTER TWENTY-ONE

In the Empty Quarter

The Empty Quarter was on the highway to Asia.
Gold, frankincense and spices were
the main products transported.

Ace and Olen were in Shisur, drinking tea and wishing they had something stronger. What was their next move? Both men knew, without a doubt, that the excavation of Ubar would be on, and Amy and Hassa would be back. They'd just missed Hassa, who'd flown back to Riyadh in a helicopter. Rashid was taking no chances with the security of his wife, or so it seemed to the villagers.

Because the Americans had been his guests, Ace knew M. Ishaq, as the governor of the area, was responsible for the safety of visitors. He would be anxious to take care of the two new arrivals.

Ace intended to use his hosts' anxiety to get M. Ishaq to explain what was going on at the mining camp. The camp's buildings were all new. The imam's village had been at the crossroads to Dubai, Riyadh and Yemen for centuries. He had to know what was going on. All the truck traffic to Yemen went through Shisur.

"Amy answered my text. She is in Riyadh at the US ambassador's residence."

He chose not to repeat all of Amy's text that said she was coming back to Shisur, with Hassa to continue the excavation at Ubar. Likely any kidnapping attempts would fail, as Prince Rashid's security team would see to that. But he would still keep an eye out for any trouble. Since the kidnappers were unknown, who could be sure anyone was safe.

M. Ishaq surprised them. "Do you want to go to Hud's tomb where the kidnapping took place?"

Olen and Ace looked at each other. No one seemed to know who organized the kidnappings even though the kidnappers had been killed. Someone, in a hierarchy above the kidnapper-smugglers, gave the okay. The two men were confident in their ability to protect themselves, but both realized they didn't know the desert or how to survive in this hostile environment.

"Well, we need some sleep and a meal before we make that decision. You have rooms?"

"Yes, yes," M. Ishaq.

• • •

The village leader was eager to have the men stay in his guest house because it would be good for his reputation. He was still seeking redemption for the kidnapping, a black mark for him and his family.

The princess's last words to him were that she'd be back. He was fortunate she wasn't kidnapped. If she'd been, his head might roll, literally. He might have kept his head, but he had lost face and was furious. Worse, his brother was dead. Somehow, Allah willing, he would avenge Hassan's death.

He knew Prince Rashid's chief of security would eventually arrive in Shisur, questioning, looking for clues. If that didn't happen, then he knew on some level the Prince was involved with the kidnapping.

Ever since the so-called mining camp opened, strangers and truck traffic had gone up and down the road. They drove through the village, never taking the road north to Riyadh. They always went south to Yemen or east to Dubai.

What the strangers were doing, M. Ishaq didn't know. But he did know they were trouble. Today the factions of tribes and travelers on the Arabian Peninsula were something he wanted to avoid. So he ignored the signs, served tea, and put travelers up for a night or two, usually when their vehicles broke down and needed repair.

M. Ishaq thought of himself as a simple businessman, the Sheikh of Shisur, the old man in the tribe, their leader. He was the intermediary between the Bedouin and the outside world. Each tribe had rivalries with other clans. The feuds could last for generations, and he brokered peace. This is the image he wanted the world to believe.

The reality was very different, but then he saw no reason to tell everything he knew. The village was his life. When the strangers were gone, the Bedouin way of life would return. The villagers would be left with simply living with the challenges of desert life.

One thing bothered him. Not the mine, which soon he believed would be covered with sand, but Ubar.

Yes, he thought, *Ubar could change our way of life.*

• • •

"Your village is very old?" Ace asked carefully watching M. Ishaq's face, as their host poured more tea.

"My family has lived here since the days of the caravanserai. In those days, the Arabian Peninsula, the Empty Quarter, was the highway to Asia. Gold, frankincense and spices were the main products. From Asia, they brought back silks and other spices. Opium was also traded, but never mentioned in history books.

"Frankincense?" asked Olen.

"Yes, in those days very valuable in perfumes, for skin care and burned in sacrifices in Egyptian temples."

"We passed mines on the road from Dubai. What do they produce?" Ace asked the question causally, but was watching M. Ishaq's face.

He and Olen had noticed more trucks going to the mine, few leaving. What, they asked themselves, was being produced and where was it going?

"The mines north of the village produce oil and gas. Gas is now as important as oil."

"No, we saw structures for mines," said Ace, "on the road from Dubai. What are they for?"

M. Ishaq shifted in his patio chair to draw on the floor.

"We are here, here is the mine, here is the border with Yemen, and here are the mountains. This is Ubar. See, there is a ridge that runs from the mountains to Ubar. It continues into the Rub' al Khali.

Today covered by sand because, how you say, climate change shifted the wind covering the sand. And the ridge is what is important. Inside the ridge, Allah has blessed the Bedouin with many minerals."

"Gold?" asked Olen.

"Yes, some gold. One time thought to be King Solomon's gold mines, now believed to be in Ethiopia. Some visiting geologists told us that many years ago."

"Geologists?" Ace sounded surprised, but he wasn't. "Surely, the Saudi government has photographed, dug, explored areas of the Empty Quarter."

"You must ask Prince Rashid and Hassa. They would know about geologists in the kingdom. They can't get into the Empty Quarter without the approval of the royals," said M. Ishaq.

"Many explorers and others were in and out of here for years, too. My father knew them. They stayed in our village, in this house."

He motioned to the doorway. Two women wearing black abayas, covering them from head to toe, brought tea and very tasty muffins.

Both Olen and Ace thanked the women, and consumed the muffins, which resulted in more muffins being brought.

"I know it's likely been a long drive for you both today."

And he launched into an explanation of sweets in the Arab world knowing his two guests were captive listeners in between bits of muffins.

"The love of sweets," said M. Ishaq, "is part of Bedouin history. In Islamic countries, sweets were a part of the culture, and a tradition. Honey, both a food and a medicine, was part of the culture from the Mediterranean to India. And we have dates."

"We love dates," said Ace, almost in unison with Olen.

"Over the centuries cooks from Babylonia, Rome and the Persian Empires created sweets mixed with flours, fruit, and nuts. In the tenth century, the court of the caliphs showed over ninety recipes for sweets. By the sixteen to eighteenth century, sugar was used to sweeten coffee and ice cream and Turkish delights were added. Emigrants took the sweets to cities around the world and baklava became universal."

When their host took a sip of coffee, Ace attempted to get the conversation back to issues that might have something to do with the search for Ubar, not sugar. M. Ishaq's reference to others told him the Saudi Royal family had hired others to conduct explorations in the sands of the Empty Quarter. So he began with the past.

"What did your father think of the British explorers?

M. Ishaq grinned a broad smile, as if remembering. "He told many stories." Then paused to sip his tea.

"Interesting men, my father said. And interested in the history of the Empty Quarter. The person here most of the time was Philby, called St. John, who arrived in 1917. My father knew him because Philby made so many trips to the Empty Quarter. He was, you would say, obsessed with it. He always stopped for tea and stayed overnight. I think he stayed in your rooms. His assignment at the British Embassy was to follow our leader and Emir, Abdul Aziz, whom he admired. And from the Emir, he learned to love our culture.

Philby became convinced of the need for Abdul Aziz to have the support of the wahhabis, the religious leaders. Abdul Aziz believed the wahhabis represented the true faith shining forth as a beacon against the infidels. To the British, that looked like treason, but not to Philby."

They were interrupted as a local shopkeeper needed to speak to M. Ishaq. Now Ace learned, to his surprise, Olen was an expert on early explorers in the Arabian Peninsula. Their friend, and partner from Mexico, had a real interest in the deserts of Saudi Arabia.

"Philby was considered a traitor."

"Right," said Ace, "like his son Kim who spied for the Russians. You begin to wonder if it isn't in the genes."

"Philby had a plan for the Middle East that included Palestine, and maybe things would have worked out," said Olen.

Ace knew the international explorers during this century, John Philby, Bertram Thomas, and Wilfred Thesiger, because they had written books about the Empty Quarter. He listened as Olen explained the Philby position, calling it the Philby legacy.

"The November 11, 1918 Armistice, assured the Arabs of self-determination. Philby felt this was a betrayal that broke his promise to Abdul Aziz for one unified Arab nation. He made that promise in exchange for the king's alliance with the Allies in the war against the Ottoman Turks, who were on the side of the Germans. He never liked the famous T.E. Lawrence who promoted the Hashemite in what is now known as Jordan."

Mohammed Ishaq returned, followed by the women who brought more coffee and sweet breads. He sipped coffee as Olen and Ace reached for the sweet breads and continued his story.

"Now, where was I. Oh, I think Philby, who lived a long time with the Bedouin, heard about Hud's tomb. He knew about Ubar, but if he went there, I don't know. My father and other tribesmen knew Ubar, but kept the location very secret. Then it was hidden for years in the shifting sand. Climate change helped us find the entrance."

And M. Ishaq paused to sip coffee.

"The royal family, House of Saud, hired geologists, and the stories of Ubar were told in Riyadh. The old generation of leaders ignored the tales, but Rashid did not," added M. Ishaq.

"A lot of time was spent by royals figuring out if Ubar was the place of Solomon's gold. Today I think none of that matters. My father said Hud's tomb was important, and that it was sacred. The House of Saud had oil in the eastern provinces. All the attention went there, and the Empty Quarter was forgotten."

"Until Hassa and Rashid brought up the excavation of Ubar," Ace pointed out.

"Yes," M. Ishaq said adamantly, "the princess is determined to excavate Ubar. It was His Royal Highness Prince Rashid who learned about Ubar, even before he married Hassa. He would come to the desert and camp, and then he got satellite photos."

The three men sipped tea and listened to the wind. If only, the wind could speak. The Empty Quarter, in the past with the old explorers and today with the smugglers and truck traffic, was anything but empty.

• • •

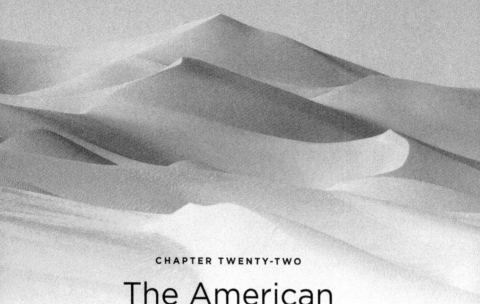

CHAPTER TWENTY-TWO

The American Ambassador's Residence

America had been involved with Islamic movements
since the nineteenth century.

Amy saw her phone light blinking. Ace had returned her text. *About time*, she thought.

Reading his text, she felt her stomach drop. He and Olen were thinking about going to Hud's tomb. She texted him back, saying since no one was sure who the kidnappers were, he and Olen could be in danger. That wouldn't stop him. She hoped he would realize there was something else going on, and he shouldn't be in the middle of it. She texted him to wait at least until she and Brewer talked to Rashid's security chief.

With relief, she read his reply. He would wait. Then she had to think. Ace would not be interested in climbing up some dusty desert ruin. He'd never been interested in ancient artifacts. Something else was going on with him, and she had no clue as to what.

She heard talking in the hallway, and in to the library came Bob Morris and Brewer escorting Rashid's security chief, M. bin Malik. Apparently, they both felt she needed support or witnesses. She noticed with interest Malik wore a light western suit, no thobe or ghutrahs for the security chief.

"Miss Prowers, nice to meet you." Then came the questions, like he was reading from a script. Amy wondered if he asked the questions so often they did sound like a script.

"What did they look like?"

"Arabs."

"What were they wearing?"

"White Bedouin robes."

"What were their accents?"

"They spoke Arabic and pigeon English, only very little."

M. bin Malik explained that the Saudi Royal guards were on alert and interviewing sources, but at this time they had no suspects. He pointed out no ransom note was received by Rashid's family or the US embassy, to get them back.

"Usually," he said, "taking Anglos for ransom was one way that bandits in the desert raised money. Our best estimate is that it was an isolated event."

He left, and Morris, Brewer, and Amy looked at each other. "What a waste of time," they almost said in unison. Brewer said his debriefing was almost as short.

"So," asked Amy, "why were we kidnapped?"

Bob threw up his hands. "Hud's tomb had nothing in it. The Saudi guards searched it after the kidnapping. Likely it has been empty for hundreds of years."

He pulled out a folder of photographs and laid them out on the table for Amy and Brewer. "We just got these in from the satellite."

"What are we looking for?" asked Amy.

No one was sure, but the photographs covered several days before the kidnapping and then the day after they were taken. The three of them looked at the string of eight-by-ten black and whites.

"What are these?" asked Brewer, pointing to tire tracks running up to the front of the tomb next to Hud's.

They looked at the first photograph. Tire tracks were clear. The last photos had no tracks, just a congested mess obviously made by the Saudi guards.

"I bet something was stored in that tomb," said Bob.

"But what?" Amy was tired of the guessing game. She believed they had stepped into some type of smuggling operation in the desert. Would they ever find out what? Smuggling was fine; only why take them to the Yemeni border? That didn't fit.

The three of them stood there just looking at the photos. Bob spoke first.

"We won't give up. I have an operative in the desert. Eventually, we'll get to the truth. And Brewer, the ambassador wants you to go back to Shisur with Amy and Hassa. Says he wants an American man on the scene, even though Prince Rashid has a large security detail going with the women. I think he has a point."

Brewer didn't flinch. "I love the desert and, maybe this time we will find the gold."

This was news to her. Gold? Amy realized she hadn't given much thought to what they would find at Ubar. Rashid and Hassa said it would be an excavation. She just assumed it was ancient artifacts. To her that meant old bones, arrowheads, but now she wasn't so sure.

"I need to do a little research on Ubar." She wasn't surprised when Bob pulled out of his briefcase another embassy briefing notebook.

"All the news that's fit to print on Ubar. Oh, and I added a short note from history on Thomas Jefferson for you both to read."

"Great, Bob, I'm still getting through the first book you gave me on the kingdom," said Amy, thinking *how much is enough?*

She knew Bob was serious. He told her she really needed to read up on the House of Saud. Hassa hadn't called to say when they were leaving, so she had the rest of the day, and maybe longer, to read.

As Bob left, Brewer flopped down on a couch and opened the notebook to the first page.

"You're going to love this paper, Amy. It's on Islam when Thomas Jefferson was president. I bet the Saudis hated it, if they read it."

Amy took the paper as Brewer, using a large magnifying glass, was giving the satellite photos a careful look. As she began to read, she saw what he meant. Jefferson was not a hero in the Islamic world.

The coast of northern Africa in the eighteenth century was ruled by pirates. Ships were targeted for their supplies and the crews held for ransom. The Muslims pirates were from the Mediterranean countries of Tripoli (now Libya), Tunisia, and Morocco. The US, along with the European countries, paid the bribes.

The United States third president, Thomas Jefferson, was sent a note in 1801 from the Pasha of Tripoli, demanding a payment of $225,000 plus $25,000 a year for every year in the future. To Jefferson, this demand was unreasonable and he sent the US fleet to stop the thievery.

The war, which lasted four years, immortalized the US Marine Corps in the Marine Hymn with the words "to the shores of Tripoli." The marines wore leather collars because the Muslims used their swords to cut off their heads when boarding the ships. Thus, the Marines became known as leathernecks.

Both Jefferson and future president John Adams didn't understand the hostility the Muslims felt for America. Both men believed in the American tradition of religious freedom. Jefferson and Adams were told that Muslims believed it was their right and duty to make war and slaves of infidels, non-believers who did not believe in the authority of Islam.

Jefferson did not understand a religion whose holy book declared war on unbelievers. Someday he foresaw Islam could be a threat to America.

Amy sat a moment to think about what she had read. This was the type of piece Sonora and the Committee would love. History repeating itself, a predictor of today. Ace would love this, if he didn't know.

She had also learned something about her own country. America, had been involved with Islamic movements since the early nineteenth century. *None of this is really new.* She shook her head, and felt relieved when Sonny came to tell her Hassa was on the phone.

The Princess sounded upbeat. "We leave tomorrow, Amy. Is that okay with you?"

It was, and Amy told her so.

"I am so happy because we need you, Amy. The Norwegian rock climbers will come a day later. They are busy on a project at their embassy, but Rashid persuaded the Norwegian Ambassador to let them assist us. We will drive as we'll need the vehicles when we're there. Rashid is going to fly the Norwegians in."

Amy knew the Norwegians were critical to the excavation, if they were to excavate without being killed. To her, the ruins at Ubar looked like they were about to collapse at any moment. Why the excavation needed her, Amy was still at a loss, but repeated to Hassa she'd be ready to go the next day.

Then she remembered Sam's request that Brewer go back with her.

"Hassa, Brewer would like to go back with us. Is that okay? He will have his own SUV."

Her friend said yes, and Amy could tell she was pleased Brewer wanted to return to the Empty Quarter. Her only question concerned whether he would bring his own security. Amy doubted Brewer would have any security.

Amy called the butler. "Is Brewer still here?"

"Yes, Miss Amy, you want me to get him?" She nodded yes.

Brewer was there in a minute. Yes, he'd have his own vehicle, and would not have a security detail.

"Amy, there is still something funny about our kidnapping. I just can't put my finger on it. None of it makes any sense. What do we know?"

Amy thought a moment. "Maybe it isn't us, but what we were going to do. I think those tracks on the sand in the photos were the key. They didn't want us to find whatever they'd hidden in the tomb next to Hud's tomb."

Brewer agreed. "They were smuggling something, weapons, drugs, booze, or something to do with the mining camp. Skip and I wanted to check that out but never got to it. No one was supposed to know the camp east of Shisur was a mine, but careful review of satellite photography exposed the mining operation. Gas and oil, it was not. Our CIA analysts are good at interpreting camouflage photography."

Amy was on her phone, texting someone. "I hear you but…"

"Sonora?" he asked.

Her answer surprised him. "No, Audrey Melville has just arrived at the Riyadh airport."

"Your stepdaughter?"

Amy explained to him she had three stepchildren, Audrey and her brothers.

"The kids were in college when we married, and the marriage was a short one. As it turned out, Sonora liked him a lot more than I did, but I did get three nice stepchildren. Audrey is the only girl."

She paused. "Brewer, like I told you, she is the archeologist, not me. Why Rashid and Hassa wanted me to come and excavate is a mystery. Audrey has the skills. Ace is in Shisur now, and even he knows more than I do about this stuff. I'll bring Audrey up to speed. She should be here within the hour."

Ace in Shisur was good news to Brewer. He and the other guy, Olen, had driven through the mining area. As a former special ops guy in the military, Ace would have noticed oddities about the camp.

"Do you have Ace's phone number? I am sure it will work if he is in Shisur, since the village has a cell tower."

Amy gave him the number, and waited for him to call her cousin.

Ace didn't disappoint them. He had questions about the mining operation. Brewer put him on speaker phone so Amy could hear the conversation.

"Yeah, the operation confused me. Brewer, I saw gooks, likely Chinese, walking around the camp. I know the Saudis hire everyone, but Chinese? Hey, they are all over Africa, but I didn't think they had a relationship here in the kingdom."

When Brewer explained that he thought the kidnapping had to do with the mine and smugglers, Ace was on the same page.

"It makes sense. The only question is what is going on in the mining camp. The worst part is, I'm not sure we should trust Mohammed Ishaq. To talk to you, I'm standing out on the patio. I have to be careful. Someone here in Shisur has to know what Amy and Hassa were doing here, and when the three of you went to Hud's tomb."

Ace paused, then said, "Olen and I are thinking about visiting Hud's tomb but haven't decided. If we go, it will be in the morning."

Amy and Brewer looked at each other. Nobody had actually gone inside Hud's tomb. Doing so would answer that question. Was anything in the tomb or was it used by smugglers? Ace said he and Olen could go tomorrow, the day the group from Riyadh was driving down.

"Watch out for the djinns," said Amy, which made Ace laugh.

She looked at Brewer. "We know better, don't we?"

"Going to Hud's tomb could tell us something," said Brewer. "But it could be dangerous. The mining camp isn't far away."

"Olen and I are prepared. A contact in Dubai got us weapons. There was no way I'd travel across the Empty Quarter without something to ensure my security. So, consider us to be well-armed and capable. We will be on the lookout for anything funny."

Amy looked at Brewer. "He was a Ranger in the army."

They heard Ace laugh. "I may not be in as good shape today as I once was, but I can take care of myself. We'll be going with you to Ubar."

Both Brewer and Amy listening on the speaker phone said yes to that suggestion. The butler interrupted them, wanting to know if they were going to the airport to pick up Audrey.

"Of course," said Amy. "See you tomorrow, Ace," and she disconnected.

Brewer smiled, adding, "this is going to be a great trip."

Amy smiled back, but in her heart, she wasn't sure. She remembered what happened last time. Was it only a little more than a week ago?

She found it comforting to have Ace and Olen going, and made a mental note to ask Ace if he had a weapon she could use. Knowing him, she was sure he had an extra handgun. In fact, he may have even gotten one just for her.

· · ·

CHAPTER TWENTY-THREE

Back to Shisur

In places, the blowing sand was so thick,
it almost covered the road.

At the ambassador's residence, Amy could barely see the swimming pool. The weather in Riyadh changed and she was surprised. Wasn't the desert always hot and sunny? Not today. Visibility was a few feet, and sand filled the air.

She went to the front entrance where Ali G was loading the SUV he and Brewer were taking to the Empty Quarter. The ambassador insisted both Ali G and Brewer go back to excavate Ubar. Amy knew he believed they'd provide protection. She wasn't sure more staff would have prevented the kidnapping. Weapons were what they needed.

The procession included five SUVs, carrying twelve men. Rashid had increased Hassa's protective detail. She thought about asking the ambassador for a gun, but didn't. He wasn't happy she was going back to the Empty Quarter. If he knew she was worried, he'd pressure her to stay in Riyadh.

Sam was worried. She understood why. He'd been her father's best friend and, after Benton Prowers's death, thought of her as his daughter.

She didn't mind. Her father would have done the same for Sam's children. One of his sons was the Prowers' family lawyer and the two families' ranches in Texas shared a border of six hundred miles for more than a century.

She motioned to Ali G and pointed to the dust-filled sky. "What's with this weather?"

"We have lots of sandstorms. All the Arabian Peninsula weather is a mess, Miss Amy. No one saw the storm approaching. A cyclone in the Indian Ocean moved south, missed the African coast, but created a void, or how you say, a depression that changed the direction of the wind. So we have dusty air."

He grinned. "Not even the djinns saw the storm coming."

To Amy, dust was everywhere, with very little air in the mix. If she was riding a camel instead of an SUV, she'd put a cloth wrap around her mouth and nose.

As if on cue, the security gates opened and Hassa's entourage, five Land Rovers, pulled into the driveway of the US ambassador's residence. Amy counted twelve security guards all dressed in thobes and ghutrahs, and Hassa's driver in the fifth SUV.

Ali G leaned over to her. "The robes are useful. You can't see the weapons they carry."

Amy smiled. Guards carrying weapons made her feel secure.

"Where are the Norwegians?" she asked Hassa.

"Rashid is flying the Norwegian diplomats, who are a married couple, to Shisur tomorrow. Today the Norwegians have to work."

Ali G took Amy's duffel bag and satchel to Hassa's Land Rover. Brewer was waiting in the Toyota Land Cruiser and pointed his arm forward, indicating they should be on their way.

Audrey Melville was holding up the trip. Amy knew she should have dragged her stepdaughter away from Sam and a tour of the antiques in his residence. The antiques made the residence receptions and dinner parties seem like more of a home and less like being in a hotel or museum. Donated by political patrons, they were worth millions.

"Where is she?" Brewer asked impatiently, just as Audrey came out the door, carrying her own duffel bag.

Wearing long billowing pants that looked like a skirt, she took off her hat to get in the Rover, and she apologized to Amy and Hassa.

"I got wrapped up looking at the antiques. My God, he has more fabulous stuff at the resident than Sonora."

She looked around for a place to put her duffel bag. Hassa's protective detail didn't do luggage. Brewer quickly stepped up and took her bag, putting it in the back of the Land Rover, and then helped Audrey into the vehicle.

Amy noticed Brewer, who had just complained about Audrey's tardiness, now seemed interested in impressing her. They were about the same age, early thirties, and Audrey was an attractive young woman.

She was as intelligent as Brewer. Whether she went for his frumpy look was another thing. Surely the CIA required a suit at some events, even in the Middle East.

· · ·

Finally, the six SUVs were off and out the guarded gates of the Diplomatic Quarter. In some places, blowing sand was so thick it almost covered the road.

According to Hassa's driver, the Saudi government used a plow to keep the road clear.

"It's like snow. The wind blows, and the sand must be cleared. This blacktop road is the main route to Shisur, then to Hadramaut and the Yemen-Oman border. The Saudis keep it clear because no one can count on the Yemeni."

They all agreed the sand drifted like snow, and were pleased to see that for the most part, the center of road was clear. So far, they were the only vehicles on the road.

"The Bedouin don't travel in sandstorms?" asked Amy.

Hassa laughed. "Only in the movies, like Lawrence of Arabia. Otherwise, they camp and wait for the storms to clear."

About ninety minutes later, they arrived at the Awad's compound. The SUVs pulled into a dirt parking lot in front of the store and its four gas pumps. Located halfway to Shisur, the break was needed to stretch their legs and take a potty break, if nothing else.

Like the first time they stopped at the store, Amy wondered about the computer setup. Why was it needed? Maybe smugglers didn't carry their own computers. To her that sounded strange because they must have computers. But who knew if they did or not?

She needed another coffee, but thought better of it. Shisur was still about two hours away. Then she realized she could go in the desert. All she needed was a big sand dune, and she ordered a large coffee.

As they traipsed into the store to the toilets in the back, Amy stopped and looked around. She loved the store. It wasn't the usual grocery store, more like a department store with food. This time she saw some toiletries she could use. After the kidnapping, she realized having tissues was as important as oxygen.

Hassa, also picking up boxes of tissues, said, "I must speak to the family. Their brother was executed, and I want to express regrets."

Amy understood and thought about the store and the family who owned it. Every traveler in and out of the Empty Quarter needed something and stopped here. It was the last stop on the road through the Empty Quarter.

With the Wi-Fi connection, travelers stopping for coffee, gas, or any of the thousands of other items, could send a message to Shisur, or to anyone camped in the Empty Quarter. As long as the camp was on top of a high ridge or dune, it shouldn't be hard to get a signal.

What about the family that ran this place? Their brother was executed. And for what? Brewer ought to know. This was his business. She felt foolish, but was curious. She walked over to Brewer who was looking at hunting gear for falcons or so the sign said.

"What do you know about the family that owns the store, the Awads? You and Skip told me you were at the execution of the brother, but your agency must have a profile on them. From what I can see, the Awads must know every traveler in and out of the Empty Quarter."

Surprisingly, Brewer didn't even blink. "We monitor the activity of the store and the family as best we can. I don't think that's classified, but appreciate it if you don't spread it around."

"What do you have on them?"

"Nothing specific." He went on to say the Awads had a chain of stores all over the kingdom. "They're a wealthy family and connected to the House of Saud. Remember when we were here before? One of the brothers was executed in Riyadh. Skip and I witnessed it. He was killed because of espionage charges against the royal family."

"The brother was a renegade?"

Brewer didn't say yes or no. "Espionage, Amy, could be almost anything. We were never told exactly what, and that's common. The Saudis rarely give any comment, publicly or privately. Just chop-chop."

He made a motion at the back of his neck. Amy grimaced.

"Even in a death case?" asked Amy.

Brewer nodded yes.

"How is Hassa involved with this family or an execution?"

"She's an important royal out of thousands of royals. Her family is from a tribe in Dubai, but she was a favorite of Hassa bin Sudairi, the founder's first and favorite wife. As Rashid's wife, she knows more of the politics of the royals than many of the princes and likely knows about her husband's Black Princes."

He looked at Amy. "The ambassador told you about that group, didn't he?"

"Yes, he mentioned them."

"What he didn't say was that Rashid's father's death was no accident, but nothing has ever been proved.

"Amy, Rashid was standing in the square next to Skip and me during the execution. So it beats me why Hassa would be consoling the family."

"I don't know either." Sam told her about the Black Princes and she didn't focus on the group. Now she had to. What else did Brewer know? After all, he was a spook.

"I hate to sound dense, but so where does Rashid fit in? I know he's a grandson of the founder of the kingdom and his father died before becoming king. I suppose today he is one of the top royals, out of thousands?"

"That's right, Amy, and the Black Princes are likely helping him get to the top. Now it's my turn at the toilet."

Amy looked around and saw Hassa talking to one of the Awads. One of the young men was following her, pushing a cart filled with what looked like all the junk food and toiletries in the store. They could use them. Mohammed Ishaq ran a clean, but basic hotel.

Mohammed Ishaq, what about him, thought Amy. He saw everything. At his village the road split, south to Yemen, and east to Dubai. He was the authority in the village. As the head of his tribe he was considered honorable and never would have participated in the kidnappings. True, his brother was killed by the kidnappers.

Was there something else going on, not with Ubar, but somewhere in that area of the Empty Quarter? Were the kidnappings a diversion from something else in the area or from excavating Ubar?

She hadn't time to discuss the Ubar excavation with Audrey. Knowing her stepdaughter, she'd done her homework. Then there were her friends, the royals, Rashid and Hassa. Soon she ought to know why they asked her to come to the excavation. Right now, she had more questions than answers.

I don't know what to think. Thank God Ace will be in Shisur. She had to share all of this with him. Not only did she trust him, but he had the right background to decipher the clues. The past always seemed so easy, and the present so tough.

Audrey joined her outside the store. "Should I pick up some stuff, too?" she asked.

"Don't worry. Hassa has enough for everyone, including the men. Did you have a chance to look anything up on Ubar's history?"

"Didn't have to. Ubar was one of the sidebar archeology subjects discussed in graduate school. We formed no conclusions because we didn't have information. For centuries, the Saudis controlled access and information to the site. We can't even confirm if it is the real route of the caravanserai. Now my bet, though unscientific, is that because of the royals' interest, it's the actual site. What we find is another story."

"Something at the site must be important to the House of Saud. Whatever it is will be something religious. A ruling class that mixes religion and politics needs religious relics to prove their right to rule," said Amy.

Before Audrey could comment, Hassa came out the door, followed by part of her protective detail. Amy knew their conversation wasn't over, but it had to wait.

Her phone dinged, and she checked her messages. Ace and Olen were in Shisur. She wasn't surprised. Ace never missed a fight, a kidnapping, or a hotel bombing. Once an adrenaline junkie, always an adrenaline junkie.

• • •

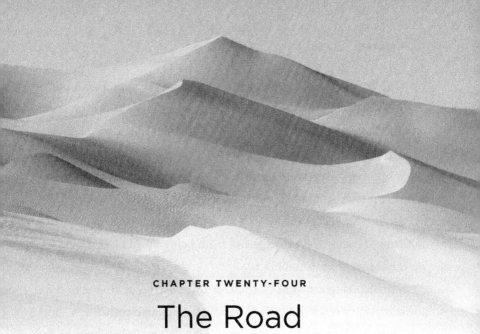

CHAPTER TWENTY-FOUR

The Road to Shisur

Historically, the Crown Prince is next in line
with the deputy crown prince second in line
to succeed the king.

"I'm back in the sand," thought Amy, watching it swirl in the wind.
The wind had picked up as they drove deeper into the desert. The land
of the Bedouin swept by in a dust cloud. Periodically, their driver slowed
as the sand covered most of the road.

Looking behind the Land Rover at the string of SUVs following
the princess attested to the concern of her husband. They could have
waited for the weather to clear and flown in with the Norwegians, but
the vehicles were needed in the Empty Quarter. More importantly,
Hassa didn't like to fly, and especially in a helicopter.

The princess was listening to music on headphones. Amy couldn't
tell if she was asleep or not. She thought about the Black Princes. She
knew Rashid well enough that if his father's death wasn't an accident,
he'd never let it go. Forming the Black Princes was the perfect outlet
for revenge.

The driver changed lanes to avoid hitting three Bedouins riding donkeys heading south. If the Bedouins weren't going to Shisur, then where? There was no way to tell.

She asked the driver. According to him, off the road back in the sand, hunting camps were common. The driver wouldn't say hunting if it wasn't true, would he?

In the rear seat of the SUV, Audrey was asleep. She had to be tired, not from the time zone change, but from being up all night, flying in on the redeye from Istanbul.

Her stepdaughter liked—no, *loved*—the desert. The chance to come to Saudi Arabia was a real coup for her. In the hundred years since Abdul Aziz founded the country, only a few archeologists were allowed into the kingdom. Audrey realized the trip was an opportunity to find an unusual artifact and publish. Archeologists lived for that moment.

Amy was skeptical of what the so-called finding at Ubar could be. The moment of truth was at hand and within a day or two they'd know.

Her problem now was how to get Hassa into a conversation on Rashid's position in succession in the royal family. She needed to know what the royals thought, not just what was in Morris's briefing books.

Words rarely escaped her, but she couldn't see how to begin. She was glad Hassa was absorbed in her music.

Reaching into her canvas bag, she pulled out the latest notebook Morris had given her. Looking at the index, she saw a chapter on the history of the House of Saud. Maybe it had information to help her ask Hassa genuine, not staged, questions.

She read that the ruling royal family of Saudi Arabia was made up of thousands of descendants, primarily from Muhammed bin Saud and his brothers who began the dynasty in the eighteenth century. Today the al Saud tribe has about fifteen thousand members, but only two hundred were in line for succession. These were the direct descendants of Abdul-Aziz bin Abdul Rahman Al Saud, Rashid's grandfather.

She paused to look out the window. The monotonous swirling sand almost made reading the notebook interesting.

Looking around the SUV, she saw Audrey was awake and had her laptop out.

"I will use it as long as I can get Wi-Fi," her stepdaughter said.

Amy flipped to the next page in the notebook and said, "We'll soon be out of range until Shisur."

Now she read something interesting. One of the rival tribes to Ibn Saud was the Al Rashid tribe in northern Saudi Arabia.

Her first question to Hassa could be Prince Rashid's name.

Amy thought a moment. Brewer told her Ibn Saud feared the British would colonize Saudi, and the Americans were the lesser of Western evils. She sighed and read on.

Fathering dozens of sons and daughters by his many wives, he married into many of the tribes in his territory. This was the beginning of the Saudi royal family.

Enough, she thought. Politics and religion were one and the same in this country.

She noticed a blinking light on the dash beside their driver. It didn't seem to be connected to the operation of the car. Some system must be used to communicate with the other vehicles for security and safety.

She looked at the seat behind her. Hassa's drooping head which had been leaning against the side of the seat, suddenly popped up. *Awake at last*, thought Amy. She waited a moment for her friend to fully wake up.

Hassa reached for her water bottle, while Amy continued to look out at the brown sandy landscape that if anything was getting browner. The area had a flatness that didn't exist around Riyadh. Enough of looking at the desert, she had to engage her friend.

"Hassa, I was going to ask you on our first trip down here, where are the huge sand dunes?"

The princess laughed. "Like you, this is only my second trip to the Empty Quarter. However, Rashid has been dozens of times to this large sand desert."

Amy saw her opportunity. "Does he travel down here on official business?"

"Oh no, he hunts. Believe it or not, looking at this desert, there are animals to hunt. Supposedly very difficult, since I have never seen any game brought back. But he takes his guns on every trip."

Amy thought it was illegal to have weapons in the kingdom and said so. Hassa said it was not a problem for a prince.

Amy could see no one was an equal to the royals in the kingdom. But she kept that comment to herself.

Hassa, took a sip of water and switched to her bottle of iced tea.

"Our politics are confusing to outsiders. In 1932, Rashid's grandfather, Abdul al Aziz, consolidated the tribes on the Arabian Peninsula. He allied himself with President Roosevelt because America was not a colonial power."

Amy said that was true. "Americans come, but don't stay."

Hassa went on to speak as if she was reading from a book. Amy listened, waiting for an opportunity to ask about Prince Rashid.

"A group of business leaders called the Ulema advises the king. More often, though, senior princes appointed their sons to senior positions in the government ministries they control, especially in defense, oil or security," Hassa explained.

For a moment, she paused and looked concerned.

"The Crown Prince succeeds the king. Next in line is the deputy crown prince. If the King is ill or unable to rule, the Crown Prince assumes power as regent. Sometimes it takes the King a long time to die. He might be kept alive for political reasons. Please don't say I said that."

Amy saw her opportunity and took it.

"You and Rashid are in this line of succession, right?"

Hassa smiled and then took her time answering. "Rashid is. My family is royal, but not in the direct line of succession. Rashid, a grandson of Abdul Aziz is in the direct line of succession."

She sipped more tea. "He's had important appointments by all the kings since his father—who was the Crown Prince—died in 1978. His father would have been king. *Inshallah.* It was not the will of Allah."

Amy asked the obvious question; how had his father died. As she listened to Hassa, she felt his death was more complex than merely a simple car accident.

"In 1958 there was a revolt by a group called the Free Princes, who wanted government reform; to take the power from the King and give it to a national council. Some royals thought my husband's father, Mischel bin Abdul-Aziz, was involved with the movement. Rashid's father was wealthy outside the royal family because of two connections. One was defense contracts in the kingdom and the other his association with the bin Laden family. His business partner was Mohammed bin Laden and together they built modern Saudi Arabia. Some say my father-in-law made the bin Laden family wealthy. Some believe my father-in law's automobile accident was not an accident."

At last, thought Amy, *her friend had said something that was missing in Bob Morris's briefing notebooks.*

"You know, Amy, it's a conspiracy theory, but nothing was ever proven. To this day, Rashid has never believed there was a real investigation into his father's death."

"What happened to the Free Princes?" asked Amy. She was thinking about what Sam had told her that Prince Rashid was believed to be involved with the Black Princes, whoever they were.

"They were exiled to Lebanon. In 1962 in Egypt, they formed the Arab National Liberation Front called the Free Princes Movement. They are not important today."

She went on to say his father's death changed Rashid's life.

"His mother was from the powerful al Rashid tribe in the north. With both parents from powerful tribes, he stayed in the line of succession. His mother died in Dubai, and my great aunt cared for her. The support of his mother's tribe, the Rashid, is still necessary to whomever rules the kingdom."

She took a moment and looked closely at Amy, almost conspiratorially. "His father, as I said, was in business with Mohammed bin Laden, and married one of the bin Laden daughters, a sister of Osama's. Rashid has a half-brother who is Osama bin Laden's nephew. You met Abdul. Rashid told me it was Abdul who got you and Brewer away from the kidnappers."

Amy was impressed, but kept her composure. This relationship wasn't in Bob Morris's briefing notebooks. She would ask Brewer about this in Shisur.

"Hassa, we owe Abdul everything. Where would Brewer and I be if he hadn't come along? Is he close to Rashid?"

"Yes and no. They see each other, but live in different countries."

Her answer sounded good, but she said it quickly, then changed the subject as she asked the driver how much longer to Shisur.

Amy was left to wonder how much was true. She noticed Audrey was listening to their conversation.

Hassa, now wide awake from drinking her bottle of tea, was full of information.

"I know everyone always wonders about the wealth in the kingdom. Rashid's father left him independently wealthy. He was fortunate to have good advisors when he was young. Following the businesses his father invested in, they made a lot of money. My husband doesn't need the stipends given by the royal family."

She laughed. "My family also made money. Royals made money selling crude oil, land sales, payoffs for contracts, simple cash handouts and huge monthly allowances. And princesses accumulated wealth, including my mother."

Audrey spoke up. "Doesn't this type of wealth make for jealousy and rivalries? Seems like it would piss some people off."

Hassa laughed. "Yes, there are feuds. It's like any family. You've been living in Turkey, so you've seen rivalries. My mother loved Turkey. We spent time every summer in Istanbul or on the coast. I loved the country, and my husband, and I have a beach home. Amy and Vince visited us there."

"It is a gorgeous country; the view of the sea, and the food in Turkey are the best," said Amy. "But we need to think about Ubar."

The radio beeped and Hassa spoke to the driver in Arabic.

"We'll be in Shisur shortly. Mohammed Ishaq has prepared a feast of grilled lamb, hummus, rice, and sweets. One of his wives makes the best baklava."

Hassa added, "And we'll have a little wine. This trip I made a point to bring several cases. They are in the back of an SUV packed carefully and covered. But no wine glasses. I thought that would be too ostentatious."

"I love Saudi champagne."

Hassa laughed again. "So do I, but we need to celebrate the beginning of the excavation at Ubar."

Amy and Audrey were both sure that was true.

• • •

CHAPTER TWENTY-FIVE

Back at Hud's Tomb

The three of them looked around
at the isolation of the area.

The sun crept across the horizon as Ace finished his second pot of coffee. Waiting for Hassa and Amy to arrive from Riyadh was boring. He knew everyone—Amy, the ambassador, his aunt—would veto his plan to visit Hud's tomb. Hassa's party wouldn't arrive from Riyadh until late afternoon. What else could he and Olen do in Shisur?

M. Ishaq followed Olen and Ace to the SUV. This time the village elder was going with his guests.

"Why?" asked Olen.

"Because I don't want more kidnappings on my watch or anyone else killed. I know the way the royal family's mind works. I'm innocent, but they blame me. The kidnappings must be someone's fault. Another kidnapping and they'll cut off my head."

Ace was curious who their host thought was responsible for the kidnapping, M. Ishaq's answer surprised him. "The royals."

"What?" Ace could barely conceal his surprise. "Anyone in particular? I recall there are thousands of them."

"Thousands, yes, and I don't know who, or I would go and say stop, please not in my village. My guess is the kidnappers had something to gain by creating problems with the Americans."

He paused. "Or smugglers did it, even by accident. The sand out here is very treacherous. Not everything goes as planned."

The thin blacktop road, with barely room for two cars, wound down the wadi, and started across the flat gravel desert to a ridge in the horizon. The ridge was a jagged line of rocks that couldn't be missed for miles around.

M. Ishaq pointed to the cliff. "The tomb."

Both Olen and Ace said, "Impressive."

They looked at each other. They needed to hear the history of the tomb, and no one would know the history like their host.

"Hud was a prophet," said Olen. Is that why his tomb is important? Still he wasn't mentioned in the Hebrew Bible of the Christian Bible."

According to M. Ishaq, that was all true. "Hud was a true prophet from the kingdom of Ad, and a fourth-generation descendant of Noah. No one in his village listened to him. The destruction of Ad is found in the Qur'an."

He paused a moment as the road momentarily disappeared in the sand, and the vehicle careened to the right. All three men were sure it was going to flip over.

"These SUVs are tough," said M. Ishaq as the vehicle righted itself. Ahead they could see where the blacktop started up again.

"Why's that spot collecting sand?" asked Olen.

"It's the wind. I'll send some workers out to clear it. We just shovel it off the road like snow. Only Allah can stop the wind."

Ace said, "Back to Hud."

"Well, Mr. Ace, Mr. Olen, it's a story told over and over. Rich people don't believe Hud, the prophet. God sent him to tell the people of Ad that God provides all that is good in their lives. If they don't believe, Hud said you wouldn't live. The people of Ad were powerful, wealthy, and arrogant. They built many buildings and monuments to show their power. Then they adopted idols for worship. When Hud told them to give up the idols or accept God's punishment, they said their Gods would protect them. Hud said all those who did not believe would die. The people accused him of being crazy and insulting their idols."

M. Ishaq paused to concentrate on the sandbars in the road, then continued.

"Hud told the people the wind would punish them. The wind would destroy everything at the bidding of the Lord. In chapter eleven of the Qur'an, Hud said, 'I call Allah to witness and bear witness my lord is the truth.'

"First came a drought, then the sun scorched the desert sands like a disk of fire that settled on the heads of the people of Ad. The wind shook everything and grew stronger every day. The people said it was a passing cloud that will bring us rain. The wind lasted eight days. Nothing was left, which is how the Lord takes care of sinners."

M. Ishaq reached under the seat and pulled out the book. He said it was in English, which was a heresy, but he had so many guests who couldn't speak Arabic that he had it translated. English seemed the logical language. Ace and Olen held the book between them and read:

We sent to the people of Ad their brother Hud, who said:
oh, my people, worship God: you have no other god.

"It goes on and on," said M. Ishaq, "but ends with: *my lord will put other people in your place, and you will not be able to prevail against him.*" At the bottom were the verses in the Qur'an: sur 11 Hud ayah 50-57.

Never letting a religious fact get in his way, Ace asked how they knew Hud was buried in this tomb. M. Ishaq said several places claim to be the site where he was buried. The most famous was the south wall of the Mosque in Damascus.

"But this is his grave. You'll see the inscriptions." He was emphatic.

There was no arguing with that. Olen and Ace looked ahead at the huge jagged rock cliff in the desert. The SUV stopped as the pavement ended in a small parking lot.

"This is where they were kidnapped?" asked Ace.

M. Ishaq nodded yes, but he was thinking of his brother, who was shot like a dog. The three of them looked around at the isolation of the area. North and west was the desert. To the south and east was a huge rock ridge. They stood there a moment; no one moved.

"I imagine this is the view the prophet Hud saw when he went to sleep at night," said M. Ishaq.

The sun was climbing high in the sky. The three men looked up at the ridge. It was a long climb in the desert sun. Neither Ace nor Olen were comfortable in the desert heat, even though it wasn't summer.

"Is there really anything to see in the tomb?" asked Ace.

Their host was honest. "No, I like to take the drive out here, have lunch, and say prayers for my brother."

"Lunch first works for me," said Olen. Ace quickly seconded that. Anything to delay the climb up the ridge in sun.

M. Ishaq said, "We can eat, climb, and be back in Shisur this afternoon. I'll get lunch out of the back of the SUV. You two set up the camp chairs and table."

He came back from the SUV with two large baskets and spread the food on the table. Olen and Ace had taken off their robes and hung their guns inside the back of the SUV. They looked at the table and at each other.

"Wow," said Ace, "If isn't the chicken that looks terrific, but the chips and salsa. And are those burritos?

"Yes, out here in the desert we do them Mexican style. By that, I mean it's just beans and bread."

Olen added, "And dates and baklava."

M. Ishaq pulled out the bottles of apple juice from the second basket. They were still chilled. "I froze them overnight."

Ace opened his mouth but before he could speak, they heard the roar of a vehicle.

Looking south, they saw what looked like a solid rock ridge. But it wasn't. Two black Humvees were heading straight at them with the flash of gunfire out the side windows.

Ace moved first, diving behind the SUV, and Olen was right behind him.

M. Ishaq shouted for them to get in the SUV. "It's fully armored."

Ace and Olen rolled to the side of the vehicle beside the door. The SUV was parked beside a large boulder. At the time, it looked like a parking place, but now they had a small fortress. Ace opened the door and took out two automatic weapons. He and Olen began firing around the side of the SUV at the Humvees.

Ace put another clip in, and with all his military training, casually asked, "Where do they get Humvees out here? Is America supplying the smugglers?"

No one answered. Olen was firing at the vehicles and M. Ishaq had disappeared into the SUV.

The Humvees stopped; they realized their bullets were pinging off the SUV and the boulder. The two vehicles squared off and all Ace could think was if the two Humvees charged, they'd never be able to handle them. The guys in the Humvees might not have his specialized training, which was in his favor. How to optimize his training was the question.

"We have to look at our options."

"What options? We need to kill them before they kill us." Olen was terse and obviously right in his assessment.

Then M. Ishaq crawled out the door of the SUV, with an automatic rifle. Ace reached over to pull it up between the hood of the SUV and the rock. It looked like a semi-automatic tactical rifle, but he hadn't seen a weapon quite like this before. It must have been modified.

M. Ishaq was back in the SUV and this time came out with a small bag. "These should be helpful."

Out of the bag he pulled three rockets and screwed one into the top of the bracket above the weapon.

"Your shot, Ace. I never practiced shooting. My brother Hassan always took the shot."

Ace leaned over to take aim. It was easy. The Humvee on his right exploded. Then he heard the whistle of a rocket and the crack as it hit behind them. They were showered by dirt and small rock particles.

"They've got a rocket launcher. With the dirt, I can't see if it's on the Humvee or stationary behind them. Someone in Saudi must be making a fortune modifying these rifles to fire rockets."

M. Ishaq had screwed on another rocket. But before Ace could take aim, the Humvee exploded.

"What happened?" It was Olen, more excited than Ace had ever seen him. The dirt and the dust prevented them from seeing anything.

"There's a vehicle coming in from the north," said M. Ishaq, looking behind them.

Ace turned the weapon in the direction he was looking. Through the dust they saw a man walking toward them. Dressed like a Bedouin, he was carrying a rocket launcher. On his back was another rocket, still unused.

"Are you okay?" he asked in perfect English. He followed his inquiry by introducing himself. "I'm Asif. I'm here to train my falcon."

Ace pulled himself up, thinking in the desert a falconer wouldn't have such a fancy weapon. But now wasn't the time to question the man. After all, he'd just saved their lives.

They walked over to the Humvees—or what was left of them.

"Smugglers," said M. Ishaq. "Let's see where they were hiding."

The tracks were easy to follow and led them to a camp tucked behind the rock ridge.

"Nice set-up," said Ace looking at a row of four tents.

They opened the flap of each one. The first was neatly stacked with boxes of scotch, bourbon, vodka and rum. Two others held crates of automatic weapons stacked side by side.

"Looks like most of the weapons are for long-range operations," said Ace. He pointed to an odd-shaped box. "Explosives and sticks of dynamite."

The fourth tent had cots. "Living quarters," said M. Ishaq. "We need to call the authorities on this contraband. They are in Riyadh, but they must have someone at the mining camp. We can call from Shisur."

Asif interrupted. "I am sorry, but I have an appointment at the mining camp. I need to get back there. Luckily, my bird has had his flight and is fed."

"No problem," said M. Ishaq. "And please come to Shisur soon, and stay at my house."

Asif thanked him for the invitation, and left after accepting Ace and Olen's thanks.

Watching him go, Ace asked the obvious. "Can we leave this stuff? It has to be dangerous to stay. No telling how many others are part of this smuggling group and may show up. We might not be so lucky twice."

M. Ishaq knew he was right. "Let's leave and I'll call the Saudi National Guard in Riyadh when we get to Shisur. This is a haul and they will want to follow up. If smugglers take it before they get here, not our problem."

"Agreed," said Ace and Olen.

None of them wanted another desert fight over the contraband.

• • •

Asif, using telescopic binoculars, watched the party depart from the valley. What the three were doing out here escaped him. But he now had something to report to Morris.

He left the ledge and headed to his SUV. Looking at this watch, he was pleased he'd be on time for dinner with the imam at the mining camp.

The imam at the mining camp must know what was going on, but he wasn't sure the imam would tell him so. Who else might know? For now, he'd pay his respects and enjoy dinner. At best, he'd get more information.

• • •

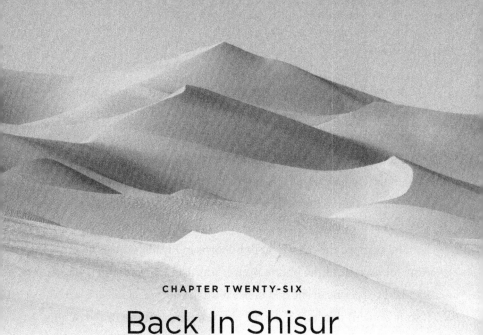

CHAPTER TWENTY-SIX

Back In Shisur

Old time explorers weren't armed
but this is a new century.

Like a jet stream high in the blue sky, the SUVs swept into Shisur
with clouds of dust trailing behind them. Hassa's staff arranged with
M. Ishaq to have rooms for everyone including the Norwegians,
whenever they arrived. Her additional protective detail would camp
out in tents behind the house. The men would pull eight-hour shifts
and guard the entire compound.

A brother of M. Ishaq's was at the doorway, beaming to greet them.
"Assalam Alaikum."

Hassa replied, *"Walaikum Assalam."*

"Please to welcome you for my brother. He will be back soon.
Princess Hassa, my wife will show you to your room. We have just
finished the large suite. We hope you will be pleased."

Hassa told him there was no need to fuss, but Amy could tell she
was pleased. They didn't know how much time the excavation at Ubar
would take. The more comfortable the accommodations at Shisur, the
better.

Brewer and Ali G were escorted to another wing of the compound, obviously reserved for men. Brewer waved at the ladies. "See you at dinner."

Then he pulled out his cell phone to make a call. "The embassy wanted us to check in, so this call is for everyone," he announced.

Amy needed to talk to him, but could see this was not the place. "See you at dinner."

She assumed the call was to Bob Morris in Riyadh. And as he turned, Amy took a look at the phone Brewer was using. It was larger than a standard cell phone. If she had to bet, it was some type of satellite phone. If so, it wouldn't depend on the cell phone towers at Shisur or the mining camp to operate. Leave it to the agency to have a phone like that. She doubted the phone could be bought in a store.

A young woman, likely a daughter of M. Ishaq's, escorted Amy and Audrey to their rooms that were side by side with a shared bathroom.

Amy had walked through the bathroom to check out Audrey's room, and asked, "What do you think?"

Audrey laughed. "I have been living in a tent on the plateau in central Turkey for five months. This is heaven."

"Didn't you get to Istanbul often?"

"Not often enough, but Ankara is near. The Konya Plain had mounds with Neolithic settlements. At Catalhoyuk, almost eight thousand people lived more than nine thousand years ago. With over a thousand structures, we'll never get them all excavated. A hundred years of digging and I doubt we will find anything of value. The natives have picked it over. Anything of significance is gone. Being optimists, we still dig, hoping."

"I hope you won't say that about Ubar. The site must have something in it. I feel it in my gut," said Amy.

Audrey smiled at her, knowing intuition had little to do with what actually existed at a dig. Still, Ubar could hold some surprises.

Amy needed to unpack her bag, but was becoming concerned about where Ace and Olen were. Obviously, they weren't at the compound. She threw her bag on the bed and walked down the hallway. At the end of it, she was in a large room that served as a living room and dining room. It was empty. She could hear people talking toward the back of the house, which must be the kitchen.

She headed that way. The kitchen opened out onto a patio with a large stone fireplace. To her left, a lamb was roasting on a slow turning wooden spit. Everything smelled great, or perhaps she was just hungry, probably the latter.

One of M. Ishaq's wives saw her and came over to ask, in broken but clear English, what she wanted.

"I'm looking for the two men who were supposed to be here," Amy said.

The woman smiled. "They go to Hud's tomb. Be back soon."

How stupid, thought Amy. Ace was bored waiting for them, so off he and Olen would go. Were they looking to be kidnapped?

Just as she was thinking that, the woman pointed to the door. "I hear a car, they come."

Amy walked to the front of the house as Ace and Olen strolled through the front door. She was relieved to see them, although realizing it had been less than two weeks since she was with them in Doha. How much had changed in that short time.

They hugged all around and then Amy launched into them. "What is this shit about going to Hud's tomb?"

Ace was smiling. "We knew you'd wonder why we went. But we didn't get kidnapped." He pulled his robe off his ample body, and Amy saw he was carrying three guns, a rifle, and two handguns, one with a long barrel.

"Got them in Dubai from an old friend."

Ace always surprised her. She was sure he used contacts from his days in special operations.

Olen pulled his robe off, and she saw the same array of weapons.

"We didn't think we should travel across the desert without being prepared. Old time explorers weren't armed, but this is a new century."

"We need to talk," said Ace. "We were in a fire fight and found tens of thousands of dollars in booze and weapons."

"My God," said Amy. "Do you want to talk now or after dinner? If I know you, eating is always a priority."

"Got that right." Ace didn't weigh nearly three hundred pounds because he missed meals.

"Amy, keep the firefight to yourself. No reason to freak everyone out. Mohammed Ishaq is calling the Saudi National Guard. He's handling it; we're out of it."

"Okay." Amy was surprised Ace was acting so causal about this incident. He had some reason, and looked beat. Smugglers were not on her radar. It was part of the desert life of Saudi Arabia. She wasn't here to stop smuggling.

• • •

They finished dinner and coffee was being served, the thin, light brown Saudi coffee that Amy had learned to love.

"This is delicious," said Audrey. "I love Turkish coffee that makes expresso seem like decaf, but this is nice and smooth."

There had been little conversation at dinner. Most of the talk was by M. Ishaq, and his concern over the trip his two guests had made to Hud's grave.

"Who is Hud?" asked Audrey. Her question told Amy she needed to get her stepdaughter up to speed on the kingdom.

Their host acted as if he'd never given this explanation, instead of several times today.

"Hud, peace be upon him, was sent as a prophet to the people of Ad. They were big people, strong, but not smart. They rejected the voice of Hud. A powerful wind destroyed them."

Then M. Ishaq changed the subject.

"Saudi Arabia has many famous tombs. Do you know Jeddah has the tomb of Eve, Adam's wife?"

The shocked looks on his visitors' faces showed amazement.

"The tomb of Hawa, upon her be peace, is in Jeddah. The city's name means the Ancestor of Women."

Amy was practical. "We need to concentrate on Ubar. I have three copies of Bob Morris's briefing notebook on Ubar, one for Audrey, one for Ace, and one for Olen."

It is nice, she thought, *once they read the notebook they'd all be on the same page.*

• • •

Audrey headed to her room and Olen went to the back patio to smoke. Amy told Ace that they needed to talk, now. The question was where they could go and not be overheard.

They headed for the door, and so did two of the protective detail. They weren't going to be alone. So, sitting on the front patio, Ace offered Amy and the protective detail the Cuban cigars that he always carried.

They smoked under a clear sky filled with stars.

"When the sky is like this, I feel I am seeing the entire universe," said Amy.

"Me too," said Ace. And the cousins went into the house to their respective rooms. Their chat would have to take place tomorrow.

• • •

CHAPTER TWENTY-SEVEN

Back in Riyadh

Two hotels had been bombed
with no apparent connection other than
they were filled with Saudi royals.

Bob Morris looked around his office. He had a conference table, a couch, and two television sets, one on CNN, the other on al Jazeera in English. He could follow it in Arabic, but he didn't want to bother Ed with the translation. He missed BBC and had put a request in for a third TV. They were all on mute, so the room was quiet. He followed the news by reading the captions for the hard-of-hearing at the bottom of each TV screen.

Hanging on one wall was a large colored picture of his father catching a six-foot swordfish off the coast of Key West, Florida. Most people thought it was him since, except for his father's beard, he was a carbon copy. On another wall, he was holding a falcon in the Saudi Arabian desert. He loved the picture because behind him was the Tarqwa Escarpment, the massive wall of desert cliffs outside Riyadh.

He turned back to his stack of cables removing the ceremonial knife off the top. Most thought it was a paperweight; but Bob knew otherwise. If there was a takeover attempt of the embassy, he would never have time to get a gun from the locked gun room. But the knife, well, he could take someone out before they got him. Never would he allow himself to be taken alive. And, for that he carried a small plastic pill bag in a shirt pocket. The idea that the Marines would protect him was only a reality in movies. The local guards might, but he figured they'd never fight to their death, certainly not his death. For proof, he didn't need to look further than the mess in Benghazi.

The first cable, a summary of drone activity over the desert, was a priority. Only drones, he was sure, could find the so-called Good Samaritan, who was a priority. Who would help two Americans, and then leave? With the headdress and a beard, it was easy to say everyone looked like someone. But Brewer insisted the guy looked like Prince Rashid. And, Amy had met Abdul in the desert and swore it was him.

Now his analysts needed to find this Abdul guy. One cable listed all the vehicles on the road. He looked at the analyst report and found something that was encouraging.

One truck was tracked from Najran up to the Jeddah road, the main interstate between Jeddah on the Red Sea and Riyadh, the capital. What piqued the interest of the analyst was that the truck turned off the Riyadh road before the escarpment and headed south. The escarpment blocked the drone from following it. The question was why a truck would turn off the main road. The route was unusual after a long trip across the desert, especially since nothing existed to the south but more desert.

The report noted a golf course was down the road. Bob knew the road looped around to the wadi behind the Diplomatic Quarter, housing all the diplomats from nations around the world.

In the wadi, the land was owned by royals, where they kept horses, goats, and vegetable gardens. The area was only a couple of miles from the royal palaces, and that of the king. The analyst report concluded that since the pickup truck was hauling goats, the driver was making a delivery in the wadi. Bob wasn't so sure the goats were the delivery. The pickup could be carrying anything.

He reached for the phone to call the general service officer—the GSO—for the embassy. Usually someone else in his office made the call, but he needed information now. He trusted Jan, the GSO, with the truck for Asif. He knew she'd see his extension number, and if at her desk, she'd pick up immediately. She did.

"Jan, I need some help. Can you get me a list of all the landowners in the wadi behind the Diplomatic Quarter? I need the royals and Saudi businessmen, the real owners, not the renters, if any."

He knew it was possible and Jan said he'd have the report in a half hour. After thanking her, he wondered what the list would show.

The next report on his desk was on the Black Princes. Few real facts existed on what they were doing, so getting a report from his staff was important. Two hotels had been bombed with no apparent connection other than they were filled with Saudi royals. Ali G thought they were connected. He was the ambassador's go-to guy, who had his finger on the pulse of the city in the strip malls, where the real Riyadh existed. Bob had learned Ali G's instincts were usually right on. Now he couldn't see what facts linked the two bombings.

With the hawala system financing terrorists, the links were impossible to trace. Sam was right about hawalas being a problem. They were everywhere. You could do laundry, trade money around the world, have a suit mended, buy yogurt, get gas, eat a sharma, sip coffee, order take-out pizza, fix a muffler, and buy a plane ticket to London or Dubai, using hawalas. The Black Princes could move money anywhere for anything.

Both hotels at the time of the bombings were hosting meetings of oil executives, which included many royal princes from Saudi. While several hundred people, including hotel staff, were killed, so had twenty-seven princes of the House of Saud.

The current king was one of the last living sons of the founder and Hassa Sudairi. The Sudairi brothers were the rulers for most of the last century. In his speech, the King deplored the deaths. Meetings took place, talking about the talent pool that was lost. The truth was twenty of the dead princes had been Sudairis holding positions of power in the government ministries, or in line to be the next king.

To Bob, the composition of the royal family was a paradox. Saudi royals were not equal. None was equal to a Sudairi. The seven sons of Abdul Aziz and his beloved first wife Hassa bint Ahmed, were chosen ones. She bore him more than any other wife, though in total he had forty-five sons that were known. The number of girls was unknown.

This ought to be a Saudi soap opera, thought Bob.

Equally important was that Hassa bint Ahmed was from the powerful Sudairi tribe, from the Najd. Her father, the chief, supported Abdul Aziz in the early years, critical to his consolidation of power in the kingdom. And finally, standing at nearly six feet tall, Hassa was beautiful. What more could any man ask? Beautiful, from a powerful family, and known as the mother of boys. The Arab culture considered the most prominent wife the one who bore the most sons.

Bob knew she'd been a personality not to be overlooked, as women usually were. She might not drive a car in the kingdom, but she advised her husband, traveled to Europe, and hosted dinners for her sons, urging them to be supportive of each other. She was no weeping willow, but a strong oak, whose sons had been king for a century.

She was dead, but her grandsons were today the Saudi power group. And Rashid was her favorite grandson. When his father died, she looked after him until he left for school in the United States. Had she or his father lived, Rashid would be king. He reached into a door in the wall unit behind him, pulling out a bottle of single malt scotch. It was four in the afternoon and time for a drink.

There was a knock on the door and Jan came in carrying a folded paper followed by Sam. Bob realized it was time for the ambassador's daily intelligence briefing.

"If Jan's here, something must be going on," said Sam.

Bob pulled out two more glasses and poured the scotch.

"Jan, what did you find?" He was confident there was something.

She opened her briefcase. "Surprise, Prince Rashid owns most of the land in the wadi. His servants farm the small plots of land."

"Gee, how did he get all that?" asked Sam.

Jan smiled. "From his father. When Prince Mischel died in 1978, he left his land, like most of his extensive businesses, in the hands of a trust. That trust makes his wives and children wealthy in their own right. They don't need any support from the House of Saud but still take their share of the royal subsidies. At the end of the day, no other half-brothers or cousins are worth more, or have as much independence from the royal family."

Bob sipped his scotch, and expressed what he had often thought.

"More often than not, the other royals, not related to the Sudairis, wanted what Rashid had. One of the ways was to form their own group, their cabal. We know about the Black Princes, who are Sudairis, but how many other similar groups are out there wanting to take control of the kingdom. My guess is that one of them is responsible for the bombings."

Sam agreed. "Some ministers have told me, with the oil crunch, many talented Saudis may move out of the country. The cuts in their allowances by almost a third have really hurt. What astounds me is they accept the reduced allowances, don't say anything, then go out and bomb somebody."

Sam reached for the bottle of scotch and poured himself another.

"The bottom line," said Bob, "without more facts we are back to Rashid, who is the likely leader of the Black Princes. Next, we have the person who helped Amy and Brewer, got local border guards to pick up Skip's body, and left hauling a horse trailer to the wadi from Najran."

All three agreed that the man who helped Brewer and Amy was the same man who had entered the wadi outside Riyadh with a trailer carrying goats. It was Abdul.

Sam sipped his scotch. "Your instinct is right on, facts or no facts. What I don't get is why he would leave when there was a substantial reward for the Americans. He obviously wasn't a local."

"And," said Bob, "we don't have any proof he's connected to the Black Princes. It's curious that Abdul didn't stay to collect a reward. Since he didn't, I bet he was carrying something else in the back of the pickup. The drone report indicated the back end was riding low, like there was a heavy load, and not just from a couple of goats."

"Two hotel bombings, each taking out royals and oil men, have to mean something. Who has something to gain? Bob, you have to be right. Another bombing is out there waiting to happen," Jan added. "The other thing is the kidnapping. Who is responsible, and I don't mean the three gofers that were killed. How did this Abdul just happen to be on the same road as the kidnappers?" Jan asked.

Sam was emphatic. "The royals are involved. I know it looks like royals are targeted in these bombings, but some of them could still be behind the attacks. The kingdom is up for grabs. The top two, the King and the Crown Prince, are ill, and no number three has been selected. They don't have a succession plan. I ask the Foreign Minister on the occasions when we meet. He says it is in Allah's hands. Someone is orchestrating the succession. I don't really care who they kill to get the throne. But they killed one of our people—Skip—and I want the assholes who did that."

"We'll get them," said Bob. He then looked at Jan who, like him, knew the chances of catching the kidnappers were slim. Still it was an odd kidnapping, though no ransom had been requested. A connection could be made to the hotel bombings.

"Jan is right. It's too much of a coincidence for the Good Samaritan to be on the road the kidnappers were on. Someone else planned this and why, for what, we are still guessing."

"So, what's our plan?" asked Sam. "We gotta know what we're going to do."

"We keep in touch with our contacts. Jan has as many as my agency. The Black Princes can't be kept a secret." On that point Bob was certain.

Sam finished his drink. "This entire country is run on secrets."

He and Jan stood up to go when Bob's phone rang. He answered it and motioned for them to stay. The call was short and Bob did most of the listening. He hung up and turned to them.

"That was Brewer. They're all in Shisur, including Ace and Olen, who went to Hud's tomb yesterday. That tomb has had more visitors in the last few weeks than in three hundred years. No kidnapping, but they were attacked by smugglers and saved by a falconer named Asif. Ace and Olen were both heavily armed. Apparently, Ace has contacts in Dubai to get weapons. Now my guy Brewer is feeling paranoid because he doesn't have a gun."

Bob knew Sam didn't care if the embassy operatives carried weapons. But experience had shown him that staff just got into trouble when guns were around. Certainly, Shisur had plenty of weapons.

"When are they going to Ubar?" asked Sam "And speaking of the trip, would Hassa know anything about the hotel bombing? The world thinks Saudi women are kept in a closet, but we know how much they run everything. She most likely knows everything Rashid does."

"Good question," said Bob. "According to Brewer, it's difficult to have a private conversation in Shisur between a man and a woman. Hassa's protective detail, some twelve guys, Somalis, according to Brewer, keep Amy and him apart or are so close they can hear the conversations. FYI, her detail is also heavily armed."

"The detail understands English that well?" Jan sounded surprised. "I thought only the staff that works for the royal family speak good English. If they are from Africa or the sub-continent, they usually don't understand Arabic. So, it's convenient for the royal family to speak Arabic in front of their servants without them understanding the conversations."

Sam had to laugh. "Unbelievable how that works."

Bob sipped his scotch. "Right now, this drink is the only thing I know for sure. When Brewer called, he told me he was at the end of M. Ishaq's garden with no one around. He said Amy indicated she has some information. How he was going to get it from her, he wasn't sure, since privacy is a premium. They're ready to go to Ubar and taking a lot of equipment, just in case they have to stay overnight."

"Oh my God," said Sam. "Overnight, are they kidding, after this kidnapping? I had a terrible time convincing the Norwegian ambassador that it was safe for his two staffers to help out at Ubar. I knew he wouldn't say no to Prince Rashid, but he wanted my assurances, and I gave them."

Bob shrugged. What could they do? The Prince wouldn't let anything happen to his wife, of that he was certain. He needed his agency to focus on the Black Princes and in particular, Prince Rashid. He was the group leader, at least that was their best assessment, and his wife was excavating Ubar. What was the connection? For now, all he could do was check out sources in the kingdom who might hear what was happening.

"Jan, can you keep an eye on the wadi?"

Her offices had an annex for the warehouse and motor pool in the wadi. It was a hub for maintenance and supplies for the entire embassy. Better yet, Jan worked out of her office in the wadi several days a week.

"Is there any way we can set up surveillance? Keep an eye on who is going in and out?" asked Bob.

"The security people could," said Jan.

Bob didn't like that answer. "I'd like to keep this between us. What about your staff? They are all third-country nationals so wouldn't have a bone in the royals' dog-fight."

"I'll manage it. No problem."

• • •

Bob had a point, though Jan wasn't pleased at being asked to spy. Working with her local staff, she had the perfect cover. Everyone, not only on her staff, but the royals' staff, who lived in the wadi would spot a plant, a spy. If something was going on, it wouldn't take the royals long to pick it up. She was not as certain as Bob that there was a royal plot to change the succession of the royal family. She did know something was not quite right, she just couldn't put her finger on it.

Often, to get supplies, she went to the strip malls in the city with her Indian procurement specialist. She could easily justify a trip this afternoon. The man who ran the store, another Indian from Mumbai, usually knew if anything was coming down.

• • •

Bob took the call from Asif, glad Sam and Jan had left. He was pleased that M. Ishaq was turning the contraband over to the Saudi National Guard. They were usually competent, and he hoped they wouldn't screw it up.

"Asif, you're doing the job I wanted you to do. Stay low and keep an eye on that so-called mining camp. I am ordering some deceptive surveillance, but you are my main man on the ground."

Closing with "stay in touch," he reached for the scotch, what was left of it. Taking out a pad, he composed a summary of Asif's conversation for his analysts. The agency was interested in booze and weapons. In the memo, he directed his analysts to use drones to survey Hud's tomb.

Who came to pick up the contraband was of interest. The dead men in the Humvees didn't work alone, and he suspected they were a smuggling ring. If he was right about the mining camp producing weapons, or just thorium, smugglers were a sidebar in the Empty Quarter.

. . .

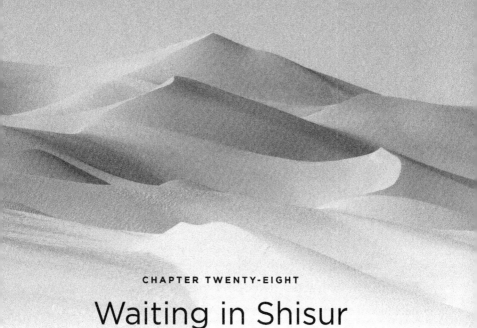

CHAPTER TWENTY-EIGHT

Waiting in Shisur

She began in the early 1950s,
though she said the search for Ubar
began many centuries earlier.

Amy stepped onto the patio, seeing a table filled with every conceivable Middle Eastern dish. She took a plate and selected lamb, rice and hummus, poured herself a glass of apple juice, and sat down. She noticed Brewer was in a corner of the yard, which was really an enclosed garden, complete with palm trees.

He pointed to his phone and then to the sky. She had to think a moment, then realized he was talking to Bob Morris. That fancy phone of his would be able to get a signal anytime, anyplace.

M. Ishaq told her communications improved since the mine operations began. They could text, even if the phone didn't work. She wondered what the truth was concerning communications.

Picking up her plate, she headed over to Brewer. They both looked at the lamb, appearing to discuss the food. For the moment, no one else was around. Hassa's protective detail was eating and the others were guarding the compound.

"I got through to the embassy. Bob and Sam were meeting and obsessing over Abdul and the drones trying to find his pickup," said Brewer.

"Brewer, something else has come up. Hassa told me Rashid's half-brother is a bin Laden. His mother is Mohammed bin Laden's oldest daughter. His uncle was Osama."

Brewer made a face, wondering to himself how his agency missed this fact.

"Wonderful. As if Rashid is not rich enough in his own right, he has a relative with access to the bin Laden fortune, and access to their network of engineers and construction staff."

Amy told him that after Hassa mentioned it, she had hurried over the connection. "She never misses discussing a detail. What is she hiding? I just know, Brewer, something else is going on. I am not sure how to get her to talk about it, or if she even would. She gave Audrey and me a long commentary on the House of Saud, but really said little."

"Trust your instincts," said Brewer. "I'll text Bob immediately to tell him. It's possible we missed Abdul's relationship to Rashid."

"It's time to get to Ubar," said Amy, as Audrey joined them on the patio.

"I'm ready," said Audrey. "I've read up on what's current on the Internet about Ubar. There are conflicting points of view, so I am anxious to get Hassa's take."

"And Audrey, you will," said Hassa, another latecomer to dinner, "but first, let's eat and talk over coffee."

The conversation at dinner was idle chitchat, and as the coffee, baklava with fresh melon, and chilled dates arrived, one of her protective detail brought Hassa a folder. To Amy, it looked quite thick.

When Hassa opened it, Amy saw why. The folder was filled with photographs.

"Now where to start?" said Hassa, and proceeded to lay out the photos in front of them. There were enough photos for each of them, including Ace and Olen, though both were busy refilling their plates. M. Ishaq brought out lanterns that lit up the backyard.

She opened the folder and took out a written document in Arabic. "This is the report that came with the pictures. These were all taken in the 1950s, but the search began years before with the old explorers.

"According to the document, the explorer Bertram Thomas said his Bedouin guide pointed to tracks between the dunes and said, '*Look Sahib, there is the way to Ubar. It held great treasure, with date gardens and a fort of red silver. Now it lies beneath the sands.*'

"On other journeys, Thomas wrote that Arabs called it the Atlantis of Sands. No one claimed to know the location, or even the approximate location. Most tales of where Ubar is focus on the Rub' al Khali, the world's largest sand desert covering almost the southern third of the Arabian Peninsula including Saudi Arabia, Oman, the United Arab Emirates, and Yemen."

Hassa looked up and asked, "Not too boring, is it?"

Amy and Audrey, sipping coffee and getting a caffeine fix, shook their heads no. Ace, Olen, and Brewer were back at the buffet table where the food kept appearing from the kitchen. They weren't being impolite because they could still hear Hassa's every word.

"Everyone remembers St. John Philby, an advisor for the British government to the founder of the kingdom, Abdul Aziz. He called Ubar, Warb. He first heard about the city from his Bedouin guide who told him of a place of ruined castles where the King of Ad lived with his horses and wives. The place was destroyed by wind and fire for his sinful ways."

"Ad," said Brewer, returning to the table, "is Hud's tribe."

Ace couldn't resist commenting. "So, some think Ubar is a myth, and others say it's true. Everyone does agree on Hud, the prophet, and the people of Ad."

Hassa was patient. "In the last decade, modern science has been a big help to settle those questions. In the early1990s, Nicholas Clapp claimed to have discovered the remains of towers at the excavation site, supporting the belief it was the site of Ubar. He knew Mayan ruins had been identified on satellite images. With his contacts, he was able to get NASA to take satellite images of the desert that identified ancient camel tracks hidden beneath the sands of the desert. These tracks were mapped. Where they intersected could be water wells and ancient cities."

She sipped more tea before continuing.

"The archeological importance of the site was proven by satellite imagery that showed a network of trails. Some of these were under sand dunes that were over a hundred meters tall. The satellite imagery showed no other place where water wells and camel trails intersected. No evidence showed the city was destroyed in a sandstorm. The fortress had collapsed into a sinkhole that was a well. The well was undermined by ground water being used to irrigate at the oasis. In other words, the city collapsed on itself."

Now Hassa became animated.

"Ranulph Fiennes, an explorer and adventurer, was a member of Clapp's expedition. He believed the spot where Ubar was, as proved by satellite photos that Clapp had gotten, was identified on an ancient map of Arabia by Claudius Ptolemy in about 150 AD."

Hassa looked around to be sure she had everyone's attention. She didn't mind that Ace and Olen were still eating. In the Arabic tradition, every time the two finished a dish another one appeared. After all, they returned to sit beside her, munching and seeming to hang on her every word.

"I am almost finished with the history."

"Will there be a test?" Ace's question made Amy wince, but she made no apology for her cousin's sense of humor.

Hassa sighed, and continued, "There's a lot of dissent regarding this site being Ubar. Some think it is in the northern part of the Arabian Peninsula. Some think it refers to a region or a group of people. Some think it is a myth. Scientists have been swayed into wishful thinking."

And she closed the folder.

"Hassa, that was a great background," said Audrey. "I did some reading flying in here and know Nicolas Clapp had no doubts about what he found. He was convinced, as are others, that over the centuries building on the stone fortress undermined the limestone base, and caused the site to collapse. He found the viper snake famous for guarding the frankincense fields in the area around Ubar. For me, Ubar is the Atlantis of the Sands."

Amy suddenly felt the chill of the desert evening and pulled her jacket around her. Even in the desert, she always had a jacket. No matter how hot it was during the day, at night the desert was always cold.

"What time are we leaving tomorrow?" she asked.

Hassa motioned to M. Ishaq, who was talking to one of his servants.

"What is the best time for us to leave?"

He thought for a moment. "Eight. That gives us time for coffee. We can eat at the site. I'll have my people bring food and set up a campfire in case we have to stay overnight."

"Overnight?" asked Amy. "Where will we sleep?" She liked sleeping under the stars, but knew Hassa would require a cot and a tent.

M. Ishaq smiled. "Don't worry. We will have cots and tents for those who want them, and most important, sleeping bags."

Amy added, "It will be a good day." But in her heart, she wasn't sure they'd find anything at the ruin. And she was even more certain Hassa wouldn't want to spend a night at the ruin.

Ali G, who'd been listening to the discussion from the doorway motioned to her. "Gold, Amy. Why is it never mentioned?"

Amy smiled. "The treasure could be something else. Remember, Ali G, the gold was likely taken centuries ago."

"So we will see?"

"Yes, we will see."

. . .

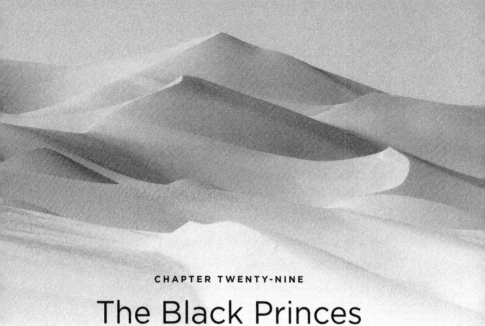

CHAPTER TWENTY-NINE

The Black Princes

Nearly half of those have been killed
in the hotel bombings.

To Prince Rashid the nearly deserted village of Dhurma, forty-five miles northwest of Riyadh, was the perfect place for the Black Princes to meet.

The National Guard, whose mission was to ring Riyadh, manning security checkpoints on the major highways, never thought about the village. Busy looking for weapons being brought into the city, small villages on the perimeter were off the radar. Today the National Guard, led by General Ibrahim, was loyal to the current king. Soon they would be loyal to him. *Inshallah.*

Dhurma, once the western gateway to the Wadi Hanifah providing water to the city of Riyadh, was now bypassed by the Riyadh-Mecca highway. Most of the younger generation had moved to Riyadh.

For centuries, the villagers supported the al Rashid tribe who controlled the northern part of the Arabian Peninsula.

My mother's tribe, he thought.

He looked around the room, knowing his heritage from both his parents made him first among equals. Surrounding him in the living room of the compound's house were his cousins, all royal princes.

They were told to travel to the village on back roads, without a security detail, and to avoid National Guard checkpoints. He even told them if they were stopped by the police or the National Guard, to go back and take another route, even if they had to cross the desert. He knew they would all be driving SUVs. None were stopped.

Rashid would have been more comfortable if someone was stopped. Now he wondered if the National Guard was doing its job.

The person missing from the circle was his half-brother, Abdul. The princes didn't need to know about Abdul, the man who would put the bomb in place. The man who was willing to die.

Three years ago, each of his royal cousins made a decision. They didn't make it out of loyalty or patriotism, but greed. Greed was why they were following him. They saw his fortune and wanted the same. Once in power, Rashid would tap them for positions of power in government ministries. Running these ministries would give them access to international contracts, to smugglers, and bribes. In a short time, each would be rich in his own right, and no longer dependent on the House of Saud for living allowances.

Rashid had invested his inheritance wisely and now his personal fortune was worth several hundred million. Not having to rely on the royal house, he was independent and had the freedom to make his own choices. The Black Princes supported him because he promised them the opportunity to make their own private fortunes, just as he had. In addition, each would get an appointment to the important ministries, oil, interior, the National Guard. With the appointment came the opportunity for them to make a private fortune from contracts or bribes.

I ought to thank the king, he thought. The latest royal announcement to reduce the allowances of royals and government officials couldn't have come at a better time. His cousins didn't want their lifestyles cut back, and that was going to happen.

To Rashid, the decrease in oil prices, which brought on the cuts, was a sign. The financial trouble in the kingdom played into his plan to take the throne. With the support of the Black Princes, he would rebuild the kingdom on solid economic principles. Beneath the sand in his country was a wealth of minerals waiting to be discovered. Desalination would provide water to grow every crop in the world.

Yes, he thought, *I will rebuild my country,* and he laughed. He also intended to make Jeddah one of the world's great shipbuilding cities. He couldn't verbalize that plan for development yet. But he'd do it.

As the red in the sky slowly faded into darkness, he heard the call to the Maghreb, the evening prayer. Rashid loved listening to the calls to prayer from the mosques in Wadi Hanifah. They echoed all the way to the royal palaces.

The princes begin to pray.

Allah Akbar, Allah Akbar, Allah is Most Great, Allah is Most Great.

Allah Akbar, Allah Akbar, Allah is Most Great, Allah is Most Great.

Ash-hadu an la ilaha ill-Allah, I bear witness that here is none worthy of being worshiped except Allah.

Rashid waited for the princes to finish. When the room was silent, he held up the Qur'an and quoted from 2:25 surah, the verse.

The Holy Book should not be doubted. It is a guide to the righteous, who believe in the unseen mysteries, and are stead-fast in prayer: who give generously from what we have given them; who trust what has been revealed to Muhammad and others before him; and who firmly believe in the life to come.

*The righteous are those who accept the righteous guidance of
their Lord; and they will surely triumph.*

He looked up at the group. He wasn't sure Allah was listening, but
to say so was heresy.

"This is our guide, the Holy Book, the Qur'an. When the time comes
for us to take power, I hope to have the original that the prophet, peace
be upon him, used centuries ago."

The cousins nodded approval. He knew they wouldn't ask how
he would obtain the Qur'an. It was best they didn't know his wife was
searching for it in Ubar. When she found it, they'd see it as a great
discovery. Only he and Hassa knew the Qur'an at Ubar was hidden
in the ruins by a Bedouin at the request of the imam in Mecca.

The imam had told the royal couple, on a visit to the Holy Mosque
in Mecca, that the Damascus Qur'an was not destroyed. Where it was,
no one knew.

He and Hassa had an antiques dealer in London search for it.
Incredibly, he found it and the imam ensured it was placed at Ubar.

The Bedouin the imam selected had worked for Rashid's mother
his entire life. Though his mother, a princess in her own right, was dead,
Rashid and Hassa knew what a friend the man had been to the family,
and visited him when he was dying.

He told them as he died he hid the Damascus Qur'an in a room
that still stood, at the base of the Ubar ruins. He died as he said the
word, "Ubar." His deathbed confession confirmed what the imam had
told them. Neither of the royal couple believed a religious cleric, and,
without the deathbed confession, would not have been sure the Qur'an
was there.

That was five years ago. Since then, they'd conspired to put together a
plan to discover the Holy Book and how to use that remarkable finding to make him king.

Impossible as it seemed, being a Saudi Royal didn't allow them to go to the Empty Quarter and start excavating. They needed a reason and Ubar's supposed gold was enough. *If the royal relatives knew the truth, they'd be all over the area trying to locate the Qur'an for themselves,* he thought.

He felt as if he had trained for this event all his life, or at least since his father had died. He couldn't dwell on that now, maybe later. Now he had to give the Black Princes just enough information to make them think they were in the loop.

"*Allah, ma'ak,* God be with you. My brothers, we are here because the Saudi line of succession is out of date. Our family numbers over five thousand and more if you count the illegitimates. Today, to be in line to rule, you have to be a Sudairi, related to Hassa al Sudairi, or your father served as King. Now the King is ill, spending time in Switzerland to get treatment. How long does he have? *Inshallah.*"

Now was the time to mention the real issues.

"The real problem is the older royals are reluctant to pass the line of succession to us, the grandsons of our founder, Abdul Aziz, peace be upon him. The Law of Governance said that succession passes to the sons of the founding king, and their children's children. The one qualification is that only the most upright be considered. Upright is not defined.

"Our rivalries usually play out in private, keeping the rest of the world in the dark. Those of us in this room must decide who is to be king. We will eliminate the challengers. We are Sudairis and our grand-mother was legally married to the founder."

Rashid paused, thinking of how to continue. He had to sound sympathetic, yet he wanted to keep their comments to a minimum.

"Fewer than a hundred Princes are serious contenders for the throne. Nearly half of those have been killed in the hotel bombings. The next attack will take out more royals, including many who expressed no interest in being king. It cannot be helped, *Inshallah.*"

He went on to say many of those killed and many still alive had been joining together to oppose the Black Princes. Everyone in the group knew other dissident princes were alive and plotting in the kingdom. So far only the Black Princes had the nerve, the will, to take the necessary steps to ensure a victory. Their competition was out there waiting for them to fail.

Rashid's expression didn't change, but he was confident in their support. Now to wrap the meeting up.

"The time is coming. In ten days, the King is hosting a celebration of what he says is two hundred years of rule by the House of Saud. No one is sure how he got that number. Poor health will keep him from the party. But—and this is important—every prince eligible in the line of succession will be there. After the event, the succession will be obvious. Don't worry. We will be safe. *Inshallah.*"

The Black Princes were silent for a moment. That was what they were today, loyal soldiers pledging loyalty to Prince Rashid, Allah willing.

CHAPTER THIRTY

Delayed
by the storm

Not only was visibility limited in the brown dust,
they had trouble breathing.

From ancient explorers to the day-trekkers of today, the Empty Quarter was always sunny, but not today. Another storm, coming in off the Indian Ocean, brought wind and with it, dust. There was a controversy among local tribesmen as to how long the area had been without rain.

Brewer was listening to M. Ishaq, who was certain it had been a year since they had almost an inch. "But not all of my tribe agrees with me. I think I'm right because well water is being used to grow the small patches of wheat, corn, and beans in the villages."

"Mohammed Ishaq, the reports I've read said the last rains came in 1977. This area is not just a desert but is considered to be hyper-arid because the average rainfall is less than an inch. Daily temperatures in the summer run about 117° to one 124° Fahrenheit with cool, sometimes very cool, nights. The winter is balmy, and it's about seventy degrees now."

He had to pause a moment, knowing the Saudi government prohibited the temperature from going above 120° F. The law was to protect businesses who had to pay time and a half if the temperature was higher. As a result, everyone, including the diplomats, had their own thermometers.

Probably not a polite thing to bring up right now, Brewer thought, watching the guests sip coffee and eating yogurt with fresh scones in the main room of the house. The village was surrounded by a severe sandstorm. How long it would last, no one knew.

• • •

Inshallah was the term used to describe when the storm might end. To Amy, that meant in an hour or next month. She was uneasy and wanted to blame the sandstorm.

She worried about Audrey. Had she gotten her stepdaughter in the middle of something dangerous? Just then Audrey walked into the room. After pouring coffee and picking up a scone, she asked what the plan was for the day.

"I see the weather, and since you're sitting here, it's going to prevent us from leaving for Ubar."

M. Ishaq said it was best to delay the trek to Ubar. "We can get there, but the problem is getting back. Setting up camp in the storm would be difficult and if we drive back…well, no one wants to travel at night in the desert."

Amy looked at their host, wanting to change the subject. "Mohammed Ishaq, I am trying to figure out where the oil is in the Empty Quarter."

Audrey selected another scone and asked, "When I read up on the Empty Quarter, I found out the desert had more oil than anywhere in the world. Of course, it's under sand dunes, but drilling in the sand has to be easier than drilling in the depths of the ocean."

M. Ishaq told them most of the oil being produced was in Sheyba, on the northeast edge of the Rub' al Khali.

"The Ghawar oil field is largest in the world. It runs across the northern part of the desert and includes an oil refinery.

"The sand dunes are not just dunes for riding dune buggies. They can be over two hundred fifty meters—that's over eight hundred feet high. Drilling can be expensive. The gravel plains you saw driving here from Riyadh, are really gypsum. The sand gets its reddish-orange color from the feldspar in it, and that's what the drillers look for to find oil."

"Feldspar." Audrey might not have said anything if it had been a sunny day, but with the sandstorm and being stuck in the house, why not. "It's about sixty percent of the earth's crust and has been discovered by the rover on Mars. Here on earth it's used for making glass, ceramics, paint, plastics, and rubber. The product lasts and resists chemical corrosion. It's also used in Bon Ami, a common household cleaner."

She took a breath and finished by saying, "I learned a lot online, but not how long a sandstorm lasts."

Brewer was bored and took up the conversation.

"Don't know about sandstorms, but in the middle of the desert there are hardened areas that were once shallow lakes. They existed from six thousand to five thousand years ago, and then others from three thousand to two thousand. Before three hundred AD, there was more rain, more lakes, and salt flats. During those centuries, the incense route linked Asia and the Mediterranean."

Amy noticed again what she thought was Brewer's interest in Audrey. They were about the same age, though he looked much older, being overweight and premature balding, a family trait he couldn't change. Most people figured him to be in his forties when he was barely thirty years old. He had spent time in Turkey, so they might have more in common than this desert.

"So, centuries ago, there were lakes," said Audrey.

"Right. The belief is they were formed by monsoons that lasted for only a few years. Fossil remains were found of rodents and scorpions. And more of a surprise was finding the remains of animals, including a hippopotamus, water buffalo, and long-horned cattle. Flint tools, including knives scrapers, borer, and arrowheads were found, but never any human remains."

Brewer ended by saying, "With no human remains or fossils found to date, it's a mystery where man came from and where he went. Maybe one day the sand will blow away, and we will find a fossil of man in a place everyone has looked for decades."

He sounded sarcastic.

Audrey said she had read about explorers.

"I am also fascinated, by the explorers. Many have traveled across the Empty Quarter and felt compelled to write books. My favorite was one by Freya Stark who went to the area alone in the 1930, and wrote *The Southern Gates of Arabia*. What intrigued me when I read it several years ago was that she was sick a lot and local people helped her heal. Most people today think about Bertram Thomas and St. John Philby, because they wrote about their travels in the 1950s. To me, Freya was the real pioneer."

Amy, listening, was pleased Audrey had done her homework. She noticed Ace was finishing up his coffee. He looked like a man who had a place to go.

They looked up as Hassa swept into the room and announced, "We must delay our trip. The sandstorm means we couldn't get back, because darkness comes early in a storm. We were prepared to stay overnight at Ubar, but we don't want to stay overnight in a sandstorm, if we can help it. So, I hope you have a book to read and I am going to have the ladies do my nails."

She left mumbling something about understanding the bad weather.

• • •

Amy saw Ace was heading for the door. "Ace, what is going on? Are you leaving?"

"Yes. This is an opportunity."

He looked around to be sure no one was paying them any attention, especially Hassa's protective detail. They were eating breakfast inside because of the weather.

"I'm going back to that so-called mining compound on the road from Dubai that everyone thinks is about mining."

"That is insane; you don't speak Arabic. And what is the purpose? They're mining. What's the problem with that?"

Ace thought a moment. "It's only an hour away. I hadn't thought about the Arabic; everyone speaks English out here. I want to see why the Chinese are there, and what are the odd buildings buried in the sand. To me, they looked like they held reactors. Ali G and Olen are going with me."

Amy could not believe what she was hearing. No way was she going to let Ace go driving off across the desert without her.

Olen arrived from his room. "Ace, I can't make it. Something I ate hit me wrong. I hate to miss the trip. I'll stay here and drink tea to stay rehydrated."

"No problem, Olen, because I'll take your place," said Amy. With his guns, Ace could shoot his way out of any situation, which could cause an incident and piss the Saudis off. She had to go, hoping she could keep him from going off the deep end.

"Without Olen, you need me as your backup, Ace. Ali G may not be able to shoot a gun. It's no fun to sit around Shisur, so I'm coming."

There was nothing Ace could say. He also knew he could count on her to handle a weapon.

Walking outside, the effect of the sandstorm hit them. Not only was visibility limited in the brown dust, they had trouble breathing.

As they were getting in the vehicle, M. Ishaq realized what was happening. He was not happy. As the village leader, he was responsible for his guests. Ace tried to reassure him. "We are going down the main road to Dubai. Even in the sandstorm, this should not be a problem. Scout's honor, we won't go off the road."

Ali G showed him the emergency kit in the back. There was a tent, sleeping bags, k-rations, a knife, water, and some type of stove. Their host knew he couldn't stop them.

"It's a terrible idea," M. Ishaq said.

"It's forty minutes away. We'll be okay." Amy couldn't believe her own voice. She sounded so convincing when she really thought going was as crazy as M. Ishaq did. Going out now was not just crazy, but dangerous. She remembered the kidnapping, but she couldn't back out now.

She quickly added, "We'll return in less than three hours. If we are not back by then, start looking for us."

What helped her stay positive when she was kidnapped was knowing everyone would be looking for her. It never hurt to have someone come looking for them if they did encounter trouble.

They were not quite fast enough. Out of the door came Hassa. "I can't believe you are going to some mining camp. Oh Amy, after the kidnapping, please don't go."

Amy gave her a hug before getting in the SUV. "Don't worry, we will be back before you know it."

Then she leaned back and almost whispered in the dusty wind, "I have to look out for Ace. You know the trouble he can get into."

At that, Hassa grinned. She had heard stories about Ace and knew he was what the Americans called a character.

I'm glad to stay here, Hassa thought to herself. *Going to Ubar will be enough ancient ruins for me.*

• • •

Bob Morris looked at his blinking phone. He hit a button and saw Brewer was trying to call him. He answered it, hearing a roar in the background. The connection was very bad. Satellite connections were weak when there was a lot of wind, and the accompanying blowing sand made it even worse.

In between the roaring, Bob understood that Amy, Ace, and Ali G were driving in the sandstorm to the mining camp. Brewer apologized for not being with them, saying he saw the car as it was pulling out of the yard. He didn't dare tell Bob he was away talking to Audrey.

"Good God," Morris said. He was not pleased they left for the mining camp. He didn't look forward to telling Sam. "Brewer, they better not get into trouble. I don't see how we can help them. I wanted you and Skip to get to the mines. You just didn't make it."

Bob knew that he and Skip had seen the buildings. The pictures they took disappeared with the camera when they were kidnapped. Both men thought that might be the reason for the kidnappings. Someone was determined to keep the activities of the camp a secret. If so, the two Prowers and Ali G could be in serious trouble.

"I can't believe they got out without me!" Brewer said disgustedly.

"The good news is that with the sandstorm, the bad guys should be off the road," said Bob. "Let me know when they return. I will be watching the clock until I get your phone call. If the lines are bad with the storm, text me."

He hung up and called Sam, who said to come on over to his office. But Bob thought a moment before heading there. Should he contact Asif, who could look out for Amy and Ace?

Bob opened the drawer of his desk and took out a handful of M&M peanuts. He always thought best with a handful of them.

No. Asif's identity needed to remain confidential. Only he and Asif knew what he was doing.

No need for Amy, Ace, or Sam to know about the imam. The camp was too important to give up all his contacts just because the Prowers decided to visit it.

Ace would be well armed, making kidnapping a low risk. That's what he would tell Sam. He took another handful of candy. Yes, they would manage, and Ace had to have weapons. If something untoward happened, he had Asif as backup.

• • •

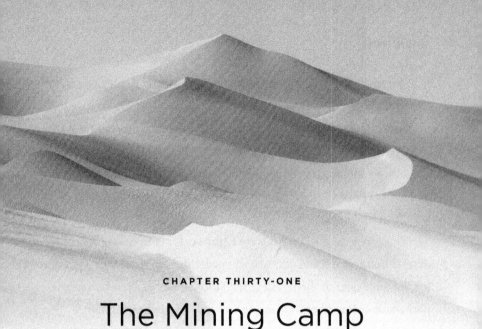

CHAPTER THIRTY-ONE

The Mining Camp

Ever heard about rare earth metals?

The drive to the mining camp was not as difficult as Amy imagined.

Her ever-resourceful cousin had high-tech glasses, which gave him 20-20 vision in the dust and sand. Amy didn't have the glasses, so to her the world outside looked like a blank wall, brown in color. Most of what she'd seen since leaving Riyadh was through a brown haze hovering about the desert.

Ace made the trip in about forty minutes, rating him a "booha" from Ali G. At the edge of the camp, they hit their first problem; visibility. The buildings were difficult to see in the dust.

After driving up and down several dirt roads, they found what Ace called the café. It was a low fabricated building where they had seen the Chinese gathering on their drive from Dubai. The proof was several dozen SUVs parked near it.

"Olen and I were sure this was the dining hall."

Once inside, Amy could see this was the original good-old-boy eatery, if you could call it that. They ordered lamb kabobs with rice, and were pleased to see beer was served. That is until they tasted it.

"Some local is making the junk. But if you chug it, the taste is not too bad."

Amy thought Ace was an optimist. "We're drinking tea, right, Ali G?"

"Yes."

"Are we looking for someone?" she asked, while thinking the kabobs had a great flavor.

"The Chinese."

That surprised her. What were Chinese doing in the middle of the desert? Before she could ask, Ace was ordering rounds of the rotgut beer for the table next to them. These men looked like eastern Europeans, perhaps Polish workers. Everyone seemed to know each other.

The next thing she knew, an American sat down at their table. He was tall and heavyset, with a light beard. She thought he belonged running one of the Prowers ranches.

So much for speaking Arabic, she thought, as he introduced himself.

"John, John Campbell."

After the introduction and another beer, John and Ace were swapping, of all things, Vietnam war stories. If Amy didn't know better, she'd think Ace and his new friend John were brothers. She never ceased to be amazed that merely talking about being in a war made you best friends decades later.

In fact, she'd been in the war; in southeast Asia, the same one they were discussing. She had worked for a nonprofit. *Do-gooders* was what Vince had called them. To her, the group was a way to get to the war zone and see her new husband. The upshot was she knew as much about the Vietnam war as anyone. She just never talked about it. Thank God, Ace and John had moved to present day and were talking about what the mining camp did.

Ace ordered more beer.

"Ever heard about rare earth metals?" John asked.

Ace and Amy hadn't, and said so.

John looked like he was just getting warmed up.

"Well, rare earth metals are used in products we all know and love. Think of wind turbines, and closer to home, iPods, cell phones, catalytic converters, fuel cell, flat screen TVs, rechargeable batteries, magnets, and radar equipment. I find it kind of humorous that the name rare earth is more like common earth."

"So they are digging the stuff up out of the sands?" asked Ace.

John held up his hands. "No, the stuff is tricky to mine, to extract, and it can be hazardous to the environment. The brown sand soaks it up, but we still have to be careful it doesn't leak into the water table."

"Water table," said Ace and Amy, almost in unison. Amy remembered what Audrey had said about the water tables below the sand. She'd been talking about Ubar, but apparently water existed in many places under the sand.

They learned that John was a civil engineer. And like a teacher, he explained why the water table was so important in the desert.

"The land only gets an inch a year, or less. Underneath is a sandstone base where the water table sits. That water supplies the oasis and the wells. If the water was on the surface, it would dry up in a month. But it's underground."

He took a moment to chug his beer.

"I supervise how we mine the monazite, because it contains the thorium, the rare earth element we need to separate out. Thorium is radioactive, only mildly so. Monazite, by the way, is a mineral that contains at least fifteen rare earth elements. Are you with me?"

He was looking at them and even Ali G nodded yes. The ambassador's go-to guy knew a lot about everything. With their encouragement, John continued.

"So why is thorium important? Because it can be used to power nuclear reactors replacing uranium fuel. The world would be safer because thorium produces very little dangerous weapons-grade waste.

It survives only a few hundred years, not the millions of years uranium survives. We have Chinese workers, because today China has more rare earth minerals than any country. They ignore environmental risks."

Amy and Ace were beginning to see how this so-named rare earth element could be used. John was a real resource.

"Other countries are looking to ramp up production of rare earths. Saudi Arabia is one, and they are not on the radar of any other countries. That's why we are here. South Africa, Australia, Canada, and now India are mining the element.

"We are interested in how India is mining because the element is sensitive to heat. Where the mines are in India is a hot dry climate, like we have here. Have to be careful, though because the Chinese workers, who help us produce the metal, don't trust the Indians."

Ace ordered more beer and saw Amy check her watch. He realized they needed to head back to Shisur.

After exchanging emails and cell phone numbers, Ace invited John to visit them in Dubai. The Prowers family and Olen's joint partnership owned a couple of high-rise condos.

"John, it's yours to use when you make your regular runs to the city."

No doubt to get real booze was what Amy thought, still amazed at this instant desert bonding. Then they were off, heading back to Shisur.

Turning onto the open road, they realized the sandstorm was ratcheting up. The dining hall was protected by other buildings. Now, the wind was blowing the sand sideways.

Ace drove slowly as the sand, covering the blacktop road was slick. Above the sound of the wind, they still could hear the pinging of sand against the windshield and sides of the SUV.

Suddenly Amy remembered she meant to call Sonora. The mining camp's communications were more updated than Shisur's. The call failed. The sandstorm had to be interfering with reception.

The drive was slow. For a moment, she felt hopeless, but it passed. Now she was focused on what they had to do. Get to Shisur, and tomorrow, if the weather cooperated, Ubar. Maybe this trip would finally end. She didn't know where to put this new wrinkle on Saudi—mining thorium.

• • •

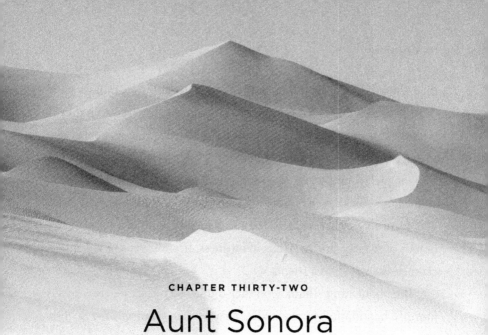

CHAPTER THIRTY-TWO

Aunt Sonora

At Ubar the ancient city collapsed on itself.
Poking around in the dirt today could cause
more destruction.

In the late fall, Berlin was cold and damp. Sonora felt the cold more when her family was in danger. With all the money in the world, with all the advancements in telecommunications, she had few options. Calling Sam at the US embassy was one.

For three generations, their families had been friends. Their Texas ranches shared borders for their cattle. Today they shared oil pipelines and drilling rigs. She knew Sam would give her a straight answer on Amy and Ace's safety. She also wanted more information on why Amy was asked by Hassa to come to the excavation at Ubar. On that point, she hoped Sam could shed some light.

It wasn't like they didn't know, or hadn't heard about Ubar. The trouble was, the site of the ruin was isolated. It almost took a military expedition to get there, let alone excavate it. How Princess Hassa's group was going to excavate, she wasn't sure.

The kidnappings told her there was a problem. Thank God Amy had been found unharmed. It was very unlucky the political officer died when his head hit a rock in the sand. Amy and the embassy men must have stumbled into something in the Empty Quarter that they weren't supposed to see. Two embassy staff had tagged along, not because they were interested in Ubar but for some other reason.

She picked up the phone to call a man in London. He was Ace's contact, but she knew he would help her and would know who she was.

According to her nephew, the two men had worked a number of jobs over the years. In Ace's old business, friends were rare, but he claimed the man was a friend.

The phone rang. Thank God they didn't use carrier pigeons any more. In her mind, she imagined an airwave across Europe, the English Channel and into the center of London, though she wasn't even sure the man lived in London. More likely, he was in some English village living a nondescript life with access to London's technology.

Finally, he answered the phone. She didn't have to explain who she was. The phone number was one Ace used, and Guy knew it was Ace's Aunt Sonora. What she didn't know was that his phone had a voice identifier on it, and when she said hello, her name came up. She was who she said she was, and he hoped Ace was all right.

"Mrs. Lleissle, I am Guy. What can I do for you?"

Sonora was pleased. He was polite. She swore his English accent was from Eton; however, she was not always accurate on English accents. Ace had faked one often enough when it was convenient.

"Guy, I have a question, and I also need information. Ace is in Saudi Arabia, in the Empty Quarter. His cousin Amy was invited by royals—royals that she and her first husband have known since college—to help in the excavation of the ancient city of Ubar. At an oasis called Shisur, she and two American officers from the US embassy were kidnapped.

"The vehicle they were in flipped in the sand, and one of the Americans was killed. It seemed to be an accident, if we are to believe what we were told. Everyone went back to Riyadh to regroup. Now they are back in Shisur and plan to get to Ubar this time. I have no idea what the royals think they will find at Ubar, but there must something going on in that desert, either at Ubar or somewhere around it. Ace told me you have access to satellite photography. I need your help. The Empty Quarter seems far from empty."

• • •

Guy realized Sonora didn't know Ace had contacted him, said he was going into the desert, and that Amy had been kidnapped. He hadn't heard from Ace since the phone call, but had put together a portfolio of information on that section of the Empty Quarter. He pulled it up to look at it while he talked.

"There are no excavations in that area. It's a dangerous place. At Ubar, the ancient city collapsed on itself. Poking around in the dirt could cause more destruction. The limestone base is unstable and really weak.

"My sources in the country tell me Prince Rashid contacted Norwegian diplomats posted at Riyadh. They happen to be two of the best rock climbers in the world. The prince asked them to assist his wife in going into the ruins.

"Why his wife thinks there is some ruin at Ubar is a mystery. Those who are watchers of the ruins know she has spent several years researching Ubar. No one can figure out why she is so interested in this wasted site that is also very dangerous. There is no profile on her. At this time, the most logical explanation is not that she is a dedicated archeologist, but that Ubar has something to do with her husband and his association with the Black Princes. What and how, no one knows yet."

Sonora took his reference to the Black Princes seriously. She knew the group. One of the Committee members mentioned them at the last meeting. There was little information on them, and her members hoped to learn more facts. At the time, what was important was the group existed.

Guy was not finished.

"Mrs. Lleissle, one more thing is unusual about that area of the Empty Quarter. Until Ace asked me, we never paid any attention to that part of the world. A mining camp just down the road from Shisur is what's new.

"Mining activity is not unusual in the Empty Quarter, but the volume has increased. Our contacts tell us it is a frenzy of activity. What they are mining is one of the rare earth elements called thorium. It could be a game-changer in nuclear reactors. Mining thorium is difficult, so the Saudis must have some experts helping them. We think they are Chinese.

"Mining activity isn't run by the Saudi government. Someone is selling the product and its being taken out of the Empty Quarter into Yemen and Oman."

He was on a roll.

"From those little gulf countries, who knows where the product goes or for what. Thorium is not that rare; the term *rare earth element* is a misnomer. The bottom line is there is a lot of traffic through Shisur, and no one can say why. One road goes east-west, one goes north-south. So we figured we could track them and see what they were doing. But we couldn't. At any point, if the vehicle is an SUV, it can go off-road, and we lose it. There have been a few runners, we call them. But frankly, if I had to make a judgment call, I would think they are smugglers of weapons, though we cannot be sure, and of course, drugs. The royals have to get their fixes even when they are in Riyadh. Actually, being in their home country probably makes them need the fix more."

Sonora knew he was right and thanked him for his analysis. They made plans to talk again. She would inform him when Ace left the kingdom.

"I like to think he is in the high-rise condo in Dubai."

Sonora said she was sure Ace would prefer to be in Dubai and ended the call. As she did, she realized what she said was wrong. Ace was happiest right in the middle of the fracas.

So all the excitement was over thorium. What were the Saudis doing with it? It was a substitute for uranium. Could they have a bomb and no one would know? One of her Committee members would know.

• • •

Guy looked at the phone in his hand. He had been honest with what he told Mrs. Lleissle, and yet had held back. With Ace, he would have told all he knew. Besides, it was only a rumor. Several years ago, one of his contacts in London was looking for an ancient Qur'an. Rumor had it that he found one. Could that be what the royals were looking to find in Ubar? If so, he'd hear about the finding. It wouldn't be the first time royal money had been used to concoct a miracle finding.

• • •

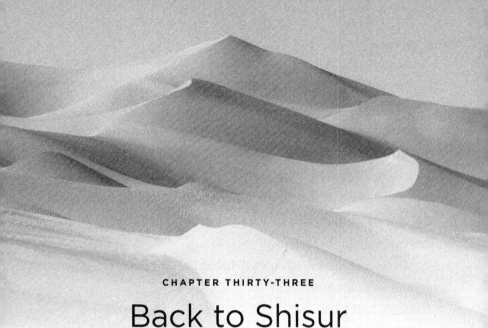

CHAPTER THIRTY-THREE

Back to Shisur

Amy realized she knew very little about weapons
but this mine was important, more so than
the excavation of Ubar.

Ace drove slowly. The sand had covered the sky, and it was like driving
in a cocoon. The sand continued to drift. His main objective was not
to get stuck.

"Amy, what is your buddy Rashid's position in the royal family line
of succession? There are supposedly some five thousand royal princes."

"That's about right," said Amy. "Only about two hundred are in the
running for the top positions of King, Crown Prince and deputy crown
prince. Sons of kings have top priority. If Rashid's father had lived, he'd
be at the top. When his father died, he lost his standing. The sons of
the next king passed him by."

Ace laughed. "So, what was written got erased."

Amy laughed, too. "I'm not sure Rashid thinks it's erased."

She paused, thinking about all that had happened.

"I was wondering about the rare earth element that you and John
talked about. If thorium can replace uranium, that means it could be
used for energy in a power plant or to build a bomb."

She waited a moment, then said, "The only buildings we saw were the tents and the café."

"Buildings for weapons are on the east side," said Ace.

"When Olen and I drove in from Dubai, we saw on the east side at least a half dozen buildings—long low stucco—and buried in the sand. What makes it so dangerous, Amy, is that countries in the world have readers set up to identify uranium when it's being transported. Thorium wouldn't be identified."

"So thorium can be transported through airports or go out of ports on ships and can't be traced?"

"Right," said Ace.

Amy remembered a conversation last year in London. She had just joined Sonora's Committee and was at a dinner party with Rashid and Hassa. It had been arranged by Sonora, who regularly hosted such parties.

"There are only so many museums you can see," her aunt had said when Amy tried to excuse herself from attending.

Sonora's usual guests included members of MI6, responsible for Great Britain's internal security. Sonora knew so many who worked in the government agencies, Amy wondered if she wasn't in some quasi-group of spooks herself.

At this dinner party, one of the guests was a nuclear physicist Sonora seated between Prince Rashid and Amy. The two men got along immediately and one of the things she remembered was Rashid told the physicist he chaired the Saudi Arabia nuclear program. More importantly, the prince invited the scientist to visit the kingdom.

"Ace, Prince Rashid heads the kingdom's nuclear program. He said that at one of Sonora's parties in London. Everyone thinks it's nonexistent, but with thorium, it might be very much alive."

"You're right," said Ace. "That mine is producing and must be protected by someone in the royal family."

Ali G spoke up. "We're in a dangerous country."

Amy realized she knew very little about weapons, but this mine was important; more so than the excavation of Ubar.

The dust was swirling in the wind as they entered Shisur and wove their way through the date palms. Suddenly there were lights above them.

"If I didn't know better, I would say it is a helicopter," said Ace.

Amy thought no one sane would be flying in this weather. But Ace was right. It was a helicopter, and it landed almost in M. Ishaq's front yard, churning up more dust. Thankfully, the windows on the SUV were closed.

M. Ishaq came over to the SUV, and Ace cracked the front window ever so slightly.

"It's the Norwegian rock climbers. Everyone thought they would come in by car tomorrow, but Prince Rashid got the Saudi National Guard to fly them in."

Ace was impressed. "Amazing they can do it in this sandstorm."

"They have a lot of practice in the sand," said Ali G from the back seat.

"A buffet is set up in the house, if you need to eat. Otherwise Princess Hassa plans to leave at eight in the morning," said M. Ishaq.

Ali G headed for the buffet, with Ace right behind him. How they could eat again amazed Amy, because she certainly couldn't. She looked around for Brewer, he wasn't in the room. Then she saw him underneath the covered patio, which had now been enclosed with heavy plastic doors.

"Cozy," she said as she entered the patio.

Brewer was drinking what looked like real scotch. Then she saw the bottle. It *was* scotch.

"I brought it with me. Don't we need to keep hydrated in the desert?"

"Yeah, Brewer, but I think the idea is to hydrate with water," and Amy, reaching for an empty glass for him to fill.

"Anything of interest turn up at the mine?"

"First, Ace bonded with one of the American contractors."

"Anyone we know?" asked Brewer.

"John Campbell."

Brewer didn't know the name. Amy was beginning to understand why the agency wanted a presence in the Empty Quarter. None of the American Embassy staff in Riyadh seemed to know anything that was going on in the Empty Quarter.

"How about thorium? Ever heard of it?"

"Actually, yes," said Brewer. "I don't know what they use it for, but I know they transport it out of the country."

"I learned from this John at the camp; it can be used in nuclear reactors. Doing so could reduce the proliferation of uranium used to create weapons of destruction. So the question we need answered is why they are transporting it out of the country?"

Brewer sipped his scotch. "We know they're sending what they mine south to Yemen and east to Dubai. But something else is going on down here. We thought that before Skip and I ever came, and I still think that."

"Ace and I don't know either. I need a favor. Can I use your phone to make a call?"

The phone was heavy, but operated like a normal phone. Amy placed a call to Sonora and waited for security to come on the line. Only their private cell phones, hers and Ace's, were set to Sonora's direct line. The security guard picked up and, in seconds, put her through to her aunt. The phone used voice recognition.

"I am relieved to hear from you. Amy. Is Ace there, too?"

After filling Sonora in on their trip and telling her about thorium, it was Sonora's turn. "How secure is this phone?"

"Our favorite agency uses it. I know you might not have confidence in it, but, Sonora, it's all we got."

"I just talked to Guy in London. I think the Black Princes are important."

Listening to her, Amy recalled what Sam told her when she first arrived in the kingdom, that Rashid was believed to be a member of the Black Princes. Now her aunt, who had access to information from many covert agencies, was talking about the Black Princes.

Suddenly a light bulb went on. She did know something. Hassa had mentioned there was a reception soon for the royals at the king's palace that Rashid had to attend. Rashid had mentioned it at the French Embassy reception. He couldn't go to Ubar with them because of the reception.

"Sonora, if the Black Princes are planning something, it could be at that reception. And, I know it's being held at the king's palace, on his grounds. It's the first time all the royals have been together since the bombing in Doha and the hotel in Riyadh."

"That is the perfect place for another bombing. Whoever is bent on eliminating some of the royals would have another target. Like the two other bombings, the royals attending the palace reception would be princes in the line of succession," said Sonora.

"I'll tell Brewer. He'll get Bob and Sam to take action."

Sonora asked. "Amy, is there anything to be done once the royals are at the reception? Try to find out from Hassa what you can about the Black Princes."

"You mean ask her directly?"

"Why not. There is nothing to lose. She will either tell you or not. As close as she and Rashid are, she must know."

"The embassy believes Rashid is the leader of the Black Princes."

"Then Hassa will know," Sonora replied.

Amy tried to get Hassa to talk about where Rashid was in the line of succession, and she skipped over it. It was unusual, as Hassa never ducked a question. She usually was bubbling over with information.

Amy had to ask her aunt a couple of questions. "Sonora, what do you know about Ubar?"

"We are not sure," replied Sonora. "Something is at that ruin that she and Rashid think they need. What that is, we can only guess."

"Agreed," said Amy. "When we entered the sunken city of Ubar on our first visit, Hassa immediately sized up the situation. She saw it was dangerous, and she knew she needed qualified people to go into the sunken cavern. Not only did she get Norwegian diplomats, but they just arrived in the middle of a severe sandstorm in a Saudi National Guard helicopter."

"This is serious, my dear. Whatever is at Ubar, they seem to need. I can't figure out why they need you, and frankly, that makes me very nervous."

Amy said, "Audrey is with us. I'm sick that I involved her, and haven't had a chance to clue her in."

"You may be better off keeping her in the dark. She's an archeologist and can focus on Ubar, not on her safety. You watch out for her safety."

"That makes sense," said Amy. With regret, she said good night to Sonora, promising to call her aunt the minute there was a new development.

• • •

Brewer knew Amy needed to talk to Sonora; about what, he couldn't imagine. Finally, she ended the call and told him about the conversation.

"Can you stay while I call Bob? He might have some questions."

With relief, Bob picked up on the first ring.

"Bob, Amy and Ace are back from the mining camp."

"I still can't believe they went in this weather." Bob was incredulous.

"Yep, it gets worse. They met some contract worker, a guy named John Campbell, in the café of all places. Or maybe the best place, because this guy told them what was being mined, and it's true."

Bob was stunned. "We had our suspicions, but are you sure?"

Neither of them wanted to say much. The phone wasn't as secure as it might be and no way to see if anyone had tapped into it.

"Well, Brewer, seems you've accidentally found what you and Skip set out to do."

"Thanks, Bob, I wish Skip was here. Now for the important part."

For a moment they were silent, both knowing the nagging question that needed answering. Who set up the mining camp? Somewhere in the array of Saudi ministries, some royal had to know about the mining camp. The question was—which one of the royals was behind it.

"Brewer, I want you to stay down there for a few days. Sam wants Amy back here, but I think she needs to stay, too. My gut says there is no way to get Ace and their Mexican partner to leave."

"Okay, Bob, M. Ishaq can put us up. Don't see a lot of guests rushing in to stay. No telling how long we will be at Ubar."

"Just keep me informed, Brewer."

As Brewer hit the off switch, Amy felt the chill of the evening. She wondered what they were going to do.

"Bob says to stay in touch, and he will try to send us another communications system."

Ace walked up, eating a dish of ice cream. "Where do you suppose they get the ice cream around here?"

"A guy at the village makes it by hand," said Brewer. "Are you going to stay after we go to Ubar?"

"Is the Pope Catholic? Of course I'll stay. In fact, if it was up to me, I'd skip Ubar and head back to the mining camp. Can't do that because it would tip everyone off involved with the excavation, and God knows who else."

Ace laughed. "Brewer, you guys are nuts. Someone is setting up a mining operation in the Empty Quarter on the road from Dubai to Yemen and Riyadh running through it. Shouldn't every royal know about it?"

"Ace, these royals are a little different. They are in the middle of a fight over succession. Maybe not many royals know about the mining camp."

M. Ishaq crossed the patio to them. "The ice cream man needs to know if we want more."

"I'd love a scoop," said Amy, knowing Brewer would follow her over for more. She almost asked M. Ishaq about the mining camp, but stopped herself. Who could say how involved he was? The camp was just down the road, and all the traffic to the camp went right by his village of Shisur.

• • •

CHAPTER THIRTY-FOUR

The Plot

*We will avenge our father and
take our place in the line of succession.*

The narrow blacktop road wound down the sides of a wadi that ran
behind the royal palaces and the Diplomatic Quarter. Above the wadi
to the east were the embassies of the international community. The wadi
was narrow with small gardens and high rocky cliffs. Somehow the royals'
staff managed to grow an array of vegetables in the plots.

To Prince Rashid, the wadi was a safe haven. Truck traffic was
frequent because the US embassy's maintenance facilities and warehouse
were located on a guarded compound in the wadi. Little attention was
paid to other traffic going to the back gate of the compound housing
the royal palaces.

For longer than anyone could remember, his family owned a small
house in the wadi surrounded by a stucco wall, the only obvious security.
Inside the house, an electronic security system, and outside, grounds
surveillance, monitored all movement. It also monitored the sky above
the wadi. Aircraft weren't permitted to fly over the royal palaces, but a
drone could.

The furniture was modern, the type found in hotel suites. His palace staff catered food for the staff and any guests. Visitors who stayed at the house were treated as royalty, and that was especially true of Abdul. Rashid wanted his half-brother to be comfortable.

The two men sat alone in the small enclosed patio. The sun had set, they'd finished the evening prayer, the Maghhrib, and were eating hummus and sipping tea. Now, Rashid knew, was the time. The plan to attack the royals at the king's reception had to be discussed. He needed to be sure Abdul understood his role. If he hesitated, Rashid would call the attack off. He and Abdul would devise another attack, likely a hotel, since the two bombings had worked so well.

"Open it," he said, handing Abdul an envelope, knowing the end for his half-brother was his beginning. He'd been willing to die to avenge their father. Now payment was due.

Rashid was watching him as he opened the invitation engraved in gold to the reception at the King of Saudi Arabia's palace. The date was a week away.

"The reception starts at noon, so time your move by that."

Rashid poured more tea. "I know you're ready to give your life to avenge what we know was the murder of our father, but we can devise another plan. You don't have to do this, nothing is written."

Rashid didn't add that Abdul's act would grease his way to the throne.

They both knew Abdul had a chance to get out of the palace complex alive. His life was in Allah's hands. To that, they were reconciled. Rashid knew Abdel was a true believer. He hoped his own cynicism of the greater power was wrong.

"The invitation will get you through the gate and onto the palace grounds. I added a map that shows the road you're to take. Caters enter the palace on that road, all of them, so you'll avoid suspicion. Drive down that road until it ends. You'll be beside the platform that holds the food for the reception. Our royals love to eat, so they will be standing near the food. The grounds are large, but at these parties, the princes cluster together. When the truck explodes, many will die instantly, and others will be too injured to be considered players in the succession for the throne."

He paused, but only for a moment.

"With the pass, you should be able to leave without a hassle. Now, I'm concerned about the fuses, because their execution will give you time to exit the palace grounds. How old are they? The heat of the desert can make them unreliable."

"I am confident they will work." Abdul sounded calm. "I've made many devices like this one. My worry, like yours, was the fuses. They were old. I went to the hardware souk here in Riyadh and bought new ones."

"Did you test them?" Rashid was upset. At this stage, they couldn't take any chances with old fuses. He knew what was sold in the souk was often old. Shops sold goods long after their expiration date.

"I took them to the desert and set a couple off. They worked. The explosives I brought in from Yemen are my worry, but they've worked in other operations after being transported across the desert. *Inshallah.*"

Rashid smiled, realizing there was nothing else could be done at this late date to verify the explosive materials would perform.

"My brother, we will avenge our father and take our place in the line of succession. *Inshallah.*"

First the bomb, then the Qur'an. Rashid hoped Hassa would find it soon. Thanks to their London contact whom Amy had introduced them to, they had—for a very steep price—obtained the Holy Book. That was five years ago. He thought it seemed like yesterday.

He recalled the anxiety until the book was delivered to the imam in Mecca. How the contact in London managed it, they had no idea or wanted to know. For two million pounds, the transfer worked.

The aging imam in Mecca had a trusted Bedouin place it in the ruins at Ubar. Now Hassa's expedition had to find it.

• • •

Bob Morris could not believe he had been, in his own words, so dumb. He tried not to be too hard on himself for not focusing on the king's reception. It wasn't his job to follow the parties thrown by the royals, though he had a couple of informants buried on the royals' staff. It was Jan Jackson's job.

She was responsible for the maintenance and warehouse facilities located in the wadi behind the Diplomatic Quarter. The road passed the embassy compound and ended at a guarded gate, the back door to the royal palaces. No vehicles went down the road that Jan's US embassy staff didn't notice. Often, she called Bob on traffic she thought odd. Usually nothing came from it. Today, she was in his office.

"The Sudanese who handle security for the King came to my office this morning. They want me to let their trucks and vans go past our guards without giving them a hassle. They know our security staff will ask questions. They told me the royals' security at the back gate of the palace would be responsible for the entire wadi and would set up several checkpoints. Just chitchatting, I asked what the King was celebrating. And they said the succession process. The only royals invited to the reception are those in the direct line of succession."

She paused, giving him a moment to think about what she had said.

"That's when it hit me. The reception is the perfect opportunity for the Black Princes, or whatever group is blowing up royals, to take out as many as they can. The reception guests are the A list. One of them will be the next king."

"You're right," said Bob. "To get to the palace, an explosive device will have to come in up the road in the wadi. My God, we need to call the ambassador. He can ask the FBI Chief, Kevin, for their monitor."

He picked up the phone and dialed an extension. "Kevin, it's Bob. Can you come up to my office, like, right now? Great."

He turned to Jan, who was looking a little confused.

"Only Kevin, the ambassador, and I know our FBI office has one of the world's new, and few, dual mode handheld explosive detection mobile tracer, or EDMT, as it's called. Don't ask me how they got it to Riyadh. It's the perfect device to monitor what's going on for this reception."

• • •

"That's why we got it," said Kevin. "But one of my guys has to operate it. Sorry, Jan, but I don't want your locals playing with it."

Bob and Jan understood. None of that was a problem, until Jan pointed out how obvious FBI agents in a van in the wadi would be. Sitting in an embassy SUV on the road, her local staff would see something was unusual. No telling who had brothers, cousins, uncles working for the royals.

"I have to be in the van with one of Kevin's men," said Jan. "If I'm there, my staff will just think I'm on some detail for the royal reception. If I'm not out there, then curiosity about the van will lead to chitchat. If the royals have a spy on my staff, as they likely do, their security service will be alerted."

"Right again," said Bob.

"Okay," said Kevin, "it makes sense. Let's do this without any paper trail. I'll be in the van with Jan. When you find out the time they plan to start bringing supplies in, call me. The actual tracer is the size of a laptop computer. We can set up in the wadi, in front of your gate, looking like we are checking on your staff. The tracer will buzz if any vehicle comes down the road to the royal palace with explosives in it."

Jan said she would clear her schedule. She pointed out, "The suppliers usually start bringing in goods the day before the party, or late the night before. If explosives are brought in, likely it will be the day of the reception, or right after it's started. The royals' security sweeps the palace grounds so they can't come in earlier. We better plan to have that van set up early on the day of the reception. I can always do business by cell phone or email."

Bob thought a moment. "If we find explosives coming into the wadi, we need to notify the royals' security."

Bob asked if Jan knew the security detail that manned the gate to the palace. She didn't. Her contacts were higher up, with the Sudanese assistants to the king.

"We will be all dressed up and no place to go," said Kevin.

Bob knew he was right. "We have one option. We don't know if explosives will be brought in; we just think they will. If they are brought in, the ambassador will have to call the king. That's how it has to come down."

"I heard my name mentioned, so did I arrive in time?" It was Sam. They filled him in.

As the US ambassador, he was the person to contact the royals. "I know we have to keep this close, but we must tell my senior security chief. He has contacts with the royals' security, and can get through faster than I can, waiting to tell the king."

Bob was counting how many staff would be involved, thinking the fewer, the better. Sam was right. The embassy security staff talking to the royals' security staff would be more efficient, getting information delivered faster.

Sam was pleased. "We're going to do what we can and hope it's enough. If not we are screwed."

Bob escorted his guests out and hurried back to his office, waving at two of his staff. "We need to get Brewer on the secure phone. The satellite is overhead for the next hour. I'm not sure how reliable his office phone is."

One of his staff had Brewer's number and made the call. The satellite connection was working and Bob connected with Brewer. The call was short, but Brewer got the information and directive. He was to keep an eye and an ear out for anything that might be related to the Black Princes.

The Ubar trip was on for the next day. Neither Bob nor Brewer believed in coincidences. Somehow the king's reception and the trip to Ubar were connected. How, they had no idea.

"Let me know the minute you learn whatever it is Hassa thinks she is going to find." Bob realized how garbled that sounded. But that was kind of how the current situation was—garbled.

• • •

CHAPTER THIRTY-FIVE

On the Road to Ubar

She began to plot how she could remain above ground while the others scrounged around in Ubar's ruins.

"Everyone have a good breakfast?" asked Hassa. She didn't wait for an answer, knowing the answer was yes. "The weather looks good, and we should be back in time for dinner."

No one was surprised to hear her say they'd be back today. Hassa wasn't the camping type.

The Norwegians were finishing their coffee. Flying in at night by helicopter certainly hadn't tired them out. They looked very fit, in a civilian version of military shirts and pants.

Then they were off in all eight SUVs. The ladies, including the female Norwegian rock climber, Jonne, were in one SUV, Hassa's security in two SUVs, another driven by Ali G, with Brewer, Ace and Jonne's husband, Gunvar. M. Ishaq and his staff were in two more vehicles, carrying supplies in case they had to stay overnight. Taking up the rear, in two more SUVs, was Hassa's additional protective detail.

"You never can have enough backup," said their host. Olen, still ill, decided to remain at Shisur.

"He doesn't have the Prowers's cast-iron stomach," said Ace, as they loaded up the SUVs.

Heading south on the blacktop, the sand blew in swirls over the road. Amy could see the large wadi through the dusty haze. She knew there were mountains to the east and west, but today dust was the look of the desert.

Though they were driving on blacktop, it was narrow, barely two lanes. The driver, one of Prince Rashid's best, stayed in the middle of the road. The sand periodically encroached in drifts on the road. It was soft, and the vehicle could slip in it like sliding on ice.

"We are traveling the route the camels used in the days of the incense trade," said Amy, silently thanking all of Bob's briefing notebooks.

"This is really historic. Sam used this quote when I arrived in Riyadh. As best I remember, it is something Thesiger said about how you always came back to the desert. It's the same climbing mountains or going to sea."

Looking out at the Empty Quarter, at the desert road heading to Ubar, Amy felt she understood what the explorer had meant.

They passed two villages of not more than a half-dozen houses. Amy was surprised to see corn and wheat growing in small fields. In one village, two camels, harnessed side by side, were tilling the field. She hadn't noticed any of this the first trip, likely because of the dust.

Hassa said it was nice to see a camel doing something useful. "To me, they are bad-tempered, nasty animals that spit at everything, but are essential to the Bedouins who live in the desert. I can tell you from my own experience, riding them is a pain. A camel can walk a hundred miles a day and go for eight days before needing water. They have long eyelashes that shade the sun and allow them to walk in sandstorms with little problem. Today our SUVs are the modern camel."

Amy and Audrey laughed. Both knew, from riding a camel, that the SUV was more comfortable by a long shot.

Audrey was opening a large map of the Empty Quarter that she had purchased in Turkey. "I was very lucky to find it. It was at the bottom of stack of maps in a book store in Ankara."

Amy, sitting beside her, looked over her shoulder. The map had little meaning to her, full of ridges and only lines for highways.

Out the window she could follow the flat wadi that seemed to be running toward a low range of mountains. Then the road split, and they veered to the west. Their caravan was the only one on the road. *No smugglers so far*, she thought.

"Hud's tomb is that direction," she said, pointing east. She couldn't forget that trip, even though she didn't see the tomb.

Jonne asked, "Is there was anything worth seeing at the tomb?"

Amy knew she didn't know about the kidnapping. The US embassy had kept a lid on the news of the kidnappings to the few who had a need to know. No one, not even the other western embassies, knew of it.

"We never got in," said Amy, trying not to think about the kidnapping, though it was on her mind often. To her, the desert they were passing through right now looked like kidnapping country.

"It's a hike up the ridge, and we don't really have time."

Hassa and Jonne began talking about caving. To Amy's surprise, in Mexico searching for Mayan artifacts, Audrey had been a caver and made a number of excavations.

"I wouldn't miss going down," said Audrey, with an enthusiasm that Amy did not feel.

"Not me," Amy replied when asked. Now, rather belatedly, it occurred to her that this excavation at Ubar was really a caving exploration, which was not her thing. She began to plot how she could remain above ground while the others scrounged around in the Ubar ruin.

Since she could shoot a gun, and knew Ace had brought his weapons, maybe she could stand guard. Anything was preferable to caving.

Besides, Hassa had asked for the experienced rock climbers, saying the sunken city was too dangerous for amateurs. To herself, Amy breathed a sigh of relief. She had to be alert and not let anyone convince her to go down into the ruin. It was fortunate that Audrey had done some caving.

The pavement stopped, and Audrey asked how far they had to drive on the sand. None of the women knew the mileage. The driver said it was about an hour to the site.

Slowly, as if out of a mirage, the high desert ridge emerged. Hassa pointed out that the ridges in this area were made of limestone.

"Limestone sunk the city. The water table runs underneath the limestone, eating away at it. Unknowingly, making matters worse, the rulers of Ubar over the centuries built more fortifications on the ends of the city with a limestone wall around it. The city was ready to sink."

"I am confused," said Audrey. "I thought the city was blown away in the wind. Not that I'm an expert on the Qur'an, but it says, the 'people of Ad who lived at Ubar, were destroyed by a furious wind.' So what's the sunken part?"

Hassa looked at their faces. "Actually, it's basic geology. An earthquake hit the center of the city and with the water table and heavy fortifications, sunk the city."

The SUV was hit by a wind gust that stopped Hassa for a moment. The vehicle righted itself and she continued.

"We know this is true. Using ancient maps and pictures from space that Nicolas Clapp got NASA to take, we saw the trade route, even from under the sand dunes. After centuries of looking for the lost city, it was found. We were all very excited back in 1992."

Then Hassa looked annoyed.

"The government of Saudi Arabia stopped all excavations. I am a royal, and from one of the largest tribes in central Arabia, Dawasir tribe. Yet, I was not able to find out why I couldn't go into the Empty Quarter and excavate Ubar, the Atlantis of the Sands, the lost Arabian city from Biblical times."

"My godmother knew, as you Americans would say, where all the bones are buried. She knew several Bedouin who had searched the area over the years. One day they never returned. The locals said it was the djinns. Then the NASA photos in the 1990s changed everything."

Listening to Hassa, Amy looked ahead of them on the road. She could see a herd of camels. At first, they seemed to weave in and out of the haze that covered the desert toward midday. Looking ahead, she swore there was a lake, only she knew there was no water out here, except for what was underground.

As the caravan of SUVs approached the camels, the vehicles came to a halt. The herd of about sixty, filled the road and with the arrival of the vehicles, hadn't moved an inch. The desert in this area was thick with a small scrub brush that was food for the herd. Why they were on the road, no one knew.

He slowed the SUV until it stopped in front of the camels. Still they didn't move. He tooted the horn and slowly inched between them. The other SUVs followed as a couple of the camels got the idea and moved a few inches to allow the vehicles to pass. Not that Amy was an expert on camel's expressions, but she thought they looked smugly pissed off.

Audrey, unmoved by the camels, hadn't forgotten the lost Bedouin and the djinns.

"In Turkey the djinns, or genies, are a common belief. Here in the desert, it is easy to believe they exist."

"They exist," said Hassa with authority. "They are good and bad and interfere when you least expect it. The Qur'an says that, too. To be mentioned in the Holy Book gives them stature."

Pausing, Hassa made sure everyone was listening. "Ubar has djinns, and we need the good ones to help Audrey, Jonne and Gunvar in their climb down to the sunken ruin."

Jonne had been dozing, but looked up at that. She laughed, but then was serious.

"When we cave, we are always careful not to upset the spirits."

• • •

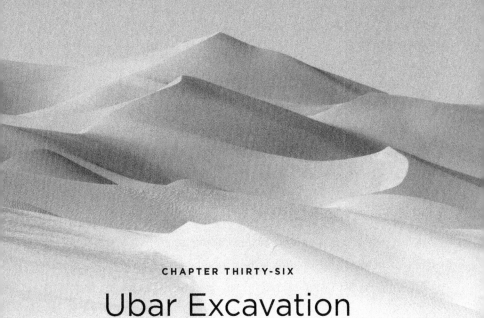

CHAPTER THIRTY-SIX

Ubar Excavation

They all turned back to the computer screen,
watching the three move around at the bottom of the cavern.

As they had talked, the haze seemed to lift and the cliffs that surrounded the Ubar ruin were just ahead of them. Amy thought the cliffs looked taller than the first time they were here, but she realized the sunlight created illusions.

The vehicles pulled up in a line next to one another. Hassa's security got out first to assess the area. After a few minutes, their conclusion was that they were alone, at least for now. Nevertheless, they took up posts around the cars and the path to the opening, holding their automatic weapons in the ready position.

Amy walked near M. Ishaq's men setting up the camp and the Norwegians fixing their ropes. Surrounding them all was Hassa's protective detail. M. Ishaq gave his staff orders to set up a couple of tents. "We will need shelter from the sun and wind, which will pick up again."

"Are we going to stay the night?" asked Amy.

"It's a precaution. I'd like to finish it up and have time to drive back to Shisur before dark. But in case there is a delay, we are prepared. Maybe the djinns will delay us."

They both laughed.

"I know we believe in djinns, but are we going to find any treasure?"

"Miss Amy, I have no idea. We will know soon, won't we?"

As for the woman they were all waiting for, she had been on the phone, supposedly to Rashid. The phone disappeared and Hassa looked ready to climb.

M. Ishaq handed out a head lantern to each of them. Amy didn't object. She had no intention of descending into the ruin, but could use one once inside the opening. The group headed up a slope about one hundred yards to what looked like an opening in the ragged rock ridge.

To Amy, whoever had found the opening was the real archeologist. "Audrey, on our first trip here, Hassa told us a nomadic Bedouin had discovered the opening. The Bedouin, who had been tending his goats, contacted M. Ishaq. The tribal leader knew to contact the royals in the Ministry of Antiquities. The site was protected from that moment on."

The group reached the top of the low-grade climb, and Amy looked back over the wadi. When land was flat, even a slight elevation made for a view. She hoped they'd finish today, but who could say.

M. Ishaq was looking at the opening as if the djinns were already there. She walked over to him. "I'm glad you prepared for every emergency."

"Thank you, Miss Amy. After your ordeal, what else can I do?"

"I know you want us back in Shisur tonight."

He shrugged, then smiled at her with what she thought was a knowing smile.

"Mohammed Ishaq, do you know something I don't?"

"No, Miss Amy. Like I said, it's up to the djinns. *Inshallah.*"

"*Inshallah,*" said Amy. To herself, she wondered how much spirits had to do with this expedition. Once again, her instinct was telling her something else was going on. She had no proof, but had to wonder if M. Ishaq was having similar thoughts.

Amy turned back to where Hassa, Audrey, and the Norwegians were entering the cave. Brewer was right behind them, but Ace waited for Amy.

"You going down in this ruin?"

Amy shook her head and said, "No way, Ace, you know I will go up, but not down, and certainly not down inside this limestone cavern."

Ace laughed. "I just wanted to needle you."

There was never a question that Ace would do any climbing. He was out of shape and no rope would support his weight. The two cousins stood at the top of the entrance and looked into the abyss.

With all the portable head lamps, the inside of the ruin was well lighted, at least at the entry point. Hassa and the cavers were clustered over a map. Amy wondered where they had gotten a map.

But it made sense. Hassa did not intend to have the team search the entire ruin. If Amy was sure of anything, Hassa wanted to be back in Shisur tonight.

Whatever was on the map created an intense conversation began between Audrey and the Nordics. Audrey was insisting on going down. "I'm an experienced caver in the states, in Mexico and in Turkey."

Finally, they were in agreement on how to proceed, and M. Ishaq's men assisted them in getting roped up. Audrey smiled and waved at Amy as she went over the edge rappelling down with the Norwegians.

Amy was looking less than happy as Audrey slipped over the edge of the ruin.

"They'll be okay," said the princess. "It's only a small area that they will excavate. Two of the men who came with Mohammed Ishaq know how to work these ropes. They're almost as experienced as the Norwegians. We have the best of all worlds. Audrey will have quite an experience to write or lecture about. That's her business, right, Amy?"

"Yep," said Amy, watching as Hassa opened a case and took out a computer.

"The climber's headgear includes a camera so we can see what they see," she explained.

Everyone clustered around the computer to watch the screen. Amy was pleased that Audrey seemed to know what she was doing, but found herself looking down the sunken ruin and then up at the tenuous stone that was above the three of them. It wouldn't take much to have the limestone roof drop on top of Audrey and the Norwegian couple.

Now she understood why Hassa didn't think this excavation would take any time at all. The princess knew exactly what and where they were to look.

· · ·

Two hours passed slowly if all you were doing was looking at the screen. For Amy, the time was put to good use because Hassa finally told her why she needed her old friend to come and assist with the excavation.

"Amy, you are the authority who will say what we found and where. What do they call it, the provenance of the finding? With the Prowers family connections and your friend, the US ambassador, the world, especially the Islamic world, will believe what was found was real. The provenance can only be proved by someone from outside the royal family."

The story Hassa told was one she and Rashid had practiced. "Our search began several decades after Hassa Sudairi died. Rashid and I were visiting the holy city of Mecca when an elderly imam who knew Hassa Sudairi told us a story about the prophet's personal Qur'an. The book had been passed down through the centuries to the imams at the mosque. Not the prominent mosques in the two holy cities, Mecca and Madinah, but at a local mosque in Damascus where the imams said the prophet practiced."

She shook her head as if remembering.

"Rashid and I were skeptical. A holy book written in 632 AD would more than likely have been destroyed by overuse. The imam said after the prophet died, the holy book was not used, rather, each imam sought to protect it and pass it on. For centuries, the book was safe. But with World War I, and the confusion with the Turkish rule and the British, an imam made a decision to move the holy book out of Damascus to a small mosque outside Mecca. No one knew he'd moved it to Ubar."

Hassa looked up at the blue sky. Rashid had been right. Practicing the story made it sound real.

"The imam at that mosque in the years before World War I was an archeologist, and knew about the ruins in the Empty Quarter south of Shisur. He had been here many times, and was sure in his own mind of his finding. This was Ubar. It was the lost city that the prophet, peace be upon him, spoke of in the Qur'an. So he had a Bedouin move the book to Ubar, and to a specific place within a sheik's house that was in the center of the city."

She said it wasn't easy to put all the pieces together, even after the elderly imam gave them the coordinates of Ubar. That was the will of Allah. A few weeks after the imam told them the story, the old man died.

"Even with our royal connections, getting the equipment and the infrared cameras was difficult. Then along came the author, Nicolas Clapp, using satellite imagery, and other Anglos were writing stories of how Ubar was discovered. We held our breath to see what they found. When it was nothing, we exhaled.

"Finally, the Bureau of Antiquities gave Rashid permission to excavate. We were so relieved, and began our own plans. The stone pillars in the satellite photos of Ubar were the key. Thankfully, we got those obsessed with finding the lost city and thinking there was gold to be found to back off. They had enough, never realizing the Qur'an was worth more than gold. We confused things by having our Saudi government stall them, and putting out information that seemed to make Shisur and Ubar one and the same. That was easy enough, as the old incense trails ran through Shisur to Ubar and on to Oman and Yemen."

"I hope I haven't left anything out." Hassa wanted Ace, Amy, and even Brewer, to understand. They were needed to verify the place the book was found, the provenance.

What she couldn't tell them was the validating of the Qur'an's provenance would assist Rashid and his ambition to be the next in succession. The Black Princes were one group who supported him; but to have the conservative religious establishments—the wahhabis, and the people of Saudi—on his side, her husband needed this Qur'an.

For sure, she couldn't mention the real fact that she and Rashid had gotten the Qur'an from a smuggler in London and given it to the imam. Did it really matter what the provenance was? She didn't think so. It was the Damascus Qur'an.

"I don't know what to say, Hassa," said Amy. "You know Rashid will have my support. All of us can validate the provenance of the book, if it's found."

• • •

Getting up, Amy walked over to the opening. She did not want to walk in too far, almost afraid that any movement would break the top off. Not being able to see the bottom of the cavern, there was no way to be sure if a piece broke off that it wouldn't hit Audrey and the Norwegians. The problem, as she saw it, was to get them back up. Hassa had safety ropes held by M. Ishaq's men. In an emergency, his men could rappel down. At least that was what Amy told herself.

• • •

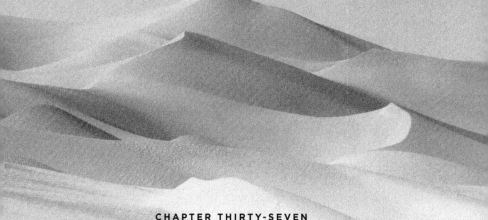

CHAPTER THIRTY-SEVEN

At the Bottom of the Ruin

No point in pushing their luck, because the crumbling limestone ceiling could collapse any time.

As Audrey's feet hit the bottom of the cavern, she turned her head lamp toward the map. Jonne and Gunvar pointed their lights around the broken stones, trying to orientate themselves. Just then, a light went on above them, lighting up the section where they stood. M. Ishaq's men had brought a set of generator lights.

Thank God, Audrey thought. No one could have predicted the headgear they were wearing was not bright enough to really see. Now the entire area they had rappelled down was in view. She took another look at the map as the Norwegians discussed if it was safe to take their harnesses off. They decided to keep them on.

"This entire area is crumbling, very dangerous," said Gunvar.

Audrey was trying to get orientated with the map, and could see the ruins had sustained more damage since the map had been made. What had once been walls were crumbling pieces of rocks. Even with the powerful lights reaching to the back of the cavern, it was still shrouded in semi-darkness.

The map showed a room, which even had the letter S written on it.

"It's very dangerous down here," said Jonne. It occurred to Audrey that they had not been fully briefed on the crumbling infrastructure that was once Ubar. But then who could have told them?

"I'm glad we left our harnesses on," Audrey added. "If something falls, I just hope it misses us and we can get hauled out of here. Looking at this mess, I think someone, not from ancient Ubar, but in this century, staged the room with the safe, if we find it."

"Ya," said the Norwegians almost in unison. "We find safe, see contents, and get out," said Gunvar.

Audrey echoed, "Ya."

They turned their lights in a circle, carefully viewing the area. Gunvar hosted himself gingerly on one of the walls. Methodically, he surveyed the area. Audrey, remembering from looking at the map before they headed into the semi-darkness, told him to look to his right.

"I see it, about fifteen feet to the right."

Audrey and Jonne carefully walked to where his light was hitting. Right in front of them, like the map showed, was what had been a room. In it was a steel safe, or file box, as it was too dark to distinguish one from the other.

"Gunvar, that's it. We'll stay here, focus the flashlights and let you, my dear, go in," said Jonne.

He moved across the ruin and lowered himself to what had been a room. "It looks like a safe, but not from the days of Ubar, that's for sure."

Gunvar reached for the safe, partially covered by debris of what might have been a wall. It wasn't locked and opened easily.

"What's in it?" asked Jonne.

"This." He brought out a package wrapped in something that resembled a plastic wrap in the shape of a book. He took it out and put it in his knapsack.

"Nothing else is in here, but remains of cloth sacks that may have held coins. Let's get out of here before something collapses on us."

They pulled on the ropes. In the silence of the sunken cavern, the wait seemed like an eternity. They could pull themselves up, but that would mean they would have to use the sides of the cavern.

No point in pushing their luck, because the crumbling limestone ceiling could collapse anytime. There was a sound of running water, though none of them could see it. They waited and hoped.

• • •

Above them at the opening, Ace was intently watching the shadows of the three at the bottom of the cavern.

"It looks like they have found something."

He turned to see M. Ishaq's men pulling on the ropes.

Amy was standing back from the opening and realized she was holding her breath. She exhaled when she saw Audrey's head come up the opening, followed by Jonne and Gunvar. She was ready to praise God, but Hassa beat her to it.

"Praise Allah, who has returned the Holy Book to the rightful leaders, the King of Saudi Arabia and Custodian of the Two Holy Mosques."

Actually, Amy didn't think she could say it better.

Brewer helped Audrey get out of her gear who turned to Amy and gave her a big hug. The wind had picked up reminding Amy of the day of the kidnappings. Below them, the desert was being covered with a slight level of brown dust. Even though Hassa's security was guarding them, Amy felt something was wrong. But then, when had she felt things were right?

Finding the book was a setup—or the entire excavation was a setup. Amy didn't want to think that was true. Hassa and Rashid were her friends. Sam warned her about Rashid being the leader of the Black Princes.

Her role in the excavation was misrepresented, to put it mildly. That she could accept. She validated the provenance, because she was at Ubar when they found the book. But everything was too much of a coincidence, as if it had been planned and staged.

Gunvar put the package on a rock and slowly began to peel back the layers of wrapping paper. Finally, in a cracked and faded brown leather case that broke apart as he opened it, came the book. The cover was crumbling, but inside they could see pages and what looked like Arabic writing.

For a moment everyone was silent, looking at a book over 1400 years old that dated to the time of the Prophet, peace be upon him.

"The book," said Hassa. She translated the name on the Qur'an. "This is the Damascus book, one of three Qur'ans that were written at the time the prophet died."

She turned a page, then was interrupted by one of her protective detail who had climbed up the incline. He spoke rapidly in Arabic. Hassa shook her head yes and turned to the group.

"Gunvar, wrap it back up. My detail wants us to get back to Shisur. No one is sure how safe we are out here. We can discuss what you found back at Mohammed Ishaq's. If we leave now, we can get back before dark. No camping tonight."

She said the last part with great enthusiasm. As she spoke Amy was suddenly aware that the sun was setting. No, it was the dust. They would be driving in a haze, but less dangerous than staying overnight.

Amy was aware Ali G was standing beside her. "You were right. No gold."

Before she could reply, Brewer was asking Audrey to trade seats with Gunvar who wanted to ride with his wife. Amy would have liked to have been in Ali G's SUV, but it would be impolite to leave Hassa. Besides, she could talk to Audrey at Shisur. Riding with the Norwegians, she would learn what they said to Hassa about the climb.

The SUVs were loaded and headed down the dirt road to where the blacktop began.

"The map showed us right where the safe was," said Gunvar.

Amy had to ask Hassa. "Did you get the map from the imam in Medina?"

"No, though the old man described the site that had collapsed. My husband is very smart, trained as an engineer, like Vince was. He calculated how much the safe could have slid down the slope over the decades and made the map. Without it, we'd be sitting here for days searching the collapsed city. It would have been dangerous, or more dangerous than it was."

"It was hard to say those ruins were once a city," said Jonne.

Then Hassa asked an odd question. "Did you see anything else?"

They shook their heads no.

Jonne started to speak, stopped, and started again.

"I had a feeling there was something more. What, I can't say."

Hassa smiled. "The djinns—they are down there. Who can say if they are good or evil? The protective detail thought the djinns were here. That's why they wanted to leave the site so soon. Camping overnight was never an option for my protective detail."

Amy looked out the window at the flat desert. They were in the middle of a world of sand where no one could find them except the djinns. She looked back at the ridge disappearing in the haze, and wondered would the djinns, the spirits, continue to live in a thousand-year-old ruin?

• • •

CHAPTER THIRTY-EIGHT

Ubar Finding

If it had been up to Amy she'd open the book
and skip the food, but she had to be polite.

To Amy, the ride back to Shisur seemed to take forever. Hassa held the knapsack with the book inside on her lap, pumping Gunvar with questions about the site. He answered each one slowly, though Amy knew his English was perfect. She thought his hesitations were too long, possibly, the mark of lies in his responses, or just an introverted personality.

Hassa persisted, asking the same question over and over. He answered it again, for the third time.

"The map listed a room and in that room was the safe."

Jonne added, "Audrey and I hung above the room on ropes with the map, while Gunvar went into the room. As the light shifted, Audrey had a good view and saw an area where the safe could be. The area looked like a building had simply dropped or sunken down."

Gunvar added another yes, and said, "Audrey has a photographic memory. She looked at the map before we went down and remembered every detail. It was difficult to see, even with the generator lights on.

We tried to scrape as much of the gravel and dirt off the top of what looked like a slab that could hold our weight. That's when Audrey and Jonne saw the safe."

Jonne said the safe was about the size of a small closet.

"Was there anything else in the safe?" asked Amy.

"I saw three bags, one with holes was empty, and the two others may have held some coins or jewelry at one time, but they were empty. The book wrapped in plastic was in the back. I grabbed it and stuffed it into my knapsack."

Gunvar paused. "We could hear rumblings and stones cracking and knew the excavation site wasn't safe. None of us put much weight on the safe or the walls. We just couldn't be sure if they would hold. Mohammed Ishaq's men did a great job of getting us back up and holding us steady over the ruin."

Hassa smiled. "You are cavers and know your stuff. The caves in the mountains on the Yemen border have been of archeological interest for many years. Mohammed Ishaq's brothers have been caving on the border for years. They're experts. No one ever came to this area, because everyone thought it was nothing but a lump of rubble."

She didn't mention that one of M. Ishaq's brothers had been killed years ago when one of the openings to an unknown cave collapsed. She knew he was thinking about that today when the three descended the ropes into the ruins of Ubar.

• • •

The sandstorm that started at Ubar intensified as they neared Shisur and because of it, M. Ishaq's family had been busy. The patio was enclosed with heavy plastic protecting dishes of lamb, rice, baba ghanoush, dates, figs and the smell of nutmeg, cumin, and turmeric mixed with sand that had crept in when the door opened. Everyone was ready to eat after such a long day.

If it had been up to Amy, she would have opened the book and skipped the food, but she had to be polite and eat. She wanted to shout, open the book, and touch it, and talk about it.

The sand battered the plastic like raindrops. Amy was wearing her sunglasses to protect her eyes, even though the sky was dark, the sand was blotting out the sun. She wondered how much change the years had brought to Shisur and the desert. To her, nothing seemed changed.

Ace interrupted her thinking. "All we need is vodka."

Brewer smiled. "I thought two bottles of scotch would be enough, but Olen and I finished those off last night. Guess it's the desert heat."

M. Ishaq motioned to one of his daughters who within minutes appeared with two bottles of Jim Beam and a tray of shot glasses.

"Just for my guests," he said, pouring one shot for Ace.

Amy suppressed a smile as her cousin chugged it down. He never drank anything except high-end scotch whiskey, but tonight would be an exception. He held up his glass for M. Ishaq to fill it again, and their host poured one for Amy and Hassa, who held up their glasses.

"Never tasted so good," said Ace.

Amy sipped it and agreed. Their host filled Brewer's glass again and two glasses for the Norwegians. Hassa proposed a toast.

"To finding our heritage."

Hassa pulled the Qur'an out of Gunvar's knapsack and placed it on the table. She gingerly opened the faded brown leather cover. To Amy, it didn't look centuries old; nevertheless, the cover had protected the book.

"Handle it carefully," said Jonne, who went on to explain that the pages were parchment. "Most likely they are made from goat skin. In Europe, they might be sheep skin, but are still fragile. All the print is handwritten. Someone copied it and then copied it again. Monks in monasteries copied the Bible the same way, over and over."

Hassa raised her glass in a toast. "To Nicolas Clapp, who persuaded scientists at the lab in Pasadena to scan the region with the radar that could see through the sand and pick out the ancient trade routes packed down by the thousands of camels that traveled them so many centuries ago."

Amy said she'd contact Clapp about their finding. Sonora ought to be able to locate him. She was curious about his role and wanted to hear his story of the finding firsthand.

I don't really care, she thought, but as odd as this excavation was, more information couldn't hurt.

With that, Hassa opened the first pages of the book. They saw an inscription.

Gunvar pulled out a magnifying glass. "It's a signature."

"I knew it!" said Hassa. "I saw one of the original Qur'ans in the Topkapi Museum in Istanbul. This signature is how the Prophet, peace be upon him, signed his name. This is his signature."

She paused a moment, then plunged ahead, saying, "This is so important. Historically there were three original Qur'ans. One is in the old Soviet State Library in Tashkent, the other in the Topkapi Museum in Istanbul. The third was called the Damascus manuscript. Many believe it was the original one, as it was dated six hundred fifty-three AD. In 1892, it was supposedly destroyed in a fire in Damascus."

She looked at the group. "But it wasn't destroyed. The father of the imam who told Rashid and I that he'd hidden it was the man who saved the Qur'an in Damascus from the fire."

Audrey spoke up and seemed to know more about ancient manuscripts than anyone.

"The books were copied by hand. Over the centuries, the Arabic script changed. What the script looks like is what dates it. Carbon dating is done on both paper and the ink used in the writing. Parchment is from animal hide, likely from goats. It can be reused so often there is a difference in the dates."

She pointed to the brass clips holding the book together. "These were used to hold the parchment pages in place because they would expand in humidity and buckle. Fortunately, there isn't much humidity in this desert."

Then Gunvar spoke, and Amy began to think everyone was an expert on ancient Qur'ans until she realized being a diplomate in Saudi Arabia meant they would be briefed on the history of the country and Islam.

"Mohammed was illiterate. The first versions of the Qur'an were verbal. His close followers put his words, his visions, in writing. And you're correct, Hassa, the Damascus manuscript was considered by all scholars to be the first Qur'an."

Then Hassa exclaimed, "I must call Rashid. Oh, what a moment, to find the prophet's own Qur'an."

CHAPTER THIRTY-NINE

Change in Plans

Don't ask me what's going on. The phone isn't secure,
so all Bob could say was there is a situation.

As she left to call Rashid, Olen arrived on the patio, looking more
like himself.

"You've got some color back," said Amy.

"Thanks. I had to have eaten something I shouldn't have. You'd
think living in Mexico would make me immune to stomach problems,
but there is all this dust."

To emphasis his point about the dust, Olen began coughing.

"With stomach problems, you never know," said Ace, "when the
wrong fly lands on your food."

Amy, sitting across from Ace and Brewer, saw Khalid, the head of
Hassa's protective detail, come into the backyard. She watched the man
look for Hassa, who was still in the house, then he headed for their table.

"Pardon to interrupt, Miss Amy, Mr. Brewer, and Mr. Ace. We just
were called by Prince Rashid's assistant. He said very important you call
Mr. Morris. The Prince wants his wife to call him. If Princess Hassa
comes, tell her to please call the Prince."

"Thanks," said Brewer. And Amy told him that Hassa had left to call Rashid. Khalid bowed and left.

The three looked at each other as Brewer pulled out his phone to call Bob. The call didn't last a minute. He clicked the off button and looked at Amy and Ace.

"Change of plans. Ali G and I are going to the mining camp and Bob says—no, he *insists*—that Amy and Audrey go to Dubai with Ace and Olen."

"When?" asked Ace.

"Now. And don't ask me what's going on. The phone isn't secure, so all Bob could say was there is a situation."

Brewer looked at them. "That's code for a big problem."

"Hassa is back from talking to Khalid," said Amy, as the princess walked over to their table.

"I can't get through to Rashid. I guess it's the sandstorm and the wind. Khalid told me he talked to his assistant. We are to return to Riyadh immediately. He said those were my husband's words."

Brewer repeated what Bob had said. Hassa shrugged.

"Khalid told Rashid we found the Qur'an. We must go. And the Norwegians are to come back with us, so he said."

The discussion was interrupted by a strong wind shaking the sides of the protective canvas surrounding the garden.

Amy got up. "I'll find Audrey, and we'll get our bags down here. Brewer, can you tell Mohammed Ishaq what's going on?"

"Yep."

In less than twenty minutes, Amy found herself hugging Hassa good-bye.

"I'll be in touch, Amy. You know the provenance and we need you to validate where we found it."

"You have my phone number, Ace's, and Sonora's."

Amy looked around. The two women were alone. "Hassa, when you get to Riyadh, let me know what's going on. Phone me, text me, whatever. I want to hear what Rashid says when he sees the Qur'an."

"Of course."

Hassa's security team came out to the patio. There was some discussion in Arabic, and they left. Hassa shrugged.

"They're ready to go; and I am a night person, so we're off."

M. Ishaq called his staff to bring more food and coffee for the royal party and the Norwegians. It was as if he knew they'd be leaving.

"You'll tell the ambassador about it, and contact Nicolas Clapp?" asked Hassa.

"Yes, I will call Sam first thing tomorrow morning, and my aunt should have contacts that will find Mr. Clapp."

They hugged. "Peace be upon you," said Hassa.

"And you," said Amy, thinking this night run out of the desert was anything but peaceful.

Amy said good-bye to the Norwegians, who told her they were ready to head back tonight. Whatever the protective detail said, they did. Never did she think Norsemen were so security conscious. In this case, it could be saving their lives.

Hassa, the Norwegians, and her protective detail were off with coffee, sandwiches, and sweets from M. Ishaq.

"I know Dubai is a little farther, but you could make it tonight," Brewer said to Ace and Olen.

Surprisingly, Ace and Olen were ready to go. "We can share the driving. Mohammed Ishaq will you get our driver? He's staying at the guest house," said Ace.

"Of course." M Ishaq motioned to one of his sons to find the driver.

Olen came to the point. "Amy, are you and Audrey sure about not going back to Riyadh?"

Amy had no idea what was going on, but she knew Olen didn't realize the royals left for Riyadh. She thought about the kidnappings, and the hotel bombings. Her instinct told her it was time to get out of here. Riyadh—and Saudi Arabia, as a whole—didn't seem safe. That was what the kidnapping had done to her.

If there was a problem, Dubai was an open city, and they wouldn't have a problem getting a flight out to Europe. The Las Vegas of the Middle East was what Ace called it. The Prowers family corporate condos seemed safer to her than the Diplomatic Quarter, even ringed with Saudi National Guard.

"Bob said we should go to Dubai, so we will. Audrey, you'll love Dubai. It will be interesting for you to see a place quite different than others in the Middle East. We can always go back to Riyadh. I'll have the ambassador send our other suitcases."

Brewer chimed in. "If there is a security alert, and I would bet there is one, you'd be confined to the Diplomatic Quarter and wouldn't see anything. Better to be in Dubai."

"I'm fine with Dubai."

Amy looked at Ace, "We won't be too crowded, will we?"

Ace laughed and poured more Jim Beam. "No problem."

He didn't know what was going on either, but knew Amy's decision to go to Dubai was a smart one. Whatever was happening was in Riyadh, not Dubai.

"Okay, Audrey, Amy, let's get your bags and get a move on. I don't know about the sandstorm, which seems to have gotten worse, but we can share the driving. Mohammed Ishaq, my friend, we need water and food."

M. Ishaq clapped his hands and gave some orders in Arabic. "More sandwiches, water, and coffee. You will need much coffee, and so will Brewer and Ali G."

Audrey looked surprised. "You guys are going to Dubai?"

"No," said Brewer, "we're going to stay at the mining camp. With the bad weather, we will follow you as far as the camp. Safety in numbers and all that."

M. Ishaq appeared with the requested sandwiches and coffee. "The storm is getting stronger. I wish you wouldn't go."

Ace had just arrived from packing the SUV, and assured him he knew how to drive in these storms.

Amy looked at Ali G. "You know a lot about the weather."

He frowned. "It's bad, Miss Amy. My phone worked coming back from Ubar, and now it won't work. I have a weather site that told me a big front is coming in off the Indian Ocean. It's like a cyclone, so the report said. Had one once in the Sudan, very bad."

"A freak storm," said Brewer. "I saw Ali G's app in the SUV. We should be ahead of it."

"But we're going east, and it's coming from the east," said Amy.

"The storm will come in from the south, and soon the satellite phone will work," Brewer said.

Amy knew she'd be a lot happier staying in the safety of M. Ishaq's house, but Ace was determined to leave. And she wasn't going to let him out of her sight. On the road, they might be protected from bandits but not from the weather. Ace was eager to drive to the mining camp. He had a reason. She'd find out once they were out on the road.

• • •

M. Ishaq watched the SUVs disappear in the dusty, darkened desert. He doubted his village had seen the last of the visitors from Riyadh. From his cousins who worked in the royal households, he was convinced as they were that something was coming with this succession business. Even in the Empty Quarter, he knew his village would not be immune from the Riyadh trouble.

• • •

CHAPTER FORTY

Back to the Mining Camp

With the blowing sand, no cars were moving
in the mining camp, nor were any people.

A few miles east on the road to Dubai, even with Ace's special glasses, the road seemed to disappear in the sand. Amy wondered how Brewer and Ali G in the SUV behind them were managing.

Ace slowed the SUV almost to a stop.

"We have to spend the night at the mining camp. This weather sucks. Apologies for my hubris in thinking we could drive through this shit."

Everyone accepted his decision, and Amy thought her intuition was right. Staying at the camp had been his intention all along. She'd known Ace all her life, and had to admit, he didn't make mistakes.

"Where will we stay?" asked Audrey.

"The mining camp is a large operation and must have temporary living quarters. The staff at the café will know."

Ace sounded like an authority.

With the blowing sand, no cars were moving in the mining camp, nor were any people. Somehow, Ace saw the café's flashing lights, obviously with his special glasses. The parking lot was full of SUVs. As they turned into the lot, Amy saw the lights of Brewer and Ali G's SUV behind them. They parked and waited for the two men to join them.

Slowly, Ace opened the door little by little, until there was enough room for Brewer to climb in, along with the sand and dust.

"We think they must have temporary quarters, and the café manager will know where," said Ace.

Brewer agreed immediately, though he knew Bob had a contact in the camp that he'd kept undercover, the imam. He saw no point in bringing any of that up unless the temporary quarters didn't work out.

Bending over against the wind, they entered the café to find it packed with Chinese, Pakistani, and Indian workers. The noise level was deafening. Everyone was eating and drinking with great gusto. Real bottles of bourbon were on the tables, but the beer was a local brew. They found a table in the back, as Ace went up to the counter to find the manager. Brewer asked what everyone wanted to drink.

"The homemade beer is undrinkable," said Amy, "so I'll have tea."

Everyone said yes but Brewer. "I'll go get your tea, but I have to try the beer."

"Quite a mix of nationalities here," said Audrey.

Amy was still curious about thorium. Ali G seemed to be an expert on all things. If he didn't know about thorium, it might be the one thing in the country he didn't know.

"Ali G," asked Amy, "when did they mine here?"

"Don't know, Miss Amy. I know the Empty Quarter has many minerals. The climate makes it difficult to mine."

"If it's so tough, I wonder what's here that makes it worth the effort."

Before he could answer, Ace and Brewer were back.

"Thorium," said Ace, seemly unconcerned that it might be a well-kept secret. "That's what they are mining here."

"What is it?" asked Audrey.

Ace quickly explained how thorium was used in communication systems. He skipped the part about being a substitute for uranium.

"Enough about what is mined. Behind the café are trailers for temporary visitors. That's us. We have three as each sleeps two. Brewer, Ali G, I got one for the two of you."

Brewer said, "Thanks." He saw no need to bring up the imam and his relationship to the agency.

"I'm ready to go to the trailer," said Olen. Amy and Audrey stood up, ready to leave.

"You all look familiar," and they turned around to see John Campbell.

After explaining they were going to Dubai, but staying overnight because of the weather, John invited them to share some real liquor and pulled a bottle of scotch out of his knapsack. When he was told they wanted to see their trailers, he invited them to his trailer when they were done.

"I'm in the row behind the temporary quarters. Hell, I'll just go with you, and we can go from there. Keep your heads down in the blowing sand."

A side door took them on a gravel pathway to rows of trailers, all identical without numbers. Luckily John was with them because he knew which ones were for temporary quarters.

"They only lock from the inside but are clean," he said, opening the door to the first one.

Amy and Audrey looked inside at a clean room, two beds and a separate bathroom.

"Perfect," said Amy. Audrey followed her inside saying good night to the rest of the group. Ali G and Olen headed into their trailers.

Amy leaned out the door looking at Ace and Brewer. "Please, Ace, don't get into anything to delay us tomorrow."

"I promise. Brewer will keep me straight." He turned to follow John to his trailer with Brewer behind him.

• • •

Campbell's trailer was only one row over from the temporary quarters. They walked down a dimly lighted gravel pathway to a trailer with a huge padlock on the door. John opened it, explaining that because of his store of smuggled liquor, he had to have additional security.

The trailer had one bed in a corner, but the room had a couch and table and chairs. Obviously, John often entertained guests. Against the wall on a bookcase was a shortwave radio.

Brewer asked if it worked. John explained, "I haven't been able to get a phone call through to Riyadh today. Don't know if it's the sandstorm or what. It's low-tech and old but usually works. It connects to my company, Azur Contracting, in Riyadh, whose offices are in the Diplomatic Quarter with the embassies."

"I really need to get through to the embassy in Riyadh." Brewer sounded serious.

John poured three glasses of scotch. "I gotta tell you, guy, this shortwave is old, and as I said, it always works. Not today. No one here in the camp has been able to get through to Riyadh. A sandstorm wouldn't cause this much interference. Something must be going on, but I'll give it another try."

He turned a switch and spoke into the microphone. Brewer and Ace looked at each other, both thinking how could they get the Azur Contracting office to take a message to the US embassy.

The stream of static blasted from the shortwave radio. "No signal," said Campbell. "Don't you guys have satellite radios, Brewer?"

"Yeah, but they only work at certain times when the satellite is overhead. Normally, my cell phone works just fine."

Brewer hesitated, then asked if John had a sample of thorium. "Just a small rock, John. I'm a frustrated geologist at heart."

John shook his head. "Can't do. I'm an administrator. More scotch?"

• • •

CHAPTER FORTY-ONE

The Royal Palace Reception

The trucks are so close to each other
how can we tell which one has the explosives.

Kevin and Jan sat in a Suburban SUV on the wadi road, watching each vehicle going into the king's palace. Between them was a thermos of coffee, helping them stay awake, a package of sandwiches, and a cooler of water. With the seats down, there was a portable toilet in the back.

They sipped coffee and watched the caravan of mini-trucks loaded with tables and chairs pass by. The vendors needed to be at the palace at dawn to set up for the meeting at noon, timed to take place after the Dhuhr, the midday prayer. Some were closed vans loaded with food, though many items, especially the meat, would be prepared on the palace grounds.

After watching a dozen trucks, Jan asked, "The trucks are so close together, how can we tell which one has explosives?"

To her, Kevin's answer was extremely casual. "We'll know which one of two or three, and get security to check them."

Jan was flabbergasted, but didn't show it. "We don't know which one? We have to go on the palace grounds to check it?"

"Yes, when several trucks are in a row, the machine can't distinguish which one has the explosives. Our security guys will get the royals' security to stop the trucks if the machine indicates a problem."

Jan refrained from saying unbelievable. She picked up the phone to call the senior embassy security officer, who, thanks to the ambassador, was on alert.

"We will immediately contact palace security if there is a problem."

Everyone was casual, as if they didn't think the threat was real. She looked back at the device, which resembled a laptop computer sitting in the back seat of the SUV.

"So it beeps?"

"Yep. My local staff checked it out using explosives and it works."

His response didn't give Jan confidence in the machine. She knew his local staff of Syrians and Egyptians. They were good on background checks, but didn't have the technical or mechanical background for managing this machine. She also knew there were many types of explosives. What explosives had they tested?

Regrettably, she wished her own staff had checked out the machine. But it was the FBI's and until the meeting yesterday, she didn't even know they had such a machine in the country, let alone at the embassy.

To her, the dual mode handheld explosive detection mobile tracer was a machine that could be used because it was a secret, but what if it didn't work… She sighed, forcing herself to remain calm.

"You know, Kevin, the hotel bombings have knocked off oil men and royal princes. Yet the Saudis think these attacks are an American problem. But the Saudis are our friends and we want to help them. It's so important we help them, and let them know what's at stake, even if they're in denial."

Kevin was unmoved. "We told them, at least the ambassador did. I was with him. The Saudi intelligence and interior ministries disagreed with our assessment."

Another line of trucks, about a dozen, carrying goats, chickens and sheep, passed by. The royal family had plenty of food at the palaces, but obviously wanted fresh meat for this royal reception.

They both turned quickly in their seats as the machine made a scratching sound, like a copy machine re-positioning itself. Kevin shook his head. "It is just re-setting itself."

"What does it sound like when it finds explosives?" she asked.

"A beep."

None of this made any sense to Jan. She knew plans made by the front office sounded well planned on paper, but often fell apart in practice. This looked like one of those times. Was there anything she could do? There had to be. Another bombing was not acceptable. Trouble was, there were so many players in the game.

• • •

Abdul left the compound and headed for the main road from Jeddah to Riyadh, turning east to Riyadh's center. He got off at the first exit and headed back to the turn to re-enter the wadi looking like any other delivery truck coming from Riyadh and not the west.

With his pickup and trailer hauling goats, Abdul waved thank you as the next truck let him move ahead in the line. He drove slowly down the winding wadi road knowing he looked like any other vendor.

Beneath goats, in the back of the truck, was the bomb, and a large amount of plastic explosive he'd gotten at Rashid's house in the wadi. From Yemen, he had brought the device to set it off. That was critical.

Yesterday, he'd made one change to the pickup. At the chemical souk in downtown Riyadh, he purchased a protective cover. The store sold them as protection for chemical spills. Thanks to studying chemical engineering, he knew the mats would conceal the explosives from equipment designed to identify them. They weren't perfect, but would confuse a machine, and buy him some time.

Rashid hadn't said how effective the surveillance might be, but he hadn't come this far to fail.

The parking spot was crucial. He needed to position the truck behind the food tent. The goats would be left in the trailer. They were sacrificial goats, going up with the bomb. On the seat beside him was the pass Rashid had given him listing the place to park. To succeed, the pass must do the trick. He had to quickly enter and pass like any other vendor.

The last guard post on the palace grounds barely looked at the truck or the pass and waved him through. *Inshallah*. He was on the grounds.

• • •

The end was coming. To Rashid that was good news. He'd planned carefully, and now would see the results. "Allah, be praised."

The helicopter landed behind the king's palace on the edge of the Wadi Hanifah, bringing his cousins, the Black Princes, to the royal reception. Scattered on the lawn were huge white tents serving fruit juices and the favorite, Saudi champagne.

Rashid picked up a glass from a waiter and walked over to his cousins.

"Ready to see my prize mares?"

He listened to a chorus of yes. They walked down a paved trail that wound to the valley floor below. It ended near a stable housing horses. There was a simple stucco house. Once inside and out of sight, Rashid hit the wall with his fist.

"We're almost finished. *Inshallah*. We will succeed."

"When?" asked one of the princes. Rashid looked at his watch.

"Within the hour, we will hear the explosion. Security will call us and we'll go back up to the palace. Here, in the wadi, we're protected from any damage caused by the explosion."

Another prince asked, "Do we stay here, or go to help?"

"We don't need to help." Prince Rashid was adamant.

"The National Guard will be there. Three units are on alert in front of the palace. They are guarding the conference and with their training, will minister to the injured, and the dead. We will arrive when the scene is still a madhouse. The photo op will show our concern. We will look competent—like we are managing the mess—and sympathetic. That will give us power."

Though it was not yet sunset, the princes knelt on prayer rugs. Rashid opened the Qur'an, thinking about the call from Hassa. She was returning tonight from Shisur. The next time he would meet with the Black Princes, they would be using the Damascus Qur'an, as the prophet had.

The Black Princes bowed. Rashid opened the book and began to read.

> "O Allah, possessor of the kingdom. You give the kingdom to whom you will, and you take the Kingdom from whom you will.
>
> "Say, 'I seek refuge with Allah, the Lord of Mankind, the King of Mankind, the God of Mankind.'
>
> "To Allah belongs the domain of the heavens and the earth and all that is between, and to Him will all return. The decision is only for Allah. He declares the truth, and He is the best of the judges. Surely, His judgement, and he is the swiftest in taking account.
>
> "And in whatsoever you differ, the decision is with Allah. He is the ruling judge. And whoever disobeys Allah and His Messenger, he has indeed strayed in plain error."

He finished and the Black Princes responded: *Praise Allah.*

The mosques in the wadi began to ring with the call to prayer. Then they heard it. The explosion blotted out the call to prayer and was louder than Rashid had anticipated. Suddenly, the air was filled with dirt, not dust. He could barely breathe. He and the other Black Princes pulled out their cell phones to call their personal security detail. If they didn't, security would wonder why.

Rashid heard his security chief screaming to him on the phone. "It looks like a war zone!" Rashid repeated that to the princes and added, "Time to go."

He led them up the path to the palace. The bomb made of chemicals used in fertilizer was lethal and a foul smell filled the air.

He felt in his pocket under his thobe for the envelope that held his speech. After he delivered it, the Black Princes would nominate him for succession. The royals who lived would be traumatized by the bombing and follow his leadership. As he reached the top of the wadi, he thought of Abdul. Could his half-brother have survived? Likely not. Later he would pray. He always would for the brother to whom he owed everything.

The Black Princes reached the top of the path and looked at the grounds. It did look like a war zone. The National Guard officers ran toward them.

General Assad, head of the National Guard, who was in charge, was adamant. "We must get you out of here," he shouted.

Rashid spoke for all the princes, "Take us to my palace. Tell us how many survived."

The General looked upset. In his hand was a walkie-talkie. Rashid thought that was rather old-fashioned, but it worked in the chaotic aftermath of the bombing.

"We don't know yet."

Two SUVs pulled up to drive the Black Princes to Rashid's palace, still called in his father's name, Prince Mischel's. *That*, thought Rashid, *will not be for long.*

• • •

CHAPTER FORTY-TWO

To Dubai

They've done it again, and it may be more
of a disaster than the hotel in Doha.

The next morning, the wind in the mining camp had nearly stopped
and with it, the blowing sand. Amy looked out at the dusty sky and
thought how unhealthy. Yet Audrey had decided to go for a jog.

"It ought to be safer than jogging at Shisur. Amy, I was really
conservative at Shisur, but here with all the contractors, I swear a dozen
have jogged by this morning while I was making coffee. Nice that
these trailers have a mini kitchen. We could stay here awhile."

Amy had no response, except to tell Audrey the group needed to
get to Dubai sooner than later. She watched her go down the path and
looking out the small window of the trailer, she saw Brewer heading
for Campbell's trailer. Ace was likely already there. Picking up the pot
of coffee, she headed to the trailer to join them.

As she walked in, she got a shush from Ace to be quiet. Then she
saw why. John was on a shortwave radio microphone and had headphones on. As she entered, he hit the button so everyone could listen
to the conversation with his office on the Diplomatic Quarter in Riyadh.

A voice on the other end was speaking. "Didn't expect to hear from you so early. We've been really busy here. Yesterday the king's palace took a hit. A huge explosion and a fireball that could be seen all over the city. What's going on is anyone's guess. Heard many royals are dead or injured. We're locked down. No one is moving on the Diplomatic Quarter even the embassy staff. One of our guys tried to leave and a National Guard stopped him. Don't know if it's for our protection, or they are suspicious of everyone."

John asked the person on the other end to keep him informed, and signed off. Now they all knew what was going on. Amy poured a cup of coffee.

"We really need to get to the UAE border before the Saudi military closes it. If we don't make it, we might never get to Dubai." Ace sounded serious.

"Ali G and I will go with you. It's my decision," said Brewer, to everyone's surprise and Ali G nodded his approval.

"If we drove to Riyadh, the National Guard might not let us enter the city."

Brewer looked at Ace. They both knew the CIA and American military would cover the mining camp with surveillance. The latest attack on the royals would make everyone more cautious with their security.

"How long can they keep Riyadh closed down?" asked Ace, adding he'd be glad to have them along on the drive to Dubai.

"Anyone can guess how long, and likely the country is closed, too. I'll bet there aren't any flights leaving from the airports."

Brewer sound like an authority, and he made sense. "Where's Audrey?" he asked Amy.

"Jogging."

"You're kidding."

"Jogging is fine here," said John.

"Let's eat breakfast at the café and be ready to leave when she returns. Can the café fix us sandwiches and coffee?" asked Brewer.

"Don't worry, there were several little village stores along the road to Dubai where we can get food and gas," Ace said.

• • •

Audrey didn't have to figure out her jogging route, she just followed other joggers. On the outskirts of the compound, she began walking. She was a fast walker and had caught up with one of the workers, a young Chinese man. With just the two of them on the trail, she introduced herself; and they walked together, talking about his work at the camp.

The walk around the entire compound took some time, and Audrey explained that her stepmother was waiting for her.

"I know I'll be in trouble."

Just making conversation, she asked her walking partner if he knew where she could get a small piece of the rock the compound was mining.

To her surprise, he said yes. "We detour as you say in America, and I can give you a small piece. May I ask why?"

She told him she was a geology major, working on a graduate degree at the University of Wyoming. "The rock will be valuable in completing my thesis."

Without hesitating, the young man turned down a gravel path to a row of buildings, all one story, but continuing on for a mile. He asked her to wait a moment, saying it would be awkward to explain her presence.

Audrey hoped this guy was for real. In what couldn't have been five minutes, he was back carrying a small bag that he said was insulated to protect them from the small amount of radiation thorium had. He carried the rock all the way to her trailer in the temporary quarters.

Handing her the bag, he asked slowly, "Can we stay in touch?"

"Of course," said Audrey with enthusiasm. "Let me get a card from my bag in the trailer."

. . .

"And that was it?" asked Amy who had just heard Audrey's story for the second time.

"Brewer, I know you're pleased, but I wonder why this Chinese worker was able to get it so easily and John couldn't."

Brewer said he couldn't be sure, but the young man probably wasn't being watched by compound security and John probably was.

"No matter how we got it, I thank you, Audrey. What the embassy experts will do with it, I have no idea. But thanks."

Just then Olen arrived. "Ace is ready to go and wants to know where all of you are. Can I carry any luggage, coffee? We won't have far to go before we hit what Ace calls a Saudi truck stop."

. . .

Amy knew Ace and Olen's Dubai driver, Shafi, was happy to be heading home. He had been sitting around the house at Shisur waiting to go back. The Mumbai native, living in Dubai, did a lot of work for Ace and Olen's business associates in Dubai, and she was sure he didn't want to lose this contact as a client.

She watched as Audrey insisted on riding in the SUV with Brewer and Ali G. Amy found it interesting that Audrey wanted to ride with the two of them. She thought there was some chemistry with Brewer and apparently Audrey also felt it. Or, it was that old proverb about the desert where strangers become friends. Time would tell, that was for sure.

They settled in their seats, not sleeping, but drinking coffee, as the Dubai driver cruised along the blacktop pavement. The road wasn't flat, but rather up and down and around the dunes.

They headed east in the late morning with the sun almost above them, each with their thoughts. Amy was the first to say she thought another shoe must drop. Ace agreed with her.

Driving across the desert was beautiful, thought Amy. They left the mining camp and the air began to clear.

"I'm not sure the group going to Riyadh will be as lucky with the weather," said Ace.

Amy was quiet. When they were settled in Dubai, she'd call Sam and hopefully find out how Hassa's trip back had been.

In her mind, Amy was going over what could have happened in Riyadh. Then she realized whatever it was maybe had nothing to do with any of them. It was a royal thing. The coffee was hot, the sand wasn't blowing. What more could she want?

• • •

Amy walked into the living room of the condo that resembled a five-star hotel. One wall was all windows overlooking the glistening blue water of the Persian Gulf. She was watching television, the English version of Al Jazeera, Doha's innovative Arabic station. They prided themselves on the latest breaking news.

"Ace," she called to her cousin, who was in the alcove pounding on a computer. "They've done it again. In fact, it may be more of a disaster than the hotel in Doha."

As he came in, the commentator described the scene at the King's Palace in Riyadh. Amy tried to call Sam.

"I keep getting a busy signal. Don't know if it's busy, or out of service; so much for fancy phones."

They looked at each other and both had the same thought. Ace spoke first. "We don't need Sam to validate that this was the work of the Black Princes."

"I agree," said Amy.

According to the news report, the ailing King was now in Zurich getting treatment at a specialty hospital. He had been dying for so many years no one could remember what was wrong with him. He didn't have many days left, Allah willing.

"The Crown Prince is in a coma." The commentator was getting his information from several sources. "The royal succession depends on the princes who are still alive."

As he spoke the screen flashed with the photo of a likely successor. It was Prince Rashid. Ace was beside himself.

"Rashid has done it, eliminated the cousins. He will be the next king, or should I say, rule as deputy premier after the death of the king and the Crown Prince, both who sound as if they are dying."

Amy agreed. "With so many of the princes dead, and the support of the Black Princes, he'll be selected to be deputy premier. It is a done deal. He may be number three, but his time is now. Once Rashid is elected, the royals should let the King and Crown Prince finally die. Then our friend will be King."

She picked up her phone. "I'm texting Hassa that we saw on television Rashid is okay. I'm telling her we are flying to Berlin at Sonora's request. We'll call her when we get there."

"And tell her," said Audrey, "we'll help if she needs any validation on the provenance of the Qur'an."

Amy said she didn't think Hassa would need any validation. It looked like Rashid would be the deputy crown prince.

"You're giving up on Rashid's sacred Qur'an?" asked Ace.

"Yes, if it really is sacred. I know my dad and Vince would go back to Ubar, but I'm different. I draw the line. Ace, the book was found. What did we prove? We have no idea if it is real or not. It has to be reviewed by an expert in London or Paris, or anywhere but in the kingdom where any so-called expert could dub any book the Damascus manuscript."

She paused. "It's over. It's written."

Ace laughed. "That's T.E. Lawrence again, saying it has been decided. To think, your Saudi royal friends didn't even need the Qur'an."

"Maybe" said Amy, "It was decided. At least no one can call me a bystander anymore."

Ace agreed.

To herself, she wondered when Hassa and Rashid would ask her to validate the finding of the Qur'an. She knew they wouldn't give up on it.

The commentator was back on the television announcing all flights into Saudi Arabia were canceled and the kingdom was temporarily closed to visitors.

Ace, Olen, Brewer, Amy, Audrey, and Ali G looked out over the Persian Gulf where the sun was setting on the blue water. Oil and gas would continue to flow. For how long, only Allah knew, *Inshallah*.

• • • • • • •

Epilogue

In Berlin, the Prowers family gathered to watch the press conference His Royal Highness Prince Rashid and his wife Princess Hassa were holding on an international news station. Their announcement was that the Damascus Qur'an had been found. Soon it would be available for viewing in a new museum built in Riyadh for ancient Qur'ans. Bedouin tribes were being encouraged to present their family Qur'ans for viewing and to be preserved in the museum. The news commentator said the provenance of the Qur'an had been verified by a London expert, Guy Melville, and an American friend of the royals, Amy Prowers.

Amy Prowers felt the vibration of her phone and checked the text. Princess Hassa was inviting the Prowers clan to London next week for a celebration on finding the Damascus Qur'an. The ambassador, Bob, and Brewer were also invited. She texted back the Prowers family would be there, but not Audrey, who was back in Turkey. Amy knew her step-daughter would never come. She believed the Qur'an was a plant and hadn't been in the Ubar ruins since the nineteenth century.

On the television screen, below the picture of the newly nominated deputy premier, was a notation that thorium had become the number one mineral purchased by Saudi Arabia. The kingdom planned to use it in power plants to produce energy, replacing oil and natural gas.

Notes for the Reader

Politics and the Founding of Saudi Arabia

Abdul Aziz was the founder of the modern Saudi nation. In 1902, he re-established the House of Saud in Riyadh. With his brothers and other followers, he captured Riyadh's Masmak Fort and killed the governor. He was twenty years old and was the ruler in Riyadh. From that time on, he was known as Ibn Saud. The next thirty years were spent reestablishing his family rule over the Arabian Peninsula, starting with the Najd Plateau in central Arabia. To consolidate the peninsula, Abdul Aziz married a daughter of every tribal leader in the Arabian Peninsula.

By 1932, he controlled the Arabian Peninsula and declared himself the King of the Kingdom of Saudi Arabia. In 1937 near Dammam, American oil geologists discovered Saudi Arabia's oil reserves. Before oil, many members of the House of Saud were living in poverty. The King died in 1953 after establishing an alliance with the USA in 1945. Only his direct descendants can use the title His or Her Royal Highness. His main rivals were the Al Rashid tribe in Hail, the Sharifs in Mecca, and the Ottoman Turks in al-Hasa.

The head of the House of Saud, also the King of Saudi Arabia, runs the country. The King nominates princes from the House of al Saud to be ministers in his cabinet. The key ministries are Defense, Interior, Foreign Affairs, and the thirteen regional governors of Saudi. Other functions of the government like Finance, Labor Information, Planning, Petroleum Affairs and Industry are usually headed by commoners, with junior members of the al Saud tribe serving as deputies. The King relies on the Ulema, which today includes members of the business community who support the royals.

Opponents of the House of Saud call the monarchy totalitarian and a dictatorship. In November 1979, dissidents seized the Holy Sanctuary in Mecca. The group included 500 heavily armed Saudi dissidents mainly from the Ikhwan tribe of Otaibah, one of the largest and most influential Arabian tribes. The group was against the corruption of the ruling House of Saud, and the socio-technological changes taking place in the kingdom. They also wanted to stop selling oil to the United States.

The royal family turned to the Ulema, the religious council, and today a government council, who issued a fatwa allowing the forcible taking of the holy sanctuary. Saudi forces, with French and Pakistani special operation units, took two weeks to regain control of the sanctuary. The world was surprised by the use of French commandos, since non-Muslims may not enter the city of Mecca. All the surviving males of the Ikhwan tribe were beheaded publicly in the kingdom.

Islam

In the seventh 7th century, Muhammed, before his death, converted most Bedouin tribes to Islam. The first Caliphs, starting with Muhammed's successor, the Caliph Abu Bakr, built towns for their Bedouin soldiers that became important trading and cultural centers. From these bases, they began to conquer new areas for the expanding Islamic Empire. Believing themselves to be the elites, they looked down on all con-quered people, even new converts to Islam. The Turks didn't like being kicked out of the Peninsula, and took Arabia back. In the twentieth century under Abdul-Aziz ibn-Saud, and the wahhabis, the Turks were defeated. Since then, religion and the kingdom are dependent on each other.

Geology

During the Jurassic age, 250 million years ago, the climate changed. Until then, inland seas had formed wadis that make up the Arabian Peninsula. Now the sea disappeared, leaving skeletons of fish and sponges buried in the sand and found in the limestone ridges around Riyadh.

The Wadi Hanifah is the largest source of water in the Nejd, and a major geological feature of the Arabian Peninsula. The rugged terrain makes the north central plateau of Arabia impassable in many places

The Wadi wraps around from north and west of Riyadh to the south. Water is produced in over eighty wells. The date palms that grow in the Wadi produce some of the tastiest dates in the Middle East. The royal family owns all the land. They grow small patches of corn and wheat for their goats and horses.

The Wadi is famous because in 1902, Ibn Saud and a small group sneaked up the Wadi to capture Riyadh from the Rashid clan. After that raid, he consolidated the tribes into today's Saudi Arabia.

The great Arabian Desert region occupies almost the entire Arabian Peninsula, an area of about 900,000 square miles, bordered on the north by the Syrian Desert, on the east, northeast by the Persian Gulf and the Gulf of Oman, on the south and southeast by the Arabian Sea and the Gulf of Aden, and on the west by the Red Sea.

The center of the desert wilderness is the Rub' al Khali, which means Empty Quarter. How the name was chosen is unknown. Some say the Europeans gave it the name, other say it came from in a book by a famous Arabian, Ibn Majid. It is one of the largest continuous bodies of sand in the world, which include everything from dunes to deadly quicksand. Camels, gazelles, oryx, sand cats, and spiny-tailed lizards are some of the species that have adapted and survive in this extreme environment. The climate is dry and temperatures fluctuate between very high heat and seasonal night time freezes.

The Bedouin and Caravans

The word Bedouin is from the Arabic 'badawwi', meaning a desert dweller or inhabitant of the desert. Historically, nomadic tribes from the Negev, Sinai, Saharan and Arabian deserts in the Middle East and parts of North Africa are Bedouin. The Bedouin specialize in breeding camels for caravans and for a fee, were caravan guides, guards, and drivers offering protection. By the nineteenth century, caravans that had linked China, India, Central Asia, North Africa and the Middle East were fading, as new sea routes were discovered. Centuries ago, Ubar was a major city on the route, surrounded by mountains, but over time the wind moved the sand. Yet satellite photos showed the old caravanserai routes remain.

The Last Request
Preface

Treasures, artifacts, stories of heroism from World War II are, seventy-two years later, still surfacing today in diaries, mementos, and old attics. Estimates state over 100,000 pieces of art, stolen or hidden, have never been found. *The Last Request* is a fictional account of what might have happened to one such piece of art.

Prologue

The past is the future of the present.
—an eastern proverb

1945 : Gracanica, a Serbian Village

The train was late.

Benton Prowers hoped that wasn't an omen. He and his partner, Brother Veilkov, needed every minute to locate the Shroud of Turin and get it off the train without being detected. *It must stop,* he told himself, *because it needs water and coal to travel through the rugged Serbian mountains to the Albanian port.*

The two men turned their heads, hearing a crunch on the snow. Someone walked toward them on the path. The two men relaxed, seeing the monk's cousin, the yardman who serviced the trains. All three heard a rumble, and felt a vibration through the frozen ground. The train slowly emerged from the darkness, billowing steam, and carrying a fortune in art and jewelry.

The Nazi guards watched from the stone bridge above the tracks as Veilkov's cousin slowly walked onto the tracks to begin refueling, trying to delay the departure without the guards getting impatient. As the engine hissed steam, Benton and Brother Veilkov slipped out from behind the stack of coal and headed for the last rail car to find a small box with the letter *M* on it. For that information, they owed a thanks to the local partisan, who loaded the train's cargo of artwork. Otherwise, they'd never find it in the short time the train was stopped.

There were no guards on the train, which did not surprise Benton. Its appearance—looking like the local mail run—served as the train's security.

Opening the door to the rail car, they found themselves looking at rows of crates stacked neatly on top of each other. *It's impossible,* thought Benton, as he and Brother Veilkov hurried through the car, looking for the letter *M* imprinted on a crate. To their surprise, it was in front of them. Veilkov's knife levered off the top. Inside was a small plastic packet.

Then they heard the hiss of steam and felt the train jerk forward. Veilkov stuffed the packet in his knapsack, and the two men headed for the back of the car. As the train cleared the water tank, they jumped off.

The guards on the bridge above the tracks saw them and shouted, "Halt!"

Using the local dialect, Veilkov shouted back, "We pick up the mail."

The halt order was repeated. Lying on the gravel next to the tracks, they weren't sure the guards could see them in the semi-darkness. Benton weighed their options to take out the guards.

The train was under the bridge when they heard a pop, the noise barely audible above the engine. The two men, experts in building bombs, knew the sound and dived behind the coal stack. A moment later, the train was under the bridge and exploded in the air. Pieces of debris flew in every direction. The guards on the bridge had no place to hide.

When the clatter of debris stopped, Benton and Veilkov hurried up the trail in the snow, the only two men in the world who knew the first icon, known as the Shroud of Turin, had not been destroyed.

• • •

1946: Gracanica Monastery

In the monastery's private alcove, monks prayed day and night to the icon *Christ in Glory.*

Veilkov prayed beside them, the Shroud of Turin concealed under his robe, remembering the train crash as if it was yesterday. He could still smell the fire and through the dust, see fragments of paintings and jewelry. Patiently he waited, knowing his timing must be perfect.

One evening he was finally alone. Climbing up the four steps to the icons on the wall, he quickly hooked the packet containing the Shroud on the wire behind the icon *Christ in Glory.*

Kneeling to pray, in the icon he could see—with insight few can claim—his own death.

• • •

CHAPTER ONE

The Key

My life has no beginning and no end.
My parents are dead and the past is buried with them.
So why am I flying half way around the world
to a monastery in Serbia?

April 1990 : Over the Atlantic Ocean

From the window of the jet, Amy Prowers watched as the sky in the east darkened. She wondered if the setting sun looked the same for her father when he died. *No, not died … killed*, she thought. Despite the findings of the Director General for Civil Aviation of Mexico who called it pilot error, she and her aunt Sonora were sure his plane crash was no accident.

On the seat beside her sat the icon book and the letter his lawyer gave her at the reading of his will. In his letter, her father said the Shroud of Turin was hidden in the church at the Gracanica monastery. He asked her to find it, and take it to the cathedral in Turin, Italy, replacing the fake one. He ended his letter with a warning: *be careful who you trust*.

Amy felt the trip could be a wild goose chase. But if her father had indeed hidden the burial cloth of Christ in this monastery, she had to honor his last request.

The note made no sense, and I don't know anyone at the monastery who could help me.

Leaning back against the seat, Amy sipped her vodka. If the real Shroud wasn't in Turin, there could be a scandal—for Italy, Serbia, and the Catholic Church. There had to be more to his request.

For years, her father traveled every few months to the monastery. She thought he was visiting old buddies from World War II. Now she wasn't sure. Why didn't he just say where he hid the Shroud? Her father always had secrets, but hiding the Shroud of Turin … for what reason?

Amy hoped someone at the monastery would know. One thing she did know: the past had not died with her father, and he was reaching out to her from his grave. Her aunt Sonora had said, "Someone wanted Benton dead. Amy, you have to follow through on his legacy or the past is lost forever."

If the Shroud is at the monastery, I'll find it, and I will do anything to find those responsible for his death. Amy smiled, remembering how her father loved puzzles. *This one may have cost him his life.*

If she was right, the letter was the first piece of the puzzle, the icon book the second, and going to the monastery the third.

The plane bounced in turbulence. Amy motioned to the stewardess for another vodka. Stretching her long legs she looked out the window as the moon disappeared in a cloud bank. The sky became as dark as the ground below.

Amy realized she faced a window of her life. She had to open it for herself. Hesitating, she opened the book *Icons of the Balkan Monasteries*.

To her surprise, a small key, almost concealed, was taped inside the cover. An odd shape and size, it looked as if it would open a small box. Tearing it off and holding it in her hand, she wondered what it opened. One thing she knew—the key was the fourth piece of her father's puzzle.

Being honest with herself, Amy resented being swept into her father's past. Whatever the key opened, she knew it would change her life.

A thought from years ago flashed across her memory. Her first husband had called her a reluctant warrior. At the time, she thought he was nuts, but today he could be right. She had a feeling she was in for a fight. The thought occurred to her that her father wasn't sure who would find his clues. Otherwise, his letter would simply tell her where the Shroud was hidden. She turned the pages in the book, looking at pictures of icons. On the last page was a Biblical quotation from the Book of Revelations.

Then I saw another angel coming down from heaven, surrounded by a cloud, and a rainbow over his head: his face shone and he held open in his hand a small scroll.

Amy skipped down to the last paragraph of the quote underlined, likely, by her father.

God's veiled plan, mysterious through the ages, would be fulfilled.

She fingered the key, watching the stars in the darkened sky. Sleep came slowly. When it did, angels blowing trumpets filled her dreams.

• • •

CHAPTER TWO

The Gracanica Monastery

*Inside her jacket pocket, she felt
the brass key. Why all the clues?*

The road to the Gracanica Monastery spiraled up a mountain ridge
and then curled to the valley below. Restless from the long plane flight,
Amy again wondered why she was here. She held the steering wheel of
the car, and reached in her jacket pocket with her other hand, reassuring
herself she had the little icon book and the key.

She had a plan. First to find the abbot of the monastery, who her
father visited during his trips. He ought to know, if anyone did, whether
the Shroud of Turin was in his monastery. If not, a buddy from World
War II, another monk her father visited called Veilkov, might be able to
help her understand the icon book and lead her to the Shroud of Turin.

She was worried about the two monks. *Secrecy always surrounds a
monastery,* she thought.

Rays of sunlight flashed between the clouds, reflecting against the
patches of snow among the pine trees on the mountains. The narrow
valley must have looked much the same years ago to her parents. The

faint whistle of a train echoed against the slope. Could that be the train her parents took out of the Balkans at the end of the war?

She knew little of their life during World War II, and nothing about icons or this monastery. Her father asked her several times to come with him on his trips to the monastery. She was always too busy and now, sadly, it was too late. Reflecting on the past was not going to help her today.

Gunfire crackled across the valley. Raised on a ranch, she knew that sound and instinctively slowed. To her right, a flock of birds rose from the trees, as if programmed in a pattern of flight. Was it hunting season? It didn't matter; she had no choice but to continue to the monastery.

The road ended at a parking lot filled with tourist buses and guards. No one could miss the guards with *Monastery Policia* printed on their chartreuse jackets. She parked the car and watched the tourists walking into the monastery.

Looking up, at the church towers, Amy recalled what she had read in the guidebook during her flight. *Historians believed the Gracanica Monastery had existed since the twelfth century. Years ago, the monastery was in Serbia, then in Yugoslavia as the Balkans changed rulers. Today, the monastery was in Kosovo, as if the average tourist knew that was the Balkans.*

When her father told her about his trips, he spoke about the people's different ethnic backgrounds and religions of the populace. He said they remembered every insult, every church, mosque, or village destroyed in the last three hundred years. To her, it all seemed absurd. Why would anyone carry all that baggage around?

A cobblestone pathway led to a church with three spiral cupolas stacked upon each other. Among the trees, other cupolas atop monastery buildings could be seen. She followed the last group of tourists through the gate as their guide, a monk, explained the history of the monastery.

He spoke English with an accent difficult for her to identify. She settled for the generic Slavic which everyone spoke in any country in the Balkans.

"Humans are God's expression of an icon as himself. A cloth wrapped around Christ's body and imprinted with his image created the Shroud of Turin, the first icon. To the Orthodox believer, the icon is a meeting point. Every Sunday, surrounded by icons, the believer becomes part of the liturgy."

She looked up at the cupola; the tiny round towers created the roof of the monastery. She had little patience with those who lived in the past. *This search*, she thought, *could be really boring.*

A gray-haired woman tourist, decked out in a pink polyester pant-suit and fitting Amy's image of tour bus travelers, raised her hand. Her question on the meaning of the word *icon* surprised Amy, since it was relevant.

She looked at the monk's expression to see if he was bored. If he had heard the question a thousand times before, he didn't show it.

"The word icon is from the Greek and means 'image.' An icon is how God reveals himself to man. The icon represents a hierarchy of saints, with the top being Christ, then Mary, then whoever the painter chooses."

"When was the first icon painted?" asked the tourist.

The monk's patience impressed Amy. How many times had he been asked these questions?

"There is a traditional and non-traditional view. According to tradition, the Evangelist, Saint Luke, painted the first icon—a portrait of Mary—in the first century AD. The non-traditional view is that the first icon is the burial cloth of Christ. The common name for the icon is the Shroud of Turin, after the cathedral in Turin, Italy where it resides."

Another tourist waved a travel book. "Local folklore says the Shroud—or the first icon, as you called it—is in this monastery."

The monk took a deep breath, as if he been asked this question many times.

"Over the centuries, rumors abound, but I assure you only traditional icons are here in Gracanica. Watch your step. The flagstones on the path into the church are uneven. Remember, it was built in 1321 by the Serbian king Milutin."

He didn't quite answer the question, thought Amy, as she watched the group follow him into the church. No one would remember the name of a Serbian king but the tourists would certainly recall the first icon, or the Shroud of Turin. If local folklore had heard the Shroud was in the monastery, her father's letter could be right. It might be here.

Beside the doorway was a directory in English and Cyrillic, the local alphabet. She took out the small book on icons and quickly compared the title page to the directory. Two of the icons in the church matched icons in the book, the icon of the *Seven Angels* and the icon of *Christ in Glory.*

She opened the book and read the quotation neatly printed in her father's handwriting inside the book cover: *the tenth chapter of Revelations, see page six.* Carefully, she turned the old pages to the sixth page.

Then I saw another angel coming down from heaven, surrounded by a cloud, with a rainbow over his head: his face shone and he held open in his hand a small scroll. But when the seventh angel blew his trumpet, then God's veiled plan, mysterious through the ages ever since it was announced by his servants, the prophets, would be fulfilled.

Why all the clues? The icon of the *Seven Angels* was in the book. Could that be the clue? If so, her father had made it simple. Find the icon of the *Seven Angels* and it would lead her to the Shroud of Turin.

She laughed out loud. *There was no way her father would make this simple. He loved symbolism, and Mayan symbolism was his avocation. Now he had her looking at icon symbolism.* She was ignorant on the subject of icons; their history and symbolism. Maybe the abbot could give her a crash course.

Looking up at the gray stone towers and dark wooden doors, she wondered what force drove men to live in a world of gray. Something inside the monastery must have appealed to these men.

She turned back to the doorway and saw a monk—she guessed in his late forties—standing against the stone entryway. With his blond hair and white skin, he looked out of place in a country of dark-haired and dark-eyed people. To her, his face and body language looked peaceful.

She had to stop this introspection … it felt ridiculous. If he spoke English, he might be able to help her at least find the abbot. Her German and French were mediocre; and she was doubtful he spoke fluent Spanish. There was no way she could communicate successfully with him; after all, she was in the Balkans. Still, Amy walked over to him, opening the book to the picture of the icon of the *Seven Angels* and pointed toward the monastery.

"It is a thirteenth- or fourteenth-century icon, and yes, it's in the church."

His English was perfect and he extended his hand.

"I am Stephan Medak, the abbot's administrative assistant. He asked me to meet you, Miss Prowers, as he's going to Vienna for a speaking engagement. You asked him to help you, and I am in his place."

She had no rational reason why, but she trusted this monk. The same instincts served her well in business, so why not now.

"I need to find one icon. I'm no expert, so I hoped he could help me. I haven't met him, but for years my family has shared business interests with his brother, the General, in Mexico."

"*I found the human shape of God and my soul found its salvation.*" Medak spoke the words and said, "I forget who said that, but it describes the icon. Icons are not what they seem to be. Perhaps you've captured their meaning by searching out a special icon."

Amy thought he might be right, but wasn't sure about finding salvation in an icon. She complimented Medak on his English.

"I studied in school and practiced with the abbot and Brother Veilkov. Let me show you the icons in our monastery church. Brother Veilkov is our expert, but he is on a retreat, so I am, as you Americans say, your guide."

Besides the abbot, Brother Veilkov was the other monk she hoped could help her. What poor timing, with both monks out of town. Shouldn't they be at the monastery praying? She kicked herself again for not coming here years ago, as her father asked. Thinking about what might have been wouldn't help her now.

Following Medak along a flagstone path toward the entry to the church, her eyes rose to the stone arches towering above the doorway. She wondered how many carved stones it took to build the entry. The monks might live a simple life, but nothing was simple about the massive church, the centerpiece of the monastic complex. From outside, it looked huge, but inside it was divided by gray stone pillars covered with religious figures. Compared to the sunny day outdoors, inside the church was cold and damp. More armed guards stood inside the entry to the church, adding to the dark mood.

"These aren't the local police force, but UN forces guarding the monastery," said Medak.

She could tell Medak knew what he was talking about.

"For centuries, this valley had a history of blood feuds among the population. Today it's a tinderbox populated by ethnic Turks, Orthodox Serbs and Catholic Croatians."

He spoke with an air of authority. Had he lived with the feuds or just studied the history? She didn't know.

Two sets of guards struck her as curious, and she wondered if that was how the monastery had escaped destruction over the centuries—being protected. The guards seemed calm, or maybe they were bored.

She couldn't tell the difference. Each carried several weapons and the word "well-armed" described them.

Medak looked at the title of the book in her hand, *Icons of the Balkan Monasteries*, and launched into a discussion of icons and frescos.

"The paintings on stone surfaces are called frescoes. When the painting is on a wooden board, it's called an icon. Both reflect religious scenes and are interchangeable. Your book is on icons, so we need to look for scenes and symbols painted on boards."

Amy's guidebook had been accurate. She was looking at huge gray stone pillars covered with paintings, and walls covered with icons hung on wooden slabs. The book also said tourists and pilgrims came to see the popular icon of the *Seven Angels* and the icon of *Christ in Glory*, the two most famous icons at the monastery.

Amy looked up at the church pillars. "Medak, why are there so many icons in the Balkans?"

"The history of the Balkans in the last century is one where hatred kills the innocents who are eager to be martyred. No matter who rules—the Turks, the Greeks, Communists—the message of icons never changes. Icons are a work of art showing the union between the painting and symbols. On a more practical level in past centuries, many of the people were illiterate. Icons are a picture and that helps them understand the Biblical message."

Amy thought his explanation interesting, realizing she was going to have to sift through a lot of information to find the Shroud.

"South of us, at every bend in the river, is a monastery. Most were built in the thirteenth and fourteenth centuries. Our monastery icons are said to be the finest of the fourteenth century. Due to good fortune or God's will, they were not destroyed, regardless of who ruled the country. I always think they remained untouched because the monks who painted them are unknown."

Seeing the icon on the church wall beside them, Amy saw one side was a portrait of the Virgin and child. On the other side was the crucifixion of Christ. The somber colors and gloomy atmosphere of the church did not appeal to her.

Medak was still talking.

"The icon is dark because the colors and lines are abstract. The message was important, and the light behind the painting shows a mystical depth that transcends time and space. The icon is different from western art, where color and nature are important."

Standing in the damp church, Amy thought about Medak's words. She realized if she ever hoped to find the Shroud among so many icons, she needed to be as honest as possible.

"My father was here before his death. He may have left something in this monastery for me. I have no idea where to look. I hope I don't sound nuts, but it's supposed to be the Shroud of Turin. The icon with the *Seven Angels* is my starting point, because my father mentioned it in a note he left with the book."

She opened the book and showed him the icon pictures. As he looked at the pages of icons, she asked the obvious question. "Did you ever meet my father?"

Medak told Amy that over the years, Benton Prowers visited once or twice a year. He said he never understood why the American came, and there was no reason for either Brother Veilkov or the abbot to explain the visits. Always, he said they intensely talked. When the American left, Brother Veilkov was unusually silent in what was already a silent life.

"I saw him when he visited Brother Veilkov, who told me they worked together in World War II. They prayed in this chapel, drank pots of coffee, and the monastery's wine. Several years ago, another man from North Africa visited. They ranted about an el Ben Alemien. I remember because the name sounded like one of the famous battles in North Africa during the war. Then the man from Africa died, and they were sad. I never knew the connection. At the time, it just seemed like three old men reminiscing about the war."

Amy knew they were her father's wartime pals: Marfkis, whose tribe, the el Alemien, ruled most of the Sahara, and the monk, Veilkov.

"Maybe this could help you. The last time your father visited, he and Veilkov sat in the alcove with the two icons, *Christ in Glory* and the icon of the *Seven Angels*. They seemed transfixed. I suppose I'm trying to read things into whatever they did."

Amy felt discouraged. "I wish Veilkov was here, he might know exactly where my father hid the Shroud."

She was still troubled. Her father had never mentioned icons to her. Perhaps Medak had hit on the truth. Everything that happened here had to do with the war. Could WW II be her starting point, not icons?

"The alcove of the icon of the *Seven Angels* is at the far end of the church."

As they walked past the stone pillars, Medak renewed his commentary. Amy thought the real message was in the silence of the monastery, but Medak's words helped her understand what her eyes were seeing.

"The symbol in the icon, a picture of Christ or the saints, is the icon concept of unity and universality. In the Hindu world, the Buddhist world, and the ancient Byzantine world, the temple is the sign of cosmology."

Amy looked up at an icon of a shadowed figure of a priest raising a chalice. Her icon book said each icon conveyed unconscious associations to show emotion. This was the mystical message, but to her, they were just pictures of religious figures. If there was a message, it escaped her.

Here in the monastery, looking at the icons, the silence of the chapel became a roar as she followed Medak down the church aisle. Maybe icons had a mystical side.

Instinctively, she glanced behind her, thinking in the movies someone was always watching from the choir loft. Not this time. Amy and Medak were alone in the corridor, looking at the walls. She saw icons on wood boards lining the walls, each with a different picture of a saint or of a scene from the life of Christ. Soft candlelight reflected against the walls, creating a haze of blues, greens and gold.

Well, she thought, *at least the floor is still stone.*

Medak brought her back to today—or rather, to the fourteenth century.

"King Milutin built the church in the fourteenth century. He was the Serbian king and the church was part of his empire. In those days, icons were the center of Christian life, telling people stories of the saints."

Amy couldn't have cared less about King Milutin. "So many centuries and the walls remember them all."

Medak laughed at her sarcasm.

"History has been bloody here, because the country is always at war. Since old Yugoslavia broke up, fighting continues almost everywhere on some level. It is still not over. The UN soldiers you saw at the entrance saved the church, but couldn't save the villagers' homes for any of the ethnic groups."

He paused, as if thinking about the war, and then pointed to the alcove.

"Here are the icons in your book, and where your father and Veilkov came to pray. The icons with the *Seven Angels* and *Christ in Glory* are the most famous icons in our monastery. Both are original icons painted by unknown monks."

At last, thought Amy. *The right icons.*

Why had Veilkov, Marfkis, the North African, and her father—all World War II buddies—met here? Was it to pray? She doubted that, which seemed out of character. But he had to have some reason.

She looked at Medak. "The Biblical quotes in the letter were specific to the icon of the *Seven Angels.*"

Opening her book, she followed her father's note inside the cover, instructing her to go to page six. On the page was a picture of the icon of the *Seven Angels*. An angel was blowing a trumpet. She faced the icon.

What did her father want her to see?

Medak tried to help.

"The icon to the right, *Christ in Glory*, is considered by critics a masterpiece of Byzantine classical art. It's so special, Russians monks copied it for a cathedral in Moscow."

Amy turned to look at the icon with a dark image of Christ, his hand over his heart. At his feet were serpents, and angels were in the background. She turned back to the book and to the icon of the *Seven Angels*, looking carefully at both. An angel held a trumpet pointing skyward and a rainbow was over the head of another angel reading a scroll.

Unexpectedly, she noticed something odd, and bent over to see more clearly. Someone had taped a card to the wall below the icon. The writing was in Latin.

"Can you translate this?"

Medak bent over to take a look.

"It says that the fourth beast is the fourth kingdom. It is a quote from the book of Revelations that Veilkov put here after your father's last visit. I am not sure why this was posted, or why no one has removed it."

Amy looked at the icon in the book and then back at the wall. Opposite the page of the icon with the *Seven Angels* blowing trumpets was a picture of the icon of *Christ in Glory*. The two icons were on the wall of the monastery, just as they were in the book. Her father left her the book as a guide to his clues. She and Medak were missing something. They had the clues, but what was the message?

Staring at the wall, Amy noticed a rough spot as if something had been removed, and took a step backward.

"Medak, is there an indentation on the base of the wall below the edge of the icon of the *Seven Angels*?"

Medak dropped to his knees and ran his hand along the beveled edge of the niche.

"Could this be what you're looking for?"

His hand brushed the light dust off the baseboard, revealing an address carved in the wood. How clever of Veilkov—or Benton Prowers. Unless someone was standing in front of the icon looking directly at the corner near the floor, they would never notice the carved address.

"It's a street address; Eleven Stradum, Dubrovnik. I know that street. It goes through the main square, the Placa, in old Dubrovnik. The square is a World Heritage site with a monastery, a church, the oldest pharmacy in the world, and several other old buildings which I don't recall."

Amy opened her notebook and wrote the address down.

"My next stop," she said, with a confidence she didn't feel.

They walked down the corridor of the church, surrounded by hanging icons and painted frescos on the stone pillars. Amy hoped she was seeing them for the last time, but her intuition said otherwise.

Outside the chapel, she heard birds singing and felt the hot sun reflecting off the mountain slope. Did time have no meaning? Her father and first husband would spend hours discussing the concept of time. At the time, she thought their discussions were trivial, but as she looked back at the monastery, she suddenly understood what they meant. Whatever happened in the past…in that monastery…in those mountains? All of it had become a part of her life today and was behind the reason her father died.

"It's a pleasant time of the day for you to leave," said Medak. He whistled and a black nondescript dog appeared.

"If you'd like a walk, we can go back to the parking lot by another trail. The view is—how you Americans say, terrific—and the dog loves the walk."

The trail took them south to a view of rocky gray peaks and isolated mountain villages.

He pointed down the ridgeline to the river.

"See the wrecked bridge below? It was blown up in World War II, and a train crashed in the river, destroying many art treasures. According to the villagers, the railroad cars were full of crates. No one knows exactly what was in them, but rumors were of paintings, gold, and jewels."

Amy looked up at the mountains, thinking of how her parents escaped from the Balkans on a train during World War II. For all she knew, they could have left on the train in valley below.

The dog barked, bringing her back to today and the tree behind them exploded. She dived behind a tall pine tree with Medak right behind her, knowing it was gunfire. Peering around the tree, she could only see foliage, and thought, *to think the world thought America was obsessed with guns.*

Medak said, "It could be a hunter who doesn't know we are here. I'm going up the trail." He started to move, then stopped, as a tall blond man carrying a rifle came toward them on the path.

When the dog leaped out into the man's path, Medak said, "I know him; stay here." As he stepped around the tree, Amy wished she had a gun. As Medak continued speaking in rapid sentences what sounded like a local dialect. She felt as if she had entered another era, like the Wild West. Her father always preached *carry a gun*, and she could use one now.

She peeked around the tree, but Medak blocked her view of the man. She could see the rifle. It was an assault rifle, not one used for hunting. Then the man was gone, disappearing into the trees as suddenly as he appeared. The dog growled, and continued to look down the trail after him.

Medak turned to Amy.

"The man says he's from Bulgaria, but I doubt he's a Bulgarian. His accent is odd, even though I have seen him around here. Claims he is hunting with a friend. Hunting is common for locals, but Bulgarians aren't common. He says he knows the abbot and his brother. I didn't want to worry you, but the abbot said there could be trouble with strangers coming to our monastery. I think we should get to your car by another trail."

It seemed an eternity until Amy saw the parking lot and her car sitting between two large colored travel buses.

Could security really exist in large numbers of tourists dressed in matching polyester pantsuits?

"Driving to Dubrovnik could be dangerous."

She looked at him as he sounded worried. Her eyes flashed as she felt the anger usually reserved for someone manipulating the family oil leases.

"My father was an old man with not many more years to live. Someone killed him and I'm going to find out who did it and why."

For a monk, Medak looked agitated.

"The road to Dubrovnik is guarded by UN troops, but rogue bandits roam the area."

He pulled out of his pocket a leather cord at the end of which hung a coin, and handed it to Amy. Amy held the coin in her hand and looked carefully at it. Medak saw she was curious.

"Brother Veilkov told me your father collected ancient coins for you. This is a so-called lucky coin that Veilkov gave me some years ago. He said it had special powers. The coin is old, from the era of Alexander the Great. When he conquered territories, he looted the countries' treasures, and minted coins in his image. No one can say if the coin was made during Alexander's reign or not. The Romans continued to make coins in his image long after his death in the third century BC."

Amy knew coins. To see what was unique about the coin, she'd need a research book and a magnifying glass, but she was polite.

"It is an elegant coin; a silver dinaz, the Roman currency. My father had one of the coins made into a necklace for me."

She looked carefully at his coin. Roman and Greek heads looked the same, but the other side of the coin was different.

"This is the god Zeus seated on his throne, holding an eagle."

Medak was surprised. "You know the gods."

"When my father gave me the necklace, I looked up all the books on Roman and Greek coins I could find. There weren't many. This coin looks different, but I'm not sure how."

Medak pointed to a small letter on the coin.

"See the letter *M* under the throne. I have seen other coins with both Alexander's head and Zeus, but they don't have that letter. I wondered if that was why Veilkov called it lucky. I hope it protects you and brings you good luck."

Amy knew the coin was old, but was less certain about the legacy of luck. Most artifacts carried either a tale of good fortune or a curse. To her, there was little difference. She thanked Medak, believing it would take more than a lucky coin to find the Shroud, if it did exist.

"I'll stay in touch." Amy waved goodbye.

"May peace bless your journey." Medak waved, feeling very little peace.

• • •

Sonora Lleissle needed to find her niece. Wearing a black pant suit accentuated with a diamond bracelet and matching earrings, she strolled among the computers and telecommunications equipment in the office of her Berlin villa, with the air of a commanding general.

She didn't have to know how the technology worked. Her staff plunked keys and got the information. Now she needed them to find Amy.

Her nephew, Ace, rolled his chair over to her with the printout of a map. A stranger would never have picked him to be part of the

Prowers family. Tall like all of the Prowers men, he weighed nearly three hundred pounds, none of which was muscle and most was hanging around his waist. No one remembered why he was called Ace.

"She left the monastery, and is likely heading to Dubrovnik with its international airlines. She isn't heading north to Zagreb, or east to Belgrade. Dubrovnik is the jewel of the Adriatic Sea, so the guidebooks say. My memories of the Balkans when Tito was alive are anything but guidebook copy. I doubt Amy is there for the scenery. It would be helpful if she replied to my texts."

Sonora let Ace's sarcasm pass. She figured he had earned it, after nearly having his leg shot off in some covert military operation, one so secret no one could talk about it. But now she needed more than a location.

"That part of the world could blow up any minute and she is right in the middle. Whatever she found in Benton's safe to take her there has to be important."

She paused. "I can't imagine what."

Ace didn't know how to reassure his aunt. The staff at the ranch said she cleaned out Benton's desk and left. What compelled her to take off for the Balkans? They were at a loss for ideas.

"She can shoot a gun, fly a plane, but likely will do neither. She likes to drive a fast car and that could be a problem on the mountain roads."

Sonora found little comfort in his analysis. "See if you can raise her on the satellite phone. When Benton was alive, the family had a rule; to carry the phone whenever you left the country."

Sonora turned to look out the glass window at the gray sky over Berlin, which fit her mood. The weapon system in the southern Saharan desert was the real problem. She and Ace should be monitoring activity at El Kanitaou and Geigner testing his ground-based laser, not worrying about Amy.

Amy going to Dubrovnik made no sense. It made even less sense that she would be running around alone.

Rarely did Lleissle think about her sister, Jarra, who disappeared decades ago in southeast Asia. She wouldn't let that happen to Amy.

• • •

Katherine Burlake

Katherine qualified as one of the first female Air Force Officers to attend the Air Force Navy Intelligence School and serve in the Vietnam War.

Living in Thailand, England, and Germany led her to the Department of State and Broadcasting Board of Governors reporting on embassy operations globally. She has traveled to over a 130 countries including Afghanistan and Iraq.

Katherine has been published in the *Macguffin*, The Face of War: A Baghdad Woman. Her vast experiences plus her four years in Riyadh, Saudi Arabia as the Embassy Senior Financial Management Officer bring in the trench experiences to her engaging novels.

Colorado is now her home.

CPSIA information can be obtained
at www.ICGtesting.com
Printed in the USA
LVOW13s0258111217
559363LV00038B/3406/P

9 780998 973432

CPSIA information can be obtained
at www.ICGtesting.com
Printed in the USA
LVOW13s0258111217
559363LV00038B/3406/P